COOPERSTOWN
PICASSO

COOPERSTOWN
PICASSO

Andrés G. López

IGUANA

Publisher: Meghan Behse
Editor: Lee Parpart
Front cover design: Lee Parpart

ISBN 978-1-77180-561-2 (paperback)
ISBN 978-1-77180-560-5 (epub)

This is an original print edition of *Cooperstown Picasso*.

For Cristóbal Pi, Uncle Toby, my second father, a brilliant, kind man who taught me to dream big, work hard, and not fear the difficult task, but tackle it boldly, with enthusiasm, energy, and resolve.

And for Kristina Wolska, my Warsaw muse, in gratitude for your perennial inspiration, friendship, and generosity. With your permission, I fabricated much of this fiction from fragments of our wonderful communications. Thank you!

"Success is not final; failure is not fatal:
it is the courage to continue that counts."

—Winston Churchill

CHAPTER 1

In the small Central New York college town of Pleasant Hills where he taught and lived, Dr. Tobias Pi concluded the poetry unit in his Intro to Literature classes the same way each semester, by teaching Shakespeare's Sonnet 55. The poem had captivated him and shaped his tastes since the first time he'd read it, back at Stony Brook University. Walking into his eleven o'clock class on this September day in 2018, he felt inspired by the cool, sunny weather and the prospect of traveling back 409 years to savor again what he saw as the most beautiful poem ever written.

Students were shocked to see Dr. Pi carrying a calico Chihuahua under one arm. The small, skinny dog wore a red, cotton vest, with the word KONG on it in bold black letters. He shivered noticeably as his large, moist eyes scrutinized his new surroundings. Dr. Pi gently placed the dog on top of his desk and faced the class.

"Hi, everyone. This is Tank, my daughter Constance's dog." Light laughter filled the classroom, as students recognized the incongruence between the dog's name and his size. "Tank loves Shakespeare, so I invited him to be our special guest this morning."

The laughter intensified. Dr. Pi put his leather coat on top of the desk and nestled the animal inside it. He leaned down to rub Tank's bony head and whispered, "Relax buddy. This won't take long. Shakespeare will make us all feel better."

Bringing Tank into the classroom had required special permission. Pleasant Hills College, a State-run four-year agricultural and technical school, had a strict policy forbidding animals on campus, other than police dogs, without authorized approval. Dr. Pi had emailed Dean O'Rourke that morning to explain that Tank had been very sick lately, and that he worried about leaving his daughter's pet home alone for several hours. The dean had granted his request to bring him into class and wished him well.

Constance had been invited camping in the Adirondacks for the weekend by her childhood friends Samantha, Lena, and Rachel, and she'd asked her father if he could look after Tank, who had kidney disease — something they'd discovered earlier in the summer when the dog was hospitalized with a bladder infection after swimming in an upstate lake. Dr. Pi agreed to watch him until Sunday.

The previous year, in October 2017, Dr. Pi had looked after Tank for a full month. It was fair to say that Dr. Pi and the dog had bonded. Tank had had lots of energy and spunk then; he'd strutted about like a Doberman and barked like a German shepherd. It was funny watching Tank patrol the grounds like an army general commanding the battlefield. His confidence and authority were visible, especially when he lifted his hind legs to mark new territory. Dr. Pi had had a good laugh over this with his friend and neighbor Randy Rover, who had helped Dr. Pi care for Tank one afternoon that fall.

"He looks like General Patton," Randy had laughed as they watched Tank take a hill of wood chips at the local dog park. "Old Blood and Guts has come back to life."

Now, however, Tank was struggling. His energy had plummeted, and it was sad for Dr. Pi to see this as soon as Constance dropped him off the previous afternoon. Constance had told Dr. Pi that Tank hadn't been drinking much water and that he could get dehydrated. Dr. Pi reassured her that he'd attend carefully to his needs and told her to go have fun.

Dr. Pi knew much about many things but not about the care of ailing Chihuahuas, and he panicked that night when Tank hardly ate any of his food. Before bed, he took Tank out for his walk, but Tank just meandered around and didn't pee or poop. When they finally went back inside, Dr. Pi noticed that Tank's water bowl remained full. He was determined to get Tank to drink something, anything. He dumped the water out and tried lemonade, then orange juice, but Tank wouldn't imbibe. Out of desperation, Dr. Pi filled Tank's bowl with milk. Tank lapped it up quickly, and Dr. Pi was relieved, praised him, and gave him much more, a decision he'd soon regret.

In the morning, as he walked down the stairs, Dr. Pi encountered what looked like a crime scene, but with diarrhea instead of blood. It was everywhere, including all over his expensive Persian rug in the foyer. "No! No!" Dr. Pi had yelled loudly as he took in the scene. He had scolded Tank, who lay huddled by the front door, but immediately felt badly for doing so, realizing it was the milk that had upset Tank's stomach. It took Dr. Pi a full hour to clean up the mess. He then took Tank outside to do any further business, but the dog was spent and still in obvious distress. He brought him back inside and tried to comfort him, speaking to him as if he were a child: "I'm sorry, Tank. I didn't mean to yell. It wasn't your fault. Please forgive me." Tears welled in Dr. Pi's eyes as he glanced at the animal's bewildered, sad expression. He cradled Tank on his lap, rubbed his bony head while drinking his coffee, and made up his mind to take him to class. Tank needed comforting, and not to be left locked alone at home.

With the dog now lying in a ball inside his coat, Dr. Pi asked the students to turn off their phones and put them away. He said he didn't want to hear "any sound, except that made by your combined minds thinking." This drew a round of laughter, and he smiled as they adhered to his request. He focused the projector, and Shakespeare's sonnet appeared on the screen.

Not marble, nor the gilded monuments
Of princes, shall outlive this powerful rhyme;
But you shall shine more bright in these contents

Than unswept stone, besmeared with sluttish time.
When wasteful war shall statues overturn,
And broils root out the work of masonry,
Nor Mars his sword nor war's quick fire shall burn
The living record of your memory.
'Gainst death and all-oblivious enmity
Shall you pace forth; your praise shall still find room
Even in the eyes of all posterity
That wear this world out to the ending doom.
So, till the judgment that yourself arise,
You live in this, and dwell in lovers' eyes.

Before discussion began, Dr. Pi had students recite their favorite lines. As they did, he glanced over at Tank and noticed that he'd closed his eyes and put his head down. Dr. Pi walked over to him and gently tucked his leather coat around his body to ensure he was as warm and comfortable as possible. Tank didn't flinch; he was asleep, completely exhausted.

Discussion focused first on the poem's form, and then on the speaker's boast — that this poem would outlive everything until Judgment Day. "How could he be so sure?" Dr. Pi asked. "Was this arrogance or naïveté?"

Kevin, a clever student who rarely spoke, ventured an insight:

"Builders used mortar to cement the stones of monuments, which would fall apart, but the speaker erects one with words — his poem, crafted so perfectly it's impossible to destroy."

Dr. Pi beamed at the young man. "Precisely. And how would the speaker achieve that?"

There was a long silence. Outside, a lawnmower chugged to life, and a delivery truck squeaked to a stop. Tank lift his head, then lowered it again and resumed his slumber. After a brief and amicable standoff, during which the students refused to give up their thoughts about Kevin's point, Dr. Pi raised more questions about the mystery of the poem's longevity:

""'Gainst death and all-oblivious enmity,' the speaker says. How does the poem survive war, fire, and nature's destructive forces? What gives it such power?"

Anna broke the long silence that ensued. "Its beauty. The precision of its form. The elegance of its sounds and rhythm."

"Yes, yes!" Dr. Pi exclaimed. "Precisely. Perfectly put. Please continue."

"Well," she said, "as Kevin noted, if the speaker is a word mason, and words are her stones, then the sounds, alliterations, and music are her mortar. The magic lies in how the words rub up against each other. We've talked about this before."

"We have," Dr. Pi said. "First week of class. Go on."

"Take lines five and six. There are three strong alliterative sounds there — the W, R, and S sounds — and many A and O vowels. These recur throughout the poem and glue the words together the way mortar cements stones. These echoes make the lines easier to remember, and the poem can live in readers' minds."

"So true," said Dr. Pi. "And why would anyone want to memorize it?"

Sarah, who sat behind Anna, raised her hand.

"Because it's about love. The speaker's head over heels in love, if you ask me. Truly insane!" The class laughed, and she continued. "Anyone who loves with such craziness might memorize it. I know I would, if I were in love like that."

"Me too," Dr. Pi said. Then, turning his back to the screen and facing the class, he recited the poem for them in as dignified a voice and elegant a manner as he could muster. His students gazed at him, amazed.

"Ah, that felt so good," Dr. Pi said. "I memorized this to impress a girlfriend's parents who'd invited me for Christmas dinner."

Everyone laughed. Tank's ears lifted slightly, then slowly came down. Dr. Pi smiled and continued: "Yes. I was that nutty once for my first love, Jennifer Amman. Unfortunately, that didn't work out. But my love of this poem remained." Dr. Pi paused. "I love it more today than ever before."

Tears welled in his eyes, and Dr. Pi struggled to compose himself as a couple of students in the front rows squirmed slightly in their seats. Though he'd mentioned Jennifer, Dr. Pi realized that his emotions were actually being stirred by memories much closer to the surface, having to do with his sister Maria and his mother Miriam — both lost to the world much too soon. His longing for them was immense, and Shakespeare's lines never failed to reopen a channel to that deep love. He walked to his desk to collect himself before concluding:

"Four hundred and nine years and going strong. Till the Judgment Day — I don't doubt it. This humbling sonnet is not a boast but a celebration of two great human abilities which have built fabulous civilizations. Using language to share wisdom and powerful ideas from age to age. And the ability to love, despite the 'all-oblivious' hatreds and wasteful wars that plague us still. Never forget the brilliant bard's words. Commit them to memory. Put their lessons to use. Let's love our beautiful languages. And one another."

Just then, Tank awakened, yawned, stirred himself free of the leather coat, and stood upright. The heaviness in the room lifted as a few students laughed and others let out oohs and aahs.

"Welcome back, buddy," Dr. Pi said. "Hope you enjoyed the lesson." Then to the students he said, "Thanks for being understanding, everyone. I appreciate it."

It was clear that the students felt that they were the lucky ones, getting to have Tank in the classroom. Several of them asked to take pictures, and Dr. Pi happily posed with Tank in his arms until everyone had their Instagram fodder and until all of the students had filed out, laughing and talking as they went about the rest of their day.

Alone now, Dr. Pi put Tank back on the desk and secured his leash, then shut the projector and packed his books. He strolled into the sunshine and headed home with Tank trotting alongside him like a refreshed thoroughbred. Dr. Pi's face was flushed, and his heart raced. The sadness that had flooded him during class was still there, but it was indistinct now — a vague malaise that he couldn't understand. He made an effort to tune into the feeling, the way he had learned to in his martial arts classes, and he realized, once again, that his mind was clinging to the sacred memories of his sister and mother. This was a pleasure and a source of pain all at once. He resolved to never stop thinking about them, no matter how much it hurt. And it did hurt.

Back at home, as he ate his lunch, Dr. Pi noticed that Tank continued to ignore his food and didn't drink anything. Tank did, however, have more energy, so that afternoon Dr. Pi let him play in the backyard while he graded essays at the picnic table. After two hours of fresh air and exercise, when they came inside, Tank went directly to his water bowl and drank a good deal. Not long afterwards, he started to devour his food. His appetite had returned miraculously, and Dr. Pi felt immense relief.

***

Constance arrived to get Tank on Sunday at one in the afternoon. Dr. Pi had some tuna sandwiches ready, and as they ate, he related his latest adventures with Tank. Constance cringed through the stories and said "Aww, my poor Tankie," as she imagined both the early morning and the classroom episodes, but in her beautiful hazel eyes there was a visible sadness, for she knew Tank's health was in decline.

As always, Dr. Pi was overjoyed to have his daughter there with him. She looked so much like Miriam, with her full, rosy cheeks and lips, long, wavy, jet-black hair, and intelligent face. Her compassionate nature shone like the trustworthy sun, a constant and perpetual source of visible inner light. Her company drew out the goodness in others. And being around her, even for a short time, made Dr. Pi forget all his melancholic forebodings.

"I bet your students got a big kick out of seeing you bring Tank in, huh Dad?"

"They sure loved him, sweetie," he said, looking at Tank, who lay on the kitchen floor enjoying the sunshine by Constance's feet. "And now he can boast that he's heard a Shakespearean sonnet. He slept right through the lesson, but many students probably did too."

"Oh Dad," Constance said. "I'm sure they loved your lesson. I'm glad you tackle Shakespeare and the sonnet form."

"Thanks, sweetie. It's challenging, for sure. Still, I feel that teaching them about even one beautiful sonnet by a master poet increases their appreciation of our language."

"I agree with you, Dad. Keep at it. Trust your instincts and expertise. That's why they pay you the big bucks."

Dr. Pi laughed and joked, "That's true. I'll do my best. I like to earn my money." Then, he added more seriously: "Studying what's been considered great for centuries, in any field, is essential for broadening a student's perspective on a particular subject. Why is this considered great? What makes it so? These questions must be answered. Imagine studying art and not mentioning Leonardo da Vinci."

"That would be a joke," Constance said, contemplating such a ludicrous idea.

"That's how I'd feel if Shakespeare were excluded from a poetry course. Any poetry course, taught in any language."

"It'd be like studying popular music and not including the Beatles."

"Precisely," Dr. Pi said and smiled. "And how's your songwriting coming?"

"Very well. Still learning the craft. Polishing the songs I've written. Adding harmonies, working on verses, smoothing out choruses. Trying different things. There's no real formula. The hardest part is finding enough time to create and develop ideas."

"Oh, I know," Dr. Pi concurred. "That's what your brother always says, and you know what an excellent songwriter Christopher is."

"We're a lot alike, Dad. I still remember when we'd stay awake late at night to work on songs to post on YouTube. We fussed and argued and debated but got it done. We had so much fun back then."

"You sure did. I remember those wonderful times."

"Me too," Constance said with a melancholy air.

Dr. Pi heard the sadness in her voice and reassured her: "They're still alive in our memories, sweetheart. They still live!"

"You're such an optimist, Dad. On this one, I think you're right."

"Thanks sweetie. It brought me such joy to hear you and Christopher play."

"Do you still write songs, Dad? Play the guitar and sing? You always talk about your fiction but never about your music anymore."

"Oh, sure I do, when the inspiration comes. I've got a couple of new songs in progress, though nothing good enough to show you just yet."

"That's awesome," Constance said happily.

"Sometimes I travel to Pennsylvania to play with Mathias, and occasionally Hutch and Fred join us, and we jam away like we did during college. Maybe you could join us sometime."

"I'd love to, Dad. That would be fun. Hey, do you ever regret not pursuing your music? Or a psychology career?"

"The music, yes. I always wonder whether the world would've loved our songs and whether we could've succeeded professionally like the band U2. We worked well together then — still do. Psychology, no. Though I love the discipline, playing with rats in a lab got old fast. I learned a lot about the little creatures, though. I felt I could've even trained one to recite poetry in due time." Constance grinned at her father's strange boast. Dr. Pi smiled and continued: "I don't regret double-majoring in English and Psych as an undergrad. But literature came more naturally, so I went with that."

They sat in comfortable silence, with Dr. Pi basking in his daughter's presence. Looking at her, it struck him how much he missed her company and how euphoric he felt when she was nearby. At length, with as much conviction as he could muster, he said lovingly:

"I'm sure glad you're pursuing your music, sweetie. It's in the blood. On both sides of the family. When I first heard your mom sing, I was blown away. Sweetest voice I'd ever heard. And her dad belted out those church hymns with gusto."

"Yeah, Poppa was simply amazing."

Dr. Pi looked at Constance intently, his face the picture of a father about to deliver heartfelt advice. "Never forget that you're an excellent songwriter and musician. And that when things get tough, 'it is the courage to continue that counts.'"

"Thanks, Dad. I'm doing my best. Churchill's words?"

"Yes. A poetic politician. Savior of the free world. Some sound advice for braving life."

"I agree," Constance said, and smiled.

By four o'clock, Constance was on her way back to Manhattan. Before she got in her car, Dr. Pi gave her a big hug and told her how proud of her he was. Within minutes of her departure, some of his gloominess returned. Nevertheless, their conversation had lifted his spirits temporarily and given him another precious memory to treasure.

CHAPTER 2

Dr. Pi was an optimist, a passionate man who'd taught for nearly twenty years. He loved teaching and felt he knew the magic needed to ensure students learned to think. It was always about connecting with them, for as he grew older, they got younger. He tried to see the world as they saw it. He wanted them to know the best that had been thought and to embrace new knowledge.

He was six feet tall and two hundred pounds — a former athlete, still on the lanky side — and he hid his age well; though fifty-one, he was often taken for a man in his late thirties. Something about his Cuban genes, that smooth, Caribbean skin and youthful mindset, kept the wrinkles at bay. A few white hairs had crept through, and his thick black mane had thinned over the years, but Dr. Pi still felt young, vibrant, full of energy.

His thinking about life and the universe had evolved a great deal. Once, he'd had a rigid mindset. There were truths and falsehoods he'd been certain of. His faith and Christian beliefs had been thumped by a strict adherence to reason, especially after studying the Enlightenment thinkers Paine and Voltaire. But now he was only sure that he knew nothing. In keeping with the Socratic paradox, his vast learning had only brought him more confusion, not clarity. The universe remained an unfathomable mystery. It was impossible to think that humans from this tiny spot in the cosmos — in one remote galaxy among an estimated two trillion — could know everything. The more he lived and thought, the more he wished to embrace contradictions, uncertainties, and mysteries. Year by year, new cosmic doors opened. Communication technology, powerful computers, and telescopes like Hubble had challenged certitudes and truths. Dr. Pi welcomed these changes fearlessly. Mathematicians and physicists provided fascinating visions of the universe. He often pondered that big picture. Nothing could be dismissed, Dr. Pi thought; nothing could be discounted. Every thought mattered. Every theory, every detail. Gathering evidence and sifting through this indecipherable maze was the challenge.

***

Despite his optimism, Dr. Pi carried a deep sadness in his heart. He'd tragically lost two women he adored — his elder sister Maria, and his mother, Miriam. Maria had died on prom night at sixteen when a van ran a red light on Ditmars Boulevard in Queens and struck her limo. Years later, Miriam had suffered a brain hemorrhage in a Long Island hospital after surgery. Some days the thought of their deaths paralyzed Tobias with such grief that he would contemplate suicide in hopes of joining them.

Maria's death had been the more traumatic of the two. Dr. Pi was only eleven at the time, and he remembered the details all too clearly. When two police officers arrived to inform them of her death, his mother had unleashed a despairing scream that still haunted Tobias; he'd instantly run to hug Miriam, who collapsed onto a couch and sobbed uncontrollably. Shortly after, Tobias went with his father Pablo, who spoke no English, to the hospital morgue to serve as interpreter and identify Maria; though she'd clung to life when she arrived, the surgeons at Astoria General couldn't save her. When they returned home four hours later, Miriam hadn't moved. Tobias was scared to see her like that. He ached inside, but tried hard to obey his father, who told him that they needed to be strong for his mother. They helped her to bed, where she lay grieving for two days. She refused to eat and couldn't speak. On the third day, Pablo brought their family doctor, Roberto, a devout Catholic, to help Miriam overcome the deep depression she'd fallen into. Roberto sat by Miriam's bedside, where he held onto her cold hands and rubbed them gently. He reassured her that everything that could have been done at the hospital to save Maria had been done. She was with God, he said confidently: "Maria está con Dios." He encouraged Miriam to eat and carry on bravely; it is what Maria would've wanted, he pleaded. Seeing a frightened Tobias looking on by the doorway, Roberto called him over and they prayed together. After much time had passed, their voices stirred Miriam's despondent spirit back to life and she said a Hail Mary with them.

Part of the crushing grief that befell Miriam and the whole family had to do with Maria's tremendous potential. She had studied piano since the age of four, and by sixteen she had emerged as a gifted performer who could play pieces by Beethoven and Chopin flawlessly. She'd even begun studying Tchaikovsky and Rachmaninoff. After her death, no music was played in the apartment, and each time Tobias passed her silent piano accumulating dust, he heard the haunting notes of Beethoven's Moonlight Sonata, that lovely melody so often elicited by Maria's delicate fingers. No one ever played the piano again. Often, Miriam would sit at the piano to cry, and Tobias would cuddle next to her and rub her back. When the family moved to Elmhurst, the piano came with them, but became a shrine to Maria, placed prominently in the living room and topped with Maria's photographs and awards and a weekly bouquet of freshly cut red roses with one white rose at its center.

The Steinway upright had been in excellent condition when they'd bought it in 1972 for a budget-busting one thousand dollars. Maria was ten at the time, and already she'd had six years of formal piano instruction: two in Cuba before the family emigrated in 1968, and four in the United States. Maria's Cuban teacher had predicted that one day she'd fill concert halls. Maria had practiced on weekends on a neighbor's Mason & Hamlin prior to getting the Steinway. Pablo had found out about the Steinway from a friend at work. It had belonged to a recently deceased Spanish woman in Flushing. Pablo and Miriam agreed Maria's talent merited the purchase.

Sitting behind the upright, Maria had joyfully filled the apartment with music. Tobias marveled at her skill. Night after night he'd stare at her moving hands, often so mesmerized by her playing that he'd neglect his homework. Sometimes, Maria would invite him to sit next to her on the bench and turn the pages of her sheet music when she nodded her head. Tobias loved doing this, and when she'd finished and thanked him, he'd hug her with all his might. She'd kiss his head and then help him finish his homework.

Tobias stumbled through the years following his sister's death, attending school but barely remembering anything that happened. His parents encouraged him to take piano lessons, but he refused. He would never play the piano, or her piano — though it was the only instrument he'd ever really wished to play. Instead, he played roller hockey after school and on weekends. Music remained in his heart, however, and when he rummaged through album collections at music stores, sadness would overwhelm him; he'd be on the verge of tears, thinking of how joyfully Maria would have browsed those albums with him. Holding a Rachmaninoff album, or listening to his uplifting, passionate melodies, Tobias's spirit would soar to Maria.

The winter he turned fifteen, three long years after Maria's death, Tobias picked up the guitar, took a few lessons, and then quit. He had no patience for formal instruction, or for the rigor of constant practice needed to perfect pieces and become a true musician. Music was a vehicle to express his thoughts and emotions, so writing songs became his passion. Playing guitar made him want to sing and train his voice; he experimented with melody and harmony, and his singing improved slowly. As soon as he knew five chords on the guitar, he'd tried to write a song. His ninth-grade English teacher had inspired in him a love of poetry, so Tobias used the guitar to get out his complicated feelings. On many late winter afternoons, before his parents got home from work, Tobias would sit at the dining room table with his guitar and write songs. Many were for Maria.

He often imagined her there playing with him, filling in the empty spaces between his guitar chords with beautiful piano riffs. He could almost hear her harmonizing with him and imagined them as a dynamic duo like the Carpenters. These moments, which could never now take place, filled his mind. He saw his mother and father smiling, reveling in their children's shared talents. His imagination was powerful, his mind transcendent. It always had been. In invented, timeless moments, his mind could defy death, destroy it, and this was both blessing and curse. When the imagined journey was over, he'd return to the painful present, and feel emptier and lonelier than before.

Years later, studying Thomas Carlyle in college, Tobias understood perfectly what Carlyle meant when he wrote: "Man's unhappiness ... comes of his greatness; it is because there is an Infinite in him, which with all his cunning he cannot quite bury under the Finite." The Infinite would always be inside, always want to journey across Time and Space, regardless of the present, the Finite, the limitations placed on the "chainless mind" — a decaying, physical body. Realists call this imaginative quest hopelessly romantic. For Dr. Pi, hopeless souls were ones without active imaginations, those who could not grasp eternal possibilities or see the mind's ability to hold the infinite universe inside. Yes, Maria was physically gone, but in his mind she lived. He could still see her play, hear her voice, and feel her when she hugged him.

But there was more. Tobias could imagine what could never come to pass, her growing up into a woman and living a full, happy life, singing songs, and composing music with him. He even saw her marrying a good man, having children, and sharing her musical gift with them. His mind gave him that power, and he would use it to get through the hard days. Milton had written: "The mind is its own place, and in it self / Can make a Heav'n of Hell, a Hell of Heav'n." How undeniably true! Maria would live within him every second of every day. She was deep in his soul — and music would bind them in that universal infinitude.

The other nightmare Tobias experienced blindsided him. Thirty-two years after Maria's death, Miriam's unexpected death in a hospital brought Tobias a grief that sapped all his energy; he floundered, became disinterested in doing routine chores, even lost his appetite and desire to exercise or sleep. What agonized him most, besides the fact of her death itself, was that it had been preventable. Her surgeon had operated for three hours to remove an enormous blood clot that extended from her abdomen to her left knee. He'd only been able to remove half of it and was to operate again the following day. Tobias was uneasy; he'd had a premonition she wouldn't make it. And she didn't. While coming off the anesthetic, Miriam was highly agitated, pulled out her catheter, and screamed from pain as the nurses tried to reinsert it. Already on blood thinners, the doctor prescribed an additional sedative to calm her, and it proved deadly. The two medications together usually worked well, but in this instance, they were lethal, and during the night Miriam suffered a brain hemorrhage.

By seven in the morning, her entire left side appeared paralyzed, and Tobias had asked the nurse to call a doctor. The nurse had said everything looked fine and ignored him. Frustrated, he found a doctor in the hallway, grabbed him by the forearm, and asked him to come see his mother. The doctor immediately sent her for CT scans that revealed that Miriam's brain was full of blood; even if they operated to alleviate the pressure, she'd never function normally again. There had been too much brain damage. She would never recover or even awaken from the coma. Their recommendation was to give her morphine for the pain and allow her to die with dignity.

When the doctors explained all of this to Tobias, he had screamed in grief and cried uncontrollably, just as Miriam had done years earlier upon learning of Maria's death. He collapsed onto a waiting room chair with his hands covering his face. After agonizing over what to do, he agreed to follow the surgeons' recommendation and let his mother die.

CHAPTER 3

On a drizzly Monday in late September 2018, Dr. Pi began the fiction unit by reviewing the literary elements. It was one of those rare days when he wasn't inspired; he felt agitated, drained, weighed down by past regrets. He did his best to get through class, for he hated letting students down. Afterwards, he felt frustrated. Back at home, he put on some comfortable clothing, and began an intense kung fu exercise routine in the parlor. He performed this ritual a few times per week, usually in the early mornings or before lunch, and often when he was sad. It exhausted him but also instilled serenity and improved his mood. He never worked out at a busy, noisy gym, preferring the solitary silence to connect with his inner self.

***

Dr. Pi was a fighter, a connoisseur of the martial arts, but his prowess was a secret shared only with Chuck, who had been a hallmate of his at Stony Brook and from whom he'd learned most of the technique he knew. If the moment ever arose when his life, or that of someone he loved, was threatened, he'd be ready to defend himself or them. He'd unleash a dormant monster that dwelled deep within every sinew of his body, one he kept caged and quiet and didn't think about.

To this point in his life, he'd used this weapon twice. Once, to save his own life, when an assailant tried to throw him off a train platform in Elmhurst, Queens, and a second time, when he'd sought out and nearly killed Eddie, an old enemy.

Dr. Pi was not proud of this ugly beast within. He hated physical violence of any sort. All wars repulsed him; thinking about their carnage made him sick. Growing up in the early seventies, watching footage of the Vietnam War every night on the evening news had scarred him psychologically — the suffering on all sides had wounded him for life.

In the fall of '78, Tobias was still reeling from Maria's death. Neither school, nor sports, nor friendships could dispel the gnawing, persistent grief that plagued him. He remembered the happy years when he'd watched *Kung Fu* with Maria, Pablo, and Miriam, and the recollection calmed his agitated mind. Tobias had instantly fallen in love with the peaceful Shaolin monk, Caine, who travels the American West in search of his half-brother Danny. Tobias recalled how moved he'd been by Caine's journey; like Caine seeking Danny, in those days he wondered whether he'd ever see Maria again in Heaven.

The day after his recollection that fall, Tobias combed through the Broadway library's books on Zen Buddhism. He borrowed several and began to read. He became fascinated with the martial arts, and immersion in the subject helped him cope with his grief. He researched its Chinese origins, its 1,500-year history, and studied the many styles of kung fu. What impressed him most was how the rigorous physical training helped develop mental and spiritual acuity. Above all, it was a sacred art, to be used only when one's life was in peril, for the inner force, once unleashed, was deadly. The ideal warrior valued life, was quiet and mild-mannered, and built a calm spiritual sanctum within. Physical strength and clear thinking were pillars of his being. A disciplined mind was a source of strength, for the art of fighting lay in one's intelligence and wit; it was about surprise and quickness most of all. Tobias read and read, studied diagrams and positions, and secretly practiced kung fu in his bedroom that long winter. He did not ask his parents for lessons but focused on learning all he could alone.

Without formal training, Tobias knew he'd be limited, but he convinced himself that would be enough. He just wanted to be ready, just in case. His natural bent was to diffuse potential crises with words, to opt for diplomacy over war. During his freshman year at Stony Brook, he saw that wasn't always possible when he witnessed Chuck get ambushed by five members of an NYC gang visiting friends on campus who'd learned Chuck was a martial artist and attacked him to test his expertise.

The fight was well underway when Tobias saw the gathered crowd. By that point, it was almost over. Chuck had been surrounded, and after brief taunts they'd come at him, all bluster and no technique. Chuck easily blocked the first combatant with his right forearm, knocking him back into a garbage dumpster. He flung his left leg in a circular swipe across the chest of a second assailant, the force knocking him back into a third. Chuck pounced on the third gang member, grabbing his head with both hands and bringing the young man's chin hard against his right knee. The other two challengers saw this and retreated into the crowd, but the first assailant would not be cowed; he ran towards Chuck again, and launched his stiff, extended legs in full karate form towards Chuck's muscular upper body. While his attacker was in the air, Chuck seized one leg and flipped him upside down. The boy's skull crashed on the grass, and he writhed in pain. Someone must have called the campus police because sirens could be heard, and everyone dispersed quickly, including the gang members. Chuck was gathering his gym gear calmly from the pavement when Tobias appeared next to him, breathless. He had run over to help, but none was needed; Chuck had a minor cut under his right eye and a red mark on his muscular bicep, but that was it. The two walked slowly and silently towards their dorm.

One night about a week later, Tobias was practicing guitar in the hall lounge, and Chuck came out of his room to listen. Chuck liked

Tobias's original songs and the way he played and sang. He told Tobias that he'd always wanted to learn to play but had never gotten lessons. He had a nice classical guitar back in Brooklyn that his grandfather had given him. Tobias thought quickly. He offered to give Chuck guitar lessons if Chuck would teach him how to defend himself better. Chuck agreed, on the condition that their pact would be kept secret, and the deal was sealed.

Tobias taught Chuck guitar on weekends. Most of their kung fu sessions were held after class on sunny, fall afternoons from October to late November and then again from early April to mid-May. They shared their knowledge and expertise for three years, usually in the secluded section of a huge open field between the infirmary and the train station. On other days, they drove in Tobias's Dodge to the isolated dunes at West Meadows Beach and worked out on the sand. Within months, Tobias's skill and confidence were growing steadily, and Chuck had learned all the major and minor guitar chords, how to pick the strings and strum, and even how to compose simple songs for the beautiful women who fawned over him. Chuck was a handsome warrior who practiced a strict code of self-defense, and he reminded Tobias at the start of each new lesson that what he learned was to be used *strictly* for self-defense, never to provoke conflict or gain advantage. Each time he'd hear these words Tobias would smile. "I know, Chuck. I know," he'd say. "I'll never forget your words or let you down."

Not long after graduating from Stony Brook, however, Tobias broke his promise. Proud of his burgeoning kung fu skills, he'd gone looking for Eddie, a boy who'd beaten him up after school for half a year in the fifth grade. Tobias had never forgotten or forgiven his torture. Eddie had dropped out of high school, peddled drugs in Astoria to elementary school kids, and still pranced around like a badass, bullying rivals and extorting money from local merchants. Tobias had found him hanging out and smoking weed on a street corner, just blocks from their old elementary school, and picked a fight by ridiculing the loser Eddie had become. When Eddie came at him like a raging bull, Tobias unleashed the fury he'd carried for over a decade. Using Eddie's momentum, he got under him and launched him into a nearby mailbox, and then jumped on Eddie's back and whacked at his neck repeatedly with swift hands. "I've never forgotten what you did to me, you low-life scum," Tobias yelled. The more he hit Eddie, the more enraged Tobias became. He shattered both of Eddie's kneecaps with heavy kicks, cracked two of his ribs, and left him hobbled on the sidewalk. Eddie cried and begged for mercy, but his pleas only hardened Tobias and made him more violent as he remembered Eddie's abuse. Before relenting, he'd repeatedly pounded Eddie's head on the concrete until blood poured down his old tormentor's head and no sound escaped the young man's lips.

When the police and ambulance arrived, Eddie was barely conscious, and a crowd had gathered around him as he lay crumpled and bloodied on the ground. The cops pulled Tobias off Eddie and pushed him back but didn't take him into custody. In their report, they labeled the episode a provoked "street fight," with Eddie cited as instigator. The officers, it seemed, knew Eddie and were glad to see him get what he deserved. In ten minutes, Tobias had done what for years the cops couldn't — get a drug peddler and extortionist off the streets. No charges were filed against Tobias and no further inquiries were made; he walked away free and unscathed. Luckily, paramedics were able to stop Eddie's bleeding. Tobias knew they had probably saved his life along with Eddie's. Though it had felt good to get his revenge, for weeks afterwards Tobias felt enormous guilt. He had let Chuck down and was horrified at how quickly he'd lost control; in mere seconds, a murderous impulse had overpowered him. From then on, Tobias vowed never again to let his emotions get the best of him. But this episode would always haunt him. Years later, Tobias learned that Eddie had been convicted on a drug charge, and while serving time at Rikers Island prison he'd been stabbed to death.

CHAPTER 4

On the final Monday of September, a foggy and windy day, Dr. Pi explained to his literature class how cleverly Hemingway uses the rare third-person objective narrator in "Hills Like White Elephants." Like a lawyer addressing a jury, Dr. Pi came out from behind his desk and moved closer to his students to share his concluding remarks:

"In the end, Hemingway shows what it's like to be faced with tough choices. The girl wants to keep her baby. 'We could get along,' she tells the American, confident that their relationship can blossom."

From the front of the classroom, John, a stocky student with a deep voice, said:

"I'm not so sure, Dr. Pi; I don't think they have a future. The man tells her plainly, 'I don't want anybody but you. I don't want any one else.' He doesn't want the baby, just the girl. He wants her to have the abortion."

Margaret, a lanky young woman with glasses who sat across from John, interrupted. "But he changes his mind, stops being a *prick*, and brings the suitcases to the other side of the tracks."

Laughter filled the classroom. Dr. Pi loved seeing Margaret's animation.

"Well, that doesn't mean anything," John insisted. "He still doesn't want the baby, even if he lets her keep it. You don't change your mind so quickly on something like that."

"You can!" Margaret insisted. "Why not? It's possible. The American feels her emotion when the girl demands that he stop talking. Right then, he understands she really wants their child, rises to the occasion, and becomes a better man. People can change."

"Too optimistic. Not convinced they can," John replied. "When he goes to move the bags, the girl tells him to come back so they can finish the beer, right? But he takes a detour, enters the bar, and has a drink alone. That tells you everything he feels right there. He's still not into it but will go along. Who's to say that the next day, or after the child's born, he won't walk out on them and find himself another girl to travel around with?"

Margaret didn't respond, as if she'd not considered the possibility John outlined.

After a brief silence Dr. Pi asked, "That's what makes this story so interesting, isn't it? Hemingway leaves us thinking about his characters' futures. He lets us make up our own minds. An ambiguous ending. Fictional works often leave us hanging, wondering what will unfold next. Life's unpredictable. John's right in speculating that the American could walk out on the girl, but he may instead grow up, as Margaret suggests, and turn into a good father, once he looks into his baby's eyes. He doesn't have to remain an emotionless *prick* all his life … He *can* change!"

The class burst into wild laughter when Dr. Pi used the vernacular (a rarity), echoing Margaret. He waited for them to quiet down and resumed:

"He could become a man, even make a commitment and marry the girl, settle down, get a job, support his family, and be happy. Outgrow his wanderlust and desire to 'look at things and try new drinks.' That gets old after a while — drinking yourself into a stupor every day is a pretty dumb way to live."

"Naw it ain't…" was the chorus he heard, mainly from his eighteen- and nineteen-year-old male students sitting in the back. "That's a great strategy," one said. They laughed, and some gave each other high-fives.

Dr. Pi laughed with them. He remembered having a similar outlook once upon a time. Realizing he'd kept his class five minutes late, he dismissed them. "Okay, have a great day everyone. Read Chekhov's 'Misery' for Wednesday."

The students filed out boisterously, still debating the future possibilities for the American and the girl. Elated that there wasn't a meeting on this Monday, Dr. Pi walked home still thinking about Hemingway's characters. He remembered at age twenty-five being faced with a similar dilemma. The prospect of having a child then had not appealed to him initially, and to this day he felt guilty for having had those feelings. He'd been cowardly and callous towards his then-girlfriend, Joanna, not heroic, as he could've been. He should've understood how difficult it was for her (for she was only nineteen) but didn't. And that bothered him. Like the girl in "Hills," Joanna was the mature one, wanted their child, and had been ready to sacrifice for their future. He'd been immature, aloof, and distant. The repugnance of his behavior then still crushed him, as he thought back. He agonized over his selfishness and stupidity then. Why hadn't he shown her more compassion? More love? For days after he learned that he'd fathered a child, he'd been angry at himself for not being more careful. But thankfully, after speaking to Miriam, she'd helped him see that one should always embrace a new life. Her words — "life engenders life" — had opened his mind to the idea of becoming a father. Months later, he was one. It was a blessing in disguise, for his son brought him joy and a heightened desire to work towards his doctorate. He and Joanna married and found a small apartment. He got his first full-time teaching job and raising Christopher with Joanna became a fountain spring of happiness.

But that was twenty-six years ago, long before the death of his parents four years apart, before his divorce, before Christopher had married and moved to Vermont, and Tobias's lovely daughter Constance had gone to New York to study at Columbia, graduated, and settled in Manhattan to pursue a music career.

CHAPTER 5

Dr. Pi walked into his old Victorian and welcomed the silence. It was cool inside and comfortable. He slid out of his Oxfords and felt his sock feet sinking into the Persian runner that led from his foyer into his front reading room. Without a meeting to attend or office hours to hold, the rest of the afternoon was his. He didn't have much grading to do. There would be plenty of time for writing, and as usual, teaching had left him full of thoughts that needed a release.

He reached into a bowl on the front hall table and picked up a piece of registered mail that he'd signed for a few days earlier. Reopening the heavy linen envelope, he reread every word of the letter, signed by his publisher, confirming the October release of his first novel, *Yellow Bird*. A little frisson of excitement ran through him as he thought about his labor of love. Finally, the world would read the story that had obsessed him for most of the past decade: a tale of adventure and spiritual growth, based on his experiences as a cab driver in Manhattan in his early twenties.

Gathering the stories and giving shape to his experiences had been a huge undertaking. He'd thrown himself into the project with gusto, unearthing as much detail as he could remember about that tumultuous time, including some bizarre experiences behind the wheel and in the community of cab drivers. But the more he thought about his story's publication, the more he wondered if it would interest anyone in this day and age. The copy editor had completed her work and the novel's cover had been chosen. It was all starting to feel real. But Dr. Pi couldn't escape the feeling that something could still go wrong. Publishers were always merging or going under or having to cancel book contracts when their authors got into trouble or said the wrong thing. He couldn't think of any reason why he would be canceled, but anxiety crept in anyway, tainting his feelings of enjoyment at having accomplished a long-held dream. He'd tried to distract himself by outlining a new novel, but on several afternoons when he'd sat to write, nothing came.

After lunch, he went upstairs for a short nap. The respite often put him in the perfect creative mindset, as did the cooler, late-September weather that had moved in. The fifty-degree temperatures and low-to-no humidity that defined these fall days was an energizing elixir that triggered thoughts. The falling leaves, browning grass, and golden colors brought back memories of vibrant life in days long gone, thoughts of love and beauty, and the desire to capture with words those strong, fleeting feelings.

Today, however, he sat at his desk for thirty minutes and again nothing came. His thoughts were scattered, his sentences labored and stiff. He didn't like quitting so quickly because he didn't know when he would have another free afternoon. He was a literature professor writing in his leisure hours whenever they appeared. Sometimes he got so busy with lecture prep and grading that weeks would pass between creative writing sessions. Sometimes this felt unfair, but he was a professor first, a writer second; he tried to make the best of his situation.

After an hour and only a few useful sentences, he quit and walked to the post office to get the mail. On his way back he enjoyed the warm fall sunshine on his face, breathed in the cool air, and felt his muscles and bones benefit from the two-block sojourn. As he approached his house, he was thrilled to see the vibrant exterior paint colors he'd chosen in summer to dress up this enormous Queen Anne in which he lived alone. He'd bought the home years earlier, for the bargain price of fifty-eight thousand dollars, and slowly restored it to its original splendor. It was among the largest houses in Pleasant Hills and was now possibly worth about a quarter-million dollars, but Dr. Pi surmised that a similar-sized house of such architectural beauty could easily sell for a half million in the wealthier nearby towns of Cazenovia or Hamilton. His home had a wrap-around porch, impressive woodworking inside and out, a huge oak staircase, and even a stained-glass bay window. Dr. Pi loved his home and felt fortunate to live in it, just a block away from the college. All fifteen rooms were his to roam through on wintry days when the snow piled high and deep, and the grey, bleak afternoons could all but kill any life-spirit within. He decided he'd paint a little today; the bottom of the side bay window was ready for some primer and fresh color. In the big yellow barn out back, at the end of the long driveway on the north side of the house, he found his brushes and prepared the paint.

He applied the primer and soon fell into a rhythm, his two-inch brush spreading the white latex evenly over all the bare spots. Dr. Pi worked as carefully and neatly at this task as he did at any other. He wanted his finished work (whatever it was) to please — that's what brought him pleasure. Yet the thing he enjoyed most about painting was that he could do it and let his mind wander. Various ideas would come; inspiration would lift him into a euphoric realm. It was also when he'd traverse again — relive, so to speak — many of the difficult experiences he'd endured. His neighbors were all at work, so the area was silent, no lawnmowers whining, no banging on metal or wood in any backyard or garage. The silence was good for thinking. Occasionally, he'd hear squirrels chasing one another over the dead leaves near the barn and stop to watch them for a brief spell. But then he'd drift back nostalgically to the days of his youth when everything seemed a busy blur.

Eventually his mind drifted to Chekhov's "Misery," and to how he'd teach it on Wednesday. Many of the short stories he taught were sad, stories that emotionally sapped one's soul — and this was one of those. A bereaved Russian cab driver tries unsuccessfully to share the news of his son's death with his passengers, who show indifference to his grief. In the end, the only one who listens (because he has no choice) is his horse. The story's irony had startled Dr. Pi when he'd first read it as an undergraduate; he'd been haunted by its subtitle, "To Whom Shall I Tell My Grief?" It was a question he'd asked himself repeatedly after Maria's death, and most recently after Miriam's, on days when his heart longed for the woman who'd not only given him life, but also saved it by bringing him to America from Cuba. Miriam believed strongly that her children's future would be wrought with suffering if the communists brainwashed them with their propaganda. So, she'd gotten her family out of that crumbling country and never looked back. After her death in 2010, Dr. Pi had so much to say about her, about the complex feelings that fermented inside him — to anyone who would listen — just like Chekhov's Iona thirsted to share his grief over his son's death. Dr. Pi knew the story's relevance, why it would benefit students, but the key always was to elevate the discussion, so what was learned could become memorable. In class that Wednesday he'd emphasize how Chekhov's "Misery" provided valuable wisdom — all the grieving soul yearns for is to speak; all a good friend need do is listen.

After he finished painting, Dr. Pi showered and decided to go out for dinner. He took out the '86 Monte Carlo from the barn and drove to Mel's in Cooperstown for a fish fry. It was a lovely drive, up Route 20, and something about that town always cheered him. He loved the old homes there — most restored to perfection and well maintained — the peacefulness of the quiet side streets away from Main Street and the Baseball Hall of Fame, and the serenity of Otsego Lake at twilight.

After dinner, he strolled through town to the lake. He avoided the bar scene where folks gathered to relax and watch the Yankees, who were in the thick of a playoff race. Dr. Pi sat on a bench and gazed at the water and the golden sunlight caressing the tops of the distant hills. Nature's beauty amazed him, and he felt calm in her presence. Given his pervasive loneliness and indelible sadness, appreciating natural beauty — wherever it appeared — cheered and soothed him. After his divorce, which was amicable and mutually agreed to, Joanna had moved to San Diego to care for her aging parents. The first year he'd missed her terribly, for he still loved her deeply. Without her company and cheerfulness, being alone in that big, old house became unbearable. The hours dragged no matter what he did, and frequently he felt like Byron's Bonivard in "The Prisoner of Chillon," chained under Lac Leman. Dr. Pi had often pondered what the rest of his life would look like. Apart from his teaching, he'd looked for noble work to occupy his time. At first, nothing had come. All he'd felt was an endless emptiness, a deep and seemingly bottomless well, full of old regrets, missed opportunities to salvage his marriage, promising roads not taken. The thought of pursuing a new relationship crossed his mind at times, but just as quickly as it entered, he'd push it out. He didn't feel he could form an intimate union with anyone ever again.

Dr. Pi noticed a woman headed toward him from the dock's eastern end. She strolled slowly, deliberately, occasionally gazing at the water as she came closer. She was dressed casually, in comfortable beige slacks and an orange silk blouse paired with a light-brown blazer. A wide-brimmed hat sat on her head, framing her short dark hair. Dr. Pi stared for a moment and then refocused his eyes on the lake. The woman stopped and sat on the bench next to his, just a few yards away.

"Good evening," she said. "It's a lovely view."

Dr. Pi was startled when she spoke, but recouped and answered, "Yes. It is. Good evening." And then, not knowing why he felt so at ease, he added, "The serenity here is good for thinking. Very peaceful."

"Yes. One can feel the years disappear in this silence."

She said nothing else, and Dr. Pi did not know what to say next, so he kept quiet and the two meditated privately. Dr. Pi muted his iPhone, worried about having it ring suddenly and disturb the woman's peaceful reverie. A good twenty minutes passed, and the woman finally got up, glanced in his direction, and said, "Have a nice night." She smiled at him and gave a little wave before walking towards the nearby restaurant's parking lot.

"Thanks. You too," Dr. Pi said and waved back. His eyes followed her as she disappeared in the distance. He'd not scrutinized her face, but only glanced over quickly. In the fading light, all he could see was a pleasant face whose features were indecipherable and not memorable, save for the lingering mystery about her.

CHAPTER 6

The next night, Dr. Pi cooked some salmon and carrots and watched the evening news. Most nights, if there was a hockey or baseball game, he'd watch that. Sometimes he read, but his eyes gave out early, so this wasn't an ordinary habit. What helped him relax at night, and what had now become a pervasive habit, was his engagement on social media with women from different countries.

Dr. Pi did not like Facebook; he found it too busy, and he had no interest in finding a date on sites such as Tinder. He was convinced he did not want another intimate relationship with any woman. He didn't mind flirting and engaging women superficially on social media, but he wasn't looking for anything serious; the pain associated with his marriage's dissolution lingered and crushed any longing for another true love. He enjoyed Instagram; he loved looking at photographs and making thoughtful comments, brief statements to uplift the people he followed — close or distant friends, family members, complete strangers living in different countries, artists, professional photographers, poets, and fitness and fashion models. The only people he wouldn't follow were those with narrow political or religious ideologies. He purposely avoided Twitter because he didn't want to get drawn into political or social debates, or anything that could raise his blood pressure. He saw all that rhetoric as a waste of his time — wolves howling at the moon — individuals with no real desire to solve problems, but who loved to force their narrow views on others. Whenever he saw mindlessness expressed on social media, he burned to engage the participants with a burst of reason, but he refrained, and thought of Paine's memorable words: "To argue with a person who has renounced the use of reason is like administering medicine to the dead." It was easier to put down his phone and pick up his guitar, or get some extra sleep, than to waste time trying to convince anyone to change their mind. Some people were too entrenched in their own stubbornness to ever see the light. Though he remained hopeful that reason would ultimately triumph in humanity's wayward kingdom, Dr. Pi believed that the best chance was to enlighten the young.

Though he'd always texted friends and family (even in the days of flip phones), initially, he'd avoided using popular social media platforms. Not long ago, he hadn't known how Instagram worked and didn't care to find out. His gut feeling was that social media was for the new generation. He couldn't fathom gaining any pleasure from staring at a screen. Then one evening his life changed — someone happened through his life and opened a door — and these days he felt grateful to have this outlet late at night. Whenever the loneliness would creep in, he'd go on Instagram, look at the photographs, and comment.

It was mid-June in 2017, on a night when he felt depressed, that Dr. Pi was first introduced to the ubiquitous app. Sitting on his front porch after dinner, staring at the twilight sky, missing Maria, his parents, children, and supportive ex-wife, his soul was in agony. He replayed mistakes he'd made, miscalculations and choices that had led to disaster. He wished fervently to travel back through the years and make better decisions. One weighed on him especially heavily. Joanna had always believed that he could be a dean or president at a bigger college if he set his mind to it and worked hard. She had encouraged him to climb the academic ladder to make more money and use his engaging personality to promote academic policies to benefit students, but he never listened. These leadership roles didn't interest him, he'd told her on several occasions; he preferred the classroom and teaching literature, he'd said, and shut their conversation down. Why hadn't he listened to her? Why had he been so obtuse? Would he have accomplished more, and would they still be together, if he'd followed her advice? As night crept in, he felt pure regret strangling him, weighing on his soul like an enormous pyramid. Just then, his next-door neighbor Raymond walked past his house, glanced at him from under a streetlight, and turned to wave at him from the sidewalk. Dr. Pi waved back at the man in the cone of light and heard himself say "Hello." The greeting came out in an odd sort of squeak, probably because Dr. Pi had just been about to cry. Ray stood still and looked at him.

"You okay?" he asked, drilling his eyes into Dr. Pi's.

"Sure. Yes," Dr. Pi said. "Fine. How are you?"

Ray hovered there with crossed arms, staring. "Not too bad," he said.

That's when Dr. Pi remembered what he had heard from another neighbor. Ray was in the midst of a divorce too. As the dusty light swirled around Ray's greying hair, Dr. Pi felt a sudden surge of empathy toward the man who he had only spoken to on a half-dozen other occasions. And although Dr. Pi was not much of a drinker, he invited his neighbor out for a drink. Dr. Pi couldn't recall the last time he'd done this. The two walked to The Castle for a beer, pretzels, and the prospect of a game of pool.

The bar was nearly empty. Ray and Dr. Pi were alone with the waitress Susan, an attractive, voluptuous blonde with a lively personality. Her flirtatious banter was exactly what they needed while they drank their beers and discussed their troubles. By his third beer, Dr. Pi was tipsy, and he stared with interest at Susan's attractive bosom and curvaceous figure. She knew exactly where his eyes roamed. It was obvious she sought a big tip because she'd take every opportunity to entice the two by bending down behind the bar.

At one point, Susan leaned over the counter directly in front of them, her folded arms propping up her breasts, and asked if they wanted to follow her on Instagram. That's where she posted her sexy photographs, she said, and winked. Ray knew her game and said he'd look her up later that night, but Dr. Pi admitted he didn't do social media. This admission perked Susan's interest. She took out her phone and showed him what he was missing out on. When Dr. Pi saw her sexy pics on Instagram he was hooked, and by the end of the night she'd created Instagram and Snapchat accounts for him, become his follower, and showed him how to access all her shots. By the fifth beer, drunk and ready to walk home, Dr. Pi was excited about this new opportunity to meet others. He paid for their drinks, and left Susan a twenty-dollar tip. From then on, he was a different man. Later that night he scrolled through Susan's pictures — a visual account of her life and travels for the past four years.

The next day he'd shared a story about his painting on Snapchat, which Susan commented on, and days later he posted his first photograph on Instagram — a bunch of baby spiders crawling over gardenias on a flower basket hanging on his porch. He received a few likes, mainly from family members, but Susan didn't like or comment on it, and he was upset. Throughout the summer, as he posted photographs, gained followers by adding hashtags (as his son had instructed him to do), and lost himself in that virtual reality, the late-night loneliness became bearable. Slowly, it started to disappear for days at a time.

CHAPTER 7

Half a year later, he was obsessed with two Russian women he followed, both in their mid-twenties. One lived near the Arctic Circle, in Murmansk, a place Dr. Pi hadn't even known existed, a city that didn't see the sun for several weeks in winter. Nora had a unique look, with magnificent dark-brown, wavy hair, a perfectly formed nose, full lips, and gorgeous green eyes. She was stunningly beautiful, dressed elegantly, and was constantly posting pictures. Many were of her snow-clad town, taken from the window of the high-rise building she lived in — with a highway close by and a bridge in the distance — while others featured her manicured hands or her black cat. The majority of her posts were of beauty products — makeup, creams, lipstick — which she advertised and sold. She wrote mostly in Russian about wellness and beauty and chasing dreams — blogs which Dr. Pi read in translation and loved. She wrote in good, clear English at times, which Dr. Pi praised. Nora thanked him for his encouragement and kindness and said his comments always made her smile (this statement alone warmed his heart and got him hooked), but that she felt more confident writing Russian. Still, one day she hoped to speak and write better in English and travel the world. Her life fascinated him; her youthful optimism inspired deep emotions. She wrote about her family, her boyfriend, Victor, how their romance had begun at university, her vacations to Russian seaside towns, and her dream to one day go to New York. Victor had his own page that seemed to be devoted mostly to books and bodybuilding.

Before bed one night, Dr. Pi replied to one of Nora's posts with an invitation: *If you ever come to New York, you have a friend here; I'd be more than happy to show you and Victor around Manhattan.* She responded with a line of hearts and happy faces and said she hoped to one day take him up on his kind offer. As he drifted off to sleep, Dr. Pi wondered what it would be like to host his foreign friends. Would this photogenic Russian couple, who seemed to live inside his device, actually turn out to be flesh and blood people? Would they fall into an easy rapport, or have nothing in common? He had no idea, but he was suddenly, wildly curious. A whole new world had opened up for him.

The other woman, Katerina, was mysterious and intrigued Dr. Pi even more. He felt drawn to her from the outset, like a paper clip in a small Central New York town being yanked across the vast Atlantic by a magical magnet in Warsaw. Katerina was also Russian, beautiful, sensitive, artistic, and above all, exceedingly courteous to him. In fact, it was the way that she responded to his posts and comments that made Dr. Pi carefully frame his remarks and weigh every word when he engaged her. He wanted to please this extraordinarily polite and beautiful young woman. He wanted her to like him. Slowly, he'd learned a little about her — that she loved music and sang Russian songs, spoke Russian and Polish and was polishing her English, saw herself as a romantic, loved autumn, and dressed impeccably, with elegance and style.

Katerina had long red hair that fell below her waist; occasionally she braided it in small sections, but never wore it up completely, or at least not in the pictures she posted. Her skin was pearl white, without a single blemish, and her large, grey-green eyes radiated a soulful richness and sensitivity. Her nose was small, accented with a simple small gold ring on her right nostril. Her lips were elegantly formed and not parted in many of the photographs, a feature that somehow captured her shyness and gave the impression that she kept parts of herself in reserve. Her body was slender, shapely, and sensuous, and her legs long and lovely. In some of her posts, she wore maroon or white lace lingerie. In a few videos, Dr. Pi saw the provocative way she moved as she sprayed perfume on her neck and outfit before heading out for the night.

A year had passed since Dr. Pi had started following Katerina. Initially he'd written brief comments on her posts, but that changed when she posted a photograph of herself in bed, looking unhappy, and shared that she'd been sad. Instantly, Dr. Pi offered fatherly advice, promissory words. He wished to lessen her loneliness. It was one of the lengthiest comments he'd ever written on anyone's post. And she'd responded with such frank gratitude that his interest in her grew. For months, he carefully worded his responses, which revealed his growing affection. Though Dr. Pi continued to praise the posts of over five hundred people he followed, it was Katerina who intrigued him. He thought of her daily, and when she commented candidly and nicely on all his posts, he realized that Katerina had stirred emotions in him that had been dormant for quite some time. He even thought of having an intimate relationship with a woman again, a desire which had all but disappeared since his divorce. The only problem was Katerina was approximately half his age and a fifth of a world away. Dr. Pi was baffled by his growing feelings for her and the new dilemma he'd gotten himself into. One side of him thought it was a foolish yearning and best to nip in the bud; the other side egged him on to continue to get to know her because somehow knowing her and having her continuously on his mind made him happy, gave purpose to his days, and filled him with a renewed desire to dream.

CHAPTER 8

On Thursday, Dr. Pi taught his Comp classes, whose focus was research paper writing. Each semester, he chose a contemporary topic of concern. This semester he'd chosen the effect of smartphones and social media use on iGeneration students, the very students sitting in his classes, who had grown up with the Internet and spent their whole young lives interacting with the world through their devices. An article linking addictive use of these devices and social media to higher rates of depression, anxiety, and suicide among teenagers had concerned him. He hoped studying this topic would help students intelligently reflect upon it.

These Comp classes were tough to teach because most students were generally shy about venturing ideas. They weren't talkative and didn't enjoy debating positions. This semester the lack of engagement had alarmed Dr. Pi. Students couldn't disengage from their smartphones. Those phones had to be on their desks or laps, and their eyes were riveted to screens. As Dr. Pi asked questions about their writing, or subjects they had interest in, few hands went up, and few eyes were visible; most heads gazed down at smartphones.

Dr. Pi's immediate reaction was to ask nicely that they put the phones out of sight. He said sternly, authoritatively (in a voice he rarely used): "I *do not* want to see them." There was some grumbling that eventually died down. He then asked the students to arrange themselves in a large circle. Chairs were moved reluctantly, and students were instantly staring at one another; some, in fact, were bewildered with this new arrangement and wondered why this was necessary. To many, it was an inconvenience. At first, they spoke only reluctantly, and when they did, their voices could barely be heard. Dr. Pi asked them to speak louder, told them they had much to say that would be useful, especially on a topic they knew so much about. Soon, most were sharing insights about their social media use, and many confessed they found it difficult to put their phones away. Several said that even while sleeping, they felt more comfortable with their phones nearby. Discussion picked up, and finally, many shared that they often felt depressed, isolated, left out by friends on social media. Others said they felt anxious and that they'd been bullied in high school. Dr. Pi saw clearly that these admissions verified the article's findings. Students agreed what they'd read was true. Dr. Pi then refocused the discussion on seeking solutions.

"We don't argue for the sake of arguing," he said, "but to find answers. And that's what all of you are going to do. For next Tuesday, you'll write a paper outlining your experience using smartphones and social media and propose ways to do so more intelligently. In what ways can we decrease the depression and anxiety that studies show is connected to social media use? Maybe this is the perfect topic to write a research paper on."

There were groans as students filed out of class, which Dr. Pi had anticipated. But he knew all of them would benefit from the assignment.

After dinner that evening and the nightly news — always a sad affair — Dr. Pi played his guitar for an hour and then prepared for bed. Before putting on a Netflix documentary about the universe (pondering stars served as his nightly sleeping pill), he scrolled through Instagram and left his usual positive comments on the posts he liked: *Lovely photograph; great scenery. Beautiful smile (happy face emoji); Nice lines; excellent poem. Love your imagery (book and pen* and smile emoji); *Fantastic painting; awesome colors. Nice job!* (*three smile emojis and a heart*). He was just about to set his alarm clock but decided to see if Katerina had posted anything he might have missed.

It was 10 p.m. New York time, and since she lived in Warsaw, it would be 4 a.m. Friday there. Dr. Pi imagined her in bed and resting soundly. She hadn't posted; he wasn't disappointed, but he felt himself missing her. He began scrolling through her photos and posts, and before he knew it, half an hour had passed. In that time, he also reread what he'd written to her and went through most of her replies. His imagination was triggered and somehow, on this night, he began to feel something much more profoundly moving towards Katerina. She was captivating him. His loneliness was suffocating sometimes, yet scrolling through Katerina's photographs, and looking at the respectful way she answered her admirers, warmed his heart. Before taking off his glasses, shutting out the lights, and tucking his head on his pillow to focus on Dr. Al-Khalili's insights on the universe's end, Dr. Pi stared another long minute at Katerina's face and her rich and warm grey-green eyes, and imagined what it would be like to hold her in his arms, to cuddle beside her through the long night, to wake up next to her in the early morning, to kiss her forehead before going off to teach, and to spend the whole day inspired by her, eagerly waiting to see her again that night.

It amazed him that this woman he'd never physically met was now a fixture in his daily life. He thought about her as if he knew her, imagined listening to her speak in Russian or Polish to friends, at school, or at the restaurant where she worked as a chef. He spent an inordinate amount of time each day trying to imagine what her life was like, what kind of upbringing she'd had, and even where she would end up in the future. He wondered whether she had a lover (*she must, because she's so beautiful and perfect*, he thought), and, if so, how he treated her. If she did have someone who treated her well, he'd be truly happy for her. But when he thought about her having a lover who didn't appreciate her, he became upset and wished to help her tear herself away from a terrible situation.

Katerina was enigmatic to him simply because he didn't know these personal details (though he wished to), and she was not forthcoming with anything about the real circumstances of her emotional life. At times, Dr. Pi sensed her loneliness. It came through in certain phrases she used — for example, being *worried about the big world around her*, and *without this hard part of life — good part can't be possible … ah, but I'm so tired to go sometimes*. But these phrases were not much to go on to get a fuller picture of her real life. Everything had to be derived from posts — photographs, captions, bits and pieces shared in her stories. Once, Dr. Pi had pressed her to explain further, to provide specific details, but she'd just written: *I do not want to burden you with that*. And though he'd left it at that, Dr. Pi wondered what was "burdensome" in her life.

The previous December she'd been just another woman he followed on Instagram. Occasionally, he commented on her posts. In one video, Katerina used a candy cane to lower her bra strap from her shoulder towards her elbow, stopping just short of showing her breast. Dr. Pi had liked it and commented:

So sensuous and lovely. Candy canes are truly useful and tasty (happy face blowing a heart kiss, and a rose and heart emojis).

She'd liked his comment and replied with a happy face and candy cane emojis and a *thanks*. On another post, of beautiful photographs of Warsaw at Christmastime, Dr. Pi had commented:

These are lovely photographs. You look fantastic. The Christmas atmosphere is nice here also. We now have lots of snow (four snowflakes, a flower, a happy face blowing a heart kiss, and red heart emojis).

She'd replied: *Thank you! (smiley face) so nice … a lot of snow (a smiley with heart eyes, and two snowflakes) in my city also snow today, but not a lot (two snowflakes).*

One photo of her lying in bed, showing just her lovely face and neck, had an erotic, artistic feel to it with a moving caption about self-actualization and the challenges faced as we grow. Dr. Pi had commented:

Wow. To wake up to this beautiful photograph was wonderful. Thanks. You look so lovely. Your skin, eyes, hair, expression — all perfect. I liked your caption also. We learn about ourselves slowly, as we move forward, and take many roads and turns. And though we never know where we'll wind up, the act of discovery makes traveling the roads before us worth it (a rose, a smiley face blowing a heart kiss, and a red heart emoji).

Katerina replied:

Thank you so much for this lovely big comment (a red heart emoji) I'm very pleased … I'm glad you can feel my caption, your words is true … life is not easy.

When Dr. Pi read her comment, he was thrilled. He realized he'd caught this beautiful young woman's attention — she'd been *very pleased.* She'd praised him for understanding her. At that point the previous December, he'd become interesting to Katerina. He was now not just one of the many men and boys who followed her. He'd put himself on her radar. Soon after, each time he posted a photograph, Katerina was one of the first to like it, and not long after that, she began to comment on his posts as well.

What verified for Dr. Pi that he'd become important in Katerina's virtual world was when, quite unexpectedly, he received a brief direct message from her:

Thank you so much for your beautiful comments always (red heart emoji) I'm always very pleased to read it!

Three hours later, Dr. Pi had replied soberly, trying not to reveal how truly excited he was that this beautiful, unknown, Russian woman had reached out to express her gratitude:

You're welcome. I always enjoy your posts. Hope you have a wonderful beginning to the coming year.

She responded with a sigh face emoji, followed by *I hope you also.* And six big and small star emojis — one whose golden points were surrounded by a blue frame. The main thing about these stars was that they were big and bold. Dr. Pi understood their underlying symbolic significance — he'd become a notable star in her sky.

Dr. Pi tried not to read too much into it but couldn't help himself. He was a lonely man. He saw it as a perfect, brief, meaningful exchange, and did not want to ruin it by adding anything further that could detract from its power.

As he reflected on those final weeks of December the previous year, he wondered whether something else might have put him on Katerina's register. One evening he'd played some old original songs on his guitar and reminisced about his grad school days when he'd played in the band Dionysus. Later, he flipped through an old photo album and found a photo of himself by a bandmate's side, and the nostalgic loneliness sliced through him. He took a photograph of it, posted it on Instagram, and described that time when his daily life was all about music and song, vibrant with youth and future optimism. Katerina had liked his post and written: *Wow! Very old style* (*a smiley in sunglasses and a thumbs-up emoji*) *I didn't know about this part of your life* (*three music notes and microphone emojis*). He'd replied: *...before I became an English literature professor, music was my passion, and I played and wrote songs for the band Dionysus. Four of our songs are up on our website: dionysustheband.com.* Katerina then enthusiastically wrote: *I'll listen!* (*a smiley face*) *I love music so much* (*red heart*). And Dr. Pi replied: *wonderful. Hope you enjoy the songs* (*red rose*).

Dr. Pi was unaware then that music was Katerina's passion, that she'd played piano since she was six, or that she currently studied ancient music, theory, harmony, and composition. She'd just said: *I love music so much.* She must have listened to those old Dionysus songs, he thought, and realized Dr. Pi shared a similar passion for music. That post on that sad night, Dr. Pi now reflected, might have been the one that opened a bright new world, a wonderful friendship with a young woman with a romantic sensibility like his, one who'd become interested in his world and would want to know more about it. Modern magic, Dr. Pi pondered, a new friend brought to him by powerful technology, electrons bounced off satellites at light speed — from a bedroom in Poland to a living room in Central New York — uniting two souls seeking comfort, companionship, and love.

CHAPTER 9

In late December 2017, Dr. Pi had been invited to celebrate New Year's Eve with friends on Long Island, but spent it alone in his big Victorian, quietly working on revisions to *Yellow Bird*. Though he felt a little down, thoughts of Katerina buoyed him. She'd become a muse — his Russian muse — who could magically make him feel calm, optimistic, and less lonely. He'd conjure her beauty whenever sadness crept in. That evening, he posted another old photograph of himself holding his guitar in the Stony Brook dorm room. The caption referenced the elusiveness of dreams, and that while his desire to become a songwriter and performer had not materialized, he'd found fulfillment as a professor — a surrogate dream. His wording was nostalgic, tinged with sadness, the end of another year stirring these bittersweet emotions. However, Katerina's comment had lifted him out of the doldrums; she'd given the photograph three thumbs up and written: *Happy New Year for you! Be happy every day and enjoy your life every day!* Dr. Pi had considered how happy he'd feel every day if he had someone as kind and beautiful as Katerina to love and care for.

Dr. Pi put down his phone and leaned back in his leather chair. His eyes traveled around his book-lined study until they rested on a framed photograph of his mother and sister sitting on a bench in the garden of their old home. The silence in the room was oppressive. Dr. Pi thought about how often he declined invitations to social events. He knew he needed more silence than most people. Silence was good for working and thinking. Yet it often led his mind to wander down roads that brought tears to his eyes, especially when he'd think about his sister and his mother — both gone — and of how scattered his once tightly knit family now was. And yet something new was growing inside of him, a nascent optimism that he hadn't felt in years. The further he got into the revising process, the more chaff he cut from his torturously long story about his cab-driving days, the more he came to believe that a lifelong dream would soon come true. And if it did, it would be because of the support of an old and true friend, Joe Rossetti, someone who'd always cared for him, and had continued caring for him, despite their separation, through the numerous years that had passed.

***

The previous October 2017, Dr. Pi had met his old college roommate in Manhattan, and they'd gone for dinner at Ogliastro's Pizza Bar in Brooklyn, where his Constance bartended. Joe Rossetti and he shared a passion for literature that still bonded them. Dr. Pi had already sent a copy of *Yellow Bird* to Joe in Kentucky where he lived with his lovely wife. Joe had liked it and encouraged Dr. Pi to send out hundreds of letters to potential agents. Dr. Pi had managed fifty-five carefully crafted queries without success.

"So, have you found an agent Tobias?"

"Not yet. I've given up. Takes too much time. With teaching, it's impossible."

"You must send hundreds out — everywhere — Canada, Australia, England. Just keep sending them. Don't quit. Someone will say yes."

"I've lost the desire. Besides, who the hell is interested? Who gives a damn about a Manhattan cabby in the late eighties? We're in the Uber age."

"Tobias," Joe said emphatically, "I read your book. It's a good story. Reminded me of *The Catcher in the Rye*. Many of the greatest novels ever written are very personal stories."

"I can't. I'm done. It's over. I just don't have the heart for it anymore."

When the waiter came to their table, Joe ordered two more beers. He looked intently at Tobias, sat back relaxed and satisfied, and then said:

"Look. Cut a hundred pages off your book by February first, and I'll show it to my editor."

Tobias was stunned.

"What? You have an editor? How come you never mentioned it?"

"Cause you're a PhD in English Literature. Figured some agent in Manhattan would represent you. Didn't think you'd need any help."

"It only means you've studied a great deal," Tobias said. "Doesn't mean you can write a good story."

"Take a hundred pages off," Joe urged. "I'll talk to my editor this week. We'll get your book out by this time next year."

Dr. Pi's heart filled with the optimism of this challenge. He felt enormous gratitude towards his friend.

"Don't mention it. I like your story. By this time next year, *Yellow Bird* will be published. Get it down to around a hundred thousand words; eighty-five thousand would be better." He lifted his glass, toasted Tobias, and guzzled his beer with gusto.

CHAPTER 10

As he remembered this exchange, and how good those beers tasted that night, Dr. Pi thanked God for having blessed him with a friend as wonderful as Joe. Now, a year later, his book was set to be released in October, just as Joe had said it would be.

Dr. Pi's excitement grew the final week of September. After delivering poignant lectures on Chekhov's "Misery" and Marquez's "A Very Old Man with Enormous Wings," Dr. Pi went to lunch with his good friend Curt Warrens, who ran the college print shop. Over the past ten years, they'd taken turns treating one another on Fridays. Curt was happily married and had four kids. He was an avid golfer, sharp-witted, funny, kind, and a Pittsburgh Penguins hockey fan. Dr. Pi was a die-hard New York Islanders fan, so sports talk dominated their conversations. Over time, the two had become close and discussed more personal matters. With Curt, Dr. Pi had shared his pain over Miriam's unexpected death, the difficulties during his separation and divorce, and the agonizing ups and downs of writing and teaching. They shared stories about their old cars, raising kids, college politics, and the challenges of relationships. For the past year, a major topic of conversation was Dr. Pi's social media involvement. As Dr. Pi had revised *Yellow Bird*, Curt printed hard copies of his drafts. When he looked at them, Dr. Pi felt optimistic that one day the novel would end up on a Barnes & Noble shelf.

Dr. Pi was in a good mood as he sat down across from Curt and cradled his pint of beer. Draft Horse Triple loosened his tongue; he trusted Curt with personal details, and though there were some things he'd *never* share with anyone, such as the brutal beating he'd once given Eddie, talking aloud about what cluttered his brain was therapeutic.

"So, whatever happened to that nurse you took out to dinner last year?" Curt asked. "Did you ever pursue that? You said she was beautiful."

"Very beautiful, attentive, and kind," Dr. Pi said, wiping a bit of condensation from his glass. "No, I didn't stay in touch. I just took her to dinner."

"Nothing in common?"

"We got along okay. Maybe I was afraid of committing to something — don't know. My heart wasn't in it."

"Can't know if it'll work out from just one date. Should've gotten to know her."

"I did. She's a practical woman. I'm an impractical man whose head's in the clouds most of the time."

Curt laughed and clinked his friend's glass. "Can't argue with that," he said. "But mate, it sounds like you decided for her."

"I've been in relationships like that before. They don't work. And honestly, any talk about hospitals makes me ill because I start thinking of my mom's death. And that's her field. It's what's important to her. I want to avoid thinking about hospitals for as long as possible."

Dr. Pi took a long gulp of beer. Curt stared at him with a knowing smile.

"Come on," he said. "I don't buy that. Didn't you tell me you'd written her a song?"

"I did. Precisely my point. She needs a man who can do much more than that, and right now that's about all I can offer anyone. A damn song!"

"What are you talking about? You have lots to offer. You have a great job, an incredible house, you're generous. Was it the age difference? What was she? Thirty-five, I think you said."

"Thirty-eight," Dr. Pi replied. He munched on some chips and decided to give his friend a more honest answer. "No, it wasn't her age. Or the hospital stuff. Really can't say. We had a nice time. I just didn't even know how to pursue it, or what to say next after I hugged her goodnight, whether to call or text. So I never followed up. Some weekends when I felt lonely, I thought I should text her, but I never did."

"Dude, you ghosted her."

"No, I did not."

"You did."

"Well, I didn't mean to. I was going on instinct. Then after a couple of months, I figured it was too late and stopped thinking about it."

"Nice," Curt said, clearly indicating that he thought no such thing.

"I did torture myself a good long while with it," Dr. Pi said, suddenly defensive. "I know I should've called or texted her and offered an explanation, but I chickened out. I still feel awful about it. Trust me, my mind's a chaotic mess these days."

"I know, man, I know," said Curt.

The waitress came over and they each ordered dessert and another beer.

"And how are things now, relationship-wise? Got anything cooking?" Curt asked.

"Well, there's this young Russian woman named Katerina," Dr. Pi replied.

That got Curt's attention. "How young?"

"Twenty-four this December."

"Holy crap. She's even younger than the nurse."

Dr. Pi smiled and pulled out his phone. After a minute of scrolling, he found one of his favorite photographs of Katerina, which he'd saved from her Instagram. She was sitting on a park bench in autumn, surrounded in all directions by thousands of golden leaves on the ground. Her smile was radiant. He passed his phone across the table and waited for his friend's reaction. Curt stared at the screen and his jaw dropped.

"Holy…"

Dr. Pi just smiled. Then he reached across and scrolled down to another photograph, showing Katerina standing behind a tall tree with her arms wrapped around its trunk. She wore faded blue jeans and a dark top and vest. Her long, slender legs and shapely body looked lovely in the late afternoon light, as did her long, cascading red hair and beautiful face.

"She's gorgeous," Curt said. "Wow!"

"She is," Dr. Pi said. "Nothing will come of it though." He sighed. "I'm just torturing myself by dreaming of someone I could never have."

"Why not? Hey, you never know."

Their desserts and beers arrived. Curt dug into his brulé, and Dr. Pi sipped his Triple.

"But it doesn't matter," Dr. Pi continued. "She inspires me. She's artistic, romantic. I love who she is. The way she makes me feel. That feeling's been missing in me a long time."

"Ever Facetime her?"

"No. She doesn't speak English."

"What? Then how do you communicate?"

"Modern technology," Dr. Pi replied and smiled. "So far, we just like one another's posts and comment on them. She translates my words into Russian, then translates her response into English for me. And I translate her Russian captions into English. It's worked out just fine for a year."

"And that's fulfilling? Isn't there a lot lost in translation? How do you even know she's a real person? Could be KGB trying to snare a lonely American and sneak a spy into the States."

When Dr. Pi's eyes widened, Curt laughed and said, "Just kidding." He reached for his beer and winked across the table. "But she could be a bot."

Dr. Pi replied quickly: "I know, right? Don't forget the fifty-second videos, also. Perhaps … I'm a gullible fool falling for a gorgeous siren." The two men laughed, ate some cheesecake, and drank another beer each before falling silent. Finally, Dr. Pi fixed his eyes on Curt's and made himself clear.

"She's real. Not a spy. I can assure you of that."

Curt raised both hands in self-defense. "Okay man, she's not a spy, or a bot."

"Remember, language is my area of expertise, right?" Dr. Pi smiled. "Besides, she's learning English, and her language has a linguistic consistency, a raw, natural honesty. I doubt a computer could simulate it. If she's not authentic, she can take me for all I've got. She's such a lovely person, I couldn't care less." He paused, took a sip of beer, and then finished: "Put it this way, if she asked, I'd give her *all* I have tomorrow."

"You're really smitten, aren't you?" Curt remarked.

"I sure am," Dr. Pi said, glassy eyed from the effects of the Triples. "Katerina's special. Thinking about her makes me happy and creative. I go through the days happier now than I have in quite some time. That counts for something, right?"

"Definitely. And what's in it for her?"

"Can't say. I'd like to know myself." Dr. Pi smiled and shrugged his shoulders. "But her comments on *all* my posts show she's taken an interest in me too. They're forthright, honest, appreciative, and she's really curious. She asks me questions…."

"Well, I've heard Putin appreciates good research," Curt interrupted, and laughed. Dr. Pi looked surprised at first, then laughed with him.

"Exactly! Can't phone in that *kompromat*. Have to dot your I's and cross your T's," Dr. Pi said, and they both laughed some more, until the professor went quiet again. "But seriously," he said. "I'll take my chances. I can't give up this friendship."

"No, no. I'm not suggesting you should," Curt said. "Friendship, huh? Sounds nice. Sounds really nice. Just be careful, okay?"

"I can't live life afraid. Katerina's the best thing that's happened in my life in quite some time. Even if nothing happens and it brings heartbreak, so be it. Heartbreak's part of life, but inspiration's rare. And I need it. Badly. To write. And Katerina helps that happen. Don't ask me how. She's a magic woman."

"I hear you," Curt said.

Dr. Pi asked the waitress for the bill and Curt thanked him for lunch. The two finished their beers and headed for the door.

CHAPTER 11

That same Friday night in late September was quiet. Dr. Pi felt lonely and exhausted. Though he had been a bundle of energy in the classroom, by week's end, after eight seventy-five-minute classes Monday through Thursday and grading papers all day Friday, plus meetings and committee work, he was spent. He thought of dining out and then catching a movie, but wasn't in the mood to go anywhere. Instead, he stayed home and ate spaghetti and meatballs while watching the ABC evening news, and then sat through an agonizing, poorly played Islanders pre-season game, which they lost. Afterwards, he felt deflated and decided to head to bed early. He put his iPhone to charge, brushed his teeth, put on his pajamas, and then went back for his phone. Its screen lit up just as he reached for it; he noticed that Katerina had liked his latest post — some old family photos of his kids when he was a young father. In one, he smiled and hugged two-year-old Christopher, and together they hugged Big Bird; in another, he and five-year-old Christopher crouched smiling around a baby carriage holding his two-year-old Constance. Dr. Pi didn't share many of these photographs publicly, but the previous night he'd decided to post for Throwback Thursday. Something about sharing some old-time happiness with the world revitalized him. Katerina's comment was direct, simple, and loving: *Your photos are very nice and cute, I feel a lot of love for them!* (*prayer hands, a smiley face, and red heart emojis*).

Her comment alone removed an entire evening's gloom. Suddenly Dr. Pi picked up his guitar. As he began to strum, his energy returned. He played one of his old romantic originals and imagined Katerina listening. It was a happy song he'd written in college for a girl named Karen. It had a bright sound in the key of G, and both the E minor and A minor chords gave the melody just the right amount of nostalgic tenderness. The lyrics perfectly fit his situation then — his longing for Karen — and now — his wishing that Katerina were nearby. Nothing had really changed with his romantic yearnings, although many, many years had passed, and the object of his affection was different. Dr. Pi sang joyfully as he strummed:

Here I sit, thinking of you,
Wondering where you are.
The night is long. The sun far away.
It's silly of me to miss you so.
But you are my life, my soul, and my hope,
And only you can make me happy.

When he finished, he played another original, and then "Nights in White Satin," one of Dr. Pi's all-time favorites — one he wished he'd written. He thought of making love to Katerina, of what her soft skin would feel like as he kissed her body. He saw her long, slender legs wrapped around his back as he tenderly entered her, while staring deeply into her grey-green eyes with eagerness and desire. Katerina would moan happily and whisper loving Russian words into his ears. He needed this woman in his real life. If just the thought of her could magically lift his somberness, Dr. Pi wondered what her physical presence could instill in him — a renewed vigor, a passion he'd forgotten real love inspires.

Before long, Dr. Pi was warmed up and his voice was clean and crisp. He played song after song, interspersing his originals with tunes he knew by The Stones, The Beatles, and Don McLean. In his parlor, Dr. Pi had colorful Christmas lights on all year, which gave the room a festive and warm feeling. By the fifth song, he imagined he was playing for an audience, what he satirically termed and told friends were the "house spirits." He enjoyed having friends think he was losing it a bit, but he knew he wasn't. This cheered him up on days and evenings that seemed unbearable because of his prevailing loneliness. After six songs, he got a cold bottle of water, then came back for his second set. He began asking the spirits for requests — always longer songs that performers never dared play: "The House of the Rising Sun" by The Animals, and Don McLean's "American Pie." Dr. Pi felt heroic and happier. Because of their length and intensity, these songs zapped his energy, and he got sleepy. He took another break after thanking his imagined audience and promised them something truly special for his final set.

It was after midnight. Dr. Pi texted his son and daughter a *Goodnight. Love you*, then ran through his photos of Katerina yet again. He'd saved many and stared at them each night before bed. He sighed, lamenting that this woman he'd been smitten by was so far away, so young, so out of reach. He felt foolish! For someone as educated as he was, these emotions seemed illogical, ones he should have nipped in the bud when they'd initially surfaced. Why had he allowed himself to want her? He couldn't explain it reasonably. It was an irrational longing. The truth was that this had happened gradually, over a year's time, until suddenly she was center stage in his world.

Dr. Pi picked up his guitar to close out his show:

"I'm dedicating this last set of originals to a Russian woman named Katerina whom I've come to adore. Strangely enough, I've never met her, never heard her sweet voice on my phone, and never exchanged any thoughts, except through Google Translate. She speaks Russian and Polish; I, English, and Spanish. Quite bizarre, you might say. Well, you're right. And yet, she inspires in me a passion and desire I have not felt for years."

He paused, reflected, and then continued:

"She's magical. My Venus. My Russian muse. So, without further ado, here's a song she's inspired called "Lady Stay." Dr. Pi began singing, tenderly at first, while softly strumming the majestic but subdued Amaj7, E7, and Bm chords. He then intensified the song's melody, using the full and bright A, D, and E major chords:

I dream of seeing your face in the twilight of a day.
Your smile so full of grace; your voice ringing with joy.
And the happiness I see in you fills me with desire...

His warm voice filled the parlor. After this song, he played three others, and the house spirits clapped their ghostly approval. At one thirty in the morning, physically and emotionally drained, he put down his guitar, blew out the fragrant candles that burned brightly on a small table, and headed upstairs.

CHAPTER 12

Before bed, Dr. Pi looked in the mirror and noticed the fatigue on his face, along with some creeping wrinkles. Though there weren't many, he remembered when he had none. He noticed his thinning hair and graying mustache. If he were younger, he knew exactly what he'd do — get on a plane the next day and find Katerina, tell her she meant the world to him, and propose marriage. There would be years ahead for their love to grow. They'd raise talented children, nurture their creativity, teach them music, art, poetry, read them stories before bed, hug them goodnight, and embrace the joys of a loving family. Dr. Pi reflected that he'd already done that, been blessed that way, and couldn't complain. He was appreciative, grateful for the many blessings of his past life. He just wished to go through it all again with Katerina.

With these longings, he went to bed. When he awoke, he felt noticeably refreshed and energetic. He stretched, yawned, took some deep breaths, and walked to the bathroom. When he looked in the mirror, he couldn't believe what he saw. He had a full head of hair, its grayness gone, as were the wrinkles. How had this happened? He looked twenty-six. He stared, then washed and rubbed his face dry, almost afraid to look into the mirror again for fear that he'd see his older self. But no. His youthful face reflected back. He rushed down the stairs, thinking he'd traveled back in time, and called for Joanna. But she didn't respond; she wasn't there. The house was just as he'd left it the night before; the candle fragrance still lingered, and his guitar lay on the parlor floor. In the dining room, he looked at the photographs of his mother and father, and at numerous framed pictures of saints on the walls. He glanced at the small statues of the infant of Prague and Mother Mary on top of the oak armoire. He thought of the house spirits he'd serenaded the previous night and wondered if they'd had something to do with this miraculous transformation.

Dr. Pi stood before Saint Theresa and prayed. He felt deep happiness and relief, grateful he'd been given a second chance to be young again. He had the urge to start a fire in the grate and did so. Soon, the living room was warm, as the flames flared brightly, and the wood crackled. He sat by the grate, stared into the light, thought about Kafka's *Metamorphosis*, about Gregor's strange transformation into a hideous roach. That was a frightening, nightmarish occurrence, but his wasn't. He wondered what was responsible for these marvelous physical changes to his body. And why hadn't his mind been affected? He was still Dr. Pi — the older man — alive in this young body.

Dr. Pi rushed into the parlor and ripped through his kung fu exercises with desire, each second feeling his revitalized body bring clarity to his happy mind. As the muscles hardened, his heart felt more joyful. He needed this new strength and vigor and confidence, to feel justified in pursuing Katerina. Now in the prime of life again, he'd give her his future. He needed this wish fulfilled. After exercising, he drank a glass of juice, ate some mixed nuts and a banana, then grabbed his guitar and played several songs. His voice was crisp, clear, and vibrant.

When he finished, he knew what he must do. He'd book a flight to Warsaw, find Katerina, get on his knees, and ask her to be his. This was the perfect time and moment. With this miraculous physical transformation, he didn't feel guilty any longer. He had the world to offer her now — his whole mind, body, and spirit. Maybe she'd accept him, move to America, have their children, and they'd make each other happy.

Dr. Pi ran upstairs to prepare for his day. He was in a perfect, jubilant mood. He pictured a gorgeous Maine sunset in summer, the pleasantness of camping with family in the woods, the idyllic peace by a still lake. He clearly saw the paradise he wanted — holding Katerina lakeside, by a crackling fire, listening to Chopin's nocturnes, or to moving Russian ballads, while their minds drifted. He saw them honeymooning in a romantic cabin at Bar Harbor, dining seaside at twilight, and ordering homemade pie for dessert.

The alarm on his iPhone rang intensely at six o'clock, startling Dr. Pi from his slumber, severing him from his dream. He walked to the bathroom and when he glanced in the mirror this time, he saw reflected back his fifty-one-year-old face. His reality was un-altered. His mind was young, his heart as passionate as it had ever been. Yet his body aged steadily as his soul grew bolder, braver, and more complete.

CHAPTER 13

On Monday morning, before his 9:30 class, Dr. Pi went to his office to pick up a packet of handouts he'd forgotten on his desk. It was 8:00 a.m. and few faculty members were around. As he walked the hallway, Dr. Jakub Jablonski exited the men's bathroom.

"Morning Jakub," Dr. Pi called cheerfully. "Ready for another week?"

Jakub smiled and waved.

"Ready as I'll ever be. Just hope my students are prepared for lab. Otherwise, it'll be a long morning."

Jakub was a lanky young man with a full head of dark hair and a pleasant face. He was only in his late twenties but had already taught college physics for a few years and held a doctorate from MIT. How or why he'd landed at Pleasant Hills College was a mystery to Dr. Pi; with such a stellar education, Jakub could teach in the Ivy League. Out of courtesy, Dr. Pi never inquired; he guessed it was probably a career choice dictated by a poor job market. Jakub wasn't very talkative, but Dr. Pi had managed to draw him out a few times with questions about physics. Whenever he could, Dr. Pi picked his young colleague's brain. The last time he'd run into Jakub, he'd asked him to explain what the "T" stood for in Einstein's gravity equation — $G = 8\pi T$. Jakub respected Dr. Pi, enjoyed seeing his enthusiasm and thirst for knowledge, and launched into a clear and detailed explanation of the variable and equation, which Dr. Pi only partially understood. But only partially understanding would never dissuade Dr. Pi, for in his estimation that was better than not trying, or not understanding at all.

Dr. Pi asked Jakub if he felt at home at Pleasant Hills.

"Everything's going well, thank you," Jakub said. "The college senate meetings are a bit long and late in the afternoon, and my commute from Syracuse is taxing in winter, but the faculty at this college are special — always kind and helpful."

"Great to hear, Jakub. You know I'm here if you should need anything."

"Thank you, Dr. Pi. Same here."

Dr. Pi paused and, simply because his mind kept dwelling on age and mortality and his desire to be with Katerina, he ventured and asked Jakub some startling questions.

"I know this is not in your area of expertise, but what's the latest science on aging? Think I can live into my nineties and stay mentally and physically strong? Hear of any magic pills or therapies out there?"

Jakub smiled. "Found a young girl you want to impress?"

Dr. Pi stared at Jakub, amazed. How could he have known? Was he that transparent? Maybe he was. Dr. Pi respected Jakub and answered simply and honestly. He wanted to talk about Katerina anyways; just uttering her name inspired him.

"You guessed it. Yes. Much, much younger than me, but we are perfectly matched in sensibility. I'm damn crazy about her, yet I'm not sure I have much left in the tank."

"Positive outlook, good diet, a daily exercise routine," Jakub said seriously. "Genetics are important, but looking at you, I'd say you have that category covered. You look great. And your enthusiasm's infectious."

"Thanks," Dr. Pi said. "Sorry for my dumb questions."

"They're not," Jakub said swiftly. "Nothing's impossible with the right mindset and proper work routine. In science, there are countless mysteries. Factors that are difficult to assess. What, for example, makes one individual live longer than another? We can understand things on a cellular, biological level, but on a mental and emotional level, things get more nebulous. How can a woman live one hundred and twenty-two years? All we know is she did, and perhaps one day all of us may be able to. Bob Hope lived to be a hundred. How? Who knows? But he spent his life laughing, entertaining people, having fun on stage. Laughter reduces stress, anxiety. Hard to weigh in those factors."

"You're right. I'm a bit surprised you know about Bob Hope. He's way before your time."

"I try to keep up," Jakub replied and smiled. "And my parents loved him."

Jakub paused and studied Dr. Pi's face. Taking a sudden risk, he said, "You seem happier this semester. Whatever you're doing, I'd say, keep doing it."

"Thanks Jakub. I am happier," Dr. Pi said with a mysterious smile that made his colleague pause.

"Another mysterious factor is love," the physicist said. "What the hell is it? We can discuss the chemistry, what compounds produce good feelings in the brain, but that doesn't explain it all."

"So right," Dr. Pi said. "I'm baffled by my strong emotions for Katerina. How they've grown. And I've never even physically met her."

Jakub looked puzzled.

"She's an Instagram crush," Dr. Pi said and laughed.

Jakub laughed with him. "Now that's a true mystery. Let's have lunch and talk about it. This relationship sounds intriguing."

"Sure," Dr. Pi said. "Next time Curt and I go to the Kettle for lunch, why don't you join us? Curt's been my therapist so far. But I can certainly use another, a scientifically minded one. And if you hear of any anti-aging pills, get the info for me."

Jakub headed towards his lab down the hall and Dr. Pi rushed to his office, where he grabbed the handouts on his desk. As he exited the room, Dean O'Rourke, who had an office directly across from his, greeted him.

"Morning, Tobias. You seem ready to go today. What are you teaching?"

"Tellez's 'Just Lather, That's All.'"

"Never read it," O'Rourke said. Dr. Pi handed him one of the copies he carried.

"Here. You'll love it. Pretty intense story."

"Thanks. I have some time before my ten o'clock meeting. How's little Tank doing?"

"Much, much better, Constance tells me. Almost his usual self. That morning he was so out of it. I was afraid to leave him alone."

"Good to hear he's doing better. And how's your Cooperstown class?"

"Fabulous students. I appreciate you thinking of me. Loving the experience thus far."

"Well, that's great news," O'Rourke said.

The two said goodbye, and Dr. Pi rushed to class, eager to read and discuss a story about the importance of one's commitments.

CHAPTER 14

The past summer, when Dean O'Rourke had asked him to consider teaching a Composition class at Bassett Hospital in Cooperstown to a group of licensed practical nurses pursuing nursing degrees, Dr. Pi had been hesitant. It was a long drive, a three-hour night class on Wednesdays, and being in any hospital awakened emotions he sought to keep buried. However, Joe convinced him this was an excellent chance to do something different and get out of the house. Joe understood his good friend's loneliness, the pain he'd suffered seeing his mother die in a hospital, and told him he'd benefit from a new experience. Dr. Pi had listened and accepted the dean's offer.

Joe's advice had been golden. Teaching the Bassett class was great therapy. His students were wonderful — mature, motivated, and eager to improve their writing. And talking with these intelligent future nurses every week helped him overcome his hospital-related anxieties. Dr. Pi looked forward to these classes and worked hard to make sure the students benefited fully from the course. Still, the mysterious factor that played into his motivation was Katerina; her power to inspire him was uncanny.

On this rainy Wednesday, Dr. Pi had left Pleasant Hills early because he wanted to browse through Willis Monie Books before class to see what treasures he'd find. The last time he'd been there he'd bought a second-state, first edition of Steinbeck's *The Pearl* for twenty-seven dollars. He revered Steinbeck, and holding any original copy of this literary master's work was like holding a gold bar from the US Treasury.

While cruising up Route 20, Dr. Pi marveled that just the thought of Katerina made him smile. This woman was embedded in his soul and tempered his loneliness. With his A6 on cruise control, Dr. Pi gazed at the hilly Central New York landscape. The drizzly mist evoked some somberness, and for portions of the drive he missed his children, both grown and with their own lives now. But just as his nostalgic feelings were about to sink him into despair, Katerina's lovely face appeared in his mind's eye, and her grey-green eyes with their natural profundity helped him rebound. Dr. Pi reminded himself that he must look forward, not back. His kids had had great childhoods, he'd done everything he could to help them thrive, and all good things must come to an end. That was a fact of life. Looking ahead was the key. And he knew he wanted Katerina in his future.

Once he descended Route 28 into Cooperstown, his stomach started growling. He parked outside Schneider's Bakery, went inside, and saw Sheriff Wilks, whom he often ran into there.

"Hi Sheriff. Getting your pastries?"

"Yes. Always before I go home. My wife loves 'em. Class tonight?"

"At six. I'm here a little early, but I love your town. Gonna browse Monie's and go eat my cookies lakeside."

"That sounds like a plan. How're the students?"

"They're quite a motivated, bright group of future nurses."

"Nice to hear. My wife's a Bassett nurse. She'll be happy to know they're doing well."

"Please tell her. Best group I've had anywhere in quite some time."

As the cashier moved to the register, the sheriff went for his wallet, but Dr. Pi got there first and handed her a twenty. "I got this one, Sheriff."

"Much obliged." Sheriff Wilks shook his hand and walked out.

"And what will you have?" the young woman said with a smile as she handed Dr. Pi his change. "Don't tell me. Three oatmeal-raisin cookies to get you through class?"

"Yes," Dr. Pi said and smiled widely. "Three magical cookies."

She handed Dr. Pi the white bag as he went to hand her a five.

"These are on me," she said. "Have a great class."

"Why, thank you young lady. And for your great service."

He put the five-spot in her tip jar, smiled, waved, and walked out the door.

"See you next week," she said.

CHAPTER 15

Dr. Pi left the bakery, entered Monie's, and browsed around. He didn't find any rare books but did buy a well-preserved Scribner's hardcover copy of *The Complete Short Stories of Ernest Hemingway* for six bucks. He carried his find to the lake, where he sat and ate his cookies. It was still overcast and gloomy, but the rain had subsided, and it had gotten cooler. He thrust his hands into his pockets and looked at the calm waters and the hills on the horizon.

As usual, his thoughts turned to Katerina. Dr. Pi was astonished how quickly she had become central to his world. He woke up thinking about her, and she remained in his thoughts until he fell asleep. Sometimes she even appeared in his dreams. He desperately wished to know something about her childhood, her parents and family. He tried to imagine a happy childhood for her, one where she'd had many friends, many warm snowy Christmases, and vacations. He wished to know what her early schooling had been like. In his mind he saw her playing an old family piano on long afternoons while the snow fell. His enchantment with her grew as he realized how much she reminded him of Maria. Tears welled in his eyes, so he closed them and said a prayer for his dead sister and for Katerina's future happiness.

On the way back to his car, he remembered the mysterious woman he'd talked to briefly by the dock a few weeks earlier. She'd piqued his interest, even though they'd not exchanged many words. For minutes, he wondered about her. *Who was she?*

***

Class discussion that evening focused on relationships, including social media ones. A few students highlighted how physical, daily life interactions suffered because of the amount of time people spent on their phones and social media. Dr. Pi understood their frustrations. Still, he challenged them by pointing out how technology had broadened our ability to make friends all over the world.

"With one device," he'd said, thinking of Katerina, "we can communicate with thousands globally and learn about their ways of life. How incredible is that?"

"It is incredible," one student had said, "but social media can also make it hard to know how to be with people in real life."

Some of the students agreed, but Dr. Pi argued that the challenge is to do both successfully — to engage those in our immediate environment genuinely, but also to broaden our circle of friends worldwide. "Adding this new dimension can enrich our humanity," he said. "People from everywhere are fascinating, and the more of them we know, the better."

"But there are many creeps out there," Patty said. "How do we know who they are?"

"Very true," Dr. Pi replied. "That's something your education provides — the analytical skills needed to differentiate between trustworthy people and creeps. You may still be taken in, but the chances of being fooled are lessened when you learn to weigh all evidence. We shouldn't live in fear of other people. Most are good."

Another student, Brendan, said, "Besides, the creeps can be in your own backyard."

The class unanimously agreed. Brendan reflected, then continued, "I agree with Dr. Pi. We need to *pay attention*, see how details stack up, listen carefully to what people say, and on social media to what they post and write."

"Good point, Brendan. Our use of language is a fingerprint," Dr. Pi suggested. "No two people write the same way. Trust me. How do you think I know who's plagiarized a paper?"

Students laughed, and several asked "Turnitin?"

"Yes, that too," Dr. Pi answered. "But all I really need is a writing sample first day of class — that's a fingerprint. Granted, a student's writing should improve and change during a semester certainly, but not radically. So if Johnny's sample has several fused constructions, or he doesn't use apostrophes or many polysyllabic words, and he submits a paper that looks like it's been perfected by a Penguin editor, I'll suspect he's not done his own work. I won't accuse him of plagiarism — I give him the benefit of a doubt. I'll invite him in to discuss his paper. In that meeting, the truth usually comes out."

"How many have you caught?" Amanda asked.

"A few each year."

"Do they fail?" Missy asked. "I feel like they should. That's a serious offense. It's like theft."

"It *is* theft. You're right. But that's not my goal. I just want them to be honest. Do their *own* work. Otherwise, they'll never become better writers. I had a college professor once who knew a friend had copied my outline simply because he'd used the word "thus" — a word he'd not used before. Dr. Houle called me into his office, said I was the only person in class who used "thus" in my writing and that he knew John had copied my work. I confessed I'd let him use my outline. He failed John, and my A- became a B-. Dr. Houle told me he was being generous and never to do it again. The sad part is that John could've earned a C+ on his own. Instead, he got tossed from the program. I always felt guilty. Should've known better."

"That's amazing," Karen said. "So you're suggesting that on social media the creeps will reveal themselves in what they say and how they say it?"

"Precisely Karen," Dr. Pi said. "We must pay close attention. Become better at deciphering how others use language. And use it better ourselves. We shouldn't close the door to making friends with countless good folks around the world just because there are some lunatics out there. We should learn to identify and stay clear of the creeps."

Dr. Pi wanted to tell his class about Katerina but held back. He was afraid he'd share too many personal feelings. The truth was Katerina was all he wished to talk about. But he kept quiet and let students continue to speak.

After class, Dr. Pi stopped for dinner at a new sports bar on Main Street called The Black Sox Bar and Grill. He sat alone at a small table by the large window overlooking Main Street. It was drizzling again, and the street's asphalt surface reflected nearby light. The bar was crowded, and he would've sat at the counter and joined the conversations about the Yankees, but he was tired and still had an hour's ride home. He ordered, then stared out the window. It seemed he dined alone quite often. He imagined how nice it'd be if Katerina were with him; they'd look into one another's eyes and playfully do their best to communicate in English. He wondered how their early days together would unfold if she ever came to visit, or if he traveled to Warsaw. A woman's voice startled him.

"How are you? Do you remember me?"

At first, Dr. Pi did not realize those questions had been addressed to him. He glanced up and saw a woman he thought he recognized.

"Hi," she said. "I think we talked briefly by the dock a few weeks back. Do you live in Cooperstown?"

Dr. Pi got up and shook her hand lightly. "Hi. Yes, I remember. How are you? Care to join me?"

"Thank you." The woman took off her long coat, hung it by the door, and then sat down across from him.

"I live in Pleasant Hills, but I teach here on Wednesday nights."

"Oh. What do you teach?"

"Writing. Literature. Just finished class and thought I'd get a bite before heading home. You live in town?"

"Just outside, on the lake's eastern side."

"Must be nice. Such a scenic, peaceful lake. Great place to think."

"I know. The dock's beautiful. Some afternoons I have dinner and go there to ponder things. Very serene."

"Care to have anything?"

"A glass of Riesling would be nice."

The waiter came over and took her order, and as he walked away the woman asked:

"Do you enjoy teaching?"

"Yes. Very much," Dr. Pi said quickly. Her features were soft and pleasant — warm, brown eyes, a small, sloped nose, full lips, high cheek bones. Her hair was cut short and blown out and styled elegantly; two long waves of it occasionally fell on her cheeks which she gently pushed back from her face and tucked behind her ears.

"I taught art as an adjunct at Hartwick for several years before my car accident. Broke my left femur and tore a ligament. Lost so much time in therapy I gave up the position. My ex-husband thought I should stay home to paint, and that's what I did. I found teaching fulfilling."

"Sorry to hear about your accident," Dr. Pi said, but didn't ask further questions. He didn't want to pry. "Ever think about going back?"

"Yes. Sometimes I've considered it, but I've chosen just to paint these days. And I work part time at the library art exhibit."

"Oh nice. I sometimes stop in to see the art. Surprised I've not run into you."

The waiter arrived with Dr. Pi's food and the woman's wine. As Dr. Pi glanced up to thank him, he noticed the bartender staring in his direction with unusual intensity. Dr. Pi scrutinized his face — eyes close together, a large eagle-beaked nose, and bushy mustache and beard. He wore a Boston Red Sox cap and a dark tee-shirt with the words Boston Strong in bright-red lettering. Dr. Pi stared long enough for the bartender to look away, wipe down the countertop with a big white rag, and then move towards the bar's far side to take a drink order. When he refocused on his guest, she said in a soft, sweet voice:

"I'm Janet Brayden, by the way."

"Nice to meet you Janet. Tobias Pi."

"Tobias Pi," she said, musing on his name. "Pie like the pastry or Pi like the number?"

Tobias laughed and said, "Pi like the number."

Janet smiled and searched his face. "And you don't mind the commute?"

"Not at all. It's only once a week. But I'd come every day if I had to. This is the loveliest town in all seasons."

"It is. I've painted it in every season. You should stop by the house some afternoon so I can show you my work. It's pretty much all about Cooperstown."

"I'd love to. Do you sell your pieces? I love art and still have many walls at home I wish to beautify."

"I do."

"Reasonably?" Dr. Pi said and smiled.

"Yes. Of course. I'm not Picasso. And I don't really see myself as a professional."

She smiled widely, and Dr. Pi saw how lovely she was. He guessed she was in her forties but surmised she could be younger. There was an exuberance visible on her face that was captivating — a peaceful, contented look that pleased him. He looked into her brown eyes and asked:

"Would next Wednesday in the early afternoon work?"

"Hmmm. Next Wednesday," she said, thinking. "Yes. That'll work."

"How about we meet for lunch at Danny's? My treat. And I'll see your art afterwards?"

"I'd love to."

Janet drank her wine and described several of the subjects she painted. She told him about the places she'd traveled to on her last European vacation. An hour later, Dr. Pi said goodbye and headed home, excited at the thought of buying her art.

Not long after he'd gotten on Route 28 North, a car with very bright lights tailgated and egged him to go faster than the posted 45 mph limit. Dr. Pi had the cruise control set and did not want a ticket. He braked and went slower to let the driver know he was too close, then resumed his speed. The driver did not relent, and Dr. Pi suspected he was being followed. Through his rearview, he could tell it wasn't a trooper. When the limit increased to 55 mph, Dr. Pi gunned the A6 and took her up to 65, leaving his pursuer behind. But as he brought her down to 55, the car caught up to him and was riding his bumper again. Finally, as Dr. Pi approached Richfield Springs, the car dimmed its lights and took a turn off Route 28. That was the last he saw of it. Once on Route 20, he set the cruise to 55, focused on keeping an eye out for roadside deer, and relaxed. A short while later, he'd forgotten the tailgater. He thought of Katerina, of her photographs and their wonderful text conversations, and smiled.

CHAPTER 16

Dr. Pi loved old cars, and each year before winter he serviced his prized Dodge Polara at Deland's Garage. Art, their master mechanic, had been schooled in muscle car technology back in the day. Dr. Pi loved bringing his machine in for maintenance and watching Art perform his expert therapy. What he loved most was hanging out with him while he worked and listening to his stories. As Art told his tall tales of racing hot rods, his eyes would light up. He reminisced about the old days with a childlike joy, remembered prepping powerful Hemi engines to cruise around town. Camaros, Roadrunners, Firebirds, GTOs — he knew them all, and as Dr. Pi listened, he longed for that bygone age when as a boy all he could do was dream of driving.

On this Friday morning, Dr. Pi had Art all to himself. It was relatively quiet at the garage and the new owner had put Art in charge. The Dodge was getting the love — a coolant flush, a new transmission line, an exhaust manifold flange, and a full tune-up. As he hung out, watched, waited, and walked around the shop, Dr. Pi took pictures of his machine and thought about Katerina. He imagined how nice it'd be spending a Central New York summer with her, going out to dinners, movies, antiquing, hanging out by nearby lakes on weekends, cruising for ice cream, and making love in the back of his

Dodge somewhere in the dark countryside under a sky full of stars as he'd once done at nineteen.

As Art worked, Dr. Pi posted several photographs of the Dodge on Instagram and Katerina immediately liked them. The exchange that followed occupied Dr. Pi for a good half hour as he walked around Deland's parking lot. Katerina wondered if he'd spent much time cruising and listening to rock music. Dr. Pi enumerated the groups he'd loved back then — Pink Floyd, The Doors, The Animals, The Beatles — and she agreed that these were *good classic rock groups*. She then mentioned much of the music she loved and listened to, especially 90s Russian classic rock. Dr. Pi became curious about that; he'd never listened to any and promised to look some up on YouTube. Katerina offered to send him some tracks by email. He direct-messaged her his email and said he looked forward to learning more about Russian music. She said she'd put together a good sample.

He received these songs on Sunday, and spent his evening listening to tracks by Zemfira, Valery Kipelov, Zhuki, and Viktor Tsoi. Dr. Pi was impressed, not only with the selections but with how meticulously she'd introduced each artist and even translated the lyrics so Dr. Pi could understand. It was obvious Katerina loved and knew much about music but also that she valued his friendship and wanted him to enjoy something she treasured. To Dr. Pi this was a true gift, a foray into a musical world he was unfamiliar with — and, sadly, that he'd never been curious about until now, and only because he'd developed an affection for Katerina. He was struck by how emotional and powerful the music was, how talented the artists; and even though he could only make out what the singers expressed thanks to the translations she'd provided, the conviction with which they sang could be heard in their voices.

Dr. Pi was struck by how tragic some of these artists' lives had been; Tsoi, a revolutionary, whose songs had been banned in the Soviet Union, had died in a car accident at age twenty-eight, and Zemfira had developed drug problems, lost popularity, and disappeared. Tsoi reminded Dr. Pi of Jim Morrison; Zemfira of Karen

Carpenter. Whether American or Russian, it didn't matter; so much talent lost to the world so soon.

The musician Dr. Pi was most impressed with was Valery Kipelov, the heavy-metal singer with a powerful voice and dynamic range; his songs were exceptionally moving. Katerina had written about him: *For me he is just like God of music, as the man who created my childhood, my youth. And even now I sometimes still listen him .... In addition to music, Valery Kipelov is a good person, simple, kind, modest. Once I was happy to be at his concert.* These words touched Dr. Pi. He could see the qualities she valued in Kipelov were exactly those he himself loved seeing in others.

The Kipelov song he loved most was "The Splinter of Ice," which Katerina had introduced as *One of the most lovely and beautiful songs about broken love.* She'd translated its chorus for him, and Dr. Pi listened to the song over and over and felt the power of its melody. He knew the feelings it described well, that painful emotional rollercoaster, that suffocating feeling when a love you trusted would sustain you has left you drained. Dr. Pi closed his eyes and felt the pain he'd experienced just a few years back when communication between him and Joanna had broken down, they'd separated, and then divorced. The shard was still in his heart, yet he knew that with every detail he learned about Katerina he grew stronger and more confident that he could pull it out once and for all. Katerina was refilling his soul with a new love, a new yearning for someone kind, modest, and genuine.

CHAPTER 17

On the following Wednesday, Dr. Pi met Janet Brayden for lunch at Danny's, and afterwards he followed her to her farmhouse. It was a cool, sunny, early October afternoon, and the two-mile drive from the village to her house was picturesque. There were golden and reddish leaves on the hundreds of trees they passed in the sunshine — century-old maples, oaks, and ashes lined the main road. Once they pulled onto her property, they drove for another quarter mile, and the splendor increased. At the end of the narrow dirt road, a huge farmhouse appeared. It was tucked neatly in a large clearing and surrounded by deep woods. From a distance, Dr. Pi saw the two-story white-and-green Federal-style home with its large twelve-on-twelve paned windows, six on top and bottom. Its main entrance with its portico was plain but impressive and elegant. And on either end of the rectangular structure, two chimneys rose above the roof line. Smoke swirled steadily from one towards clear blue sky. On the farmhouse's southern side stood a large red barn with two elaborate old doors, a huge gray cupola, and a fancy weathervane. Behind the barn, acres and acres of abandoned farmland stretched to the horizon; everywhere else thick woods barricaded the house from the outside world. Both house and barn were in fantastic shape, and Dr. Pi recognized that maintaining such a place must cost thousands yearly, not including property taxes.

His gut feeling was that Janet Brayden must be from old money, unless of course she was a very successful painter and not telling him.

"What a gorgeous place, Janet," Dr. Pi said as he got out of his car. He surveyed the property carefully. "Wow. Absolutely beautiful. So inspiring. What a lovely house and barn."

"Thank you. Dad bought it a little after World War II. He farmed on it for over forty years. I grew up here an only child. He died of lung cancer in 2010," she reflected somberly, then added, "My inheritance," and fanned her arms widely across the property.

"Same year my mom died," Dr. Pi said and fell silent.

Janet waved for him to follow her, "Come."

She led him to her fully renovated kitchen in the back and prepared some coffee. She then tossed a few cherry logs into the wood stove and sat across from Dr. Pi at a small table nearby. He admired the room's décor and the cabinetry's craftsmanship. Everything reflected impeccable taste and attention to detail, including the granite counters, Viking stove and other new appliances, woolen, fluted curtains, and the large French doors through which one could survey the deep back woods.

"This area is lovely. So comfortable. The renovation must've cost you a fortune."

"It was pricy. But since this is where I spend most of my time, other than in my art studio and the library gallery, I thought it'd be a good investment."

"Most definitely," Dr. Pi said. "I've been thinking of redoing the entire back of my Victorian. Should've done it years ago for my ex-wife Joanna, but with raising a family, it wasn't financially practical. Something like this would be so nice."

Janet got up and poured their coffees. "Cream and sugar?"

"Yes, please."

"Oatmeal-raisin cookies or a Danish?"

"Cookies. Thanks. How'd you know? That's what I have every Wednesday before class. Get them at the Schneider's Bakery on Main Street?"

"Yes. My favorite place."

"That's my pit stop, though today this is it. Thank you."

The two relaxed and enjoyed their coffees and dessert.

"Do you live alone also?" Janet asked.

"Yes. For four years now."

"Been two for me. Dated much?"

"Not really. And you?"

"No. My ex-husband's made it difficult. He spreads rumors about me in town. I think he has everyone convinced I'm crazy."

Tobias looked surprised. "What? Really? Why?"

"That's a really good question," she said, her eyebrows rising. "I think he just can't stand the thought that I'll marry someone else who'll move in here. He tried to take the property from me. Hired some powerful Manhattan lawyers, but a will's a will."

"Thank goodness for that. You must have taken precautions."

"Before he died, Dad had it amended, created a trust, so if my marriage failed, I'd be able to keep the farmhouse and maintain it. He never liked Ebenezer. Didn't trust him."

"Sounds like a smart move."

"It was. My ex-husband's related to some moneyed Manhattan real-estate brokers. He wanted to sell the property after father's death and invest the money in the city. I told him I didn't want to leave Cooperstown. I grew up here, was comfortable, and wanted to keep the property my father adored. He couldn't care less about my feelings."

"That's terrible."

"Well, our marriage had been strained for several years already, but after Dad died Ebenezer became cruel. Had no compassion whatsoever for the pain I suffered. Ridiculed and belittled me to the point I finally sought a divorce."

"And good riddance, it sounds like."

"Absolutely. I have a protection order against him; he can't come within a mile of this property without risking arrest. But that doesn't stop him from continuing to harass me. So the rumors in town are that I'm mad. He doesn't want anyone near me. And he has his little spies everywhere in this town, keeping an eye on my movements."

Janet stopped, drank her coffee, while Dr. Pi wondered what else to say. He could sense she felt trapped, isolated, and at the mercy of Ebenezer.

"He sounds obsessed. It can't be easy living with someone like that still around. Has he ever violated the order?"

"Yes. One night he came to the door very late and scared me to death, knocked aggressively, said he wanted to talk, to reconcile. I told him to go away but he wouldn't listen. I could tell he was drunk and phoned Sheriff Wilks. Ebenezer was arrested, spent the night in jail, received a heavy fine and warning from both the judge and the sheriff, but he's continued to spook any man who comes near me."

Dr. Pi felt awful for Janet and wondered whether the car that had tailed him on Route 28 a week earlier had been her psychotic ex or one of his spies. He told Janet about his experience.

"I'm so sorry, Tobias. I'm almost certain that was him. I should've warned you. But just how do you tell someone you've just met and are getting to know that your ex-husband's deranged?"

"Oh I'm not worried about him, Janet. He just distracted me by shining the high beams on that sinuous road. That's all. He won't do anything. He'd be smart not to try." Suddenly Dr. Pi recalled the bartender at the Sports Bar also staring him down and inquired about him.

"Is the bartender at The Black Sox a friend of your ex's?"

"Oh no. That's Anthony DiCarlo, an old childhood friend. He looks out for me. I've known him since the sixth grade. He was probably wondering who you were. Anthony's had it out with Ebenezer a few times. Fought with him on several occasions. Last summer, Anthony threatened to have his cousins come up from the Bronx and deal with Ebenezer if he didn't leave me alone. But Ebenezer's a stubborn man."

"I don't know how you can deal with him — sounds sick to me. But you can't live afraid, I always tell people. Can't let the goons win; you just can't."

"I agree. Sorry to tell you about my nightmare life. Hope you won't be scared away. Do you still want to see my paintings?"

"Of course. Would love to. Don't worry, not much frightens me these days, except maybe hospitals — but that's a long story. And that fear's almost gone. Thanks for telling me your ordeal. I'll keep my eyes open. The coffee was delicious, by the way. Thank you."

Janet gave Dr. Pi a tour of her studio. It was a grand room painted a soft salmon color with beautiful crown and window moldings in white enamel. The afternoon light that came through the refurbished windows gave the entire space warmth, a magical glow that awed Dr. Pi and made him think nostalgically of decades gone by. The curtains were light blue trimmed in a rich red, and the parquet floor was covered with a huge oriental rug of the finest quality and design. The rug alone Dr. Pi surmised must be worth fifteen thousand dollars, the eight curtains another five thousand. Two of the walls were lined with bookshelves replete with literary, artistic, and scientific volumes — a book lover's paradise; the other two with lovely landscapes by Church and Cole and some traditional portraiture. Even from a distance, Dr. Pi recognized paintings by Hudson River School masters. On walls beside the doors, ornate, polished brass sconces held slender candles that when lit would give the space a romantic ambiance. In two corners, Stickley end tables displayed decorative porcelain vases full of fresh-cut flowers; in the other two, Tiffany lamps rested on their dark mahogany tops. An elegant Stickley mission-style writer's desk graced the far-right end of the room, which overlooked the forest out back. What a great spot to think and write, Dr. Pi thought, and he imagined himself sitting in that spot composing in the early mornings. In the opposite corner, facing the house's front windows, a black baby grand Steinway piano stood with its top propped open, ready to be played. On the end closest to the kitchen and den from which Janet and Dr. Pi had come, Janet's paintings rested against a wall on the floor, her easel nearby. Dr. Pi could not believe his eyes. The room itself was an architectural and decorative wonder. He was instantly smitten and moved by its grace.

"Janet, this room's majesty lifts my soul. So, so beautiful. I'm speechless."

Janet smiled proudly.

"Are those Cole and Church paintings?"

"Yes, good eye! Two of father's prized possessions. He paid handsomely for them at auction."

"I bet. They add such warmth to this incredible room."

"So glad you like it. Dad loved this room. He was an *enlightened* farmer, a book lover and art collector. Most of these volumes were his. I've only added a few since he died." She glanced at Dr. Pi playfully. "Guess who his favorite author was?"

Dr. Pi smiled, thought, loved the look on her face. Up close, in the afternoon light, he saw the magnificent brown of her eyes, and the smoothness of her white skin.

"I'd say Franklin, or de Crevecoeur." He paused, reflected. "Though something tells me Thoreau was a favorite."

"Yes. Yes," she said joyfully. "Loved all three. *You're good*! And *Walden* was his favorite book. He thought Thoreau a genius."

"He was. The reason I didn't put him first is because Thoreau liked simplicity, a more austere living environment. This house, this elegant room, tells me your father had a more elevated taste than Thoreau. *Way more elevated.* Franklin, on the other hand, was a dignified statesman who traveled the world, appreciated European courts; though he was a self-made man, he had a taste for the more refined things in life. And de Crevecoeur wrote a book on the American farmer."

"So well-assessed. Dad would've loved you."

"Your dad sounds like a wonderful man." He smiled. "I'm sure I would've loved him."

"He did have great taste, in just about everything. Each summer, we sat through numerous performances at Glimmerglass. He loved opera and traveling to Lincoln Center twice a year to hear the philharmonic. He knew just about every merchant in Cooperstown, loved baseball, and donated big sums to help build the Hall of Fame.

You'd never know he was a farmer by trade, or an ingenious investor in computer technology companies. Bought thousands of shares of Apple stock when the company was in its infancy. Different than Thoreau, certainly, but an honest, practical man at core. He saw the future and embraced it."

"A visionary, for sure. Wish I had his investment insight; I'd be retired from teaching and writing full time. Glad you've kept his house so perfectly. That piano reminded me of my sister Maria who died at age sixteen. She would've loved this room."

"I'm sorry. That's truly sad."

"A piano virtuoso. Someday I'll tell you about her. If I start now, I may not make it to class tonight."

"I understand."

"And that desk is a writer's paradise. I could see myself sitting there in the early mornings clicking the computer keys effortlessly. Everything's impeccable. Gorgeous. I think you'd better show me your paintings now, or I'll definitely be late."

"Of course," Janet said. "They're right over here." Dr. Pi followed her and listened attentively as she described each painting and the inspiration behind it. In the end, he bought two, each for seventy-five dollars. He knew they were worth more because of the elegant frames on which they were mounted, and offered more, but Janet refused to take extra.

"I need to move these," she said. "You're doing me a favor by finding spots for them. This room has gotten cluttered, and I can't allow that to happen."

"Well, I truly appreciate it. My walls will welcome their beauty. These are amazing. Thanks."

The first painting was of Otsego Lake at twilight, by the dock, the place where they'd first met. The colorful canvas was alive with its reddish, glowing sky and brown, distant hills, and towards the front dozens of lovely small leisure boats at anchor rested in calm waters. The entire piece evoked tranquility, peace, and an eternal autumnal splendor. The second painting was of St. Patrick's Cathedral at

Christmas. Dr. Pi fell in love with the vantage point presented, which highlighted the hundreds of revelers, churchgoers, and shoppers gathered on the sidewalk and up the front steps towards the opened massive front doors. One saw the warm, yellowish lighting inside the church, from its huge hanging lights and candlelight, and the viewer's eyes were taken towards the grand altar in the deep distance and its manger and other Christmas decorations celebrating Christ's birth. Dr. Pi's joy when he spied this piece was instant: "This one's just magnificent, Janet. I want it. I'll never tire of looking at its magic."

"You like it that much? I'm flattered."

"Goodness, yes! It fills me with hope — its light, the people, the intimacy and warmth of the busy city. An inspired and inspiring piece."

"Consider it yours."

"Thank you." Dr. Pi pulled out his iPhone and checked the time. "I better get going."

"Okay. Let's stay in touch."

"Most definitely."

They exchanged numbers, and then Janet helped load her paintings into his car. As he drove towards Bassett hospital, Dr. Pi thought about Janet's difficult situation. Her loneliness reflected his own. He felt happy with his purchased paintings and the new friend he'd made.

CHAPTER 18

Yellow Bird came out in mid-October just as Joe Rossetti said it would, and for days Dr. Pi felt like Jesus walking on water. Published novelist! A big dream had been realized and the book's publication changed his life, including his relationship with Katerina. He couldn't believe it had actually happened, that now anyone around the world with internet access could purchase a print copy of his novel. The last thing on Dr. Pi's mind was the money he'd make if it sold well. What was most important was that the project had been finalized, that his story would be read, that all those hours and years of hard work — more than seven, since he'd gotten serious — were worth it. Most of all, he was thrilled to leave his children a record of his emotional journey from when he was younger. Though *Yellow Bird* was certainly a fiction informed by real experiences he'd had while driving a taxi at age twenty-two, the emotional core of the story was a true rendering of Dr. Pi's person — the way he thought, felt, and saw the world then. He'd changed some over the years, but not much. The virtues he lived by, his outlook on life, the essence of who he was, were etched into his novel's framework, fingerprinted in the words he'd chosen and deliberately organized to tell his story.

His journey to publication had been exhaustive and often deflating. No matter how much he did, there was still more to do. By mid-summer 2018, Dr. Pi was in the home stretch and had finalized his draft. Though he'd been given full discretion over the final text and permission to ignore his editor's advice, he realized that 99 percent of the time, she was right. He stopped questioning, trusted her, and made the suggested changes. On one of those hot July days when he'd spent hours tweaking sentences, he'd looked around his office at the stack of papers and novel drafts Curt had printed. *What a mess*, he'd thought; writing was rewriting, a laborious, time-consuming process — exactly what he taught students. He took a few photographs of his messy office. In the evening, he relaxed by watching a Yankees game, and afterwards created an Instagram post using those photographs. He needed to share his frustrations with others, to say something publicly about the journey he was on. In the post, he wrote with conviction:

Writing is rewriting. Pruning and polishing and trying to make perfect … how many drafts? I've lost count. How many months? I've lost track. Many! Agony? A little, certainly, not to mention the torture I've put others through who have read these drafts willingly and offered suggestions … My hope is that soon, very soon, I'll be ready to share the product of this labor with the world.

Katerina had been sympathetic and commented compassionately:

Oh how many books and many papers! … I can imagine how much work it was … interesting photos of the process. I always like to watch something about process … it's so cool that you're writing a novel, it's so romantic to sit and write … I wish you success.

Dr. Pi asked if she'd read it when it was published. She said she'd be happy to:

I will wait till summer's end! … For me it will be hard to read a book not in my native language … I can imagine … but I'll try because it will be very interesting … (why people all over the world can't speak the same language …) but well it's all no matter. More important that you could finish it as well as you want.

Dr. Pi had offered encouragement: *I'm certain you'll understand it perfectly — your English is excellent. There's no rush. You can read it at your leisure — as long as it takes … I just hope you and all who read the story will like it.* And Katerina had offered encouragement of her own and an interesting explanation of the process she used to communicate with Dr. Pi: *Yes I will, and I sure all who read your novel will like it … (my English is good just because I use online-translator when I don't understand some words … usually I don't understand 20– 30 percent) and I also like to touch books, not read only, and I like to smell books … wish you inspiration.*

Dr. Pi made up his mind to send Katerina a dedicated copy of his novel when it came out. He was impressed with her desire to communicate, with her thoughtfulness, and honesty — she loved to not only read but also touch and smell books. He did also. Real book lovers love everything about books. She was being truthful and understood the artist's chief desire: to be read and enjoyed. And despite the difficulty of reading a book not in her native language, she'd try it because it would be *interesting*. These comments were endearing, and from that night on Katerina became one of the most important people Dr. Pi followed — and in his life! All her thoughts mattered to him. From then on, he went out of his way to communicate with her as elegantly and thoughtfully as he could.

As soon as the novel was available, he ordered four copies; one he kept and three others he sent out to Instagram followers, among them Nora in Murmansk and Julia-Kate in Canada, who'd offered to promote his book. But the most important was Katerina. He direct-messaged her on Instagram and asked for an address where he could mail her a copy. She replied enthusiastically, sent him the address of a close female friend, and he rushed to the post office. *Yellow Bird* was on its way to Poland, to be read by his Russian muse.

When she received it a week later, she messaged Dr. Pi: *I have! I have!* Her enthusiasm gave him such a lift — he felt he'd just received a gift himself, and he had. In Katerina he realized he had a true friend. This woman whom he had never met had expressed immense gratitude; she was committed to reading his novel no matter how long it took, using a translation app when necessary. Dr. Pi felt deep joy that anyone would go to such trouble to read his story. His affection for Katerina grew tenfold. Not only was she physically beautiful, but he'd fallen in love with her mind and soul.

The biggest surprise came when Dr. Pi saw Katerina's post to celebrate his gift. He had just finished teaching on a Thursday afternoon in mid-October. It was a beautiful day, sunny and relatively cool. Before heading home to lunch, he opened Instagram and saw a photograph of Katerina on her bed reading *Yellow Bird*; she wore a knitted, light-gray sweater, and stared intently at the opening pages of the book. Her red fingernails were perfectly done, her long red hair cascaded down her back, her bare legs and feet crossed before her. The bedsheet was light pink and decorated with blue and yellow flowers. On the upper-left corner of the post, a smaller photograph highlighted the novel's cover, her lovely hand and red nails caressing the book. A second photograph showed Dr. Pi's dedication, and at the bottom, on the inside tip of her index finger as it held the page open, he could see a tiny heart drawn in ink. Dr. Pi's heart swelled with love for Katerina; it was obvious she had planned the photographs and post carefully.

Dr. Pi floated out of the building, feeling as happy as he could remember feeling in months, if not years. The light breeze almost seemed to be caressing his face. He breathed in the cool air and noticed, with pleasure, how alive he felt. He couldn't wait to repost Katerina's photograph. As he crossed the campus with his phone still cradled in his palm, he looked at her post over and over, wanting desperately to thank her in person for thinking of him and helping him spread word about *Yellow Bird*.

Once home, before sitting down to lunch, he stood before a photograph of St. Teresa of Ávila and thanked her, in a heartfelt prayer, for giving him a friend as wonderful as Joe who'd helped him make his dream come true, and for bringing Katerina into his life.

CHAPTER 19

In late October, Janet texted Dr. Pi, inviting him to come to her house for dinner after his next class, and he accepted. Dr. Pi offered to bring a bottle of wine, and though she didn't tell him what dish she'd prepare, she said red wine would be best.

On the drive to Cooperstown that Wednesday afternoon, Dr. Pi's thoughts turned, as they so often did, to Katerina. It was overcast and gloomy, but thinking of her relaxed and cheered him. Some of Katerina's sexiest posts came to mind, especially one where she was skimpily clad on her bed reading to her stuffed bears. Dr. Pi's heart beat faster as he pictured the lovely silhouette of her slim, delicate body. He wondered what it'd be like to touch her smooth, white skin, and imagined himself in that room with her, about to make love. He felt himself getting aroused. The lovemaking seemed so real in his mind that after he snapped out of his reverie, he felt as if it'd actually happened.

Once he got to town, he found the liquor store and purchased an expensive bottle of French red wine. He felt especially cheerful this evening. Not only was he carrying the euphoria of his developing relationship with Katerina, but he was also looking forward to getting to know Janet. His students were perceptive and told Dr. Pi they sensed he was extra happy. He gave them credit for his good mood, telling them the papers they'd written were especially good. He thanked them for their hard work and asked that a few of their papers be shared in class. Karen and Meg read theirs, a fantastic discussion ensued, and the rest of the class unfolded perfectly. Dr. Pi only floated away in his mind a few times during the reading of the papers, and somehow managed to keep his fantasies of Katerina in check for the rest of the hour.

Shortly after nine, Dr. Pi drove up Janet's driveway and parked near the kitchen, where she came out to greet him wearing a long green dress that showed off her lovely shape.

"Don't you look lovely," Dr. Pi said, handing her the bottle of wine before leaning in to kiss her lightly on both cheeks. As he did so, he noticed her enticing perfume.

"Why thank you," she said, and he thought he noticed her blush. "So do you," she added, stepping back for a moment to take in his attire: a solid pink Brooks Brothers long-sleeve shirt and dark blue dress slacks. His ankle-high Brunello Cucinelli boots gave him a hip, casual look.

As he followed Janet inside, Dr. Pi was struck by the room's ambiance. The curtains were drawn, and the overhead lights and lamps were off, while candles of all shapes and sizes flickered from surfaces throughout the living room and dining room, creating pockets of moving shadow and dancing golden light. The wood stove radiated a comfortable warmth and its glow seemed to draw them in. Classical piano music was playing at such a low volume that it took Dr. Pi a moment to recognize that it was a piece by Chopin. The table was set and the food ready to serve.

Janet held up the bottle and looked at Tobias almost sheepishly. "I know most people serve red wine at room temperature, but I love it chilled," she said. "I hope you don't mind if I pop it in the freezer for a few minutes before we eat."

"Of course not," Tobias said. "We can do what we want."

As she smiled at him and crossed the kitchen, he watched her lithe movements, which looked like those of a former dancer. He also took note of the fact that she was wearing light makeup and had blown out her hair, and he was touched by the effort she had put into her appearance. He could see in her big brown eyes that she was excited to see him, and that she was not afraid of letting him know.

"Thanks for inviting me," he said. "Once again, your house looks incredible."

"Thank you. I've been looking forward to seeing you again. Hope you like Chicken Parmesan."

"Very much. It's a favorite. How'd you know?"

"Just a guess," she replied. "Based on the paintings you bought." She laughed, and Tobias laughed along with her.

"Well, that's a very impressive and unusual skill, and I'm starved. Just hope the French wine is to your taste. Had I known I would've picked an Italian vintage."

"If it's strong, it's perfect. Come."

She prepared their plates, and they walked to the table and began eating. Not long afterwards, Janet got the chilled wine and poured two glasses. They talked for over an hour about many topics: his teaching, her job at the library, the beauty of Cooperstown, places they'd vacationed and loved, especially the beautiful Acadia National Park in Bar Harbor, which was one of the places Janet was currently painting.

"So have my paintings inspired you? You took two favorites."

"They have," he said. "I glance at all my paintings before I sit to write. Art inspires more art. We'll see what kind of influence they have as I write my second novel. The first — *Yellow Bird* — is done and out. Just last week."

Dr. Pi knew he wasn't being totally truthful because lately it was Katerina who inspired him and not any paintings on his walls. Nevertheless, what was correct was that the art he surrounded himself with did provide warmth, evoked nostalgic feelings, and elevated his mind. Katerina, however, provided the spark. He wrote with her in his mind and heart, and it was a deep-seated longing for her, as yet unfulfilled, that made the words flow.

"Congratulations! That's fantastic!" Janet cried, "So where's my signed copy?"

"Next time I see you, I'll bring you one," he said. "Promise."

"What's it about?"

"My cab driving days in Manhattan at twenty-two. Youthful love, pain, adventure, and the cosmic machinery's mysterious, bizarre workings." Dr. Pi smiled and was relieved when Janet smiled back at him with wonder in her eyes.

"Can't wait to read it. Sounds *heavy* … but interesting."

"Definitely heavy," he said and laughed. "I'm really glad it's done. A first effort, an amateur work … yet honest."

"I'm sure," she said. "What's the topic of your second novel?"

"Modern relationships, including virtual ones."

"Now *that* won't be easy."

"I agree," Dr. Pi said. "It has been quite challenging thus far. But first I must promote *Yellow Bird*."

"Well, I'll help spread the word. I'll let you know what I think once I get my *signed* copy," she said, and smiled warmly.

"Thank you. I'd love to hear your thoughts."

"And if you need inspiration for your next story, I have plenty more paintings you can take off my hands. I sell some smaller pieces at an antique shop in town and at the library, but the big ones are here."

"I'll buy some for my children. They love art."

"Oh, how many do you have?"

"Two. Both talented musicians. Constance is pursuing her music dream in Manhattan. She writes songs, sings beautifully. Loves art. Studied Comparative Lit at Columbia. And Christopher lives in Vermont with his wife and their lovely seven-month-old daughter."

"Magnificent. Your daughter's chasing her dream. That's wonderful."

"It is! She's a dreamer like her father. Plays guitar, sings in an indie band, The Chilling Misers. And to pay bills, she bartends at a Brooklyn pizza bar and is a part-time nanny."

"Nice band name. She sounds like a motivated young woman. Much like my only son Phillip. I nicknamed him King Phillip because of his resourcefulness. His energy. He's a classical pianist, composer, and conductor. Spends most of his time working for the New York Philharmonic and in the summers runs the Glimmerglass program and stays here with me."

"Wow! He sounds like quite a young man," Dr. Pi said. "How old?"

"Twenty-seven," Janet said. "He was my gift, an unexpected gift. But that's a long and painful story to tell that I doubt you'd be interested in."

There was a momentary silence and Janet finished her wine. Dr. Pi drank what remained in his glass, and then poured Janet and himself another full glass. He sensed Janet had much that she wished to talk about.

"All stories interest me, Janet. I'd be more than happy to listen. Does Phillip spend time with his father when he visits in summer?"

"No. That's the source of much of Ebenezer's hostility towards me," Janet said, her voice becoming thin and almost lifeless. "Phillip can't stand his father. Wants nothing to do with him. He's called the police on him a few times when he's been here with me and Ebenezer has come by uninvited."

"Sounds like a difficult situation."

"It is," she said. Janet drank her glass of wine much more quickly this time, and then poured a third glass. Dr. Pi refused a third when she offered because he had to drive home.

"Why was Phillip your unexpected gift?"

"Because I was told I'd never be able to conceive. Getting pregnant was a miracle, really. Dr. Reilly even said so. I'd had two abortions in little over a three-year span. Ebenezer insisted we weren't ready to have children and convinced me to terminate the pregnancies. I told him I thought we could manage, that I was mentally ready and wanted the children, but each time he said no, the time wasn't right. He was busy traveling, investing abroad."

Janet paused and turned away. When Dr. Pi noticed her face glistening with tears he got up and went to her, putting his hands on her shoulders.

"I'm sorry," he whispered. "So sorry."

Janet took Dr. Pi's hand, squeezed it, then got up and escorted him to the couch in the adjacent room. He sat next to her. Suddenly she leaned in and put her head on his chest. It had been a very long time since Dr. Pi had been this close to a woman, but instinctively he let her nestle into him and tried to comfort her by running his fingers gently through her hair. Janet kept quiet, but her soft breathing let Dr. Pi know she felt more relaxed. After several minutes, she resumed her story:

"Ebenezer coerced me into having the abortions, and then when he decided we were ready to have children, I couldn't get pregnant. They ran all sorts of tests, but none could pinpoint what exactly the problem was. I did finally get pregnant, but it ended in a miscarriage. And this made Ebenezer furious. He blamed me. Showed no compassion. Said it was the yoga exercises I did and my poor diet. He said so many nasty things. We fought daily, and I took anxiety medication for a while."

Dr. Pi nodded and made sure she knew he was listening, but he didn't speak until she had gotten a good bit of the story out of her system. Finally, she sat back up to look at him. He smiled and patted her hand in a gesture of compassion, and she looked briefly confused.

"Think I'll top up my glass," she said. "Would you like coffee or dessert? I picked up some gelato," she added, her voice hopeful.

Dr. Pi declined, and she got up to pour herself a fourth glass of wine. When she returned, she sat back down next to him and looked into his eyes.

"Thanks so much for coming tonight. For listening. I appreciate your company."

"You're welcome. Dinner was delicious. Thanks for inviting me. Your story is very sad, but since it ended with Phillip's birth then it ended well, even if your marriage didn't survive."

"Yes. Phillip's my miracle. After I got off the medication and Ebenezer stopped blaming me, we were able to get back to a more peaceful existence. Things stabilized. And it was during those calm, quiet months that I got pregnant. Ebenezer became more supportive, and we had several good years when Phillip was small, and even into his early teens. Things flared up again when Phillip turned fifteen and Ebenezer sent him to a military boarding school. Phillip hated it. But that's another long story."

Janet reached for Dr. Pi's hand, the same one that had recently patted hers. When he gave it, she pulled him towards her, and then reached in and kissed his lips. It was a short, soft kiss at first, but seeing he didn't object, Janet kissed him again, this time more passionately. It'd been a very long time since Dr. Pi had kissed a woman. Though he wasn't emotionally attached to Janet, the kiss felt good. He ran his hands down her back gently, and the two hugged and kissed more aggressively.

Suddenly Dr. Pi realized where this would lead and felt uncomfortable. Though he was aroused and did want to continue, he thought of Katerina and his emotions became confused. Right then, he knew he had better not go through with it. Janet was in a vulnerable state, and he did not wish to take advantage. He didn't feel like having casual or convenient sex. Besides, he thought, she had had quite a bit of wine and might regret her decision. He also knew he'd feel guilty. He wasn't ready for a commitment or a relationship, at least with Janet. All he knew for certain was that it was Katerina he longed for. So on this night, he chose to honor a fantasy over a real-life opportunity. He stood up and announced he had to head home.

"Thank you for dinner, Janet," he said, in as warm a tone as he could muster. He brought her close, gave her an affectionate hug, got his coat, and walked towards the door. She followed.

"I had a nice evening," she said. "Let's do it again."

"Sure. I'll stay in touch. Need to steal more of your paintings."

Soon, Dr. Pi headed slowly out of her driveway. What Janet had shared about her abortions stayed with him, and he thought about

"Hills Like White Elephants." Though in the Hemingway story the reader is left with hope that the man has changed, and that the couple's future could be bright, in Janet and Ebenezer's case, despite the promise inspired by Phillip's birth, it seemed the relationship was doomed early on. What weighed most heavily on Dr. Pi was the pain the women had been put through because of the callous behavior of their men. Dr. Pi was sickened hearing how Ebenezer had coerced Janet into aborting two children, and then later blamed her when she couldn't get pregnant. Ebenezer should've hated himself, not her! His behavior was cruel and selfish, and just thinking about how he punished Janet made Dr. Pi flush with anger. He wanted to comfort Janet, but felt that if he'd slept with her, he, too, would have been acting selfishly. Dr. Pi also wondered if kissing Janet, even briefly, counted as a betrayal of Katerina. He felt it did. He'd already given Katerina his heart; the truth was he wanted her and no one else. He did like Janet, wanted her friendship, loved her paintings, and house, and felt sympathy for her situation. Still, the inspiration that constantly flowed to him from Katerina surpassed all of that. It seemed ridiculous even to him that this woman could have such power over him. But it was true. He wanted no one else. For Dr. Pi, this virtual relationship with Katerina was more real, more inviting, more inspiring, than the real-life connection he'd just shared with the lovely, talented, and vulnerable Janet.

As soon as Dr. Pi turned left out of Janet's driveway, a car was on his tail, following too closely, and with its bright lights on.

"Aww, damn it! I don't need this shit right now. Fuck!" He thought it must be Janet's ex-husband or one of his cronies out to harass him again. "Doesn't this asshole give up? What the hell does he want?"

Dr. Pi never panicked in precarious situations; his experiences growing up in Queens had prepared him for adversity. His gut instinct was to fight. And after what Janet had shared about this heartless prick Ebenezer, there was no way in hell he was going to be intimidated.

"All right," Dr. Pi said to himself, "let the jerk follow me out of town. If that gets him off, more power to him."

Dr. Pi slowed down, cranked on some Zebra, and focused on the narrow road ahead. He was a half mile from town. Suddenly, out of a driveway 600 feet ahead, an old rusty dark-blue F-150 pulled onto the road and stopped. Dr. Pi slammed on his brakes and skidded to a stop as dust swirled around him. Dr. Pi anticipated that the car tailing him would crash into his bumper, but it didn't. In his rearview, he could see the car had stopped about ten feet behind. He recognized this was a set up; he was about to get ambushed and thought quickly.

Dr. Pi locked his A6's doors and gazed ahead to see who occupied the Ford truck. Through the darkness, he could see two forms inside the truck's cab. The driver pushed open his door and stepped out with what appeared to be a baseball bat in his hands, while the passenger slid into the driver's seat. Dr. Pi was not going to wait for him to get any closer or to hear what he had to say. He looked at the narrow embankments and realized there wasn't much room to pass on either side, but despite the brush and steepness of the ditch, he felt if he drove fast enough, he could get through. His Audi was a Quattro and that gave him an advantage. Two years earlier, on the way back home from his friend's house in Pennsylvania, he'd been blinded by headlights, lost control, and gone off the road into a similar ditch. The Quattro had saved him; the car had bounced from side to side and maintained traction, and ultimately, he'd regained control and stabilized the Audi onto the main road. He knew what these cars could do. And because of its 3.2-liter engine, this one was much more powerful than the 2.8 he'd driven then. His best chance was to blow by the truck by entering and climbing out of the ditch.

"Here we go, baby," Dr. Pi yelled, while "Tell Me What You Want" wailed out of his Bose speakers. He threw his car in reverse and punched his accelerator to the floor. His wheels spun, lifted a great deal of dust, and the A6's rear end crashed into the front end of the car behind him.

"Minor damage to my bumper, dude, but a leaky radiator for you!"

The bang was loud and the driver behind him blew his horn, but just as Dr. Pi anticipated, the car was disabled. The radiator didn't blow, but the Audi's impact had jammed the car's left fender into its wheel, rendering it immobile. Within seconds, Dr. Pi slammed his shifter into drive and gunned it. The engine roared as he headed around the truck's rear-end and into the ditch. Dr. Pi knew he had to maneuver like an Indy driver by turning right first and, once in the ditch, cutting quickly left to climb back onto the road. He did this expertly. Just as he anticipated, the Audi bounced in and out of the ditch and back onto the main road past the truck blocking his way. The all-wheel drive system was amazing; each tire took a turn gripping the road and as long as he maintained his speed the car would not get stuck. Dr. Pi knew he risked snapping a spring, or damaging the exhaust system and steering control arms, but what other options did he have?

The truck's driver was so surprised at Dr. Pi's clever stunt that he did not pursue him. Besides, they had to help their buddy figure out a way to get his car moving before the sheriff arrived.

Dr. Pi drove to the sheriff's office in town to file an accident report. Sheriff Wilks was not there, but the officer on duty took down all the information and reassured Dr. Pi that Wilks would be notified in the morning. Dr. Pi wrote him a personal note and offered to return to town on Thursday afternoon to see him, if necessary. The officer on duty said he'd investigate; Dr. Pi left his Audi in the lot and drove up the East Lake Road with him. When they arrived, both car and truck were gone, but the skid-marks made by the A6 were still there. However, any debris from the damage Dr. Pi had done to the car behind him had been removed, so there was no evidence left to determine who'd tried to ambush him. Dr. Pi had a good suspicion it could've been Ebenezer and his cohorts, but it was impossible to prove.

Before heading home, Dr. Pi texted Janet to tell her to be careful, and to let her know of his little adventure after leaving her house. She texted she'd see Sheriff Wilks the next morning. For precautionary measures, the officer escorted Dr. Pi out of town up Route 28 all the way to Route 20. Once there, Dr. Pi blew his horn to thank him and drove home. Surprisingly, his Audi made no noises as he drove, and when he'd looked underneath its chassis at the sheriff's office, he'd noticed no damage. If something did get out of whack, he was sure sooner or later he'd find out. But for now, Dr. Pi felt a deep pride in his German machine. It was a tank, a powerful beast of a car that had potentially just helped save his life. He was also very proud he'd grown up in Queens.

With Zebra cranking, he cruised to Pleasant Hills with Katerina on his mind.

CHAPTER 20

After classes the next day Dr. Pi called Sherriff Wilks and explained what had happened the previous night. Wilks said the accident report was clear and thorough, and that he'd already begun investigating. But he did not elaborate. Dr. Pi thanked him, and then brought the Audi in to Pierce Auto for an oil change and to check the front end for damage. While the owners serviced the car, Dr. Pi told them of his late-night adventure. Craig discovered a bent lower rear control arm on the passenger side and a bent rim on the driver's side. Luckily, there was not much rear-end damage, just a scratched-up bumper, which a little touch-up paint could camouflage. Dr. Pi had the front-end parts replaced; he wasn't charged for the oil change. Pierce Auto always cut him a good deal.

Later, he texted Janet to see how her meeting with Wilks had gone. Wilks, she replied, had talked with Ebenezer, and he'd denied any involvement whatsoever. Wilks reminded him of the restraining order and the consequences of violating it. Ebenezer had expressed shock that he was under suspicion and told the sheriff to stop harassing him. Janet said the sheriff had no physical evidence connecting him to the incident. They were trying to locate the old rusty dark-blue F-150 truck that had blocked the road, but they weren't sure if it was even registered; it could be an unregistered truck used primarily on a private farm. Dr. Pi thanked her for the update. She thanked him for coming to dinner.

Dr. Pi reflected on Janet's difficult situation. He sympathized with her but realized that forming a close friendship with Janet could have serious consequences. What, for example, would those thugs have done to him if he'd not reacted quickly? Would they try something else the next time he came to town? Dr. Pi hated injustice and didn't want anyone to intimidate him; still, his gut feeling was that perhaps he should back off and not exacerbate things. He worried that maybe he'd make matters worse for Janet by continuing to visit, but reflected that by not visiting, he would let Ebenezer claim victory by isolating her.

Later that evening, wishing to disconnect from reality a little bit, Dr. Pi got lost in a well-played Islanders game, which they won. The agitation from the previous night lingered; though he'd had a nice time at Janet's, the events afterwards soured his recollection. Dr. Pi picked up his guitar. He cycled through several of his own songs and for a brief spell he was cheered. Singing was therapeutic and calmed him. The acoustics in his home office were excellent, where piles and piles of papers covered his desk, mostly from the multiple drafts of his novel. The sight of all that paper, which had been a source of dread during the final months of the process, now filled him with a sense of triumph.

He put his guitar away, picked up a copy of *Yellow Bird*, and fanned through its pages. What a journey it had been, getting this book into the world. So many years spent wrestling with competing creative directions the story could take. It felt good to know that where the story's characters had wound up in the end pleased him. He flipped to the end and reread the novel's final lines; in doing so, he wondered whether readers would continue to think about his characters once they put the novel down. For Dr. Pi that was the mark of a great novel, one where readers would miss its characters long after they'd finished reading.

He put the book down, went upstairs, and got ready for bed. Settling under the covers, he picked up his phone and scrolled through his notifications. Right away, he saw that Katerina had posted a video on Instagram. He clicked on it hungrily and was immediately drawn in by its simple but seductive scene of Katerina, in a loose-fitting sweater and tights, reading in a chair, and then reaching up to gather her hair into a loose bun. He played the video through half a dozen times, becoming more mesmerized with every viewing, and noting new things each time: a little pot of what could have been lip gloss sitting on the edge of her night table, a blue apothecary bottle, and a row of books above her head. He marveled at the effect the video had on him. How could such a simple scene leave him breathless with desire? He wanted to reach through the screen and touch her. He wanted teleportation to be a thing — to be taken apart and put back together again, to show up at her door and hand her his beating heart. Unable to do any of those things, he did the one thing he could do. He thought carefully, then wrote:

Riveting! (Heart emoji) Your video mesmerizes me with its beauty and passion. Your face is so beautiful, your ears and hair so cute, your red lips moist and gleaming — I wish to taste them just once, your magical eyes opening a door into your romantic soul. Katerina, your natural beauty inspires. But what is most special is that the person within is equally magnificent. You're warm-hearted, kind, understanding, and those virtues fill me with love and desire. (A queen emoji in between two red hearts and then a kissy face).

Dr. Pi was shocked that a minute later Katerina had liked his comment and responded enthusiastically to it:

I think it's the most beautiful words I have ever heard…

Dr. Pi replied:

thank you so much. (A red rose emoji) That means the world to me. (A red heart emoji) They're just for you, inspired by you. You've captured a part of my soul, Katerina, which I gladly relinquish. (A smiley face emoji) That hasn't happened in a very long time. It amazes me to realize I can still feel that way. You're such a special woman (A red heart, kissy face, smile, and prayer hands emojis).

Her subsequent response let Dr. Pi see how humble Katerina really was, and how important he'd become to her:

but I didn't do anything special! (*A bewildered girl and a shy monkey emoji*) ... *but I promise I will take care of this part of your soul* (*Wings, huggy face, and white cloud emojis*) *of course you are also in my soul* (*Red heart emoji*) *reading your comment is the last thing I do before sleep, and I go to sleep with a big smile* (*Sun emoji*).

Dr. Pi was euphoric. He finally had answers to the questions he'd had for weeks: *Did Katerina really care for him? And if so, how much?* He realized through her words that he was in her soul also, and important enough to occupy her thoughts each night before bed. When she thought of him, she smiled. Right then, Dr. Pi knew what he'd do for Katerina on the following day.

CHAPTER 21

Dr. Pi knew Katerina was about to turn twenty-four in early December, two days after his own birthday. Like him, she was a Sagittarius. Dr. Pi was falling in love and trying to find any and all connections he shared with Katerina to keep himself from accepting the truth — that she was far too young and that the logical thing to do was abandon all hope of making her his. His romantic outlook scoffed at this reality. What he felt for Katerina was immense, overwhelming, difficult to fathom. But these emotions were strong, as real as anything else he saw or touched in the physical world, and hard to ignore or crush, even though in fleeting moments he felt guilty for wanting to act upon them. It was clear to him that she felt strongly for him also, and this made it difficult to abandon the chase, his desire to make her happy, and his belief that his love was what she needed.

On Friday morning, he drove to Cazenovia Jewelry and found exactly what he thought Katerina would love, a beautiful fourteen-karat gold ring with a garnet stone accented with tiny diamonds. Dr. Pi had studied Katerina's hands and fingers from her photographs; her ring finger, he'd guessed, was the size of his left pinky. He asked to see the ring and luckily it fit his pinky perfectly. He purchased it and left the store brimming with confidence that

Katerina would be thrilled. He then drove to Clinton and looked around its specialty stores for other gifts she'd like. He found a handmade canvas bag with a cute cat on its front and purchased a few small, scented candles. When he got home, he found the most personal item he wanted her to have, one which he kept in a special place — a pea-green, broad woolen scarf that his mother had knitted. The year before her death, Miriam had knitted many of these as Christmas gifts to special people they knew. A few had not been given away, and Dr. Pi had saved them for special future friends. Katerina was one of them.

Later that morning, he mailed these gifts to Poland. In a small, cute card Dr. Pi had written loving lines expressing his growing affection. One phrase he'd written, "I'm in trouble now," foreshadowed what was to come. Once that box was in the mail, Dr. Pi knew his intentions could not be mistaken — he'd mailed her his heart. He had two feelings that fateful day. First, he felt energized, confident, eager to profess his love unmistakably. But the second was a devastating and frightening fear, as if he were falling over the edge of an immense waterfall into millions of swirling gallons of water, without a lifejacket, or the slightest clue how to swim. For seven days, while the package traveled the globe, he wondered how it would be received. At times, he felt reassured he'd done the right thing, yet often he worried it was a foolish gesture. Still, he held on to the hope Katerina would understand his desire. Life experience had taught Dr. Pi one thing — sometimes, you have one chance to make an indelible impression on someone, only one. And thus, you'd better not miss it.

Just as he'd hoped, Katerina was overwhelmed with his romantic gesture. After receiving his gifts, she messaged him and expressed such shock and happiness that Dr. Pi felt like running to the post office and sending her another gift box. Elatedly, he read the beginning of her message over and over:

dear dear dear Tobias I have your gifts I am so happy!!!!! (Forty red heart emojis) oh, you bought me a gold ring ... (surprised face and hands-on-cheeks emojis) I'm just in shock!!! Seriously ... this is so big gift so I have no words just ... and I don't know what to do now ... I'm confused and incredibly happy at the same time! you just can't imagine ... (four shy monkey emojis).

Katerina's candor brought an enormous smile to his face. Her words ignited his heart and amplified his desire, the way sunlight passing through a magnifying glass makes a leaf catch fire.

Dear Katerina, he wrote back, *I am thrilled that you like your gifts so much and your exuberant response (your lovely, warm, heartfelt words), gives me immense satisfaction and true joy ... Your genuine reaction is my gift! ... And I appreciate the 1001 kisses and hugs. So much!!! I will feel them the rest of the night and always!*

She then sent him seventeen red hearts followed by words that etched themselves in Dr. Pi's brain, much like Egyptian hieroglyphics carved into stone:

I really want to hug you ... (not just write) ... it's you an amazing, beautiful, talented, kind, thoughtful person ... not me (a smiley face) and I don't know why you are so good with me but I appreciate it very much! I'll sleep in your ring — so much I love it and happy (a smiley with heart eyes) thank you very much again! (Six red hearts) ... I am very happy today!

A few days later, when he least expected it, Dr. Pi received a special gift from Katerina: a DM containing a gorgeous, artistic photograph of herself on her bed. It resembled a Titian Renaissance painting celebrating the female form, in hues of white and red, and best of all, it was for his eyes only. That fact alone let him know he wasn't imagining her affection. She felt strongly for him, cared about his feelings, and wanted to thank him.

Dear Tobias! (A smiley face) I have a little gift for you — in gratitude for your gifts, and for your kindness to me. You wrote that you liked one of my Instagram pics with bear very much, and you like the profile of my body. I created the same photo, but more special and only for you (Red heart) yes, maybe I'm just a little girl, and I can't give you also a gold ring ... but I want to give pleasure to your eyes.

And I want that you too feel my gratitude to you — you are the first and only one man in my Instagram, whom I sent such a special photo (Red heart).

Dr. Pi thanked her, expressed his happiness, and wrote back that he'd treasure her gift always. From that moment forward the only thoughts which occupied his mind were: *I've never wanted a woman this much,* and *How do I make Katerina mine?*

CHAPTER 22

Dr. Pi invited Curt and Jakub to lunch at the Copper Kettle. He gave his friends dedicated, signed copies of his novel, and he'd also brought an extra one for Heather, their favorite waitress.

Jakub was happy to have been invited; he rarely left Crawford for lunch, but Dr. Pi insisted that he join them and said it was his treat. Jakub knew Curt well and shared his taste in beer. The two ordered IPAs and Dr. Pi his usual heavy Draft Horse Triple. They ordered a calamari appetizer to share and began discussing the latest gossip. Dr. Pi sat quietly and listened as Curt and Jakub discussed spring construction projects and new retention strategies. Like all colleges, Pleasant Hills faced dwindling enrollment and deficits, and had to devise ways to attract and keep students. Dr. Pi had taught for many years and heard new proposals with an open mind tinged with suspicion. He hated the faith some administrators placed in statistics and the recommendations of high-priced consultants. They never seemed to take what Dr. Pi thought of as the most obvious and important step: hiring bright, qualified, energetic professors who would passionately engage students in discussion, raising difficult questions and seeking solutions that forced them to think creatively. Dr. Pi was confident that if there were more great professors around, students would not only stay long term but actually attend their classes.

Many regarded his view as simplistic, archaic, and detached from the new demographics and realities of the modern (or was it now postmodern?) world. Dr. Pi scoffed at their excuses, at tasks professors were required to complete yearly, the countless hours spent on surveys, reports, and mind-numbing meetings and training sessions, when what they really needed was to be left alone to find exciting ways to engage young minds. And to make matters worse, the politically correct culture promulgated at every level in academe was having a corrosive effect on freedom of thought and expression. Dr. Pi often wondered what John Stuart Mill would say about this ridiculous academic environment, which limited one's speech and use of language. These days there were good words and bad words, acceptable views and unacceptable ones. A free, genuine exchange of ideas and opinions was no longer possible. Professors had to watch carefully what they said, or risk being dragged through the mud (by the PC police) for saying something regarded as insensitive by a dominant and vocal minority. What got Dr. Pi through the semesters, year after year, was knowing Mill was right when he'd written: "All silencing of opinion is an assumption of infallibility." Everyone should be allowed to speak freely — even idiots. Especially idiots! At least then, one would know who they were and stay clear of them. Dr. Pi passionately hated any effort to control language, ideas, or opinion. He, in fact, had once told his children in earnest that George Orwell was a god and that *Nineteen Eighty-Four* should be considered a bible for everyone who revered free thought.

Heather brought their beers. Dr. Pi toasted to Jakub.

"Thanks for joining us. All good since I last saw you?"

"Yes," Jakub replied, "Thanks for the invite. Just a few more weeks till Christmas break, then I'll have to start the job hunt again for next fall."

"What?" Dr. Pi asked. "Why? I thought you were on a tenure track."

"I was. But my wife and I can't make ends meet. She only works part-time, and I don't make enough. She wants to move west or south, for me to give up teaching and work for an aeronautics firm. More money in business."

Dr. Pi felt the tops of his ears getting hot. He remembered a similar situation when he was an undergraduate at Stony Brook — a true injustice. The university had not renewed Dr. Schiavone's contract, arguably the brightest literature professor Tobias had ever had, but at semester's end Schiavone had told him he was leaving academia and going back to school for a corporate law degree. Tobias was disillusioned. He couldn't believe someone with a doctoral degree in literature from Yale couldn't find a job at a university. Though he understood and respected Schiavone's decision, he lamented how many students would be deprived of his brilliance.

"You have a dammed degree from MIT," Dr. Pi said adamantly to Jakub. "*MIT*! Not some Joe-blow bullshit credentials from an online degree factory out west. Where is Pleasant Hills going to get anyone as qualified to replace you? Don't go, Jakub. We need you here! Students need you. I need you, damn it. Who the hell am I going to talk physics with if you go? You're the best hire we've had in years. Have you talked to anyone about getting a raise?"

"A raise?" Curt scoffed. "What the hell's that? Union's still at the table."

"No, seriously Jakub. I'll help you negotiate. The students love you. Every single one I've asked has told me so."

"Wish I could, Tobias. Just doesn't pay the bills." He paused, reflected. "Besides, Jill doesn't like the cold. She wants to live someplace warm and sunny. Not everyone is cut out for the bleak northeast."

"The springs, summers, and autumns are glorious here," pleaded Dr. Pi. "It's a clean and great place to raise kids. I raised two of them."

"Can't stay," Jakub said conclusively. "Next semester's my last. I guess if they raised my salary ten thousand, Jill might overlook the long winters, but I doubt that's in the college's budget. Besides, dozens of other professors here also deserve more cash."

"Not many with an MIT degree," Curt said. "Everyone should be evaluated on their own merits, but often the extra cash doesn't find its way into the most deserving pockets."

"I understand you, Jakub," Dr. Pi said. "You need to do what's best for you and your wife. What I lament is that students are the ones who'll lose out. If it were me running the place, I'd take the thirty grand Pleasant Hills paid that consulting firm for their golden retention report and give you half that money to stay here and inspire our kids. Of course, that's not how our world works these days."

They ate quietly for a few minutes, and then Jakub changed the subject.

"So, how's the diet and exercise routine going, Tobias? And your Instagram crush?"

Dr. Pi smiled.

"Eating well, as you can see. Fish, chicken, salads, soup. Only an occasional beer to raise my blood pressure." He smiled and raised his glass to toast his friends, then continued.

"I exercise at home. Ride my stationary bike, walk a lot." He wanted to tell them about his kung fu routine but didn't. "Can't seem to get to the gym to lift weights. That's not me. But perhaps I should. Been threatening to join Curt one of these days."

"Definitely threatening," Curt said, laughed, and then drank his beer.

"Katerina's got me inspired. I've started work on a new novel — about her, relationships, and the loneliness of growing old. I'm writing, every chance I get. She's a magic muse." Dr. Pi wished to show Curt and Jakub the photograph Katerina had sent him, so they'd see how beautiful she was, but that was private, for his eyes only, not a trophy to be shown off to friends. Besides, his attraction to Katerina went beyond her physical beauty and sensuousness. If his friends thought him a foolish, lost, and lonely old man, so be it, he reflected.

"Think you'll go meet her soon?" Jakub asked. "Poland's only thirteen hours away — one long sleep on a plane and you can meet this woman in person. You could see if the chemistry between you is real."

"And if it isn't?" Dr. Pi asked, then answered, "I lose the romantic fantasy, the inspiration, everything. Physicists need to move the argument forward always. I understand. For the moment, I'm happy where I am — immersed in my idealistic reverie. Think she's fine where she is too. Why rush things? We're getting to know one another slowly."

Curt chimed in, "Wouldn't it be better to meet, though? I'm sure she'd be more alluring in person. Pictures and videos don't tell the whole story."

"Don't forget our words. It's more than just a physical thing for me."

Dr. Pi paused, and then added: "You're right, Curt. Guess I haven't thought seriously about going there yet. Maybe I'm taking it too slowly. I just don't want to presume or rush things. It's a friendship I want to keep and not ruin. Besides, I'm sure she has someone. Haven't asked her, but I'm certain she does. Someone her own age. Anyone as beautiful as Katerina I'm sure has many suitors."

"A friendship, huh?" Curt said and smiled.

"Yes. For now, at least," Dr. Pi said. "And I have another friendship brewing in Cooperstown."

"Another Instagram-crush?" Jakub asked.

"No, no," Dr. Pi said. "A local artist I recently met by the lake. I bought a few of her paintings. She's a very nice woman."

"Twenty-three too?" Curt asked.

"I'd say in her forties."

"Sounds promising," Curt said. "Now we're talking. An artist, closer in age. Right up your alley. Right down the road too. A much more suitable prospect. Good looking?"

"Very. *Classy.* Educated, talented, and kind."

"So you've actually been on a date?" Curt asked.

"She had me over to dinner."

Dr. Pi described in detail his unfolding relationship with Janet, her precarious situation with Ebenezer, and the close call he'd had after leaving her home.

"Except for the creepy ex-husband," Jakub said, "she sounds perfect — a bright, creative, beautiful woman, with whom you can converse in person without a translation app."

Dr. Pi laughed and agreed. "We've become good friends. Hasn't replaced Katerina, though."

"No, of course not," Jakub said. "You must have your fantasy! Your '*idealistic reverie.*'"

"Yes! I guess I must." Dr. Pi smiled and took a long sip of his Triple. "But who knows? The universe is evolving, right? Mutability is the law of nature. Practicality might win out. Maybe Janet will eclipse my Russian muse. Hasn't happened yet. But she's awfully nice to me."

"It would save you a trip to Poland," Jakub said. "That's big savings."

"It is," Dr. Pi agreed. "But why must I choose? I'd rather keep both as friends. Makes my life fuller, less lonely. Perhaps that's all I really need at my age anyways — some good friends."

"Absolutely," Curt said. "Just watch out for that disgruntled ex. He sounds like trouble."

Jakub left to prepare for his 2 p.m. lab, while Dr. Pi and Curt lingered and ordered another couple of beers instead of dessert.

"I'm serious about you watching your back," Curt said. "You never know what a jerk like that is capable of."

"I handled it pretty well, but yes, it's nerve wracking," Dr. Pi admitted.

"What you need is some expert advice. You should ask Johnny Rocket over there for some tips." Curt pointed towards the far end of the bar where John Bellows, a tall, handsome, middle-aged professor in Pleasant Hills' criminal justice department, drank his beer alone while waiting for his lunch.

"I met him once," Dr. Pi said. "He stopped in my office to tell me he liked my painting of George Washington crossing the Delaware. I didn't know he had a nickname."

"Did you know he used to be in the FBI? He's apparently a marksman, karate black-belt, a real-life James Bond."

"That's awesome," Dr. Pi replied. "Wait here," he said as he got up, walked over to Bellows, and invited him to join them. Bellows agreed right away and brought his beer and his leather messenger bag over to their table.

Before long, Bellows's lunch arrived, and Curt and Dr. Pi sat with him while he ate, enjoying their beers. Bellows sported a military-style crew cut, slightly grown out, and a serious demeanor. He had intense brown eyes and an intelligent gaze — the look of someone who'd spent a lifetime reading people and situations, much like Jakub's scientific attentiveness to detail, but with the added weight of years spent investigating crimes and human nightmares.

"Been taking good care of George?" Bellows asked Dr. Pi, referring to the framed painting that leaned against a bookshelf in Dr. Pi's office. "I hope you've found a spot for the painting. Our first president shouldn't really be leaning against a bookshelf."

Dr. Pi laughed and said, "You're right, and no, I haven't hung it yet. Actually, I think it might look better in your office. For a little advice, it's yours."

"I'd love it. Advice? Shoot."

Dr. Pi went right into the Ebenezer saga, explaining Janet's situation and the close call he'd had with her seemingly homicidal ex in Cooperstown. As Tobias spoke, Bellows' expression grew more and more serious, until he finally held his hand up.

"This is really pretty bad," he said. "These kind of repeated displays of aggressively threatening behavior are highly correlated with violence." He invited Dr. Pi to stop by his office as soon as possible. Trade secrets, he said, should be discussed while sober and in privacy.

"Make it soon," he urged. "And get me the guy's full name. Let's discuss the best way forward. Sounds like your buddy's bound to make a mistake that'll land him in trouble. Stop in and feel free to bring George with you."

Dr. Pi nodded his agreement and cradled his Triple. Worry settled onto his face as he took a small sip of his beer and stared ahead in silence. Everything about Janet was suddenly seeming too real, including this man from her past who was doing everything to make his life hell.

"I'll come see you next week," Dr. Pi said. "Thanks."

CHAPTER 23

Dr. Pi's favorite part of the year were the days leading up to Christmas. With the publication of *Yellow Bird*, the heating up of his friendship with Katerina, and their impending birthdays on December 9 and 11, this year promised to be extra special. Even better, the snow had come early to Central New York, adding a romantic ambiance to the coming holidays, and making the whole place look like a wonderland. In the classroom, he felt inspired, motivated to make discussions meaningful and memorable. Walking to class on these cold, snowy mornings, he reflected on how fortunate he was, how much he still loved teaching, how wonderful it felt to share ideas and insights freely with students.

In Lit class, he discussed Tillie Olsen's "I Stand Here Ironing," a complicated narrative which explores the psychology of a mother/daughter relationship. As the narrator irons clothing, she tries to make sense of the experiences that have shaped their lives together and concludes "I will never total it all." He loved teaching this story because Olsen illustrates how mysterious and unpredictable human experience is. Unlike the exactitude of science or mathematics, with their formulas and precise answers, our lives are fraught with unknowns, and quite often, the sum of all our experiences just doesn't add up into neat conclusions. And that's precisely what makes our lives worth living — there is always the expectation, the unpredictability of what's to come, and the promise of something bewildering, possibly magical. This story's truthfulness yanked students' hypnotized heads from their phone screens and sent their hands into the air, and this filled Dr. Pi with joy.

Certainly, Dr. Pi's endured pain — the deaths of Maria and Miriam, and the breakup of his marriage — had been at times unbearable, and yet, somehow, hope had reappeared, much like new buds in a burned forest. And the epicenter of that hope, the source of his renewal, was undeniably Katerina. In these early days of December, he learned many new things about her life and some of what she'd lived through up to that point. Each detail increased his compassion and affection for her; it seemed everything about her elevated him, invigorating his desire to live.

Two things he'd learned after her birthday touched him: one, that she no longer had any family left in Russia, and two, that she planned to work this Christmas at the restaurant and not celebrate. Russian Christmas was after the New Year on the Epiphany; in Poland, as in America, it fell on December 25. Though she'd mentioned that ordinarily she celebrated both, Dr. Pi had the impression that this year she was melancholy and might not feel up to it. Right then, he decided to send some Christmas presents to cheer her. It immediately occurred to him that he'd get her the latest Bose headphones — a musician would appreciate them. He also picked up some soaps and a beautiful handbag decorated with line drawings of long-necked cats. Then he bought two lovely Christmas cards, stuffed them with two hundred dollars' worth of Polish zloty that he'd picked up at his bank, and sent the package off that afternoon. That night he messaged Katerina about the coming gift. Though she initially seemed bewildered and playfully reprimanded him for sending it — telling him the birthday gift had been plenty — she ultimately thanked him for his thoughtfulness and expressed sincere satisfaction that he'd done that for her.

That evening, Dr. Pi graded several papers before he started to yawn. It wasn't even nine, but these days his eyes tired quickly, and there were so many fused constructions in his students' writing that he wondered whether they thought a period was optional; it seemed a mark headed for extinction, like the wall-mounted phone. Commas were now frequently used as periods, and the semicolon was forgotten like a distant, unknown relative on permanent vacation.

Dr. Pi never drank coffee late at night anymore because it disrupted his sleep, and on this night, quite strangely, he couldn't muster the energy or the enthusiasm to pick up his guitar. Preparing for bed, he suddenly thought about Janet, and felt badly that he'd been brusque and disinterested when she had kissed him. Kissing her had felt good; feeling her soft breath on his face had aroused him. And yet, he'd backed out of it. *Why?* he wondered. Did his lack of feelings for her stem solely from his growing affection for Katerina? Or was he afraid of getting physically involved with a woman again? *Why not give Janet a chance?* he thought. She seemed to be into him, and she was undeniably attractive. They had a lot in common. Sleeping with her might be exactly what he needed.

He found a science show on Netflix to ease him into sleep, then set his alarm, but before putting the phone away he decided to invite Janet to a nice restaurant.

Hi Janet, he texted. *Any chance you can have dinner with me tomorrow and let me purchase a few paintings to give away at Christmas?*

A response wasn't immediate, and Dr. Pi felt guilty; perhaps he'd hurt her feelings and ruined the prospect of a good friendship or more. He watched his program and frequently glanced at the phone's screen, but there was nothing. After a half hour, he gave up, texted his children goodnight, lay back, and promptly fell asleep. At midnight, he awakened and shuffled to the bathroom to pee. He glanced at his phone screen and saw Janet's reply:

Sure. Tell me where and when you'd like to meet? And please don't forget my signed copy of Yellow Bird. *I'm dying to read it!*

Dr. Pi thought of answering but realized she was probably asleep. He'd reply the next morning. That night he dreamed about Janet. He was dressed like a king and was carrying a blooming rose bush with bright yellow blooms as he approached a broad garden that she tended. She looked up at him and stopped her planting. In her eyes he saw tears. He was surprised when she extended her hands to receive her gift. She carefully planted the rose bush in silence, and then smiled. And she said, "I thought you'd never return. I'm glad you did. I have a surprise for you inside. Come." Just as she escorted him toward her house, hundreds of birds flew into the sky from the nearby trees. That was all he remembered when he awoke. He texted Janet, and they agreed to meet for dinner that evening at The Inn at Cooperstown.

Driving to Cooperstown, Dr. Pi felt especially joyful. Not only was he happy knowing that the gifts he'd sent Katerina would liven up her Christmas, but he was also buoyed by an eagerness to see Janet. He looked forward to holding her in his arms and perhaps tasting her soft lips again. He understood her situation was complicated, at best, and he mused about how most artists' lives were often tumultuous and chaotic, even without a jealous and possibly violent ex-spouse in the mix. Still, that wouldn't deter him; he'd deal with Ebenezer if he had to. He wanted to get to know her. Suddenly he envisioned Janet's beautiful farmhouse as an oasis — a refuge from loneliness, where an intelligent, talented woman would welcome him and share her treasure.

At five-thirty that evening, the two sat by candlelight in a lovely dining room corner table. From a plastic bag, Dr. Pi took out a dedicated, signed copy of *Yellow Bird* and handed it to her. Janet read his inscription to her, and then the book's dedication to Dr. Pi's parents and children.

"Truly lovely words for your parents and children," she said and smiled. "Thank you."

"You're welcome. Just hope the rest isn't too disappointing."

Janet perused the epigraph from *Don Juan*.

"When a writer begins with Byron's words for inspiration," she said, "it's a sign of good things to come."

They both ordered the Friday fish and chips special and decided to share a bottle of red wine. Since it was early and not yet crowded, their dinners came quickly. Both loved the haddock's freshness and taste enough to send their compliments to the chef, and for a good while they spoke of their favorite foods and restaurants. Janet's face was aglow with happiness. The twinkle in her eyes expressed gratitude at being invited out, something she'd not expected after Dr. Pi's sudden departure on their last visit and the near ambush that had followed.

Though Janet usually dressed conservatively, tonight she wore a sheer white, low-cut blouse which invited Dr. Pi to stare at her bosom. He couldn't resist her physical loveliness, especially as the wine relaxed him. She noticed and became more flirtatious as the time passed.

"You know I don't paint nudes?" she asked playfully. "Just landscapes. Iconic places. Sometimes I think I should though."

"I'm well aware of that," he said, and smiled broadly, realizing that Janet had seen him looking down her blouse. "Landscapes will do; they're pieces for friends." He paused, then continued, "Forgive me for staring. You look so lovely tonight."

"Piqued your curiosity?"

"Yes, immensely."

"Often takes a while, especially when it's been a while. Believe me, I know. But you're welcome to come back to my place for a closer look. Unless of course…" she paused, "you're in a rush, or worried about Ebenezer, and just want to browse quickly through my paintings and leave."

"I'm not worried about him, or in a rush … and I'm very eager to see more of you," Dr. Pi said.

Janet's eyes lit up. She reached for his hands and held them.

"I have some chilled wine for us. And you're welcome to stay, if you don't have other plans?"

"None. It's Friday. I came to see and be with you. Make up for being so cold the last time."

"You have someone? That was my impression. Sensed you felt guilty going further."

"Yes, sort of. A little guilty." Dr. Pi drank his wine and then explained. "I've developed feelings for a Russian woman living in Poland. A very beautiful…" He stopped.

"How young?" Janet asked. "On Facebook?"

"No, Instagram. Just turned twenty-four."

"That's really young. Perfectly understandable though. I'm sure she's lovely." She sounded dejected.

Dr. Pi wished to show Janet a photograph of Katerina but, sensing her disappointment, thought it inappropriate. After all, he'd come here to get to know her, and make up for his rudeness their prior visit.

"What do you text about with someone so young?" Janet asked glumly.

"Music mainly. She's a classical pianist."

"Marvelous. Just like my son."

"And bits and pieces about the photographs we each post," Dr. Pi continued. "It's funny, but it doesn't take much to feel you know someone well, to see them as a friend. She knows I'm much older. Said she'd scrutinized my page and didn't care. That she preferred texting a mature man. Friends have said it's someone catfishing, preying on a lonely man. But I know she's real. Ninety-nine percent sure."

"I see," Janet said. "Perhaps there are some deep-seated daddy issues. And you're a surrogate father figure. A professor full of wisdom."

"Maybe," he said, and laughed gently. "If that's the case, I can be there for her."

"Nothing wrong with it," Janet insisted. "If you fill that void, and the feelings between you are mutual, it's perfectly fine. I can see why she'd be interested. You're handsome, smart, and kind."

"Thanks Janet. That's nice of you to say." He smiled, hesitated, and then asked jokingly, "Are you interested?"

"*I am*," Janet said immediately in a sexy, provocative manner. She smiled and brushed her legs against his under the table.

Dr. Pi took a big sip of his wine and collected his thoughts. He felt a bit uncomfortable, wondered how to get out of this conversation without ruining the moment. It seemed to him that Janet didn't care if there was a Katerina. Janet was an attractive, confident woman and well-aware of her own powerful charms.

After some minutes, Dr. Pi said, "I've developed strong feelings for Katerina over the past year. I *am* a vulnerable, lonely man. In this crazy head, I crave another chance at a youthful love. A totally new beginning. And fantasy. I've always been a stupid fool. Silly to want a new love's magic at my age. It's illogical and utterly ridiculous."

"It isn't!" Janet said adamantly, the alcohol animating her. "You're not stupid at all. And those are *wonderful* desires. I've felt that way too."

"After you and I kissed last time," Dr. Pi said, "I felt as if I'd betrayed Katerina. Someone I've never spoken to in person. It's idiotic! Katerina and I aren't officially in a relationship. I don't even know if she has someone. Haven't asked, but I suspect she does. We've not agreed to anything. We're still just getting to know one another. I've sent her a few gifts. It's a budding friendship more than anything else. I'm well aware she's much too young for me. But she reminds me so much of my dead sister Maria, who also played the piano. Who I loved so dearly and miss. When we were kids, I'd often tell Maria one day I'd marry someone just like her, and she'd squeeze me tightly till I almost couldn't breathe. And somehow texting with Katerina triggers those sacred memories and brings me immense joy. It's hard to explain."

Dr. Pi stopped, sensing how stupid he must look and sound to Janet. This was not something he'd come to discuss — his Instagram crush.

"Sorry to hear about Maria's death."

"Thank you. It's an old and painful wound."

They fell silent for a spell, but then Janet surprised him:

"There's nothing idiotic about your feelings," she said. "I understand them perfectly. I've gone through it. Loneliness takes us onto strange roads. Believe me! And beauty is very appealing, especially a young person's beauty, when one has an artistic temperament like we both do."

"You've had an Instagram crush too?"

"No," Janet said.

Just then, the waiter arrived to remove the dinner dishes and presented their dessert menu. Each ordered the cheesecake, and another bottle of wine. The waiter left, and she resumed:

"A Facebook fling," she said, and smiled.

"Ooh."

"With a former student."

"Double ooh, and ouch," Dr. Pi said, and shook his head — no — in disapproval.

"Yeah. You're right," she said. "Believe me, I'm not proud of it. He found me on Facebook. He pursued me, said he wanted desperately to meet, to show me his art, and he expressed an eagerness to see mine. I was weak, and *very* lonely. Ebenezer and I had separated, and he'd started seeing an eighteen-year-old who worked at the pizzeria. He wanted to hurt me. Made sure I saw her with her hands all over him when we'd meet in court. Sadly, I wished to get him back."

"Eighteen?"

"Yes. Just turned eighteen, a mere child."

"There's a lot I don't know about this man. I know he was cruel to you, and that he's money-hungry, but he's a lot stranger than that. Brayden's your maiden name, correct? Not his?"

"Correct. His last name's Lancaster. Ebenezer Hendricks Lancaster. Of the Manhattan Lancaster family."

"Mr. Ebenezer Hendricks Lancaster," Dr. Pi repeated slowly, trying to commit the name to memory. "And what about your fling with your former student?" How'd that turn out? How old was he?"

"Didn't last long," Janet said. "Twenty-four. Same as your crush. After just a few weeks, he got attached, bought me fancy lingerie, and talked about marrying me or at least moving in — to work on art, of course. There was … *lots* of sex." Janet smiled as she thought back. If her intention was to make Dr. Pi feel jealous, it was working. Right then, he imagined sleeping with her and his heart raced.

"My son didn't like him though," she continued, "or it might have lasted longer. Phillip was livid with me when he figured out what was going on. So I broke it off soon after."

The waiter arrived with their desserts, poured each a glass of wine, and left the bottle. Janet excused herself and went to the bathroom. After she'd walked away, Dr. Pi typed Ebenezer's full name on his phone's notepad so Rocket could investigate him. Ebenezer sounded even creepier than Dr. Pi had first thought.

When Janet returned, they ate their desserts, and continued to drink.

"How did you meet Ebenezer?" Dr. Pi asked.

"While working at the library art exhibit. He was visiting the Hall. That's how most people wind up in this town. Wish I'd called in sick that day rather than meet that jerk. But I can't regret Phillip, so I guess to have my son I had to endure all that pain."

Janet's voice thinned with emotion, but she pushed on.

"He was dressed elegantly. Suit, tie, polished black shoes, big, broad smile. Oozing money. Self-assured. And I fell for his suave rap — his thick, sly *bullshit*! This deal and that deal, lucrative schemes he used to make his company money. Money's all he talked about. Sounded smart, knew how to woo me, and screw me too — that very night at the Otesaga Hotel where he stayed. I cheated on the boy I was seeing then. A dumb little *tramp*, that's what I became as I let that son-of-a-bitch rip off my panties and ruin my fucking life."

Dr. Pi found it strange hearing Janet speak so vulgarly, but the alcohol had brought her hidden pain to surface. He felt badly for her, reached for her hands, squeezed them, and said ever so gently, "You're *not* that, Janet … not at all … I know for sure … but *he is* everything you've said *and worse*."

"Thanks," Janet said and fell silent. He wished to make her pain disappear. He got up, hugged her, and then whispered, "Come. Let's get out of here."

She kissed his cheek and got up. Dr. Pi paid their bill, and the two walked onto the wide, beautiful porch of The Inn. It was cold but still outside. Janet suggested walking around town a bit until the effect of the wine wore off and before driving the short distance to her house. They strolled arm in arm down Main Street, gazing at its Christmas decorations, and stopped to look at the Baseball Hall of Fame before veering left towards the lake. The closer they got to the water, the darker the streets became, as they left behind the houses with their glowing picture windows and colored Christmas lights. For a few moments Dr. Pi tensed up, as he wondered whether Ebenezer or one of his thugs might jump out from behind the bushes to surprise them. He pushed the thought from his head and stopped at the darkest corner by a long wall of tall cedar bushes. Gathering Janet in, he wrapped his arms around her waist and kissed her passionately. It was a long, intense kiss, followed by several shorter, playful ones, and when he backed away and looked into Janet's eyes, he saw tears.

"I've craved that all night," she said softly. "You're a romantic, complicated man."

"A strange man," Dr. Pi replied. "Even to myself."

"That's a turn on," she said. "Join us for Christmas this year, Tobias. Say yes, right now. Just Phillip, his fiancée Veronica, you, and me. It'll be fun. A Cooperstown Christmas at my house, and I'll do all the cooking."

"Sounds fantastic," Dr. Pi said. "I'd love to, Janet. Yes, of course I will. My son will be at his in-laws, and my daughter will be with her mom. I had planned to write and spend it with the house spirits this year, but your offer is *way* more appealing. Thanks."

"Perfect," she said happily. "For a moment I thought you'd say you'd already booked a flight to Poland."

"Did I sound that lost and desperate?" Dr. Pi asked. "Don't think I know Katerina well enough to do that yet."

"No. Not lost or desperate," Janet said. "But flying to see her would be a true romantic gesture. A *big* chance to make a statement."

Janet looked at Dr. Pi and smiled slyly. Then she kissed him, this time much more passionately.

"I want to sleep with you now," Dr. Pi said and squeezed her. "Let's head back."

"Sure," she said.

Once home, Janet locked the door behind them, and he helped her off with her coat, then ripped his off aggressively and took her hand as they walked quickly towards the loveseat in the living room. Dr. Pi unbuttoned Janet's blouse and brought his mouth to her bosom. He felt the soft skin of her chest on his cheeks, nose, and mouth, and felt her heart beat fast. Her body's fragrance aroused him into a frenzy. He moved his hands under her long woolen dress, searching along her slender legs, feeling their delicacy, and Janet moaned. She unbuckled his belt, pulled his zipper down, and seized his member. Dr. Pi's hands, meanwhile, moved past her moist upper thighs, higher, felt how wet she was, and rubbed her gently. Not long afterwards he was inside her, enjoying her warmth, kissing her body everywhere, out of control. It'd been a while since he'd felt this pleasure. He looked at Janet's lovely face, into her brown eyes, kissed her lips delicately again and again, and thrust more wildly. She was afire, full of lust, desire, and he, a volcano set to blow in her. Beckoned by this beautiful artist, soon he released the dormant, explosive madness which for months had raged only in his mind.

Janet took control, dragged Dr. Pi up to her bedroom, pushed him on the bed playfully, jumped on top, and the two made vigorous love again. He kissed her curvaceous body. She caressed his face, whispered her pleasure, kissed him tenderly, and held him firmly, appreciatively. Exhausted, they finally fell asleep with their limbs entangled. In the middle of the night, when the room got chilly, Janet pulled the sheets and comforter over them. At dawn, while Dr. Pi lay still in a sleepy stupor, Janet climbed on top of him and goaded him awake. It'd been years since he'd had sex with a woman who knew what she wanted, and who wanted *him*, openly and unapologetically. She took lovemaking to a level he remembered experiencing only in his youth.

Janet wanted to cook them breakfast, but Dr. Pi insisted on treating her to brunch in town. By eleven they were sitting at the Lake

Front Restaurant & Bar, where they ate quickly and drank their coffee in silence. Finally, Janet jabbed him humorously:

"Think your young Russian girl can love you like that when you meet her?"

"Not sure," he said and smiled. "I've imagined her in a more innocent manner."

"C'mon," Janet said. "You don't expect me to believe that? Having sex is the first thing that runs through a man's mind. That's why you follow that floozy."

Dr. Pi braced at the term, with its connotations of looseness — a quality he couldn't imagine in Katerina. "That might be true of other men," he said seriously, "but it's not me. When I think of Katerina, I imagine a slow romance. Gifts, flowers, songs…"

"Oh God. Sounds pathetic. What if when you meet her, she jumps your bones like I did? Would you be disappointed? Throw her out of bed?"

Dr. Pi smiled slyly, thought of Janet's naked body, of how amazing she'd made him feel.

"Must say I'd be surprised. Same way you surprised me," he said, taking refuge in a sip of coffee before admitting the truth to himself and Janet. "I think I'd be thrilled. And no, I wouldn't throw her out of bed."

Janet smiled as though she'd won her point, then drew one finger slowly along his hand as it rested on the table. "So … you enjoyed it? Us? Last night?"

Dr. Pi shot her a wide-eyed look that said "You know very well I enjoyed it."

"It was fine. It was adequate," he deadpanned, dragging out the moment until she laughed out loud and smacked him lightly on the arm.

"It was amazing," he clarified.

"Good, because I was just trying to help you out. I figured if you were going after a twenty-four-year-old, you'd need to practice. *A lot!*"

Dr. Pi laughed. "That's very thoughtful of you," he joked. Then he looked at her gratefully and said, "Thank you."

"You're welcome."

"So how'd I do? Can I pull it off?"

"Think you'll need to come over and practice. A month perhaps, maybe two, before going to Poland," Janet said and winked.

"Can we start this afternoon?"

"Most definitely. Not bad for someone who's been fantasizing wildly about phantoms abroad, but there are things to improve."

"I like your generosity," Dr. Pi said, as the waitress handed him the bill.

"And I like yours," Janet said.

CHAPTER 24

Dr. Pi stayed at Janet's house Saturday and was set to leave late Sunday afternoon, exhausted but happy. He'd lost track of how many times they'd had sex, but he was clear on one thing: everything about being with Janet felt right. Her bedroom prowess was intense and adventuresome, but what made Janet special was her intelligence. She could talk for as long as he could and listen attentively just as long. No matter what the topic, whether art, baseball, metaphysics, or Pink Floyd, the thoughts she shared captivated his interest. Her curiosity was equal to his, and she could be funny one moment and profound the next. He'd wanted to stay Sunday night (he could get used to her pampering, he thought) but decided against it, since he had to give a final exam Monday morning.

Before leaving, Dr. Pi asked to see the paintings Janet had for sale. He wished to buy at least one, he told her. Janet showed him a painting of the snow-covered Swiss Alps and another of a Sahara sunset. These were inspired, she explained, by memories of the half-year she'd spent traveling after her divorce was finalized. She and Phillip (who took an unpaid leave from work) had visited several European cities, Northern Africa, and Brazil.

"Just beautiful," Dr. Pi said, as he examined the blend of yellows and browns in the desert painting. "I can feel the heat there and imagine the endless dunes and sand. Spectacular, but not a place I'd ever wish to visit. Seems so bleak."

"I loved it," Janet said. "It *is* bleak, yet ironically, it's also full of life. Something about the landscape captured the loneliness I felt then, even though Phillip was there to cheer me. Did I do it justice?"

"You did. It's just not somewhere I'd ever go. Now South America, on the other hand, I do wish to see someday. Any paintings of Brazilian beaches? Lovely blues and greens?"

"Haven't gotten to those yet. Soon. Something you're particularly looking for?"

"No. This Swiss Alps painting is perfect." Dr. Pi reached for his wallet. "Will a hundred suffice?"

"This one's *free*. You've spent enough money on me this weekend. And you can consider it a thank you for my copy of *Yellow Bird*."

Dr. Pi smiled, pulled her close, and kissed her. "Thank you."

Just then, they both heard a vehicle coming up the driveway, followed by a loud brake squeal and the sound of an engine shutting off. Not long after, there was a knock on the back kitchen door. Janet looked a little bewildered.

"Excuse me," she said and went to answer. Dr. Pi listened intently from the other room while he stood still, gripping his gift painting. He heard Janet talking to a man with a deep voice but could not make out any of their conversation. At one point, however, she raised her voice and said, "We *agreed* on Monday. I have company."

Immediately afterwards, their voices died away, and the door closed shut. When Janet didn't return, Dr. Pi put the painting down and walked into the kitchen. Through the window, he could see her escorting a burly man towards the barn. They disappeared inside for several minutes, then came back out, and Janet closed the barn door. The man carried a fairly large, yet slim, wooden box under his arm, and walked with quick strides towards his Subaru. He was middle-aged and sported a bushy mustache and beard. He wore a backwards Red Sox baseball cap, an un-zipped Patriots' winter coat, carpenter's overalls, and construction boots. He lifted the car's hatch, placed the box inside, slammed it shut, and drove off.

Dr. Pi greeted Janet when she walked back in.

"Everything okay?"

"Yes, yes" she said. "I'm sorry. That was my good friend Anthony who came to pick up a painting. He was supposed to stop by tomorrow."

"He looks familiar," Dr. Pi said. "Think I've seen him before."

"You have," Janet said. "He bartends at The Black Sox Bar and Grill."

"I remember now," Dr. Pi said. "The night you introduced yourself, he gave me the evil eye."

"He's a dear friend, Tobias. He looks out for me. We do a little business together. He sells my antiques downstate through his Bronx connections. I have a barn full. Sometimes paintings too."

"I'm sure you get good money for them in the city," Dr. Pi said. "Is he upset that I'm here? Looked like he left in a huff."

"Oh no, no," Janet replied. "Anthony knows you're my friend. He's just pissed because the manager changed his work schedule last minute and he has to bartend tomorrow. That's his day off usually. It's why he came by today."

"Must be frustrating for him," Dr. Pi said.

"Very."

Dr. Pi reached for Janet's hand, pulled her closer, smiled, and asked playfully, "So, as my students say, am I a *friend with benefits*?"

She laughed, kissed him softly, and then said, "Yes, one with *excellent benefits*! Wouldn't you agree?"

"Yes," he replied helplessly and kissed her. "I love that term. And this strange new world."

"I'm glad. Come," Janet said, "I want you in me once more before you go. Let's make it an even six, shall we?" She unbuckled his belt and yanked him back upstairs to her bedroom.

On the ride to Pleasant Hills, Dr. Pi wondered about Janet. She was so different than when he'd first met her. He thought about everything she'd shared about Ebenezer and his cruelty, her travels, her business ventures with Anthony, and her affair with a former student. She now seemed much more mysterious. And she really liked having sex. Dr. Pi couldn't recall the last time he'd slept with a woman so often in such a brief time, not even when he was twenty. He felt proud he'd kept up and not disappointed Janet. But though Janet had made him feel wanted and very much at ease, something about their intimacy felt odd. There was an inner restlessness gnawing at him — a vast, dark void and an emptiness deep inside. Leaving her house, he hadn't felt a deep desire to stay. Already he knew that he didn't miss Janet, who'd given him everything on a golden platter, the way he missed Katerina, whom he'd never touched. The truth of that realization bewildered him. While eating dinner with Janet on Friday, he *thought* he knew her, but just forty-eight hours later he wasn't so sure.

That night his legs and lower back felt like jelly after so much sex. He set his alarm, texted his children goodnight, noticed he had a direct message on Instagram, and checked it. Katerina had sent him a photograph of a large, impressive tray of bread she'd made at her restaurant.

Bread by my hands, she'd written proudly underneath the picture, and it looked delicious. His heart filled with love and longing. Dr. Pi knew she was a talented chef who'd attended an advanced high school culinary program in Irkutsk before coming to Poland after graduation to study music, and for a moment he wished he could taste a piece and compliment her in person.

But she'd written much more. *We had a party at the restaurant tonight after work, just for the employees, and I met a man, an investor in our restaurant. He said he heard about me, wants me to be head chef at his new restaurant. Is a big opportunity, but not sure about it, don't want to betray my boss and leave him. Thank you for sending me a Christmas gift. I am so happy about it. (A smiley face and three heart emojis).*

Dr. Pi realized Katerina must be asleep, but he texted her back right away, elated by her news. *Sounds promising, a great opportunity to become head chef. I know you must be torn about leaving your restaurant but think about it. May be financially a smart choice. And you're welcome; I just hope the box arrives before Christmas. Have a great day tomorrow."* (*A smiley face blowing a kiss and three heart emojis*). Dr. Pi put down his phone and fell asleep.

CHAPTER 25

After his exams the next day, Dr. Pi went home for lunch, did his kung fu exercises, showered, ate, and then returned to his office to organize materials for Tuesday's exam. When he saw Johnny Rocket's door was open, he rushed to grab the Washington painting and brought it to him happily.

"George is here for you," Dr. Pi said. "Told me he'd like to hang on the wall of a true Patriot."

Rocket smiled and waved Dr. Pi in.

"Well, that I am, for sure, though 'These are the times which try men's souls.'"

"Tom Paine's famous words from *The American Crisis*," Dr. Pi said. "Moving and true. Every generation has its challenges, as does ours."

"Yes. And we must meet them head on."

"I agree."

"Having the great general here to inspire me will help," Rocket said. "Thanks. When my wife visits again, she can find him a permanent spot. For now, we'll put him here."

Rocket took the painting and placed it on top of a tall bookcase. "From this perch," he said, "may he guard and bless this office."

"Hear, hear," Dr. Pi said.

Bellows smiled and then turned to Tobias with a look of curious concern.

"Did you get the full name of the creep?"

"I did," Dr. Pi said.

Bellows handed Dr. Pi a small pad and pen. "Write it down. We'll see what my boys can dig up."

Dr. Pi wrote *Ebenezer Hendricks Lancaster* and then returned the pad and pen. Bellows glanced at the name before opening his drawer and shoving the pad inside. He put the pen in his shirt pocket, then turned his attention to the painting.

"In Washington's day," Bellows noted, "there weren't many who thought fighting the British — the greatest war machine the world had ever seen — made any sense. Imagine, a ragtag bunch of revolutionaries taking it upon themselves to fight the British Empire, whose soldiers were better fed, better equipped, and better organized. It made *no sense whatsoever.* A suicide mission."

"That it was," Dr. Pi chimed in. "But it made perfect sense when the nation's freedom depended on it. For without liberty, those few determined life was not worth living."

"Precisely!" Bellows exclaimed. "Thank goodness we had those few enlightened ones to lead the way, especially General George." He nodded at the painting. "Otherwise, this great nation wouldn't have been realized."

Dr. Pi replied. "Imagine how sure of his argument Thomas Paine had to be to ask ordinary men and women, some with families, children, and businesses they could potentially lose, to *risk it all to fight for freedom.* General George was a great, great leader. But it was Paine who persuaded Americans who were against the war to be bold and unafraid. For wherever fear reigns, freedom can't be attained. That was Paine's logic — and thank God for that!"

Bellows, beside himself with joy, slapped Dr. Pi on the back.

"Wow! Do you go off like that in class? I see why students like you."

"Thank you," Dr. Pi said. "Only when I'm teaching poetry! Or talking history. I suck the rest of the time. I'm just an old, worn out, and lonely-ass professor trying to make it to retirement."

"Bullshit! You've got years to kick still, young man."

"Perhaps," Dr. Pi said. "Cause *that's* when I'll retire — when I'm *done* done. As long as I don't lose my mind first, I'll be in that damn classroom teaching students to think for themselves."

CHAPTER 26

A week later, at the Dean's retirement dinner in Cazenovia, Dr. Pi felt down. He didn't like these goodbyes. Though they were celebratory occasions, it was hard to see great friends leave, and to think of his own eventual departure from academia. Dr. Pi couldn't fathom — though he knew it was coming — the day when he'd no longer enter a classroom to teach poetry and writing. He was solemn and subdued, though outwardly he tried to be jovial, all the while feeling the gloom of passing years. Everyone had aged so much.

It was in this very hotel, twenty years earlier, that he'd agonized over what lesson he'd teach for his job interview at Pleasant Hills. Joanna had encouraged him, as she recognized his building anxiety, and his son had played with the Ninja Turtle toys he'd brought on the trip from Long Island. Dr. Pi hadn't received his doctorate yet and felt the pressure of needing this job to support his family. He decided to teach Wordsworth's "We Are Seven," and, the next day, he'd moved expertly through the lesson, feeling his success as students became engrossed and engaged. There had been no iPhones or other distractions then — just chalk, a blackboard, and lots of raised hands to call on. Tonight, he found himself here, forty semesters and nearly four-thousand students later, full of nostalgia. The sadness lingered while he stared at the flames in the lobby's fireplace, occasionally smiling as other professors arrived and said hello.

After the Dean gave a speech and expressed his heartfelt gratitude to colleagues, Dr. Pi's sadness subsided. He sincerely hoped one day when his turn came to say goodbye that he could find such appreciative words. Dean O'Rourke, he knew, had done his best to steer a deficient ship, with a very diverse crew, through turbulent waters and often changing weather; as captain, navigating was a challenge, sometimes a thankless job — and there were some who didn't like him — but he'd tried. And that was all one could do.

Before long, Dr. Pi was eating, drinking, and chatting with colleagues. He met Johnny Rocket's wife and took a selfie with Bellows that he'd later post on Instagram, along with other pictures from this festivity. He had five hundred followers to keep happy, some who'd never seen a Dean's retirement dinner, and Dr. Pi would show them what one looked like.

Partway through the evening, Rocket leaned in and told Dr. Pi he had some information about Ebenezer.

"Can you meet for a drink at the Kettle 'round two tomorrow? I'm coming in to tidy up my office and then we're traveling to Florida."

"Sure thing," Dr. Pi said.

After dinner, Dr. Pi felt solemn again. He'd had a ginger ale with dinner, so he was sober and fit to drive home. He really wasn't sure what accounted for his emotional turmoil. Certainly, it was in part the nostalgia, in part a recognition of how quickly one's life flies, in part a sense of regret that after all those years of marriage and all the wonderful things he and Joanna had accomplished together that still their marriage had ended. Seeing Rocket and his wife had filled him with joy. They glowed when they talked about their two children! Dr. Pi wondered whether a new relationship for him was possible. With Janet? Katerina? He wasn't sure.

His cellphone buzzed. He sat in a chair by the fireplace and looked at its screen. It was a direct message from Katerina, in response to the best wishes for a wonderful day he'd sent her that morning:

Thank you, Tobias. You are a really good man. Your words always make me smile. I'm glad I have you. I don't want to lose you.

Dr. Pi smiled inwardly. Simple words had such power, he reflected. He knew he needed to continue steering his ship. He wasn't done. His journey was ongoing.

You won't lose me. I'm here, he texted back. *I'll always be here for you. (A smiley face, followed by a heart emoji).*

***

At 2:10 the next day, Bellows and Pi sat with their beers in a private corner booth.

"Snow's not letting up this year," Bellows remarked. "The kids don't want to go to Florida. Christmas on the beach isn't their cup of tea. But their grandparents will spoil them, so hopefully they'll have a good time. Clara misses her folks and needs to get out of Syracuse. A break from this bleakness will benefit us all."

"Absolutely," Dr. Pi said. He handed Bellows a copy of *Yellow Bird*. "Your gift. Thought you'd read it by the fireplace after Christmas, but I promise it'll be just as good while lounging on the hot sand."

"Thank you," Bellows said. "That's thoughtful of you. Selling well?"

"Not sure. I'll find out when I see a royalty check. Just glad it's done and out."

Dr. Pi then asked, "Learn anything about Ebenezer?"

"He's harmless," Bellows said. "Just a jealous, disgruntled ex-husband, I think. Clean record. Nothing on him. Not even a damn speeding ticket. No arrest record. Attends church, donates to several charities — the Cooperstown police and fire departments, Bassett Hospital, the Hall of Fame. Has worked for two Manhattan-based real-estate investment firms over a twenty-year period. Traveled abroad extensively early in his career. Attended West Point Military Academy. All indications are that he's a stellar citizen — a patriot."

"No restraining order?" Dr. Pi inquired.

"Nope," Bellows said.

"Wow," Dr. Pi uttered. "Not what I expected. Not the picture Janet painted of him."

"I was surprised too," Bellows said. "There might be something missing. My former colleagues will keep digging, I can assure you. If there's anything there, they'll find it. My hunch is you're safe. Probably doesn't appreciate you seeing his ex-wife. That's understandable."

"Yes. True." Dr. Pi thought about the previous weekend he'd spent with Janet. Their relationship was now much more intimate; he'd been invited over for Christmas and was going to meet Phillip. He felt guilty, recalling how jealous he'd been when any man came near Joanna after they'd separated.

"I don't think he poses any real threat," Bellows reassured him. "If they're divorced, he'll have to move on eventually. She's trying to, obviously, but he's not."

"Thanks. I'll keep my eyes open. I appreciate the help. Lots of *gray area* in personal problems. Two people in a relationship often see different truths."

"Tell me about it," Bellows said. "That's why I listen closely to my wife and hear even what she doesn't voice. The key is to keep the harmony, sacrifice for one another when it's difficult — for love, for family, for country."

"Amen. You're a true optimist," Dr. Pi said happily. "And a damn romantic like me."

"That's why I took a liking to you. We're a lot alike."

"We're teachers. To move forward, we compromise."

"I'll toast to that," Bellows said. He raised his glass, and they clinked to their unfolding friendship.

CHAPTER 27

Dr. Pi drove to New York City to visit Constance and bring her some Christmas cash before she left for San Diego to see her mom. He played with Tank and took him out to do his business but noticed that the little guy seemed disoriented. His kidney disease had worsened, and it was painfully obvious that his energy had diminished since he'd visited Pleasant Hills the past September. Dr. Pi thought wistfully of the month he and Tank had spent together the year before, and of their many adventures in the old Dodge and Monte SS. The two had forged a loving bond, and it was hard for Dr. Pi to see Tank struggling. Constance and Dr. Pi focused a lot of loving energy on Tank during the short visit, but still managed to go out for breakfast, lunch, and dinner, play guitar, sing songs, and listen to Celia Cruz. In the late afternoon on the twenty-second, Dr. Pi drove back to Pleasant Hills.

On the way home he encountered a slick Taconic Parkway and lots of blowing snow. Tucked in his Audi's warm cabin, sheltered from that outer bleakness, Dr. Pi reflected on how fortunate he was to have two such bright, talented, and industrious children. He thanked God that in his life he'd experienced so much love and happiness. The loneliness drifted in and out like the snow, yet the despair he sometimes felt never crushed him. Even when he wanted to cry, when he felt the weight of all the mistakes he'd made in his marriage and life sucking the air out of him, Dr. Pi managed to take a deep breath and rebound. On these long stretches of highway, he thought a great deal, but the culmination of all that thought was a feeling of gratitude — for he recognized he was a very lucky man.

Once home, he texted Constance that he'd arrived safely and thanked her for the visit. Then, just before retiring a little after midnight, he checked on the status of Katerina's gift. The box had left Kennedy on the twentieth; it was now the twenty-third, and no update was available. Dr. Pi realized that it'd probably not arrive by Christmas.

In the morning, he checked again, but there was no further news. He messaged Katerina, apologized that his gift might not arrive on time.

***

On Christmas Eve, Dr. Pi drove to Café CaNole to buy a tiramisu cake and some Italian pastries. Not long after returning home, it began to snow heavily. He received a text from Janet asking when to expect him. Phillip and Veronica had already arrived, and it'd be nice to dine by 6:30. Dr. Pi texted her he'd leave shortly. He noticed an entry in his inbox and opened his Gmail. Surprisingly, it was from Katerina.

Merry Christmas, Tobias. My gift to you. Classical music for your pleasure. I recorded this week at my university. My favorite Mozart, Fantasy in D minor. And my own piece I call Snowfall in Siberia. Hope you enjoy. Sending my love (a red heart and a smiley face).

Dr. Pi was thrilled and sent his brief but effusive thanks, with a promise to write more soon. He then charged his phone, loaded the cake and pastries into the car, and headed to Cooperstown. As he drove through the near-blinding snow listening to Katerina's tracks, he was struck by her flawless rendering of Mozart's emotional piece, but mostly by the elevating beauty of her original composition.

CHAPTER 28

State Route 20, the Old Cherry Valley Turnpike, was a scenic, safe road and well-plowed in winter. There were long stretches with two lanes going east and two west and a broad grassy divider between them, yet in some locations in and out of small towns, the road narrowed to two lanes with no divider. Dr. Pi was familiar with Route 20, knew its tricky and dangerous spots, and was adept at watching his speed and navigating in a variety of weather conditions. In the fall, as he traveled to his night class in Cooperstown, he'd encountered various challenges. One night, the fog outside of Richfield Springs was so thick, he'd almost gone off the road twice; another time, he'd meandered carefully in a deluge, so much water falling that his wipers had been on the fastest setting for twenty minutes straight. The most dangerous part was near a swamp just past Mount Markham High School where the road iced up; no matter how attentive one was in trying to locate these patches of black ice, they were nearly impossible to see, and so dangerous that even an all-wheel drive vehicle with studded snow tires would struggle.

The snow fell abundantly as Dr. Pi passed Waterville, and the wind began to whip it into enormous swirls that impaired his visibility. Heavy winds carried snow over wide-open fields and across the highway, and several snowdrifts made the path ahead perilous.

Little daylight remained. Dr. Pi reduced his speed to 40 mph. He'd not seen one snowplow yet and wondered whether to turn around. He felt safe in the Audi and on Route 20, but Route 28 might pose greater problems since it was narrow and sinuous. Not wanting to disappoint Janet kept him moving and focused. The further east he traveled, the fewer cars he saw. It was Christmas Eve, and he guessed most folks were already tucked by fireplaces drinking hot brandy and watching *It's a Wonderful Life.*

Despite the weather, Dr. Pi looked forward to his first Cooperstown Christmas. He welcomed the opportunity to be with others for the holiday. He'd just passed the red barn restaurant outside of West Winfield when he noticed a pair of large, dim yellow lights behind him. It was the first vehicle he'd seen in over ten miles, and it was far enough back that he couldn't tell if it was a car, SUV, or truck. He ignored it and refocused on the road ahead. He passed through the swampy section easily; there was no black ice, just lots of snow. Once past the juncture for Route 51, Dr. Pi had to accelerate, for the road ahead became gradually steeper. He was now doing 50 mph; through his rearview he could see the lights behind him had gotten closer. There were only two lanes on this part of Route 20 and there was no divider. As he looked ahead about a quarter mile to the top of the hill, a tractor trailer came over the crest, traveling very fast. Its rear end seemed unsteady, the tires were losing traction, and the trailer swayed more wildly as it got closer.

Dr. Pi gripped the wheel tightly and glanced in the rearview, then fixed his eyes on the tractor trailer coming at him. There was no place for him to go should the trailer jackknife, no driveway or road to turn into, and only a deep ditch from which he wouldn't be able to emerge without a tow truck's help. Feeling vulnerable, and realizing he'd probably be killed if the trucker lost control, Dr. Pi accelerated up the steep incline. He sensed he had only seconds before the rig would swing into his lane, so he pushed the pedal to the floor. Even with all the snow on the road, his Quattro system kept the car balanced and his new Nokian tires gripped well, and in seconds the 3.2-liter engine had taken him from 50 to 60 mph. His calculation was precise, and his instinct had been right, for just as his Audi passed the swaying truck's rear end the trucker lost control. The rig swung violently into the oncoming lane, into the spot of highway where Dr. Pi's car would have been had he not sped up. Unfortunately, the driver behind him didn't have a chance to get out of the way, and a fully loaded trailer, like the bat of a big slugger, smashed into the vehicle head on, knocking it back twenty yards across the slick highway and wedging it into a deep ditch. The truck came to a halt. Dr. Pi saw the impact through his rearview and heard the loud crash. Stopping his Audi at the highway's crest, he turned around and drove back down towards the accident, stopping ten yards behind the truck. With hands shaking, he found his phone in his coat pocket and punched in 911, then rushed to the struck vehicle. The truck's driver also trotted towards the badly mangled, old, blue Ford F-150 in the ditch. It lay on its side, its metallic hood and fenders twisted grotesquely, steam rising from its burst radiator.

When the 911 operator picked up, Dr. Pi cried into his phone: "There's been a terrible accident on Route 20, just east of the Route 51 juncture. Send an ambulance. Please hurry."

"Any fatalities?" the operator inquired.

"Not sure," Dr. Pi said. "A jackknifed tractor trailer collided with another vehicle. Looks like an old Ford pickup. It's in a ditch. Going to see about the passengers now. No fire visible."

"Please stay on the line, Sir, so we can pinpoint your exact location."

Phone in hand he waded through the thick waves of snow towards the disabled truck. In minutes, he'd joined the driver of the tractor trailer, who'd not been hurt, as he struggled to open the Ford truck's door to extricate its pinned, unresponsive driver. The middle-aged man bled profusely from deep cuts to his forehead, sustained on impact with the windshield.

The trucker saw Dr. Pi on his phone and barked out: "Driver's unconscious, but still breathing. No other passengers."

"One unresponsive driver," Dr. Pi wailed into his phone. "Alive but bleeding profusely. Please hurry."

"Help is on the way," the operator said. "If possible, apply pressure on the wounds to stifle the bleeding."

The rig's driver couldn't open the Ford truck's door, but he could reach into the cabin; the driver's window had been smashed to pieces.

"Door's jammed. They'll have to cut him out," he yelled. "I need something to stop the blood."

Dr. Pi thought quickly. Though he had rags in his car, getting them would take time. He thrust his phone into his pants pocket, took off his leather coat, unzipped the wool sweater underneath, and handed the sweater to the truck driver who carefully wrapped it around the man's head to slow the bleeding. Huge snowflakes fell hard, and in seconds Dr. Pi's shirt was soaked.

"His breath is steady," the trucker said to Dr. Pi, who'd thrown his leather coat back on. Then the trucker addressed the victim with a frenzied plea: "Don't die on me, man. I'm so fucking sorry! Please don't die!"

"Wasn't your fault," Dr. Pi reassured the trucker. "This snow's to blame. He'll make it! Just keep the pressure on."

Minutes later, Dr. Pi heard loud sirens; through the falling snow, red and yellow lights approached. Several police vehicles arrived, and fire department rescue personnel rushed in to extricate the man. With the Jaws of Life, the rescue squad began cutting the old F-150 open to remove the pinned driver. Not long afterwards an ambulance arrived, and its crew prepared an IV, began a blood transfusion, and got a stretcher ready.

While the truck driver talked to the officers, Dr. Pi pulled out his phone and called Janet. He explained what had happened and told her to take care of her guests and start without him. He'd get there but didn't know when. As he spoke, the rescue squad removed the unconscious victim from the wreck and placed him on the stretcher.

"So glad you're not hurt," Janet said with feeling. "We'll wait for you. Please drive carefully."

When his turn came, Dr. Pi did his best to report everything he remembered before the accident and what he'd seen unfold through his rearview. The temperature had dropped, and without his sweater Dr. Pi shivered as he spoke. The officer noticed, asked him to step into his cruiser, cranked up the heat, and took down the rest of Dr. Pi's statement. Afterwards, he thanked him for stopping and doing what he could to help. He told Dr. Pi that detectives might contact him after Christmas as the investigation unfolded.

CHAPTER 29

It took Dr. Pi over an hour to reach Janet's house after leaving the accident site. He drove the entire way on Route 28 at 25 mph. The roads had not been plowed and the high snowdrifts made the trip difficult. As he maneuvered the sinuous road, the only thought on his mind was how close he'd come to disaster. His airbags might have saved him had he been struck, but by the looks of the crushed pickup, his car could have sustained equal or worse damage. Dr. Pi felt relief as he finally descended the steep road into Cooperstown at around a quarter to nine. Fortunately, the town roads had already been plowed, and Janet's driveway was passable.

When she greeted him at the kitchen door with a big embrace and a delicate kiss on the lips, Dr. Pi heard beautiful piano music coming from the grand room. He recognized it immediately as his favorite Rachmaninoff piece — Piano Concerto No. 2 in C minor. He stepped into the bright kitchen at the height of the concerto's second movement — the Adagio Sostenuto. Its emotional melody was intense, vibrant, and soothing, and Dr. Pi listened with longing. He stood as if in a trance, concentrating on the melody's movement, and didn't even take off his coat. He could see Maria's fingers delicately depressing the piano keys, her hands gliding effortlessly across them. He was sitting next to her again, a boy turning the pages of her sheet music, close enough to hear her breathing. He was looking at her beautiful face, yearning to do good for others, to be a loving young man.

Janet noticed his far-off gaze and placed her hands on his chest, gently bringing him back into the moment. She unzipped his coat slowly and said, "That's my King Phillip. Whenever he's here, this house comes to life."

"That's so beautiful," Dr. Pi uttered, still mesmerized. "He's a fabulous pianist. Sounds like Ivo Pogotov. How graceful and serene. I've needed to hear just that melody all afternoon."

"Phillip knows Ivo. They've played together in Moscow. Ivo's an amazing pianist. And so is my dear Phillip."

"He is. He plays with energy and emotion," he said. "Like my dear Maria once did."

Janet noticed tears in his eyes and changed the subject. "Here, let's take off that wet shirt, Tobias. Let me toss it in the dryer. Get you comfortable."

He unbuttoned his shirt and gave it to her, still intent on listening to the piano, not wanting to miss one single note. Janet tossed the shirt into the dryer in a back room, returned, and wrapped one of her woolen sweaters around him. He slipped into it quickly, happily, still focused on the rising and falling piano notes coming from the adjoining room. He followed Janet to the kitchen robotically, hypnotized by the music. She made him a cup of tea, placed it before him, and then sat down next to him and held his hand. At length, the piano piece ended. Snapping from his trance, Dr. Pi looked at Janet and smiled.

"It has been so long since I've heard that piece played with the proper emotion. I enjoyed it so much."

"I'm truly glad," she said, then reached over and kissed him. "Thanks for trudging through the storm to join us. What a frightening accident you described, Tobias. So fortunate you weren't hurt."

"Yes, very. I got lucky," he uttered in a low voice, reflecting on the horrible scene.

"Did the pickup's driver make it?"

"I don't know," he said. "He was unconscious but alive when the paramedics arrived. He'd bled a great deal." Dr. Pi filled Janet in on a few details he'd not mentioned over the phone, especially how the moments before the crash had unfolded. In remembering those precious seconds, he realized how close he'd come to not seeing Constance and Christopher ever again. Suddenly he lost focus and stopped speaking.

Janet saw his expression change, understood his inner strife, and purposely changed the subject. "You must be hungry," she said, and got up.

He nodded yes.

"Come get your shirt and we'll eat."

Dr. Pi followed her, threw on his shirt, and felt its wonderful warmth. Janet brought her son and his girlfriend Veronica to the kitchen, introduced them, and then everyone proceeded to set the table. Janet re-heated the Christmas ham and poured four glasses of red wine. She'd made mashed potatoes with a delicious gravy, cream corn, and spicy Mexican rice. In a short while, all four sat at the circular mahogany table serving themselves and enjoying the warmth emanating from the cast iron wood stove nearby, while the snow continued to fall outside.

King Phillip was a truly handsome man, in youth's prime. He reminded Dr. Pi of a young Daniel Craig, with his short, dirty blonde hair, intense blue eyes, and rugged, unshaven look. He had a strong brow, Grecian nose, firm jaw, and the inquisitive look of an older, wiser man. His lanky, muscular frame gave him an imposing stature. Only his long, delicate fingers seemed out of place with the rest, as though the hands of a piano player had somehow wound up on the body of James Bond. He and Veronica, who sat next to him, seemed mismatched. She was recognizably much older, a woman in her mid to late thirties, with a pleasant, curious face, too tan for December, and her bleach-blonde hair gave her a Southern California surfer look. Like Janet, she had an intelligent beauty, and had been divorced. Within half an hour of knowing her, Dr. Pi also gleaned that she was a talented cello player and an assertive woman — maybe even an aggressive one — with strong opinions and a strong personality. The contrast between her style and Phillip's calm disposition made Dr. Pi wonder how the two had found each other.

Dr. Pi liked Phillip immediately; he felt as if he'd known him a very long time and marveled at his talent and physical stature. Dr. Pi realized with a slight jealousy that this was the type of man Katerina deserved to have in her life: someone handsome, talented, and in the prime of life. Intuitively, Dr. Pi recognized they'd be perfectly suited.

"Glad to see you're OK," Phillip said to Dr. Pi. "Mom told us about your close call."

"I got lucky. If I hadn't sped up the hill last minute, I probably wouldn't be here."

"So scary," Phillip replied. "Our trip up the Taconic was also treacherous; the roads outside Middleburgh were almost unpassable."

Dr. Pi raised his glass and toasted his company. "Thank you all for letting me share this holy evening with you. I heartily appreciate it. And for that beautiful piano playing, Phillip. Mesmerizing."

"Glad you liked it," Phillip said. "He's one of my favorite composers."

"And mine," Dr. Pi replied. "Hearing him always triggers sacred childhood memories. Will you play more Rachmaninoff after dinner?"

"Sure, if you'd like."

"And some Chopin for me?" Janet looked at her son lovingly. Dr. Pi observed the glow on her face, the admiration, the contentment that his presence brought her.

"Of course, Mom. But I thought we'd watch *A Christmas Carol* like in the old days."

"Oh, yes please," Dr. Pi said joyfully. "Dickens energizes the spirit, especially at Christmas. But I'm with Janet. A little Chopin first would be perfect."

"More wine, everyone?" Veronica asked, and before receiving any answers, she filled all their glasses full.

The four took deep draughts of wine and filled their plates with second servings of the delicious ham and Mexican rice. Janet threw a cherry log in the wood stove; before returning to the table, she dimmed the lights, and asked what her guests wanted for dessert.

"I brought dessert, Janet," Dr. Pi said, and went to get the cake and pastries from his car. Janet brewed coffee, and Dr. Pi helped her clear the table, load the dishwasher, and bring dishes and cups for their dessert.

"This is such a lovely cake, Tobias," Janet said. She cut large slices for everyone, and Phillip and Veronica noted how delicious it was.

Dr. Pi was elated his choice had pleased everyone. After dinner he felt sleepy, mostly from the stress of the trip. He thought about the injured Ford driver and wondered whether he'd made it. He hoped Constance's plane trip to San Diego had gone smoothly. Though he rarely drank coffee this late, he had some of the Colombian brew, and the caffeine and sugar in the cake perked him up. Soon, he felt rejuvenated and eager to hear Phillip serenade their company.

A beautifully decorated Christmas tree, a six-foot blue spruce with a piney, woodsy aroma, stood in the parlor behind the piano. Its multicolored lights blinked, its tinsel gleamed, and the huge star at its top shone bright and cheerful. It gave the stately room warmth and added to its elegance. Janet lit the candles of the wall sconces and turned on the Tiffany lamps, whose stained glass produced a beautiful, romantic aura. Phillip and Veronica snuggled in the loveseat, while Dr. Pi and Janet sat separately in the Stickley mission recliners across from them. Dr. Pi took out his phone and texted Constance.

All good, sweetie?

Yes Dad, she replied immediately. *Hanging with Mom and Tank.*

Fabulous, he texted. *Have a great visit. All good here.*

Dr. Pi glanced at Phillip and Veronica. The two kissed, and Veronica rubbed Phillip's inner thigh. Both were a bit tipsy.

"We need more wine," Janet announced. "Don't move." She went into the kitchen for a cold bottle. While waiting, Dr. Pi checked his

Instagram. He noticed Katerina had added a picture of a beautiful Christmas table laden with food and wine and a bottle of Polish vodka. Plates full of bread and salad sat on a white lace tablecloth. The China and crystal glasses gleamed. The entire table layout was elegant, artistic. But the most important detail was that it was a table set for two. *She must have someone*, he thought. This realization brought on competing emotions. He was happy she was celebrating Christmas, for a week back she'd said she wasn't planning to and was going to work instead. Apparently she'd changed her mind, and from the looks of it, she must be happy, because she'd created a gorgeous table. Whoever she'd dine with would enjoy the intimacy of her company in a cozy setting. Though Dr. Pi felt a bit jealous that it wasn't he who was there with her, he commented on her story: *Beautiful table, Katerina. Artistic. Lovely photograph. Enjoy!* (*a smiley face, a red heart, a rose, and a kissy face*). Dr. Pi lamented being so far away from Katerina, knowing so very little about what she was doing at that moment and with whom. His heart felt heavy. But why? He chose to snap out of it. He reminded himself that he wanted the best for Katerina, for her to be joyful on this precious night. Soon, the jealousy disappeared. Seeing Phillip and Veronica quietly talking and teasing each other made him smile, and not long afterwards Janet returned with the chilled wine bottle.

Janet filled his glass, then asked her son and Veronica if they wanted some.

"Oh yes," Veronica replied. "Want to keep this boy in the best of moods."

"Working on making my grandchild tonight?" Janet asked playfully, the alcohol in her blood animating her bold inquiry.

The question surprised Dr. Pi. Veronica's response, which was quick and pointed, revealed her annoyance, and that a tension existed between the two women.

"No plans for that," she said brusquely. "That would ruin our careers." She paused, then added: "We need to play. We have no time for raising children."

Phillip stopped rubbing Veronica's back, grabbed his glass, and downed half his wine. He stared ahead blankly, saying nothing.

Dr. Pi saw the sadness that suffused Janet's face and heard the disappointment in her response.

"I understand, sweetheart. It's not my business anyway, and it's your choice, of course. I'm here to help if you need it, though."

"We know, Mom," Phillip snapped. "We'll figure it out. Plenty of time still."

Dr. Pi sought to diffuse the tension.

"So, who plowed your driveway, Janet?" he asked curiously. "That last stretch was the easiest part of my trip. All the town roads were clear as well."

"My friend Anthony did. He stopped by the last time you were here. Remember?"

"Oh yes," Dr. Pi said. "The bartender."

"Why's he still coming around, Mom? Didn't he cause enough trouble between you and Dad? That creep should know to stay away."

Dr. Pi realized he'd triggered more tension inadvertently and felt badly.

"He's a good friend, Phillip. Nothing more. Remember, I'm alone here. Anthony helps me."

"I know, Mom. I'm sorry."

Veronica turned to Dr. Pi and said, "Janet showed us your new novel. It looks interesting. Love the cover. What's it about?"

"My *first* and *only* novel," he replied and laughed. "I wanted to explore whether experiences are meaningful or just chance occurrence."

"I believe life is meaningful," Phillip interjected. "Things happen for a reason."

"I agree," Janet said.

"Me too," Dr. Pi concurred. "People enter our lives for a reason. I'm very glad, for instance, that Janet invited me to celebrate this special night with you."

"We're all glad you could join us, Tobias," Janet said. "Sorry to take you away from your new story."

Dr. Pi laughed. "Don't be," he said. "It's been floundering lately. I needed a break from writing, believe me."

"And what's that one about?" Veronica asked.

"Relationships. And the gray area that often defines them. How we manage the tough times and maintain our love."

Phillip planted a big kiss on Veronica's cheek. He then got up, gave Janet a kiss on her cheek also, followed by a long, hard embrace. He walked over to the grand piano and collected his thoughts.

"For you, Mom," he announced, and then began to play with great feeling several of Chopin's nocturnes in succession. King Phillip's prodigious talent was a powerful tool. And he knew how to use it. Wine or no wine, he was inspired! Each note hypnotized and elevated the spirit to a calm place far above petty, human disputes. The magical notes floated upward, bounced beautifully off the walls and ceiling, and fell on their ears like a soft rain from heaven.

The room was *alive* with music. And in every note, Dr. Pi felt Maria's presence. It seemed that forty years had not passed by. Only the music mattered, and as long as Phillip kept playing, Maria was there next to Dr. Pi, still playing, forever fifteen.

***

At a quarter to one, King Phillip stopped playing, gave Janet another kiss and a long embrace, whispered "I love you," and he and Veronica went to bed. After they'd left the room, Janet asked if Dr. Pi would stay up with her. He helped her tidy the parlor and kitchen. They then sat on the loveseat to drink more wine.

"Sorry you had to witness our little family drama earlier," Janet said. "I'm so embarrassed. Let me explain."

"No need to," Dr. Pi replied. "It's none of my business, really. You love your son; he loves you. And you both love strong-minded Veronica. Phillip's found someone very much like his mother."

"Yes. A bit selfish like me. We're a lot alike. That's probably why we butt heads."

"You're not selfish, Janet," Dr. Pi interrupted. "Quite the opposite."

"Thank you, Tobias. For understanding. I feel guilty that Phillip's father and I couldn't make things work."

"Wasn't your fault. You did your best, and you raised a good boy — talented, loving, and happy."

"He *is* wonderful," she said, and started to cry. Tobias hugged her, ran his fingers through her hair, and rubbed her back gently.

"Shhh, shhh. They'll figure it out. Veronica will be his pillar. Like you've been all these years."

"I made so many mistakes," she continued. "So, so many!"

"Who hasn't?" Dr. Pi asked. "We're *all* imperfect."

Janet felt a need to traverse the lonely landscape of her past life, and Dr. Pi listened sympathetically.

"Phillip doesn't like Anthony," Janet said sadly. "He's angry with me for valuing his friendship, as you saw tonight."

"But why?"

"Phillip believes my marriage fell apart because of Anthony, but that's not true. It was already doomed. Ebenezer and I were separated when Anthony and I reconnected."

"Have you told him?"

"Yes. He just doesn't buy it. Thinks Anthony and I had something going on that led to our separation. But Ebenezer's callousness towards me was there from the beginning."

"You've mentioned that. And that Anthony was a childhood friend."

"Anthony was my first love. The boy I was dating when I met Ebenezer. The one whose heart I broke when I cheated on him with a stranger."

"I see," Dr. Pi said, shocked at her revelation.

"It was a terrible thing to do," Janet admitted. "But I did it. A youthful mistake, a decision I've wished to reverse. But without it, I wouldn't have Phillip. So how can I regret the error that brought me the greatest blessing in my life? Yes, I'd have another son. Perhaps, a daughter. Or maybe several children with Anthony or another man. But not Phillip. And I couldn't see my life without *him*."

"I see your point. It's like a double-edged sword. We're bound to get cut, no matter what choice we make."

"Agonizing," Janet said and drank her wine.

"I have regrets as well. Made many poor decisions, despite my education. We're fallible. Nothing to do but carry it all inside. Appreciate our blessings. *We must do that!* And accept the rest — the grief, the misery. Hold it stoically, the best way we can."

"I guess," Janet said doubtfully.

There was a long silence. Dr. Pi drank his wine and the buzz felt good. He wanted to know more about Janet and what she'd experienced, about her love triangle with Anthony and Ebenezer, so he finally got up the nerve and asked, "Would you tell me the rest of your story?"

"It's not elevating," Janet said. "Just a big mess."

"It often helps to get it all out."

"Would you hold me?"

"Of course," he said and wrapped his arms around her. He felt her warmth, her heart beating fast, smelled her pleasant perfume, and saw the satisfied look on her face. "Tight enough?"

"Yes," she replied, and began.

"Anthony had moved up from the Bronx with his parents when he was twelve. The family settled in Richfield Springs, and Dad hired his father Samuel to work on our farm. He was an excellent farmer, and Dad took a liking to him. He was invited back the next summer, and he brought Anthony with him. That's when I got to know him. Tragically, that winter his parents were killed in a head-on collision on Route 20, just outside of Albany. Anthony was put in foster care for a few months, but Dad decided to look after him. He moved in with us, we went to high school together, and did farm chores together. The following summers, he worked full-time for Dad, who encouraged Anthony to save all his money. We ate dinner and studied together, spent endless hours roaming our property, talking, and forging a deep friendship. Dad treated Anthony like a son. We were one happy family. During one summer vacation, our friendship blossomed into romance.

"Anthony was very handsome then, before he began to gamble and drink. He had a rough, attractive, Italian look, with dark eyes and gorgeous olive skin. He was well-built, and awkwardly romantic; in summer, when I went into the fields to find a spot to paint, he'd take a break from work, bring me bouquets of colored wildflowers, and sing in a labored, terrible voice old Italian songs he'd learned from his grandfather. I laughed and told him to quiet down, that the other workers would hear, but he said they all knew he was in love with me. He told me I was beautiful and wanted me in his life forever. I was young, impressionable, and new to romance. No boy had ever professed his love for me so confidently. Anthony was the first and won my heart. It was awkward at first because we'd grown up like brother and sister. Dad encouraged our friendship. I'm not sure if he knew we were in love, but if he did, he never interfered. I worked at the library in town part time, took private painting lessons, and life seemed perfect. I was happy then, and we were very much in love.

"We'd secretly dated a year before Ebenezer seduced me and changed my life forever. I've already told you about him."

"You have," Dr. Pi said. "Please continue."

"I'd just turned eighteen, and I was going through a wild phase, drinking, and partying. I was immature. I hated myself for sleeping with Ebenezer the day I met him, but instead of realizing I'd made a mistake and rectifying it, I told Anthony what I'd done, broke up with him, and continued seeing wealthy Ebenezer, who was ten years older. Anthony was furious. Told me I'd live to regret my betrayal. Still, he stayed to work on our farm and help Dad, while I went off to college. Not long afterwards, I dropped out, married Ebenezer, and five years later gave birth to Phillip. Ebenezer hired a full-time nanny so I could finish college; eventually, I earned my MFA. Anthony married a local woman, started a family, and settled on the outskirts of town. For years, he ran a small garage and helped Dad at our farm on weekends. I saw him occasionally when I visited. When we stopped farming, he left the area, worked in New York City a few years, but then returned to Cooperstown. He and his wife were having marital troubles at the same time Ebenezer and I had separated. One day I ran into Anthony in town; we had drinks and talked for hours. Our passion reignited briefly. He left his wife for me. The deep bond we'd had was still there. But I couldn't tolerate his hard drinking. When he was drunk, he'd berate me for betraying him. I couldn't take it. He wanted to move in with me, but I refused. Broke it off. After struggling for years in a failing marriage, I preferred living alone…"

"I understand that perfectly," Dr. Pi interjected.

"I told Anthony I wanted to remain friends but that my romantic feelings weren't there anymore. He couldn't accept it, stormed out of the house, and didn't speak to me for six months. Then one day he sent me flowers, a card with an apology, and invited me to dinner. Said he treasured our friendship and wanted me back in his life. He'd cut back on his drinking. It doesn't help that he now works as a bartender. Still, he manages his problem. We've been close ever since. He helps me a great deal, Tobias."

Janet stopped, looked inquisitively into Dr. Pi's tired eyes, and asked, "Bored yet?"

"Of course not," Dr. Pi said. "Me? Never. Your story's fascinating. Except for the time, place, and explicit sexual seduction, it reminds me of Heathcliff, Edgar, and Catherine's tale in Brontë's *Wuthering Heights*. Familiar with it?"

"Never read it," Janet said sadly. "Now I wish I had. Might have learned something. I'm sure Brontë knew human suffering."

"She did," Dr. Pi said. "The *best* English novel if you ask me. Poetic prose of the highest caliber. A timeless tale. Youthful love, heartbreak, poverty, wealth, betrayal. Human suffering in the eternal scheme of things. That book has it all. You'll think about it years after reading it."

"I'll definitely read it," Janet said and smiled. "Soon as I'm done with *Yellow Bird*."

"Jesus, Janet!" Dr. Pi cried. "Forget my book. Read Brontë's first. There's no comparison. Priorities!"

Janet laughed, then hugged and held Dr. Pi tightly for several minutes.

"What's that for?" he questioned when she finally let go and looked at him.

"Are you always this animated about literature? Sifting through your literary catalogue as you experience or talk about life?"

"I guess," Dr. Pi said. "Is that a turn off?"

"Quite the opposite," she replied, kissed him, and smiled.

"Well, continue your story," he said eagerly. "You were just getting to the good part before I took us on a tangent. I want to hear the rest — Anthony's run-ins with Ebenezer."

"Nah, you've helped dispel my gloom. Thank you. And to tell you the truth, I have other things on my mind now," she said, running a finger along his chest and looking up at him coquettishly. "You'll get the rest later. Suffice it to say, they hate each other."

"That's not good," Dr. Pi said with concern. "And they *both* must hate me."

"Worried?"

"Nope," he said adamantly, feeling brave, and just a bit drunk.

"*Well good*! I wish to create a *new* story. Pull down your pants. Here, *feel this*."

Janet grabbed his hands and guided them up her thighs so he could feel how wet she'd gotten.

"C'mon. I'm serious, Janet," he pleaded. "Please finish your story."

"I want you first," she said. "I'll tell you the rest tomorrow." And she proceeded to seduce him.

CHAPTER 30

Christmas Day was sunny and clear but very cold. Heavy snow had blanketed the ground overnight, and there were snowdrifts everywhere on Janet's property. Phillip and Veronica were the first up, and they prepared breakfast. Before long, the wonderful smells of coffee, eggs, and sausage roused Janet and Dr. Pi. They felt a little hung over from all the wine they'd drunk, and weren't keen on waking at 9:30, but the delicious smell of food enticed them. While they ate, a snowplow could be heard scraping the driveway clear. Mindful that Janet had company and would probably like to attend church, Anthony had come early, and soon the path down the moderately steep hill to the main road was free of snow. He even cleared off Janet's Beamer and the Benz SUV. Only Dr. Pi's Audi was left untouched.

The four decided to attend Christ's Mass at the Episcopal Church at noon. After breakfast, Dr. Pi threw on his boots, coat, and gloves, shoveled the back steps, cleared off his car, and brought in the small Samsonite with his clean clothes. While waiting to shower, he texted Christmas greetings to Constance and Christopher, checked the status of his package to Poland (no new updates), and sent Katerina a direct message on Instagram.

Merry Christmas, Katerina. Sorry the package hasn't arrived. Hopefully soon. Wishing you a wonderful day.

It was afternoon in Poland, and not long after he'd texted, Katerina replied, *I will wait and wait, if tomorrow or next day doesn't matter. It will come. I am happy. Thank you, and for liking my dinner table. Have a nice Christmas.* (*Christmas tree emoji, Santa Claus face, smiley face, red heart, kissy face*).

Dr. Pi smiled broadly and continued staring at his phone. He wondered how her day was unfolding and wished he could be there in person to wish her Merry Christmas. He flipped through his photographs of her, paused on the one that was for his eyes only, then searched for the classical recordings she'd sent him. Phillip, meanwhile, finished a Mozart piece he'd been playing. Dr. Pi walked towards the piano and complimented him.

"Is Mozart your favorite?"

"Yes," Phillip said. "Mom tell you?"

"She didn't. It's just the way you play. You move through the notes as if it's your own piece."

"Don't I wish," Phillip said. "Pure genius. Soon as you hear three notes you know it's by Mozart. I've studied works by many great composers, but he's the best."

"I have a Russian friend who feels the same way," Dr. Pi said happily. "She's a classical pianist, studying the works of Shostakovich and Glinka at a Polish academy. She composes and plays beautifully. Loves Mozart. Care to listen to a recording she sent me?"

"Sure," Phillip said eagerly.

Dr. Pi found the track on his phone, and Phillip helped him connect to the room's speakers using Bluetooth. In seconds, Katerina's rendition of Mozart's Fantasy in D minor played. Dr. Pi saw Phillip's attentiveness, the way he concentrated on the slow, sad melody. When the piece ended, Phillip smiled broadly.

"Wow. She's fabulous," he said. "Plays with genuine emotion. What's her name?"

"Katerina Kotova," Dr. Pi said. "Can I play you one of her own compositions?"

"Absolutely," Phillip replied, and Dr. Pi played the track.

Katerina's piece, one could tell, was inspired by Mozart, but its uniqueness was unmistakable. It began slowly, with long notes that drew a listener in to a painful feeling, as of someone suffering and near death. But then gradually the number of notes increased, the piece moved faster, and in that rapidity, it seemed the pain was being shed. A spirit was being liberated and was soaring into an angelic realm — a vibrant, visible paradise, nearer and nearer to God. At its conclusion, the long notes returned, and somberness increased; the pain lingered and crushed the heart. Yet now it was a different pain, one felt by relatives already grieving at the loss.

"Simply amazing," Phillip said with surprise. "How old's Katerina?"

"Just turned twenty-four. Super talented, isn't she?"

"Goodness, yes," Phillip acknowledged. "She has a graceful, elegant style. And that original piece is absolutely beautiful."

Just then, Veronica came down dressed in a gorgeous white lace dress, kissed Phillip, and ordered him up to shower. She told Dr. Pi that Janet was also done, her shower vacant, and the two men went to get ready. Soon, Janet came down, prepared fresh coffee, made Veronica a cup, and joined her in the parlor. She showed Veronica her latest paintings. They talked about Phillip's travel commitments for spring, the hectic pace of Manhattan life, and the Glimmerglass concert schedule for the following July. Several wonderful shows had been planned, including one in the Pavilion showcasing an adaptation of Tchaikovsky's *The Queen of Spades* with piano accompaniment.

"I'm sure King Phillip pushed hard to include that one," Janet said proudly.

"Yes," Veronica said. "No season's ever complete for him without including something by a Russian composer. I think he hoped to play the accompaniment himself, but he's such a professional. Always on the lookout for the latest talent in the States or abroad. He wants to book Ivo for that show. But he's gotten no commitment from him yet. Ivo's quite busy."

"I'm sure," Janet said. "With Ivo's reputation, I doubt a small venue like this will appeal to him. Unless he likes baseball."

The two laughed, and Janet continued, "Phillip should find out what team he likes and send him some souvenirs. If he's a Yankees fan, perhaps tickets to a game. You can offer to give him a tour of Manhattan, then bring him up. He can stay here, practice, and relax. It would make Phillip very happy, I'm sure. You and I should make that happen."

"I'd love to, Janet. When we get home, I'll look into it. I'm certain Ivo would love to come to New York. Phillip would be thrilled to have him play."

***

The four drove to the beautiful, snow-clad Christ Church on River Street to hear mass. Attending an Episcopal service was a totally new experience for Dr. Pi, and he enjoyed seeing his friends' happiness and watching young and old parishioners celebrating Christ's birth. He prayed for his children and for Joanna and her parents, and asked Christ to help humanity overcome evil, spread peace, broaden minds worldwide, and nourish imaginations. With intense conviction, he said special prayers for Miriam, Pablo, and Maria. Deep in his heart he knew Christ's way, Christ's love, was the road to salvation. He reached for Janet's hand, squeezed it, and prayed for her, Phillip, and Veronica. He then closed his eyes, thought of Katerina, and prayed that her life in the years ahead would be full of blessings.

When they returned to Janet's house, Phillip and Veronica changed into their snow gear and went snowshoeing. Afterwards, fully exhausted, but reveling in their time together and away from the usual hectic pace of their daily lives in the big city, they made a snowman by the barn, gathering twigs and branches to give him his features. Dr. Pi helped Janet make dinner, and the two talked continuously about art, literature, music, and the chaos in American politics. Not once did either mention their own unfolding relationship. Though curious about Ebenezer's and Anthony's run-ins, Dr. Pi didn't ask Janet to finish her story as she'd promised the previous evening, and Janet avoided the subject altogether. Light conversation was preferable on this lovely afternoon, and as the bright sun disappeared, and evening crept in, they drank tea by the woodstove, enjoyed the peace, and listened to Christmas songs on Pandora.

After dinner, Janet asked Dr. Pi to occupy her guests in the kitchen while she went into the parlor to prepare Phillip's special surprise. Dr. Pi cleaned the kitchen with Veronica and Phillip while the three chatted about music and books and the challenges Dr. Pi faced in the classroom.

In a short while, Janet called them, and everyone filed into the parlor. She inserted a big tape into an old VHS player, planted a kiss on Phillip's cheek, and announced:

"For my King Phillip. His favorite version of *A Christmas Carol*. Voilà! Mr. George C. Scott as Ebenezer Scrooge."

"Thanks Mom," Phillip said happily. "Just like in the old days."

Surprisingly, it was also Dr. Pi's favorite film version of the classic story, and he smiled while thinking of Dickens's storytelling magic. No Christmas, he thought, would be complete without recounting Ebenezer's spiritual awakening.

The four squeezed onto the love seat and watched the film. During its climactic scene, when Ebenezer reads his name on a grave, Janet sighed, sniffled, and said regretfully, "If only your father had seen the future and changed … we might still be together. I wish he'd treated me kindlier, more generously, and compassionately. If only he'd been a true Ebenezer …."

"There's still time, Mom. While he lives … it can still happen."

Janet didn't respond, covered her face with her hands, and leaned back. She suppressed tears. Dr. Pi saw how past pain still haunted her.

"Besides," Phillip continued, "I'm grateful for *this* moment, shared with Veronica, Dr. Pi, and you. If Dad had seen the light then, *we* wouldn't be together. It was what it was and is what it is. This is the moment that matters."

"You're right, Phillip," Janet said. "I'm sorry."

"Don't be sorry, Mom," he reassured her. "Just be grateful."

CHAPTER 31

Phillip and Veronica planned to stay with Janet a few more days, and Dr. Pi chose not to overstay his welcome. Janet begged him to stay longer, but he refused; he said he needed to get back to his writing and that he planned to travel to Long Island to visit his good friends Will and Adriana, who'd invited him for New Year's. He asked Janet if she had any paintings he could buy as a surprise for his friends. An image of horses in a field would be perfect for their daughter, Nicole, and the husband and wife were big fans of boat scenes. Janet escorted Dr. Pi to her barn and showed him an older collection of hers he'd never seen. He was impressed with many pieces. Horses, she admitted, were one of her earliest subjects, and as a teenager, bucolic farm scenes and animals had been a focus. And there were several pieces of small boats on Otsego Lake. Dr. Pi picked two of the most colorful oil paintings and squeezed a couple of hundred-dollar bills into Janet's hand.

"It's too much, Tobias," she said. "Half of this is fine." She tried to return one of the bills, but he pushed her hand away.

"Please," he insisted, and kissed her. "Thanks for a wonderful Christmas."

"Thanks for coming," she said, and hugged him. "Text me when you get back."

"I will."

"Here, let me show you the rest of this big old barn before you go."

Janet showed Dr. Pi around the huge, insulated, and heated barn where she kept the costly antiques and numerous paintings she sold with Anthony's help, many by famous artists. There was only one door through which she didn't take him. It had a huge lock and Janet didn't have the key on her. She said it was an old tack room, which she'd show him next time. In one corner, just beyond the locked room, Dr. Pi thought he recognized Warhol and Pollock paintings.

"Are those originals?" he asked.

Janet hesitated before answering. "Yes. But they're not my favorites. Probably should be hanging in the house, but they don't go with my décor. I'm looking to sell them."

"Must be worth a fortune."

"Anthony's searching for a buyer. I may ask Phillip to inquire among his city friends. I just made up my mind to let them go. Should hold on to them, but the taxes on this place are staggering."

"Why not use an auction house? Christie's or Sotheby's can get you the best price. Buyers and investors from all over the world. They're the pros at selling art."

"Don't want to pay the fees or do the paperwork. Besides, I want someone to own these who'd truly appreciate them. Not all art lovers are wealthy. That's what Dad used to say."

"Tell me about it," Dr. Pi said. "Nothing hangs on my walls that's worth more than a thousand. To look at a great master's painting would inspire me daily. I agree with your father."

"Do you want them? We can work something out."

"Me? Oh no, Janet. I can't afford either of those. I'd have to mortgage the house." Dr. Pi laughed, and Janet smiled. "They're not my favorite paintings. But if you decide to sell the Church or Cole hanging in your parlor, please call me first. I'll go beg my bank for money."

"Those will remain where they are while I live. Long as I can keep this place. Two of Dad's treasures."

"I understand," Dr. Pi said.

"Care for any of these antiques? Look around. Everything here's for sale ... *unfortunately*. Had I been wiser, not traveled so extensively, or spent so lavishly, I could keep these items for Phillip. I have only myself to blame."

Dr. Pi didn't reply right away. He sensed Janet was under intense financial pressure and thought it inappropriate to meddle further in her affairs.

"You're doing your best," he said at length. "You maintain your house beautifully. So, what are you asking for the Warhol?"

"I knew you were interested," she said, and smiled. "Fifty thousand. I'll hold it for you. Promise."

"What?" Dr. Pi questioned in disbelief. "That's worth three or four hundred thousand easily. Maybe more. Auction it off. Even after fees and taxes, you'll make four to five times what you're asking. Trust me. Help yourself out."

"Ok," Janet said sadly, and then added in a more subdued voice, "I'll think about it."

Dr. Pi didn't say anything further. He realized Janet needed to spend time with Phillip and Veronica. He loaded her paintings into the Audi, gathered his belongings, said goodbye to Phillip and Veronica, gave Janet a big hug, thanked her again, and left.

***

On the drive back to Pleasant Hills, Dr. Pi tried to honestly assess his future with Janet. His feelings were complex. He certainly admired her. She was a lovely, intelligent, kind, and talented woman. An artist, who lived in an elegant home, in the most beautiful of towns. Perfect, really. Storybook. Almost too perfect. He loved her company, had enjoyed their conversations, their intimacy, even how they worked together. Making Christmas dinner with her had been fun. Despite these positives, he didn't have deeper emotions for Janet; his feelings for her were not like those he had for Katerina — a woman he'd never met or been with.

Dr. Pi was baffled, and wished he could feel differently, but he didn't. Maybe it would take more time. Or perhaps he was just deeply impractical. He had to consider that possibility, given the facts. Janet was the right age; Katerina wasn't. Janet was close, accessible, as Curt and Jakub had pointed out. Katerina was a world away, inaccessible, part of his romantic imagination. Dr. Pi wondered if perhaps what bothered him was Janet's baggage. She did have a chaotic past: the tumultuous marriage, the Heathcliff-like Anthony who was still hanging around. Something didn't feel right. Janet was a mystery. What exactly was she looking for? What did she want? Why had she gravitated towards him? Did she just want a friend with benefits? While drunk, she'd told him she wished to start "a new story," and sex seemed central to it. Did Janet want more? Need more? And did he? How far was he willing to go with this? He was grateful that she'd invited him for Christmas, and he'd had a pleasant, happy time. Now, though, as he drove away, he didn't miss her much, or the sex, and he was happy to be headed home. He felt terrible about it. He couldn't fathom his own messy emotions. They were indecipherable — a mysterious black hole that funneled inward with gravity's force towards the core of his being.

It was a quarter past three and he had just hooked left onto Route 20 at Richfield Springs when his phone rang. A Detective Florio wanted to question Dr. Pi about the accident he'd witnessed on the twenty-fourth. The last thing he wanted was to return to Cooperstown on the following day, so he opted to meet Florio and Wilks in forty-five minutes at the station house. He made a U-turn on Route 20, pulled into the Sunoco station, gassed up, got himself a coffee and muffin, and headed to Cooperstown.

Detective Florio's interview was straightforward. He explained he needed to fine-tune his accident report and verify the details Dr. Pi and the tractor trailer driver had already given. The driver of the blue Ford pickup had died from his injuries. Dr. Pi was saddened to hear this and expressed his remorse. Florio called Wilks in, and the two shared with Dr. Pi that there was an investigation underway to determine what the dead man was doing in the area. He drove with a fake driver's license, and they were still trying to determine his identity. They were certain he wasn't a local, or from Central New York, but possibly from New York City or Long Island.

"Here's the reason we wanted to speak with you," Wilks said. "The blue Ford pickup in question matches the description of the vehicle you reported had blocked the road on the night you were almost ambushed. The unregistered pickup had phony plates, and a loaded shotgun was found behind the passenger's seat. We don't know where the driver was going, or what he was up to, but he was behind you. May have been following you. Could be a coincidence, but it's possible someone may be looking to hurt you, or worse."

Dr. Pi was in shock and tried to assess this information. He had a strange feeling that it wasn't a coincidence and that someone was out to get him. He thought of Ebenezer and then Anthony and considered sharing his suspicions with the sheriff but kept quiet. Besides, when the sheriff questioned Ebenezer previously, he had denied involvement. Dr. Pi thought it best not to speculate and to let the police conduct their investigation. Professor Bellows had found nothing incriminating on Ebenezer either and Anthony was Janet's close friend. Why would either of them want to hurt or kill him? Because of his friendship with Janet? Jealousy? It made no sense. Maybe it was all a coincidence, as Wilks had stated. Better not to jump to conclusions.

"Thanks for the heads up, Sheriff Wilks," Dr. Pi said. "I'll keep my eyes open. I don't have any enemies that I know of, here or elsewhere, and you've already talked with Ebenezer."

"I have," Wilks said. "But I may speak with him again. In any case, I'll keep you posted as we investigate."

Dr. Pi shook Wilks's and Florio's hands and walked to his car. He sat for a few minutes to assess what he'd just learned. He thought about texting Janet but decided not to. He didn't want to stress her out or detract in any way from the time spent with her family.

It was five minutes to six and Dr. Pi was hungry. Danny's was closed, but The Black Sox Bar and Grill next door was open, so he ordered a meatball sub and sat at the bar to drink a beer. There weren't many customers, and Anthony was not bartending. For some odd reason, Dr. Pi wanted to see him, look him in the eye, maybe strike up a conversation to feel him out. He was confident that he could see through anyone and decipher their motives. All they needed to do was speak. Language was a fingerprint of their personalities, mental make-up, and motives — in short, of their characters. Speaking with Anthony, Dr. Pi thought, would help him verify whether Janet's portrayal of him was true and accurate or, perhaps, completely off the mark. Even though Janet had known Anthony for a very long time, even loved him once, and still did business with him, it was possible that she didn't fully understand him, or his motives. If he could just get Anthony in front of him, it wouldn't take Dr. Pi long to know how the man felt about him. Who was Anthony? What made him tick? Did he not want Dr. Pi around Janet? It was difficult to focus on anything else after being told by Wilks that someone might be out to hurt him.

With no chance to act on this investigative itch, Dr. Pi focused on his dinner and his beer. His sub had just arrived when a tall, thin man with curly black hair and a well-groomed beard walked into the bar and stood at the second stool over. He wore a Red Sox cap and a canvas coat with the words Bassett Hospital in decal letters on the back. The man tipped his cap to Dr. Pi, then sat down and ordered a beer. Dr. Pi nodded back at his new bar mate and raised his pint glass.

"Work at the hospital?"

"Sure do," the man said. "Twenty years in the maintenance department."

Dr. Pi asked about a couple of nurses from his writing class, and the man thought he might know one of them but couldn't be sure. He introduced himself as Tom Bunting and moved to the next stool over, where he shook Dr. Pi's hand and learned his name.

From there the two men struck up a conversation that took Dr. Pi away from his troubles for almost half an hour. They skirted pleasantly along the surface of things, talking about how deserted Cooperstown was in winter, during the off-season, and about the Red Sox's chances of coming back as champions again in 2019. Dr. Pi treated his new friend, a big Sox fan, to a beer. It was Dr. Pi's second, and he was feeling its effects. He knew he shouldn't have had more than one because he still had to drive home, but the beer lifted his mood, and his new friend seemed happy to be offered a free round. As they chatted and discussed the Sox's prospects, Dr. Pi got carried away and told a humorous story about his first trip to Fenway when his children were little. It was on Christopher's birthday.

"It was a beautiful night," he told his new friend. By then Bunting had moved closer, and Dr. Pi could see that the man's intense blue eyes were bloodshot. He was social and talkative, and a good listener, and Dr. Pi was in a mood to talk.

"Boston was trailing the Twins late. Think it was ten to seven in the bottom of the eighth, but don't quote me on that. My memory's foggy there. You can Google it later on. My wife and I decided to leave and get our one-year-old, Constance, to bed. Mind you, we still hadn't checked into our hotel. We didn't even know where the hell it was. We got up to leave and beat the crowd out when a passionate fan, a big, burly man sitting next to us who'd eaten like ten hot dogs during the game, turned and said to his wife, 'See, it's over. They're gonna lose.' His exasperation moved me, and to lessen his anxiety, I told him the Red Sox would come back to win. He looked at me and said, 'You really think so?' And I said, 'Sure,' as confidently as I could manage, as if I had a crystal ball. He wasn't sure what to believe, so I dug in and said, 'They'll come back. We'd stay, believe me, but we gotta get this little girl to bed. The Sox'll win.' By the time we'd squeezed past him and were about to leave I could tell the man felt better.

"Well, we drove and drove and couldn't find the damn hotel. At one point, my son Christopher said he wondered how the game had turned out, whether my promise to the man had come true, so he turned on the radio to find out the outcome. We thought the game would've been over by then. An hour had passed. But the game was still going on. Christopher found the actual station, and we heard the play-by-play announcer's super-excited final call."

"Wow," Tom said. "That's crazy."

"Yeah. Nuts. Game was in the bottom of the ninth. Boston had the tying and winning runs on base, and just as we tuned in, *at that precise moment*, the batter hit a line drive in the gap to deep center field, both runners scored, and the Red Sox won. We couldn't believe it and gave each other high fives in the car."

"Fuck yeah!" Tom cried. "Go Sox!" He took a big gulp of his beer and stuffed a bunch of pretzels in his mouth.

"My son, I remember, commented on how happy the big man who'd eaten the hot dogs must be. I just smiled. Thought of how memorable this night would always be to Christopher."

Though a loyal Yankees fan, Dr. Pi picked up his beer and said to Tom, "Here's to the Boston Red Sox."

Grinning ear to ear, Tom raised his glass, clinked Dr. Pi's, and said, "To the Sox! That's a hell of a fucking story Tobias. Was nice to hear, buddy."

"And true! Think the final score was 11–10, or 12–11. Something like that. You can Google that too. A great comeback on a gorgeous summer night, in a game which time has since swallowed. But it lives on in my memory, Tom. My kids' first vacation. Our first time at Fenway. On my son's damn birthday. Think the man upstairs was working His magic that night?"

"He sure was!" Tom cried. "Hey, thanks for the brew."

"You're very welcome my friend." They toasted again and gulped down the rest of their beers.

Dr. Pi finished his meatball sub, which by now was cold, said goodbye to Tom, and shook his hand firmly. He paid the bartender for his meal and their beers, placed a twenty-dollar tip in his palm, and walked out. He chose to walk down Main Street for a bit to sober up.

Telling that story to a stranger had cheered him briefly. As he walked, he reminisced about other fun family vacations to Salem and Marblehead, Massachusetts, and thought about beautiful Joanna. He missed her and yearned to relive all the wonderful times they'd shared with the kids. He felt proud that they'd been good parents who'd worked as a team to bring their children joy. But as he sloshed through snow and passed closed stores, he remembered what he'd learned earlier from Wilks and was bewildered. It was disturbing. Could someone really want to kill him? Agitated, he strolled towards the lake, a place which always calmed him, and stopped by Council Rock Park.

It was dark and quiet and isolated. A chain across the stone posts blocked the stairway down to the lake-level terrace. Dr. Pi knew he shouldn't walk down and risk slipping on the icy steps, but he wanted to be closer to the water. He climbed over the chain and carefully descended the concrete steps towards the big, white, painted Native arrow below. The arrow itself was obscured by snow and darkness, but Dr. Pi nodded to it anyway, sat solemnly on a bench, and stared at the lake's dark waters. It was cold and slightly breezy, and he could feel the chill grip his muscles and bones. He shivered as he thought about the dead pickup truck driver, and then meditated on Maria's and Miriam's deaths. He concentrated on the sound of the lake's small waves as they lapped on shore rocks and did not hear quickly approaching footsteps behind him.

Seconds later, Dr. Pi felt the cold barrel of a handgun pressed hard against the back of his skull, and from the corner of his left eye he vaguely saw a hand reaching in to wrap around his neck. Fear made his instincts take over; he knew his life was in peril. Time slowed, his heart pounded, body tensed, and snapshots from his life flashed in his mind. He saw Maria playing her piano, Miriam collapsing after learning of Maria's death, Miriam and Pablo consoling him in the sad weeks and years that followed. The images were clear, intense, illuminating, and none were more vivid than Christopher's and Constance's births, his cherished children whom he adored more than life itself, and now sensed he'd never see again, should a bullet blast through his brain.

In the milliseconds that elapsed, as Dr. Pi anticipated the assailant's finger squeezing the trigger, he determined he'd never let it happen. Ever! He must fight! And now! His life just couldn't end there. Not that way. His fear transformed to anger, then to courage and resolve. Like the bolt of lightning Chuck had once trained him to become, Dr. Pi threw his head down away from the barrel, pivoted slightly left, and brought his right hand up like a claw. In one smooth, rapid motion, he clutched his attacker's left hand, pulled downward with all his might, and flipped a big body over him and the bench he sat on. The gun slammed against the terrace floor and flew out of the assailant's right hand but luckily didn't discharge.

In the dimness, Dr. Pi discerned a man's shape on the ground and stood poised above him in his praying mantis kung fu posture. As the stunned figure tried to rise and attack, Dr. Pi swung his left leg and connected with his head. It was a solid blow, a blunt, hard shot against Dr. Pi's lower shin and foot. The assailant's head hit the terrace floor, and Dr. Pi could see that he was disoriented. One more kick to the back of the skull could have broken the man's neck and possibly ended his life. And Dr. Pi would be acting in self-defense. But he hated violence, and as he stood over his assailant, he remembered Chuck's words. His life was no longer in danger, his attacker was out of commission, and that was enough. Dr. Pi turned and ran swiftly up the slick, concrete steps, stumbling once, but regaining his balance and momentum quickly. He jumped over the chain at the top of the stairs and did not look back or stop running until he reached his parked car on Main Street. With shaking hands, he let himself into the vehicle and drove straight to the police station to report the assault.

Wilks wasn't there, but the officer on duty sent a squad car to Council Rock Park immediately. When the officers arrived, however, Dr. Pi's assailant was gone. They combed the area with high intensity lights but couldn't find the weapon. Dr. Pi wrote a report of what had occurred but made no mention of the kung fu technique he'd used to save his own life — that was his secret. He'd fought off an individual who'd pressed a gun to his head, and the weapon had not discharged when he'd heard it hit the ground. That was all anyone needed to know. Their job was to go find the fuck and prosecute him. The duty officer noticed that Dr. Pi was bleeding from his shin and tried to convince him to go get checked at Bassett Hospital, but Dr. Pi just wanted to get home. He asked for a bandage and patched up his gash in the men's bathroom, then thanked the officer and left the station. He drove out of town carefully, vigilantly, conscious of all vehicles near him, making sure he wasn't being followed.

Now he knew for sure someone wanted to kill him. Why, he wasn't sure. His gut feeling was that he should stay away from Cooperstown and stop seeing Janet for a while. Still, he knew himself. He'd have a hard time doing that because he wouldn't live his life afraid. He was proud that the kung fu he'd learned, and Chuck's intense training, had paid dividends so many years later. His age had not betrayed him because his mind was still sharp and clear. His agility and inner fortitude had taken over. Though fear reared its ugly head often, Dr. Pi knew that one's survival depended on two things: living intelligently and undaunted. He'd continue to do both.

When he got home an hour later, he was still a bit on edge. He turned on the lights one by one, checked every room in the house for intruders, and even went down into his basement. There were no signs of a break in, so he finally went upstairs. He cleaned his wound with peroxide, showered, and slapped a fresh bandage over a wad of gauze. Once in bed, he went through all his rituals, which helped comfort and calm him. He put on a science documentary, texted his children goodnight, and flipped through his Instagram. When he realized that Katerina had not posted anything or sent him any messages, his stomach did a little flip. He couldn't understand why he missed her so much, or why knowing that she was well and happy mattered to him. But it did. He suddenly had the urge to text Janet, to share everything that had happened since he'd left her side. But he didn't want to worry or upset her. All he wrote was: *Night Janet. Thanks again for a most wonderful Christmas. Enjoy each moment with King Phillip.*

The second Dr. Pi's head hit the pillow he was sound asleep.

CHAPTER 32

Dr. Pi received a call early the next day from Sheriff Wilks, and they arranged to meet. He drove back to Cooperstown, talked with Wilks about the assault, and together they walked to Council Rock Park where Dr. Pi showed Wilks how the attack had unfolded. Investigators had searched the area for evidence, but thus far neither a gun nor any other clue had been found. The process was hampered by a fresh coat of snow that had fallen overnight. Dr. Pi and Wilks returned to the station house, had coffee, and discussed matters further.

Dr. Pi shared his suspicions with Wilks. He wondered whether Anthony DiCarlo had had anything to do with the assault. He recalled Anthony's hard stare the night he was bartending, when Janet had introduced herself to Dr. Pi at The Black Sox Bar and Grill. He thought, too, about the story Janet had related about Anthony's infatuation and lifelong devotion to her and remembered how Anthony had left in a huff on the Sunday he'd shown up unannounced to pick up a painting the weekend Dr. Pi was at her house. And most recently, when Anthony had come to plow the driveway and clean off the cars Christmas morning, he'd left Dr. Pi's Audi untouched. Dr. Pi sensed Anthony's jealousy. Could it be Anthony who wanted him out of the picture? Away from Janet? When Phillip had questioned her on why Anthony was still coming around, after the trouble he'd created in her marriage, Dr. Pi thought there was much more information he wasn't privy to.

"So, what can you tell me about Anthony, Sheriff? Is he violent? My gut's telling me he doesn't want me around Janet."

"Could be. I'll certainly have a word with him," Wilks said. "No history of violence that we're aware of, and no reputation for being violent. Keeps to himself mostly. Last year, though, he did have a run-in with Ebenezer, threatened him in public, but not much has happened since."

"Janet told me about that," Dr. Pi said.

"Yeah," Wilks continued. "It was a source of town gossip for weeks. Course everyone round here knows about the rocky past of those three. But that was many years ago."

"Janet told me about that too. Says she and Anthony are just good friends now."

"Don't doubt it. The real hostility is on Ebenezer's part. He's bitter over their divorce settlement. Judge ruled in Janet's favor. Honored her father's will. She got to keep all their property. He got nothing but their small lake house. Shortly after the ruling, he showed up at the farmhouse one night fuming mad. Demanding she return his paintings. She called, and I came to escort him home. Been quiet since."

"Is there a restraining order against him?"

Wilks looked puzzled. "Not that I'm aware of," he said.

"I see," Dr. Pi said, as he recalled what Bellows had shared about Ebenezer.

"I'll talk to Anthony. Far as I know, though, he sticks up for Janet at every turn. Can't see what he'd have against you, since you're her good friend."

"I'm sure you're right Sheriff," Dr. Pi said and got up. "I'm just on edge. Wish I'd asked to meet him the day he came over when I was at Janet's. I could have felt him out."

Wilks's phone rang and he picked up. As he listened to someone speak on the other end, he signaled for Dr. Pi not to leave. Dr. Pi sat back down and stared at the sheriff.

"Thanks John," Wilks said into the receiver. "Yeah, have forensics take a look."

Wilks sat down and looked at Dr. Pi with a bewildered expression.

"What's up, Sheriff? Find anything?"

"Why yes, Dr. Pi. Two teeth — a front tooth and a canine. Under the snow. Between the slabs of slate. They're being sent to the lab now for analysis. We'll be able to get DNA from the dried blood at the root. How hard did you kick this guy?"

"With all my might. My life was threatened."

"You a black belt?"

"No. I studied the martial arts informally as a kid."

"Informally?"

"Yes. Out of books. And at college a good friend taught me proper technique."

"Not easy to knock two teeth out with one shot," Wilks stated. "That's, of course, if those teeth belong to your assailant. But I'll bet my life they're his. Surprised he got up. Do you still train? Attend a gym?"

"No sir," Dr. Pi said. "I don't train formally or go to any gym. I try to remember what I once learned. Only for self-defense. That's all."

"How bad is your shin?"

Dr. Pi lifted the bottom of his jeans, removed the bandage, and showed Wilks his wound. The small red gash was slightly swollen.

"May want some antibiotics for that," Wilks said.

"It'll be fine," Dr. Pi said. He reattached the bandage, rolled down his pants, and got up to leave.

"Glad you can still bring it," Wilks said.

"Me too."

Wilks promised to keep Dr. Pi informed on the ensuing investigation, and said he'd look in on Janet. He asked Dr. Pi to stay vigilant and call him immediately should anything else happen. Dr. Pi thanked him, and they shook hands. He left the station house and drove back to Pleasant Hills.

That evening, he received a call from Janet. Wilks had stopped by and told her what had happened. She was upset that Dr. Pi had not called her or mentioned anything in his goodnight text.

"Didn't want to worry you," he said. "Nothing happened to me. It sucks knowing someone's out to hurt me, but I'll deal with it. Just be careful please. Okay?"

"I will. You should've called me," Janet insisted. "Or driven back here."

"Probably should've. Didn't think it was a good idea. *Someone* doesn't want me around you. That's my gut feeling. I'm just going to stay home a few days and write. Not yet sure if I'll drive down to Long Island."

"OK," she said. "Don't worry about me. Wilks has my house under surveillance, and Phillip's decided to stay till New Year's."

"Great," Dr. Pi said. "Enjoy him. Don't worry about me either. I doubt anyone will come visit me at Pleasant Hills. Better not. My house is booby-trapped."

"What about your Russian girl? Are you flying to Poland?"

Dr. Pi laughed. He recognized some jealousy in Janet's tone.

"Didn't plan to. I'm sure she has better things to do than await a visit from me."

"Just wondering," Janet said seriously and then added tenderly, "I'm here for you."

"I know," Dr. Pi replied. "Thank you. I'm here for you too." Right then, he knew Janet had developed feelings for him. "And thanks for the fabulous paintings. I'll text or call you soon."

"You better," she said.

CHAPTER 33

Dr. Pi made an honest effort to write the next few days but couldn't. He just wasn't inspired. His new story wasn't going anywhere. He'd begun writing about Katerina in early December and had forged a beginning of sorts. But the idea of finding his way to Katerina, even in his fiction, now seemed a remote and ridiculous proposition. The words wouldn't come. Did it have something to do with meeting Janet? Sleeping with her? Having his life threatened? He couldn't pinpoint the reason, but each time he sat down, he wound up staring at his computer screen for long stretches of time, and thoughts of death swarmed in his mind. He knew death was always close and wondered when and how his life would end. He wasn't afraid to die because he felt Maria, Miriam, and Pablo would be on the other side to greet him — and he wished so desperately to see them once again — but the thought of leaving Constance and Christopher was unbearable. He needed to be there for them. He would have to fight to live, for their sake.

Dr. Pi remembered an incident that took place the previous December during finals week. During his Comp 101 exam, he'd noticed that Marcus Bale was behaving oddly. Normally calm and quiet, Marcus was agitated and fidgeting in his seat. He had asked for permission to go to the bathroom, went, and returned more aggravated. He tugged at his hair, threw himself back in his chair, scribbled a few lines in his booklet, and then put his head down on the desk for over ten minutes. Dr. Pi could tell he was exhausted. He'd tapped the young man on the back and asked if he was okay. Marcus had nodded, and tried to focus, only to put his head back down. This time, Dr. Pi left him alone. He decided to let him rest and talk to him afterwards.

When everyone had finished and walked out of class, Marcus apologized to Dr. Pi. Tears welled in his eyes; he said he was angry at himself for not studying, but he couldn't concentrate. He'd just fought with his mother the previous night. Said she didn't know what he was going through, that he just didn't want to do any of it anymore; he didn't see the point. The signs were clear to Dr. Pi. Marcus was in trouble. Dr. Pi asked Marcus to sit and tell him what was wrong.

Marcus began, and Dr. Pi soon realized that his situation was complex — something a counselor needed to hear, not him. Marcus spoke of how his friend had died in a car accident, how he'd survived, but how the boy who'd driven the car that he and his friend were in had been reckless, how he'd also survived, hadn't served any jail time, and now walked around town happy as could be, smiling, looking forward to his future, pretending the accident hadn't even happened, never admitting guilt, or regret, or remorse.

Dr. Pi did his best to calm and comfort Marcus and asked if he'd come with him and see a college counselor. Marcus said he already had a counselor he was seeing in Oneida, but he felt it wasn't helping. Dr. Pi in the most relaxed manner possible told Marcus to trust him; he knew Cheryl at the Health Center personally. She was patient and kind and great at her job. She would be able to help. Marcus wiped the tears from his eyes, debated, and finally told Dr. Pi he'd go. As they walked over to the Health Center together, Marcus's grief continued to pour forth from the depths of his wounded soul. Dr. Pi understood his agony, having been there twice himself. Marcus was only eighteen; he deserved a chance to live. Dr. Pi waited with him until Cheryl escorted him into her office.

The following semester Dr. Pi ran into Marcus, who thanked Dr. Pi for introducing him to Cheryl. He was still seeing her weekly, and it was helping. He was more focused on school now, working only on weekends, and his relationship with his mother had improved. As he walked to his class that morning, Dr. Pi felt elated that Marcus had gotten the help he'd needed in a time of crisis, and he was proud that he'd been there for him.

Dr. Pi realized that, like Marcus, he'd now entered a vulnerable period. He felt himself sinking into depression; it was odd that the loneliness bothered him now when he had both Katerina and Janet. He shut the computer and walked around the house aimlessly, occasionally looking out the window at the bleak, frigid landscape. He felt like visiting someone, anyone. He knew he could get in his car and travel back to Janet's and felt for some moments a need to feel her in his arms again, but then changed his mind. For several moments he stared hard at Miriam and Pablo's wedding picture in the china cabinet, then at Maria's photograph sitting before her piano. Tears flowed down his face. He wanted to join her and his parents. It was unfair that Maria had been taken so soon, that Miriam had died because of a doctor's mistake, and that he'd not been by Pablo's side when he'd taken his last breath.

This one memory about failing his father, till now buried in his unconscious, jolted Tobias with profound regret. Pablo and Miriam had been living in California with relatives when Pablo died suddenly from complications after suffering a stroke. Pablo was eighty-seven at the time, and Tobias hadn't seen his aging parents in over two years. He had planned to visit but felt he couldn't extricate himself from his scholastic and familial duties. Joanna had urged him to drop everything and just go. But he hadn't. The family flew to Santa Clarita for Pablo's funeral, and for weeks after returning to Pleasant Hills, Tobias's guilt was unbearable. He felt shame for abandoning his father who'd always been there for him. Though they had talked on the phone often, Tobias knew it wasn't the same as if he'd gone to see him. Joanna had been right. If only he'd listened to her. Miriam moved back to New York three months later, and Tobias did his best to look after her until her death in 2010. It felt strange at this moment, after so many years, that this one regret would surface to suffocate him.

Finally, Tobias calmed down, wiped his tears, drank some cold water, and felt a little better. Photographs of Christopher and Constance, their baby pictures and graduation portraits, revealed the reason he must endure, break out of this depression, and move on somehow into an uncertain future.

A few weeks earlier, thoughts of being with Katerina had fueled his spirit with an amazing optimism. He'd imagined starting a family with her, loving her devotedly, and bringing more talented children into the world. Now that all seemed ridiculous. But what had happened? Why not pursue that dream in earnest? Why feel guilty about wanting to love someone who made him feel alive inside, full of desire and energy?

What he yearned for was an impossibility, a fantasy. He wanted to retain all the wisdom he'd acquired over the years and forge a new beginning, a new life devoid of the mistakes he'd once made, one in which he'd know beforehand which decisions would prove fruitful and which ones would be painful. A life full of nothing but success and happiness and joy. Fantasy or not, this was the vision that elevated and motivated him. His children presented him with the practical reason for living — so he could love and support them. But Katerina provided that mystical, magical, intangible spark, however impractical it seemed. Katerina was a pure inspiration; her image alone had reawakened his mind to a belief in endless possibilities. And though he was physically attracted to her, his longing had nothing to do with sex. It had more to do with her energy, which was ethereal, magnanimous, and luminous. Dr. Pi knew he needed it desperately.

At once, he rose from the couch, picked up his guitar, and for the rest of the afternoon sang his soul out of solitude.

CHAPTER 34

When Constance returned from San Diego, Dr. Pi told her he'd be visiting, loaded his car with Janet's paintings for his friends, and drove to Brooklyn on the thirtieth. Being in Constance's company had a soothing effect on Dr. Pi. And seeing Tank's tail wagging wildly from side to side made him smile. The night he arrived they ate at a local Dominican restaurant, then returned to Constance's apartment for a long night of playing guitar and singing songs. Tank seemed a little subdued and stayed cuddled up by Constance's feet.

On the thirty-first, Dr. Pi drove with Constance and Tank to Will and Adriana's house on Long Island. Will, Adriana, and their daughter Nicole admired Janet's paintings, and said they'd find perfect spots for them. The New Year's Eve party was lively in that Colombian-Cuban household. The music, food and drink, and wild dancing were all spectacular. Even Tank was rejuvenated briefly and spent a good bit of the evening ripping into a pork bone — a hopeful sign that he was doing better. After a delicious dinner of pork con mojo, mondongo soup, grilled camarones, and plantains in garlic sauce, they had flan for dessert, with coffee and more drinks, and all the women began to sing and dance in the living room. Nicole, Marta, Estella, Adriana, and Angelica joined Constance and Tank in the celebratory dance-a-thon.

Will and Dr. Pi relaxed on the couch, where they chatted about the Islanders, the Yankees, and politics, and snapped photographs and video of the twirling, excited women. Dr. Pi kept one eye on his phone the whole time, until Will playfully poked him on the arm in an attempt to bring him back to the party.

"What's so interesting?" he asked. "That your lady in Poland?"

Dr. Pi smiled and put his phone in his pocket, but it was too late; Will jabbed a finger in the air and began to lecture his friend on romance.

"Katerina sounds fine," he said, "but what you need is a Colombian woman to spice up your life." He waved one hand across the scene, gesturing to the women in the room like Vanna White showing off a grand prize on *Wheel of Fortune*. "Spanish women," Will joked, "won't let you slouch or slow down. Trust me. I know."

Dr. Pi was laughing and starting to object when Will doubled down on his advice.

"I tell you," he said, alcohol weighing his words, "a Colombian woman will set you straight, my friend, and get the pecker up. You'll have no time to think or look at pictures. Estella's as hot as they come. That's some woman right there. Perfect for you."

In that moment Estella, Adriana's sister, who was divorced and single, was performing some sort of made-up flamenco move while Nicole, Angelica, and the others laughed and vamped alongside her. Dr. Pi couldn't argue with Will's point. Estella was beautiful, vivacious, and had a most wonderful personality. For a spell, he considered Will's suggestion, sensed he was right, and wondered whether he should get up to dance with her, or flirt a little. But thoughts of Katerina and Janet made him hesitate, not act and embrace the moment.

When Will eventually wandered off to the kitchen, Dr. Pi went back to his phone. He checked the USPS website often and got angry because his package had not arrived in Poland. He felt it might be lost. He also flipped through Instagram. Katerina had posted some wintry pictures from Irkutsk, the Siberian Russian town where she'd been born and was visiting. In her caption, she celebrated the real winters there, versus the milder, mostly snowless Polish winters, but she didn't mention why she'd traveled there. Perhaps to see old friends, Dr. Pi thought. Instead of focusing on the ongoing fun in front of him, Dr. Pi's mind wandered to Irkutsk, a place he knew little about. He googled Irkutsk, read about its Orthodox Christian churches, and then fantasized, as always, about joining Katerina at church, listening to a Russian mass by her side, marrying her in such a sacred, majestic place. While he was doing this, he missed at least two attempts by Estella to catch his eye. All of the activity in the room had been reduced to a blur.

Sensing how lost Tobias was, Will brought him a cold Heineken, pulled him up off the couch, and waved for him to follow.

"Come, brother," he instructed. "I want to show you something."

Tobias stuffed his phone in his pants pocket, took a big gulp of beer, and followed Will through the kitchen door to his garage out back. Will raised the garage door to show Tobias his new toy, which he'd purchased in early September, just weeks before joining the Latin American Motorcycle Association (LAMA).

"Voilà," Will said proudly. "You're not the only one with an exotic, foreign beauty. Here's *my* Russian queen, Natasha. Got the wife's permission to keep a concubine." Will smiled devilishly, then asked: "Well, what do you think? Isn't she lovely?"

Tobias fell in love instantly when he saw the gleaming chrome and polished, metallic black paint of the brand new, 850-pound, 2018 Harley Davidson, Road King special, a low rider, with a 19-inch rim tire up front and an 18-inch one in the back. A steal, Will told him, at 23K. Even though he'd never driven a motorcycle, the bike's majesty awed Tobias, and all that came out of his mouth at first was, "WOW! WOW! WOW!" Tongue-tied, he moved in for a closer look.

"You need one of these, Tobias," Will urged. "To join my sisters and brothers when we ride on the Island and upstate by you. People from all walks of life are in our club. It'll be fun."

"Are you nuts?" Tobias asked, bewildered. "You know I've never driven a motorcycle. And that I don't have a license. I'm too old for that."

"No, you're not!" Will insisted. "Hey, what happened to all that *proud* talk about being a Renaissance man? You used to chime on that idea ad nauseam. Now you spend your life glued to an iPhone. Give it a fucking shot!"

Tobias considered the proposition for some seconds. He didn't like being called out. "Okay, maybe I'll try it next summer. But only if you'll teach me."

"Of course, I will. That's the spirit," Will said, satisfied. "Lots of gorgeous, athletic, and smart women ride bikes these days. I'm sure you'll meet many — or maybe we can invite Estella to join us. She may want to learn as well. Best thing I've done in quite a while is join LAMA. We ride, celebrate the love of motorcycles and family, do charity events, tour the city and countryside. We have a blast!"

"Why'd you name your bike Natasha and not Sally Mae?" Tobias joked. "I thought Harleys are American?"

"They are. Very American!" Will said emphatically. "Guess, like you, I need my own Katerina." He then added slyly, "Only Natasha's a little nastier than your glamorous gal, if you get my drift. A different type of woman. With a hundred thirty-one horses, she awakens my soul. Adriana loves her and rides with me. Screams in my ears the whole damn time. It's brought us closer."

"Glad you're both having fun," Tobias said. "Hey, thanks for having us over tonight." Tobias reached in and gave Will a big embrace, then added: "Constance, Tank, and I appreciate it a whole lot."

"Very welcome, brother. You're all a part of our family."

Will closed the garage door, and they walked back inside to rejoin the women.

Dr. Pi sent Katerina a direct message wishing her a happy New Year and safe trip back to Poland. There was no immediate answer; on his world clock, he saw that for Katerina it was almost noon on New Year's Day. Again, he wondered who she had visited in Irkutsk, who she was with, and why she had gone. Tank meandered to the couch by Dr. Pi's feet and rubbed his head on his legs. In the past, he'd just jump up; now he waited to be picked up. Dr. Pi finally shut off his phone, placed Tank on his lap, talked to him lovingly, and softly petted his small, bony head. Will brought Dr. Pi another beer, and soon everyone sat to watch the Times Square ball drop, see the televised celebrations worldwide, and toast to a fantastic 2019. By 3 a.m., the women retired to their bedrooms; Will and Dr. Pi fell asleep on the couch with Tank cuddled between them.

Dr. Pi drove Constance and Tank to Brooklyn in the early afternoon on New Year's Day. Tank was exhausted; he ate, drank a little water, and went immediately to rest in his bed. Constance and Dr. Pi walked to a nearby Indian restaurant, and Dr. Pi snapped pictures of Brooklyn's beautiful brownstones and churches to post on Instagram. The samosas, chicken tikka masala, and korma were delicious and spicy, and for almost two hours they talked about the present and near future, writing songs, and Constance's performances with The Chilling Misers. Her hazel eyes lit up when she told her father that at Ogliastro's Pizza Bar she'd met an intelligent, resourceful young man named Bernardo whom she cared about and had recently started dating.

"That's wonderful, sweetheart," Tobias said joyfully and smiled, and Constance expressed her growing feelings.

"He's so attentive and kind, Dad. Thoughtful and respectful. You should see how lovingly he plays with Tank. I wanted you to meet him yesterday, but he had to work. And today he's helping his uncle. So maybe next time you visit I can introduce you."

"Sure, sweetie. I'd love to meet him," Tobias replied, elated to hear Constance's happy news. "Next time I'm down, we'll have dinner together."

Tobias paid for dinner, left a big tip, and thanked the owner for being open on New Year's Day. They then walked home several blocks battling the blustery wind and freezing cold.

Anytime Tobias and Constance were together, they reminisced about good times past, and the promise of the years ahead. Dr. Pi lingered as long as he could, but by six he was on the West Side Highway. Before leaving, Dr. Pi took Tank out for a walk, tucked him back in his bed, rubbed his back gently, and said goodbye. He hugged Constance, held her tightly, pressed two hundred dollars into her hand, and slowly descended the brownstone's steps, not wanting to leave.

Minutes into the drive home, Dr. Pi gripped the wheel with a nervous tension that he hadn't even known was there. As he pitched himself forward in the seat and focused on the road, tears ran down his face, and he was engulfed by a vague sense of regret. He tried to sort through the reasons for this sudden wave of emotion but couldn't immediately understand it. Part of it had to do with already missing Constance and Tank. It churned his stomach to be away from his daughter for another long stretch, and to think that he might never see that little dog again!

But there was more. As an 18-wheeler passed him at high speed, images flashed before his eyes, of Katerina, of Janet, of pastoral scenes in which cars crash and vehicles go up in flames and charred bodies are pulled from the wreckage. Even Estella flashed across his mind — a dancing, beckoning figure, one of many missed opportunities. And then he lit on the true source of his worry. Like the rows of trees and the other scenes outside his car window, life was passing him by. It seemed to him that these days, he was never living fully in the present moment as he should be. He was too distracted to embrace the passing time with full focus. Being away from his children was difficult and home was lonely. Try as he might, however, he couldn't honestly imagine a life with Janet. Instead, the closer he got to home, the more he thought of Katerina. He couldn't wait to reach home, jump into bed, and DM her.

CHAPTER 35

The next day, Dr. Pi and Katerina texted for a few hours, covering more ground in this one session than at any other point in their comms. They discussed her trip to Russia and her work at the restaurant, and Dr. Pi ruminated about the fact that his present still hadn't arrived. He was hopeful it would get there in time for Russian Christmas on the Epiphany, but promised he'd send her another gift just in case the first had gotten lost. Katerina told him, emphatically, that wasn't necessary, that she was sure the first would arrive, but Dr. Pi insisted he loved sending her gifts.

Dr. Pi asked Katerina about her classes, and she shared that her final exams were on January 14. She still had much to study, but with the long hours spent cooking at the restaurant, it was impossible to practice and keep up with all the work. At one point she mentioned how often she had no energy to do both. She explained how her hands and fingers would swell while cutting meat and preparing dishes, and this made it almost impossible to play the piano (*My hands and fingers like a stone after these days, I can't play and have no time to study ... and just ... I have no strength.*). Dr. Pi wished he could somehow alleviate this difficult situation. He thought about how much he wanted to support and take care of her, so she didn't have to work at all and could concentrate fully on her studies. He wondered whether Katerina would be willing to come to America, live in his big, old house, and let him be at her beck and call. He thought about this many times but didn't have the courage to ask her if she'd be willing to join him.

Dr. Pi asked about her trip to Irkutsk, whether she'd returned to see loved ones she missed for the holidays and whether that trip had made her nostalgic for the past, her childhood, and the good old days of innocence and fun. He even asked how old she'd been when she'd left Irkutsk but not why she'd decided to leave permanently to live in Europe. Dr. Pi stopped short of inquiring if she'd gone back alone or accompanied; he didn't want to meddle or appear jealous. Still, he knew that was a very long trip to be traveling alone. Katerina's answers were not what Dr. Pi expected; she was forthright, honest, and suddenly the air of romance he'd pictured in his mind about her past in Irkutsk burst from his mental balloon.

About Irkutsk, she wrote, *No, I don't have a family, and I also have no friends in Irkutsk, because I don't live there for many, many years, it was just nostalgia ... 17 years old, I felt nothing. True. Just nothing. I enjoyed the winter more, than felt anything.*

Dr. Pi was startled, pained. Sympathy swelled within him. If she no longer had any family, he wanted her to join his, and fill that void in her life.

Dr. Pi mused for many minutes before responding, and then wrote plainly that from then on, he'd consider her a part of his family. Katerina paused and then asked why he was so interested in Irkutsk, and he responded it was because the most beautiful woman he knew had been born there. Also, because he'd read that it had some of Russia's most beautiful churches, and he adored architecturally stunning cathedrals. Katerina told him that was a curious and *cute* detail to know about him. Dr. Pi replied that maybe one day they'd visit Irkutsk together, and that perhaps she'd give him a tour of the city's treasures.

Katerina asked about his writing, and he admitted he hadn't written much for several days. He didn't mention anything about his affair with Janet, or the assault at Council Rock Park. He joked that his inspiration — *she* — had been offline for a while, and that he'd lost his desire to sit for hours in front of the computer. Katerina expressed amazement that she *inspired* Dr. Pi's writing (*I never before in my life could ... imagine that I will inspire someone and be the hero of the novel!! It is my great pleasure* [*A smiley emoji with red heart eyes*]). It was true, Dr. Pi admitted, but he also stressed that *writing is a pretty boring process.* Katerina expressed her wish to be in his presence while he wrote:

Why do you think that watching you write is boring? It's very — cozy! Imagine: a light of lamp in the room in the evening, the silence, the key clicks. You sit at your table and write. I lie near on the sofa and doing something else. I do not speak. I keep silence. But I am in this atmosphere: the light, the key clicks and people, and you, who concentrated thinking. It's super cozy! Super peaceful. Super warm. I like it very....

Dr. Pi was amazed that she could imagine spending such a pleasant evening with him. He told her he wished to do so much for her, and she replied candidly:

Don't ask yourself what you can do for me ... just be and that's enough! (*Thank-you hands and three red heart emojis*).

He went to bed that night happy, fulfilled. It would be a blessing, he thought, if he could feel that way every single day for the remainder of his life.

The next morning, he called USPS and started an inquiry about the package he now considered lost. The last tracking message showed it leaving Kennedy Airport on December 20. He went to his local post office and told them about the package, and they reassured him that sometimes it could take up to a month to get there; rarely did packages get lost. Though comforted to hear this, Dr. Pi decided to send Katerina a new package anyways, so he spent the afternoon shopping for cool gifts — more specialty soaps, woolen winter hats, more fancy bags.

For Russian Christmas, Katerina posted a photograph of herself cradling half a dozen yellow tulips. Her eyes were closed, and she smiled with sincere satisfaction. She looked beautiful with her long red hair pulled back in a ponytail, and in her right hand she held a white gift bag and a greeting card with the phrase "I Love You" written across it in big, bold, colorful letters. At this moment Dr. Pi realized what he'd suspected all along but did not want to acknowledge — Katerina had someone else who loved her. Strangely, Dr. Pi's reaction was joyful rather than sad. He was truly happy for her.

He wanted to know if his guess was correct, so he decided to ask her. If she did have someone, he wondered what his role in Katerina's life should be. He had many questions: Why was she drawn to him? What purpose did he serve? Should he just let her be? Stop thinking of her romantically?

The next night, Dr. Pi asked whether she had someone, and she responded: …*in short, I have.* But she didn't write more about it, and Dr. Pi did not press her to elaborate. The confirmation was enough, and they'd continued writing back and forth for another two hours, as if that fact about her life — that there was *a significant other* in it — wouldn't affect the course of their friendship. However, the revelation did deflate him a little.

The next day, Dr. Pi was busy at the college organizing his materials for the spring semester. Late in the afternoon, as he walked home, his phone vibrated, and he stopped to see who it was. Katerina had sent him a direct message. It was just a big, red heart. Dr. Pi smiled, tucked his phone back in his pocket, and continued walking. She was thinking of him and that made him happy. In this strange new world, Dr. Pi mused, an emoji heart sent electronically from over four thousand miles away had the power to make him smile and feel a deep joy; he felt like someone seeing the sun reappear after several days of rain.

Dr. Pi arrived home, got comfortable, and began making dinner. As the chicken cooked slowly in the wok, he drank a cold beer and looked at his phone. Janet had texted asking how he was doing, and he sent her a quick reply: *All is well, thanks. Been getting ready for school. Hope all is well with you.*

Later, after dinner and TV, he wondered how to respond to Katerina's red heart. His feelings for her hadn't changed. It didn't matter that she had someone. He felt no jealousy, though, and was just happy for her. He wanted to let her know that and expressed exactly those emotions in a carefully worded message. An hour passed before his phone beeped and he read Katerina's reply:

Thank you very much for your words ... I was afraid very much that you never write to me again ... and I waited all day, but then could not resist and sent you the emoji heart.

Dr. Pi replied in earnest, *Aww. You're so sweet. (Red heart emoji). I'm here. I care for you deeply. I want to cheer you, inspire you, and make you (Smiley face emoji) happy. Write to me anytime. Trust that my emotions for you are true. (Red heart emoji) ... The main thing is that you study, do well on your exams — that would make me happy...*

I don't know how to say in English ...just you have your place in my heart and all another is no matter and can't to change it ... It's all different things.

Thank you, Dr. Pi wrote. *I wish to keep my place in your heart (Red heart emoji). I don't ever want to leave it.*

I will care about your feelings and I will try never get you upset, she replied. *I will be with you as long as you want — and you always can write to me, talk with me about all what you want. My feelings about you is warm (Red heart emoji) ... I love to know that I have you (Red heart emoji).*

You have me, he reassured her. *And always will.*

And you have me.

The exchange ended. And soon Dr. Pi went up to bed. He put on his universe documentary on Netflix but couldn't fall asleep. He wanted and missed Katerina so much. He wondered who held her that very moment. In whose arms did she feel secure and at peace? If only she could be in his, he thought. If only.

After an hour of tossing and turning, he shut off the television, grabbed his phone, and listened to the Russian rock songs Katerina had sent him. Suddenly she was there next to him. It was so thoughtful of her to share these songs. Oh, how he yearned to understand each lyric. He felt the emotion in Kipelov's voice, the strong way he caressed those strange, intense words; his sincere enunciation of them, and the detectable pain that Dr. Pi felt as he listened, reminded him that experiencing heartbreak is an inescapable part of life — the same for everyone, regardless of their culture or the language they speak. A clause from Kate Chopin's "The Story of an Hour" floated to him in the darkness: "What could love, the unsolved mystery, count for…!" Chopin was so right, he thought. Love will always be an unsolved mystery, but though impossible to explain, one knows when it has seized the heart and mind and is in full control. That moment, Dr. Pi realized he wished to love Katerina forever, though she loved someone else. And soon, his sadness lifted. He placed his phone on the dresser, put his universe documentary back on, and within minutes he was sound asleep.

CHAPTER 36

Early on January 8, Dr. Pi received a call from Sheriff Wilks asking that he come to the Cooperstown stationhouse later that afternoon. They were waiting on DNA results in his assault case, but he didn't want to discuss the matter further over the phone. Dr. Pi was shocked but relieved to hear that perhaps this mystery might be solved and the albatross hanging around his neck removed. Dr. Pi had emailed Professor Bellows about what had taken place. Bellows, like Wilks, had urged him to stay away from Cooperstown and be vigilant at home. Bellows promised to research Anthony. As each day passed, when Dr. Pi got on the computer to check the status of Katerina's packages, he also looked for a subsequent email from Bellows. Thus far, none had come. But now, finally, it appeared Wilks knew something definitive. After lunch, Dr. Pi showered, got dressed, and drove to Cooperstown.

When Dr. Pi arrived at the station house it was 3:30 p.m. He was told by the clerk to sit in the waiting room. Sheriff Wilks and Detective Florio were not yet in. He'd be meeting with detective Florio first. Dr. Pi wondered what news Florio had to share. Right then, quite unexpectedly, he received a brief but urgent text from Janet.

I need to see you, she wrote. *Anthony's been arrested in Manhattan. I'm worried.*

I'm at the Cooperstown station house waiting to see detective Florio, he wrote back. *I'll be over soon as I'm done.*

Thank you, she wrote.

He put away his phone, and for several minutes stared ahead blankly, wondering why Anthony had been arrested, but more importantly, why Janet was worried. What did his arrest have to do with her?

The street door opened, and Sheriff Wilks walked in. He greeted Dr. Pi and proceeded towards the clerk's door. A tall, well-dressed, older man entered behind Wilks. "I'll be with you shortly," Wilks said to him, and then headed to his office. The man nodded, took off his long, black woolen coat, hung it on a corner coat rack, and sat across from Dr. Pi. He wore an expensive blue Armani suit and sported a bright red tie. He had long, curly blonde hair, parted in the middle, which fell well below his chin, California surfer-style. It was a cut one wouldn't expect to see on an older man. His eyes were a striking, rich blue, his brow and nose elegantly formed. He nodded a welcome to Dr. Pi but didn't say anything. He then reached into his pocket, pulled out his phone, and soon became absorbed. Dr. Pi noticed his swollen mouth and wondered who he was, how he'd been hurt, and what he was there for.

Just then, the clerk came into the waiting area, and when she told "Mr. Lancaster" that Wilks had just received an important call and would be delayed a few more minutes, Dr. Pi realized he sat across from Ebenezer. She then turned and said, "Dr. Pi, Detective Florio has also been delayed; he said to tell you he'll be here in twenty minutes."

"Thank you," Dr. Pi replied, and she went back into her office.

"So, you're the famous Dr. Pi," Ebenezer said sarcastically. "Glad I finally got to meet you." He reached forward and extended his hand towards Dr. Pi. After a pause, Dr. Pi reached up and shook it.

"Nice to meet you," Ebenezer said. "You a medical doctor at Bassett?"

"No. A literature professor at Pleasant Hills. I taught a writing course at Bassett last fall."

"Oh. Heard you've been harassed and recently assaulted. I can assure you, I had nothing to do with it, Dr. Pi. That's why I'm here. I've told the sheriff I'm not involved."

"How'd you hurt your face?" Dr. Pi asked, recalling the kick he'd given his attacker.

"An accident. A two-by-four fell on me in the shed. Should've been more careful."

Dr. Pi didn't respond right away, and Ebenezer asked, "How long have you known my ex-wife Janet?"

"A few months."

"And her thug friend, Anthony?"

"I've seen, but never met, him."

"Bet my life he has his city friends after you. Doubt he wants you near her. They're childhood friends. Past lovers. Last year, that ass threatened me. What's your business with Janet?"

"I've bought some of her paintings. We've become good friends." He paused, and then added, "Sorry about your divorce. Relationships are never easy."

"We were doomed from the start, as they say," Ebenezer admitted. "Had some good years. Have a wonderful son. Struggled a bit, but who doesn't? Then that mobster Anthony came back into the picture, and everything fell apart. Course I've never shared the details of our breakup with my boy. No sense in making him view his mother differently. Though I'm sure he's surmised some of it."

Dr. Pi wanted to tell Ebenezer that he'd met Phillip and that he was a wonderful and talented young man, but he didn't think it appropriate. He also yearned to know more about Anthony's role in the demise of his marriage from Ebenezer's perspective. Dr. Pi remembered Phillip questioning Janet on why Anthony was still in the picture and coming around after all the trouble he'd caused. But this information was much too personal to ask someone he'd just met.

The door opened, and the clerk told Ebenezer that the sheriff was ready to see him. Ebenezer got up, but before he disappeared through the door, Dr. Pi asked if they could meet for a beer sometime — his treat.

"Sure thing," Ebenezer said. He took a business card from his wallet and handed it to Dr. Pi. "Call or text me at that number. I'm in town for another week."

"Perfect," Dr. Pi said. "Good luck in there."

"Thanks," Ebenezer said. "This won't take long."

Ebenezer was right. Not long after entering to see Sheriff Wilks, he emerged back into the waiting area, put on his long coat, and smiled at Dr. Pi.

"What'd I tell you?" he asked. "Free to go. Glad to have met you, Dr. Pi. Give me a call, and let's grab a beer soon."

"I will," Dr. Pi replied, and got up to shake Ebenezer's hand one more time before he walked out the door.

Five minutes later, detective Florio walked in, apologized for being late, and asked that Dr. Pi follow him into his office.

CHAPTER 37

Dr. Pi sat in Florio's office and wondered what the news would be. Florio excused himself momentarily, walked out the door, and minutes later re-entered with Wilks.

"Here's what we know about your case, Dr. Pi," Wilks said. "Ebenezer's not our man. Thought there was a good chance he'd attacked you. That the bruises on his face were from your kick. But the DNA on the teeth is not his. Different labs have concluded the samples don't match. And there's no record he's ever owned a handgun. Ebenezer's slate is clean."

"He just told me he had nothing to do with it," Dr. Pi said. "Said a wood beam hit his face. Sounded genuine."

"Yes," Florio said. "Quite a coincidence, I must say." Florio glanced at Wilks and continued. "We thought he was lying. What are the chances? On December thirtieth, we visited his lake house and became suspicious when we saw his swollen mouth. He showed us the work he'd been doing on his back deck steps and explained how the shed accident had happened. We took a DNA sample to verify his story."

"We called you in to file charges against him this very afternoon," Wilks said. "We were that sure. Now we're back to square one. The perpetrator is still out there, so please, watch your back. You're obviously capable of doing that, but stay vigilant."

"I will, Sheriff," Dr. Pi said and got up.

"You sure you don't moonlight as an MMA fighter?" Wilks asked and smiled.

"I can assure you, I don't, Sheriff," Dr. Pi answered and laughed. "I fight ignorance in the classroom. Try to awaken young minds."

"Soon as we have anything new, we'll be in touch," Florio said.

Dr. Pi thanked them and left. A strong, cold wind picked up as he walked out of the stationhouse. He drove to Janet's, eager to know what she knew about Anthony's arrest in Manhattan.

**

Janet greeted Dr. Pi at her kitchen door in a sexy red negligee. Her intentions were obvious, and the look on her face revealed her desire. Few words were exchanged as Dr. Pi entered the room. She grabbed his hands, escorted him into the parlor, and they sank onto the loveseat as they both struggled to free Dr. Pi of his clothes. Her body's warmth felt good as his hands roamed her sensuous curves. Two weeks of absence had ignited their desire. Dr. Pi realized he'd missed their intimacy. He knew this wasn't romance; it was a raw, physical lust that propelled them both forward, and the two savored sex in the same way they'd enjoy a tasty glass of wine after weeks of abstaining from alcohol. Afterwards, they lay back, satisfied. Janet pulled on her lacy panties and covered her body with a woolen blanket that she retrieved from the arm of a nearby wing chair. Dr. Pi pulled up his pants, tightened his belt, and snuggled under it with her.

As they luxuriated in the cozy warmth of the blanket, they stared up at Janet's ceiling, with their heads tilted and touching. Sex had momentarily removed the lingering loneliness that pervaded their individual lives. After a long silence, Janet turned towards him and spoke.

"I've missed you so much."

Her voice's tenderness and the eager look in her eyes enthralled Dr. Pi; he kissed her and savored her lips' softness. When the kiss was over, he whispered, "And I, you." The words flowed out of him naturally.

Suddenly she asked him pointedly, as if bewildered, "Why did you abandon me?"

The question both surprised and bothered Dr. Pi, and he answered directly.

"I had a gun pressed to my skull!" he exclaimed. "Someone tried to kill me. Sheriff Wilks told me to stay away. I shouldn't even be here. Can you understand that?"

"Yes," she said softly. "I'm sorry."

"Who the hell would do that?" Dr. Pi continued. "And why? Can you tell me?"

The questions hung in the air a bit, but she didn't answer. Instead, she offered comfort and an explanation.

"I'm so glad you weren't hurt. Forgive me. I've just been worried and lonely here without you."

"Common sense said to stay away. I've been on edge these past two weeks. I've answered your texts. I haven't abandoned you. Or committed to any serious relationship with you or anyone."

"No. You haven't," she agreed. "That was selfish of me to say." Janet leaned in and kissed him. When their lips parted, Dr. Pi had calmed down.

Dr. Pi's instinct told him Janet was keeping something from him. There was certainly information he felt she wasn't sharing. He debated whether to dig for it, tell her what he knew, and what he suspected. Then, suddenly, he came right out with his emotions. He pressed her to reveal whatever secret she guarded:

"Look Janet, I'm surprised I came here tonight. Someone doesn't want me near you. In fact, someone wants me dead." He paused, and then said bluntly, "And it isn't Ebenezer. I know that for a fact."

Janet looked shocked but said nothing.

"My guess is it's Anthony who's wanted me to stay away," Dr. Pi said. "Am I right? Why was he arrested? Tell me what you know — and why you texted me that you were worried. What does his arrest have to do with you?"

"How do you know it's not Ebenezer?" Janet asked defensively. "He's a pest. He spreads rumors about me and won't leave me alone."

"Because DNA doesn't lie. Wilks has conclusive evidence Ebenezer didn't attack me. So, tell me, was it Anthony?"

Dr. Pi searched her face, but she seemed to have become frozen.

"Well?" he demanded, angry now. "Tell me the truth."

Janet looked down and back up again, and finally said "Perhaps…"

"Perhaps what?"

"I mean … it's possible Anthony didn't want me getting close to you. He was upset the Sunday he came to pick up a painting and you were here."

"Why didn't you tell me that? You said he was upset about his work schedule. Why did you lie to me?"

"Because his feelings didn't matter. I didn't want to get any deeper into our little soap opera. I told you most of it. We're just business partners now. That's it. He had no right to tell me who I could have over or sleep with. He has a wife. What we once had has long been over. He had no right to be jealous. Of you, or anyone else."

"Why was he arrested?"

"I don't know. He just called to tell me he'd been taken in." There was something vague in her reply. A missing element. Dr. Pi seized on it.

"You *do know*, Janet," he said adamantly. "And you should tell me. You said you cared for me. This jealous man may be directly or indirectly responsible for an attempt on my life. You owe me an explanation. You owe me the truth."

Janet sat silent and thoughtful. She debated and finally said, "You're right, Tobias. I do. It's a long story." Her brown eyes watered. "I'm in a lot of trouble. Let's eat dinner first, and then I'll tell you everything. Promise."

As the first few tears spilled down her cheeks, Dr. Pi's frustration softened. He agreed to do as she asked. He was starved, in any case, and so he followed her into the kitchen and sat at the table. She excused herself, went upstairs to freshen up and dress, and then returned to join him wearing dark-blue corduroy pants and a maroon woolen sweater. She heated some leftover beef stew and corn, toasted and buttered slices of wheat bread, and poured two glasses of wine. Dr. Pi helped her and kept off the subject of Anthony's arrest. Soon they ate and drank and chatted about Phillip and Veronica and other lighter matters. Dr. Pi was eager to hear more about the circumstances of Anthony's arrest; his instincts were telling him that there could be serious consequences for Janet. But he swallowed his suspicions along with his stew and waited for her to take the lead.

CHAPTER 38

When they had finished eating, Dr. Pi helped Janet clean the kitchen. They did not converse much; once Janet had shared all of her news about Phillip and Veronica, Dr. Pi's frustration gradually crept back in, and there was an obvious tension between them now. He did not appreciate Janet's skirting the truth when she'd talked about Anthony, and he clearly remembered the way Anthony had stared at him from the bar on the night that Janet had introduced herself. The stare, harsh and intense. But Janet had brushed it off and diverted Dr. Pi's attention towards Ebenezer as the cruel culprit behind all her troubles. What could she be hiding?

Dr. Pi refused a second glass of wine and opted for coffee instead; the wine had made him sleepy, and he was mindful of his hour-long trip back home. He was sure Janet would ask him to stay over, but he'd lost his desire to do so. It was crazy how his emotions fluctuated around Janet. A little over an hour earlier he'd made love to her, and now he was eager to head home. She'd lied to him about Anthony, and that might have cost Dr. Pi his life.

Dr. Pi became impatient and finally broke the silence.

"Why did you come over to my table at The Black Sox Bar and Grill?"

She reached for his hands, held them tenderly, and looked into his eyes.

"Because I'm a lonely woman," she replied, her voice cracking slightly as emotion overwhelmed her. "I found you handsome. And yes, I wanted to sell you some art."

"How'd you know I loved art? Did you guess?"

"No. I knew."

"How?"

"I'd seen you at the library a few times before, perusing the art exhibits. We hadn't met, but I overheard you talking with my assistant Juliet one afternoon about the pieces on display. I sat inside the office. You carried on and on about them. You sounded so enthusiastic; it was obvious you appreciated art. And I thought, perhaps, I could sell you some of mine."

"So you followed me to the dock on the night we met?"

"Yes. I wanted to get to know you. I'd just finished dinner in town, and I saw you walking towards the lake, so I followed you, and introduced myself."

"I remember," Dr. Pi said. "You made an impression. Said the lake's serenity made the years disappear."

"It's a magical place," Janet said. "I wasn't lying."

"I know," he said. "I love it there too. Very much."

"One day my ashes will be scattered over its tranquil waters."

Janet's remark surprised Dr. Pi, and he was silent for some seconds.

"A very peaceful resting place," he said at length.

"Yes. I do love it," Janet said with emotion. "Since the day Dad took me fishing there for the first time. I must've been four or so and had never been on a boat before. We stayed out till twilight, and I still recall the lake's serenity. The awe it inspired has never left me."

"What a wonderful memory," Dr. Pi said. "You caught my fancy the night I saw you there. Seemed you were in a trance. A beautiful, mysterious woman had sat by me. I was at a loss for words. And quite lonely myself."

"I didn't want to be too forward that evening, hoped you'd be as talkative as you'd been with Juliet. But you were rather quiet and subdued. So I left and figured at some point I'd run into you again. I'm glad I did — at the bar and grill. And that I've gotten to know you."

"All just to sell me some art?"

Janet hesitated, thought carefully about her response, and Dr. Pi knew there was something she worried about sharing.

"At first, yes," she said. "I didn't realize I'd be swayed by your charm and fall for you. I'd wanted a real bond with a man for a very long time. Over Christmas, when I saw how well you got along with Phillip, I was hooked."

"He's a remarkable young man. A great pianist and a wonderful son. You're very lucky."

"I am."

"But we're getting off topic. You were going to explain Anthony's grudge. What does Anthony have against me?"

"It's not you, specifically," Janet said. "Anthony doesn't want me to have anything intimate with *any* man."

"Why not?" Dr. Pi asked. "You said he has a wife."

"He does," Janet said. "But he says he can never let me go. He wants us both."

"You should've told me," Dr. Pi said angrily. "Would've been nice to know what I was up against. So the jealous bastard followed me around, almost ambushed me, and recently tried to kill me? Is he that deranged?"

Janet was silent.

"Do you sleep with him too?"

Dr. Pi knew he'd crossed the line and apologized. "I'm sorry, Janet. That's none of my business."

"I did sometimes, before I got to know you," Janet said, flustered now. "Then I lost my desire to keep playing that game. Told him I wanted to start something new with you. Urged him to focus on his wife. Thought we could continue our business enterprise together. That he'd understand. But he berated me, told me to let you go, that you didn't have the kind of money we were looking for…"

Janet stopped abruptly, realized she'd said something she shouldn't have. Dr. Pi caught it and asked with concern:

"What kind of money is that? What's your business enterprise?"

As he asked these questions, all the pieces suddenly came together for Dr. Pi, and he sensed that from the beginning Janet and Anthony had been trying to set him up for something sinister.

"Are those antiques you sell stolen, Janet? Was that Warhol a hot item? That's why you won't auction it off? Is that what Anthony does in the city, sell stolen art and furniture for you? Is that what he's been arrested for?"

"Not stolen items. No," she said immediately. "I'm not a thief, Tobias," she added, saddened that he could think that of her. "The antiques we sell are our cover. What we've done is a lot worse. Come, let me show you."

CHAPTER 39

Janet escorted Dr. Pi to the barn. They sloshed through huge snowdrifts, freshly carved by the howling wind. As Janet unlocked the door and they stepped into the barn's cozy interior, Dr. Pi was reminded that the entire space was heated, even though there were no animals inside. He had noted this detail before, but thought it was just to help preserve Janet's pricy furniture, antiques, and art. Now his mind was firing with possibilities, and he struggled to stop himself from hitting her with a barrage of questions. Too much pressure might spook her, and he needed the full truth.

Janet walked over to the room that Dr. Pi had not seen on his initial tour — what she'd told him was an old tack room. She unlocked the door and flipped on the light to reveal a large, windowless room full of wiring and high-tech equipment. The walls were painted white, and the floor was a polished, knotty pinewood. On a large oak desk in one corner of the room sat a computer and some other electronic gadgetry, including what looked to Dr. Pi like a digital projector. In another corner, an easel displayed a painting in progress, and next to it, various paint tubes, brushes, and other painting paraphernalia were strewn upon a small table. On the floor, leaning against the walls, there were various sized canvases. A large camera stood atop a high tripod and faced what looked like the

Warhol painting that Janet had previously shown to Dr. Pi. Several paintings, in diverse styles, hung on the room's walls, many he thought he recognized. One looked like a Picasso piece imitating ancient cave art — a strange-looking bull, its strokes striking in their simplicity. A second appeared to be a Pollock, with its signature splotches of chaotic color. A third resembled a Rothko with its abstract color field.

Janet went to the desk and laid her right index finger on the computer's keyboard. The screen lit up instantly to reveal a close-up of a painting. As he stared at the detailed and amplified brush strokes, Dr. Pi realized that they belonged to the Warhol painting that the digital camera was aimed at. Before Janet offered an explanation, Dr. Pi surmised what she was ready to confess; all the pieces of an elaborate con artist's scheme came together. Suddenly he knew what her enterprise was, and sadness overwhelmed him.

"This is how I've wasted my life since my divorce, Tobias," she uttered in a trembling, thin voice. "I forge art. I'm a phony. Anthony sells it to naïve, unsuspecting investors looking for bargains. He has mob ties in the city. The furniture and antiques serve as a cover. The money's in the forged art. Of course, when you work for organized crime, the family makes most of the profit. It was all my idea; Anthony offered his help."

Dr. Pi was stunned, in complete disbelief that Janet would do this. After a prolonged silence, he moved in to inspect the hanging paintings, and asked:

"So, are these copies you've made of masterpieces?"

"No. Those are the original pieces I study and replicate with the help of this technology. One per week. For each, I generally receive two thousand dollars. Anthony gets five hundred for transport. They usually sell for about ten thousand a piece, so you know into whose pockets the rest of the money goes. Occasionally, Anthony gets a good lead and swindles a naïve investor for fifty to a hundred thousand, and at twenty percent, we have a much bigger payoff. The market for fake art is huge. Some are sold in Manhattan, but others are sent to major cities across the US, even shipped around the world. It's a sophisticated underground network. Anthony says lots of artists do what I do. The only competition comes from expert copies made in Asia."

"It's too big a risk Janet," Dr. Pi said, frustrated at her foolery. "How'd you come by these originals?"

"The pieces hanging here were purchased legally by Ebenezer and by his father, James Morgan Lancaster. Ebenezer's an art connoisseur. His father was a Manhattan real estate broker and an art collector." She pointed disdainfully at the Picasso cave painting. "Except for that emaciated bull, which is a rare Picasso that Ebenezer acquired at a private estate auction in Barcelona years ago, all the other expressionist paintings were bought by James Morgan in the late forties and early fifties from the original artists, de Kooning, Rothko, Pollock, and Krasner."

While Dr. Pi stood there in stunned silence, Janet continued.

"Ebenezer's father wasn't just investing. He loved abstract art. He believed in the movement, socialized with the artists in Greenwich Village and on Long Island, and supported them financially. He purchased many pieces in cash for under ten thousand dollars. The world's never seen these; they do not appear in any of the artists' catalogues raisonnés. They've hung on private walls nearly seventy years."

"Wow," Dr. Pi exclaimed, still getting his bearings. "And now they're worth millions."

"Yes," Janet said, then resumed her story. "James Morgan gave them to Ebenezer shortly after we were married; he was a very generous man. And happy his son had married an artist."

"The ideal daughter-in-law," Dr. Pi mused aloud.

"Well, I'm not so sure about that," Janet said sadly, "but Ebenezer got my father's permission to bring the paintings to Cooperstown, and then paid to refurbish and heat the barn and this old tack room to display them. They were to provide inspiration for me. This would be my special room, Ebenezer said — my oasis. And this is how I've repaid him."

Janet choked up and started to shiver. Her eyes brimmed with tears. Dr. Pi felt sympathy for her and reached in to hug her.

"Is all the art in this room Ebenezer's property?"

"Yes. Everything here; even the Cole and the Church in the parlor belong to him. Dad was a well-read and cultured man, but he didn't buy art. I lied about that. He liked Renaissance paintings and landscapes but hated abstract art. That's why these paintings wound up in this room."

"I see," Dr. Pi said, assessing the situation. "And the proof of ownership papers?"

"I have the provenance for each painting. When Ebenezer moved out, he didn't take the paintings or papers from our safe. I don't know why. I was angry at him and hid the papers. At our divorce settlement, I told the judge they didn't exist. Years back, when our marital troubles began, Dad amended his will to protect me, claimed that everything in the house was his, and bequeathed the estate to me. The judge honored the will. Ebenezer was only awarded our lake house and its contents. It made him furious; he contested the will but couldn't produce proof the paintings were his. James Morgan had given Ebenezer the paintings and their provenance while he lived, but they were never mentioned in his will, so Ebenezer couldn't prove he'd inherited them. I lied to hurt Ebenezer."

"I can understand why he'd be fuming mad, Janet," Dr. Pi said. "And see why you can't sell these at a public auction house. The papers you hold prove the paintings were purchased by James Morgan Lancaster and gifted to his son, not to you, or to the two of you as a wedding present."

"Correct," Janet said, in a tone of self-scorn. "I've acted despicably. Instead of giving Ebenezer back his rightful inheritance, I kept everything to spite him, and concocted this foolish scheme to make money. I spent thousands on this sophisticated equipment. Wasn't long before I knew I'd made a huge mistake. Been stuck living this lie since."

"But why?" Dr. Pi asked with dismay. "You're an excellent painter. You should be promoting your own unique pieces, not swindling people with fake copies of others' art. That makes no sense, Janet."

"It does when you've run up the debt I have. I've squandered the money in Dad's trust, burned through the prenuptial amount I received, and the alimony and library income I get aren't enough to cover my expenses. Soon, I won't be able to pay the taxes on this place. Foreclosure's right around the corner. I'm royally screwed."

"So, what's stopped you from selling these originals on the black market? I'm sure Anthony could find buyers quickly. What you'd get for just one of these would take care of all your financial needs. You know that."

Janet did not reply. She walked away, paced slowly across the room, and reflected. She stared hard at the chaotic colors of the valuable paintings as she passed them, and when she walked back towards Dr. Pi, he could see tears running down her face. She reached for his hands and held them, looked into his eyes with sadness, and finally spoke:

"My conscience won't allow me to do it," she said, quite subdued. "They're Ebenezer's — his father's gift. I can't let them go. Believe me," she continued, annoyed at her recollection, "Anthony pesters me to sell them all the time. It's the only part of Ebenezer I have left, and I need to hold on to it."

"How'd you get involved in this forgery business?"

"Please don't judge me," she pleaded. "I saw no other way out. I was desperate."

Tobias looked into Janet's brown eyes as tears ran down her face. He tenderly ran his fingers through her short, dark hair.

"I don't judge, Janet. I know life, and what a mess it can quickly become. But this is beneath you. You're a true artist — a talented painter. Your work's as good as anyone's. When did you lose sight of that?"

"When my marriage ended and all of the joy bled out of me," she said, and buried her face in Dr. Pi's chest to cry.

Janet sobbed with great intensity. It seemed she still loved Ebenezer immensely; that love had been buried within, hidden under a stoic, uncaring façade, but it lay there nevertheless, just waiting to be re-acknowledged and re-animated. Quite surprisingly, Dr. Pi also understood that Anthony's love for Janet was identical to — the mirror image of, in fact — the love she felt for Ebenezer. It was ironic, sad, and disheartening that true love of that magnitude could bring such suffering. But this volatile triangle was real, destructive, all-consuming, and its participants would be forever entangled in its tentacles, in the paralyzing grief such strong bonds brought.

Dr. Pi held Janet tightly until she stopped crying. Finally, she composed herself and said with a matter-of-fact disdain, "The former student I dated taught me how to forge. He said he'd read about an eighty-million-dollar forgery scandal in the art world that had gone undetected for years. He wanted to get in on the action. The forger was a struggling artist who lived in Queens and taught math. He had reproduced near-perfect versions of abstract expressionist paintings. The woman who trafficked the fake art was apprehended, confessed to the FBI in 2013, and the artist fled the U.S to avoid prosecution. Ten lawsuits were filed against Manhattan's Knoedler gallery, where the fakes had been sold. Nine were settled quickly. One went to trial, but in the end, the case was settled before a verdict was reached. The gallery closed, but to this day, the art dealer who was fooled into believing the fakes were originals maintains her innocence."

"That's an incredible story, Janet. Seems impossible that something like that could happen."

"It's a true story, Tobias," Janet said, reflecting on the trouble that could lay ahead for her. "My former student said he became obsessed with making some quick money this way. He had already perfected his craft for over two years when he got me into it. Of course, I never showed him this tack room or these original pieces because I didn't trust him. He was equally fascinated with art robberies, especially with the mysterious art heist at the Isabella Stewart Gardner Museum. After sex, I'd pick his brain. He'd devised a way to dissect the sequencing of a master's strokes and also assess the exact formula for blending colors. Showed me how to age a canvas to a specific period. With that knowledge, all I had to do was practice. Piece after piece, I perfected my forgery skills."

"Well, it's good that this art was acquired legally."

"Yes," she said. "What's not good is what I've done."

"Why isn't the Picasso on display inside the house?" Dr. Pi asked curiously. "That's got to be your most valuable painting."

"I don't like it. That ugly bull doesn't fit the parlor's décor," Janet replied and softly smiled. But then she said honestly, "Picasso and Warhol, believe it or not, are easier to copy than Cole and Church. Less involved."

Janet paused, reflected, and, suddenly aware of all her wasted effort, said, "I was getting really good at it too. Now Anthony's been arrested. Soon they'll come for me."

"Perhaps not," Dr. Pi urged. "He loves you too much to turn you in, and I know nothing about this. Just dismantle this room immediately."

"You're not mad?"

"A little disappointed, and definitely surprised. But you haven't murdered anyone. And those who purchased your copies, what they thought was stolen art, are equally guilty — and stupid, I might add. Just stop forging. Get rid of all this crap. Paint your own stuff."

"It won't bring in the money I need," Janet insisted. "For taxes, maintenance, heating costs, insurance. Plus, I owe over three hundred thousand dollars and can't manage the payments anymore."

Dr. Pi was shocked at Janet's admission but responded optimistically. "There are legal ways to restructure debt and lower payments. This property must be worth eight hundred grand."

"No. Not that much," Janet rebutted.

"Close to it," Dr. Pi insisted. "And it's in fabulous shape. I'm certain some bank will offer you good refinancing terms. The rates are very low now. I'll help you find a good deal."

"With my poor credit, I doubt it, but thank you. I'd appreciate your help."

"May I invest in your art?"

"You already have."

"A more substantial investment? Say yes."

Janet's eyes lit up. "Yes," she said, relieved.

"Good. I'll loan you twenty thousand at zero interest. To pay your most pressing bills. That'll hold you until you can refinance."

"I don't deserve it," Janet said, chastened. "Why such generosity when I've lied and deceived you? You should be furious. Tell me to go to hell."

"Probably should," Dr. Pi said sharply. "Let's just say I foolishly believe in your innate goodness. And your talent. And your ability to rebound. Though I really should be running like crazy from you."

Dr. Pi shook his head, held her firmly, and looked into her eyes.

"Can't believe you were ready to swindle me too. In on this with Anthony from the start. I thought this elegant artist was genuinely interested in me, and all along she was reeling me in like a hooked fish to sell me a forged Andy Warhol. Do you know how little a literature professor makes?"

"You're anything but poor," she said. "The real problem is I didn't offer you the right paintings. Had I tried to sell you the Cole or Church, you would've hocked everything for it, begged, borrowed, and stolen to own either."

"Maybe begged and borrowed, but never stolen. I follow the commandments."

"Oh really? You know, I'm now tempted to let you have them for free. But only if you'll do me a big favor."

Janet pulled Dr. Pi closer, unbuckled his belt, and they made love on the hard pine floor.

***

It was late, and Dr. Pi's reignited lust made him lose his desire to drive home. Eager for his company, Janet convinced him to stay. They trekked back to the house, had more coffee and a snack in her kitchen, and then cuddled under a blanket in the parlor. The loveseat faced the Cole and Church paintings. Dr. Pi stared at them intensely, and the bucolic peace of the Hudson Valley captured by each artist in its natural, pristine splendor elevated his spirit. Majestic art raised the mind's expectations far above the realm of human frailty and failings. Dr. Pi reflected sadly on the situation Janet had gotten herself into. She was in a predicament and could possibly wind up behind bars. Would Anthony betray her? Would the police trace the forged pieces back to her? Why had she stopped believing in her art? Her own paintings were beautiful and inspiring. If only she'd continued to trust that others would appreciate her vision, love *her* art, perhaps she wouldn't be in this mess. But it was obvious to Dr. Pi that the circumstances of her chaotic life, especially her reckless spending and volatile relationships, had contributed to the wayward path she'd followed. He was sympathetic and wished to understand and comfort her. He had a hunch that Janet carried a deep guilt that crushed her daily and had done so for a very long time.

"Janet," Dr. Pi uttered softly, "I know this is personal, and if I'm totally out of line please tell me to mind my own business, but I'd like to know more about your two abortions and the strain on your marriage when Anthony re-entered the picture. Can you trust me with what actually happened?"

"I can," she said swiftly. "If I were a Catholic like you, I'd confess to a priest and ask forgiveness. I'm tired of lying to myself. I'm totally to blame for everything. It's really simple. Here's the painful truth."

Before she could continue, Dr. Pi said, "Save it for a reverend then. That may be the catharsis you need. I'm sorry for meddling, for pushing you back to that trauma. Forget it. And forgive me."

"I don't want a priest or reverend," she said adamantly. "I want *you*. I'm the architect of my own destruction. I want you to hear the ugly truth, Tobias. It's not complicated at all."

Janet took a sip of her coffee, placed the cup back on a small end table, grabbed Dr. Pi's hands under the blanket and held them tightly, then began to speak.

"I betrayed Anthony. That's where it all began. I seduced Ebenezer, not the other way around. I was bored, eighteen, and stupid, and swayed by Ebenezer's looks and money. Anthony didn't deserve it, but I broke his heart and didn't care. The night I told him we were over he was so torn up about it I slept with him one last time, just days after I'd slept with Ebenezer for the first time. I was promiscuous and foolish. Anthony went away, I married Ebenezer, and soon after found out I was pregnant. I chose to have an abortion. Ebenezer urged me not to; he was heartbroken I did. Of course, I never told him I'd slept with Anthony just days after I'd agreed to marry him. I didn't know who the father was, so I kept my secret and terminated my pregnancy. And it happened a second time, just twenty months later. Ebenezer was on a long business trip to Europe. I'd left college, was bored at home, and on a visit to town I ran into Anthony. He'd married a Bronx woman, moved back upstate, and settled just outside of Cooperstown. We had lunch at Danny's, got a room at the Cooper's Inn, and had sex the entire afternoon. He asked me to leave Ebenezer, and said he'd leave his wife. The two of us could start a new life together. He was convincing and sincere, but I couldn't do it. He left the hotel angry, and after that day I didn't see him again for several years.

"I didn't use protection when I was with Anthony. Mindless, careless, call me what you will — I was all of that, and worse. Well, when Ebenezer returned from his long trip, I slept with him repeatedly, and weeks later I learned I was pregnant. And again, I panicked and decided to have another abortion. I tried to hide it, wasn't going to say anything to Ebenezer, but he saw the pregnancy test I used, which I had left in the bathroom, and asked me about it. He was very happy, wanted us to have our first child, but I said I wasn't ready. It broke his heart yet again. He was furious, asked why I was being so selfish, and didn't talk to me for days. I couldn't tell him I'd cheated on him and might be carrying Anthony's child. After the second abortion, I fell into a deep depression. Ebenezer was supportive, made sure I had counseling, and lined up someone to look after me when he went on his long trips."

"So, everything you told me about Ebenezer's cruelty is false?" Dr. Pi asked.

"Yes," Janet said directly. "Everything. I've accused him of things he never did. He never dated an eighteen-year-old to make me jealous or tried to take this house from me. He's been kind and generous since the first day we met. I lied to gain your sympathy."

"There's no restraining order?"

"None. I lied. He did show up at the house once shortly after the judge's ruling. Demanded I return his art. I called the sheriff, who came and escorted him away. He never bothered me again."

"What about the miscarriage when you finally decided to have a baby? Was that a lie too?"

"No. That's true," Janet said forthrightly. "For three years, I couldn't conceive and in that time I had a miscarriage. Once again, Ebenezer was supportive, attentive, and kind. He never blamed me or my lifestyle, or my yoga exercises. I shouldn't have lied to you about him. He's a good man. Always has been."

"So you didn't seek the divorce?"

"No. He divorced me. Years after we'd had Phillip and attained stability as a family — we really were happy for quite some time — Anthony came back into the picture, and I cheated on Ebenezer again. This time he found out, and he told me it was over. My life quickly went downhill after that…"

Janet's voice constricted when she said that, and she stopped speaking and looked down, refusing to meet Dr. Pi's eyes. He put his arm around her under the blanket and they stayed that way for a long time, in silence.

It was clear to Dr. Pi that Janet's heart was heavy with the weight of all she'd done, the mistakes she'd made, and lies she'd told. He resolved to do his best to understand and offer comfort. He knew his own life was riddled with failure as well. Imperfection bound us all, and tolerance and forgiveness were the only virtues that could save us from the madness of our messy lives. In Janet, Dr. Pi saw something of himself. Both of them had battled through life's incomprehensible maze and made serious mistakes along the way. As he did his best to offer comfort, he knew he must continue to love unconditionally. It was the one precious human action, for it was love that could elevate us from the finite to infinite. Dr. Pi's heart swelled with compassion, and he looked deeply into Janet's eyes.

"I'll do everything I can to help you," he said. "You're not alone. I won't abandon you. Let's figure out how to steer you out of this mess."

She nodded and thanked him. That night they slept intertwined like a leafy, growing vine. But they did not make love.

CHAPTER 40

In the morning, Janet spoke candidly about her situation. She felt terrible about lying to Dr. Pi and putting his life in jeopardy. She was now very sure that Anthony had orchestrated both the earlier ambush and the latest attempt on Dr. Pi's life. She recognized now that Ebenezer had had every right to leave her, for she'd taken advantage of his goodness and not deserved it. And because of the guilt she carried at having betrayed Anthony initially, she'd overlooked how far he had fallen. It shocked her to realize that his behavior had deteriorated to the point where he could consider murdering someone out of pure rage and jealousy. While Janet agonized about her errors, Dr. Pi thought of how he could best help her.

"I should've told you last night," he said, "that yesterday afternoon I met Ebenezer at the police station. Seemed like a nice man, just as you described."

Janet was shocked and asked: "Why was he there?"

"Well, he was briefly considered a suspect in my assault. But DNA analysis has cleared him, as I mentioned. We talked, and I offered to buy him a drink. He gave me his card."

"Why's he up here?" Janet asked, bewildered. "He never visits till spring."

"He's been fixing up the lake house. Said he's headed back to Manhattan soon."

Janet was suddenly subdued. She stared ahead for a bit and then glanced down at her coffee cup. She seemed deep in thought, no doubt feeling the strain of all the pain she'd put Ebenezer through.

"I think you two should try to reconcile," Dr. Pi ventured. "Moving ahead amicably, as good friends, like Joanna and I have, is the right thing to do. You have a wonderful son together. You can make amends, Janet. Despite the hurt, something tells me he'd be receptive."

"I doubt it," she said quickly. "He should hate me. I've ruined his life."

"Youthful mistakes. You're a loving woman and mother. I've seen it. You said he was kind in your times of trouble. I'm certain he'll forgive. You need to heal."

"I do," Janet said, and reached for his hands.

"Let me text him. We'll show up together."

"No, please. It's too risky. He'll be angry."

"He won't," Dr. Pi said confidently. "He craves the peace as much as you do. Trust me. We all do."

There was a brief silence. Janet looked bewildered.

"Okay," she said at length. "I'll go." She covered her face with her hands and began to cry again. He wrapped his hands around her and kissed her head.

"Shhh, shhh," he said softly. "It'll work out. I'll be there for you."

***

While Janet showered, Dr. Pi found Ebenezer's business card and called him. He explained he'd be headed home soon, might not return to Cooperstown for a while, and wondered if instead of a beer he could drop by for a late coffee. Ebenezer seemed happy to hear from him, said he wasn't busy, and gave him directions; his lake house was at the end of Cooks Road, off Route 28. Dr. Pi considered asking Ebenezer if Janet could visit with him but chose not to. His instinct told him Ebenezer wouldn't mind, and if he did, they could both just leave. He thought it was a chance worth taking. Janet needed the peace, a chance to start to heal from what he'd recognized was still a big wound, and he was sure Ebenezer carried regrets of his own that he wished to get beyond. Dr. Pi anticipated that his presence would serve as a buffer, the needed catalyst to make the reconciliation happen. He told Ebenezer he'd be there around noon.

Janet came down a half hour later dressed impeccably. She wore a beautiful, long, red-and-blue striped woolen skirt, a navy-blue blouse, and snug, high black boots. Her make-up and hair were done perfectly. Judging by her look and attire, Dr. Pi knew this meeting meant the world to her. In her arms Janet carried several cotton blankets, and Dr. Pi wondered what these were for.

"I've decided to give Ebenezer what is rightfully his," Janet announced happily. "Would you help me take down and wrap up the Cole and Church paintings?"

Dr. Pi was surprised but recognized the appropriateness of her action, one that could pave the way to a brighter future between her and Ebenezer.

"Of course," he said happily. "That's a wonderful gesture, Janet."

"And he can also have the Picasso and Warhol. They're his. He acquired them and can do with them as he pleases. He can pick up his father's pieces whenever he likes. They mean nothing to me anymore. None of this does. He can even have this property. I destroyed Ebenezer's happiness, his peace of mind, the loving family he did his best to build. I'm culpable and crave his forgiveness. Even if I wind up in jail for the wrong that I've done, as long as I have his support, I can endure what's coming."

Dr. Pi was moved by her confession, and relieved that she'd come to terms with her past turmoil and was ready to move beyond it.

"I understand perfectly, Janet. Be glad to help you," Dr. Pi said enthusiastically. "Let's get started. I told Ebenezer I'd stop in around noon. That gives us plenty of time to get these paintings properly protected for transport. I'm sure he'll be more than surprised at your loving action."

"Ebenezer deserves them. He's a good man. The father of my beautiful son. I want nothing more than to shed the guilt I've carried. If he can't forgive me, I understand. But I must try."

"Forgive yourself first," Dr. Pi said.

"Thank you for filling my emptiness with love. You've helped me more than you know."

He took the blankets from her hand, put them down, and then reached in and gave her a long hug. "Let's do this."

In less than an hour, the four paintings were wrapped carefully and loaded in Janet's car.

CHAPTER 41

At a quarter past noon, Dr. Pi pulled his A6 into Ebenezer's narrow driveway, and right behind him Janet followed in her Beamer. She parked next to him and waited some minutes before exiting her car. Suddenly she had some misgivings, her emotions overwhelmed her, and she felt like backing out of this and driving back home. Ebenezer came to the door to greet Dr. Pi, who'd gotten out first and knocked. The look of surprise on Ebenezer's face was nothing compared to his visible happiness when he recognized Janet's Beamer. Dr. Pi spoke immediately, hoping to allay the moment's awkwardness.

"I know this seems strange, Ebenezer. Forgive me for not being totally honest over the phone. Coffee's not why I came. Janet wanted to return your property. Thought I'd help her do that."

Ebenezer did not speak right away. He was baffled, completely taken aback. Ebenezer's bright blue eyes watered, and his expression softened.

"Thanks for helping her. Glad you both came."

Ebenezer opened the door wide, stepped past Dr. Pi, climbed down the front steps quickly, and approached Janet's car. He waved to her lovingly, motioned for her to step out, and when she did, he embraced and held her tightly without uttering a word. Janet was speechless also. She squeezed him and held on in complete disbelief.

Dr. Pi looked on, mused joyfully, and smiled. In the bright sunshine, their loving embrace glowed with an ethereal calm and splendor, as if two spirits that had been wrenched apart by unforeseen misfortune had suddenly found each other again and desperately grasped the peace missing since the other's departure.

"Welcome," Ebenezer said, as he looked into her eyes. "So good to see you, Janet. Come."

He held her hand, and together they joined Dr. Pi on the landing.

"The coffee's ready," Ebenezer announced.

"I brought your paintings, Ebenezer," Janet said. "Will you help me bring them in, Tobias?"

Ebenezer remained silent, and Dr. Pi realized there was much they needed to iron out in private. Right then, he knew he wouldn't stay long, just long enough to help Janet through the meeting's initial awkwardness.

"Sure thing," Dr. Pi replied and walked back to retrieve the paintings with her, while Ebenezer cleared a spot for them in the front room. With meticulous care, he unwrapped the paintings and leaned each one against the far wall, then folded and returned the blankets to Janet. She placed them on a small couch.

"Thank you," he said sincerely. "It's very nice of you to bring these to me. I appreciate it."

"You're welcome," she said. "I wish I'd never kept what wasn't mine."

Ebenezer said nothing further. He reached for her hand and ushered her to the table.

***

After Ebenezer served coffee, Janet reached into her bag and handed him several documents.

"Those are the ownership papers and purchase receipts for all the art. I hid them and denied they existed in court. They prove the pieces I brought and your dad's collection, which I'd also like to return, are your property, not mine. I apologize for how I behaved at the settlement, Ebenezer. You didn't deserve it. I acted cruelly. I'm sorry for many things. You had every reason to want to leave the marriage. I hope you can forgive me."

As Janet spoke, her voice thinned. She was on the verge of breaking down. Dr. Pi didn't anticipate Janet being so forthright, but he was proud of her, for it took guts to make that admission. Ebenezer saw her distress and reached for her hand. She gave it as tears pooled in her eyes.

"I'm the one who should be asking your forgiveness," Ebenezer replied and squeezed her hand tenderly. "I gave up on our marriage and shouldn't have. Mere bumps on the road I could've endured."

"I betrayed you," Janet admitted. "I'm a despicable person."

"No. Perhaps you made a poor choice. We all do. Perfection's a fancy. Just not possible in this world."

"I acted terribly," Janet insisted. "And I'm truly sorry."

She started crying heavily. As Ebenezer consoled her, Dr. Pi left the table and entered the bathroom but could still hear their conversation.

"You're a wonderful person, Janet. You gave me the only priceless gift I've ever been given — our Phillip! He and you have been and still are my treasure. My *only* treasure. Not that art.

"I should've worked harder to save our marriage," Ebenezer concluded. "I regret not holding on. Not envisioning our family's future happiness. Not plowing through our temporary turmoil and seeing our coming joy. If you can forgive my failure, and the pain I've put you through with the divorce, I'll move ahead a happy man."

"I've never stopped loving you," she said adamantly.

"Or I you," he replied and placed a gentle kiss on her forehead.

Dr. Pi exited the bathroom when he heard the conversation cease. He told them he needed to drive to Manhattan. His daughter had just texted him that her dog was very sick. Dr. Pi shook Ebenezer's hand firmly and wished him well. He hugged Janet tightly. He felt strange, as if he'd reached the end of a tumultuous story — one whose characters waited in purgatory with Dante and wondered if they'd ever see paradise.

CHAPTER 42

Dr. Pi drove east on Route 20, then took Route 145 towards the Catskills. He knew there was much more Ebenezer and Janet needed to iron out alone. He placed his iPhone to charge on the passenger seat.

Dr. Pi stopped for gas in Cobleskill. He went to the bathroom and grabbed a bag of chips and some water. Before pulling back out on the road, he texted Constance: "Headed down, sweetie. Love you and Tank. See you soon."

When he crossed the Rip Van Winkle Bridge in the late afternoon and saw the Hudson's majesty, Dr. Pi was overcome with sadness. The beauty of the cold, distant river filled him with dread. Its waters were restless, perpetually unsettled, stirred by strong winds — not unlike his own hectic life or Janet's. He reflected on Janet's tumultuous past, the consequences of her decisions, and the heartbreak she'd experienced. He couldn't judge her because he knew all too well the strange things that love, and our emotions, make us do; he was aware of the bizarre and costly decisions he himself had made which had plummeted him into despair. Like Janet, who'd not been able to sever her relationship with Anthony once and for all, and who had let that get in the way of her marriage, Dr. Pi realized he'd held on to the memory of his first true love, Jennifer — the one for whom he had memorized Shakespeare's sonnet — much longer than he should have, and that this had damaged his relationship with Joanna right from the start. He'd not given Joanna all his heart initially because his romantic yearning for Jennifer was still there — in the songs he'd written her and continued to sing, in the joy she'd brought him, which he lamented losing. He wasn't mature enough then to see that Joanna had sacrificed everything for him — leaving college at nineteen to have Christopher, putting her life on hold to try and make him happy. In contrast, Jennifer had broken off their relationship, left him heartbroken, and not looked back. Just as Anthony kept creeping back into Janet's life to disrupt it, Jennifer haunted Tobias's every waking moment, so from the outset Dr. Pi didn't build a strong enough foundation for his marriage to go the distance. Though his love for Joanna had grown steadily and he had become a devoted husband, Dr. Pi's initial casualness about their relationship didn't reassure her that she, and *no other*, was the only one who mattered, the only woman he truly wanted. The first cut *had* been the deepest, Dr. Pi realized, for him and Janet, and the wound had crippled each.

Dr. Pi recalled that after his divorce, and the emotional trauma their separation brought, he and Joanna had forged an enduring friendship based on respect and a mutual belief in the eternal grace of God. The only way forward was to forgive, be open-minded, and continue to hope for and move towards something better. It seemed to him that it was right for Janet and Ebenezer to embrace each other again, to put past pain behind them, and seek a healing empathy for one another. Where that left his own relationship with Janet was uncertain; however, everything about Janet and Ebenezer's meeting seemed right, appropriate, and Dr. Pi hoped it would bring each something good, fulfilling, and energizing.

As he drove off the bridge, Dr. Pi recalled how quickly he'd fallen under Katerina's romantic, powerful spell the previous December, and how crazy he'd become while longing for her love. In those first few weeks after *Yellow Bird was* published, when he was riding high, she'd inspired him, and he'd purposely overlooked how young she was while he'd fantasized about starting a new life with her. He'd sent her two Christmas gifts that hadn't even arrived, and then he'd learned she had someone. Even *that* hadn't deterred him from continuing to communicate with her. He knew he was important to her — she'd *told* him so — but he couldn't fathom why, or what void he filled in her life. Nevertheless, he realized her inspiration was *still* alive within him, and the mere thought of that connection made him feel less lonely.

Once in Brooklyn, Dr. Pi spent a frustrating half-hour searching for parking; after circling the block six times, someone pulled out directly in front of Constance's apartment, and Dr. Pi slipped his car into the tight spot. He had several flashbacks to living in the city; each day had been a battle, a struggle, and though he loved and appreciated people, competing with so many for even the smallest of things — a parking spot, a seat on a bus or subway, an open lane while in traffic, even a place in line at the supermarket or DMV — frayed his nerves. Moving to Pleasant Hills had been liberating. Not having to deal with crowds and the aggressive hordes of people had been like escaping from a perpetually raging fire. But now here he was again, years later. It was his daughter's turn to deal with the daily madness, expense, and ridiculous social rigmarole of city life.

He climbed the narrow, rickety steps to Constance's second-floor apartment swiftly. The pungent smells of cigarette smoke, cooking food, and basement dampness rose through the building's seams and assaulted him on the way up. Once inside, he held Constance in a tight embrace for a full minute. When he finally pulled away, he noticed a visible sadness in her eyes.

"How's Tank?" he asked.

"Not good," was her quick response. "He's not eating or drinking. Looks like he's given up."

Constance walked her father into the small living room, and he saw Tank curled up in a ball in his little bed. As soon as Tank heard Dr. Pi's voice, he raised his head and perked up his ears. His big, soulful eyes gleamed a greeting, but Dr. Pi could tell he had almost no energy. Tank brought his small head back down, but his eyes stayed riveted on Dr. Pi. Constance picked him up and removed the warm blankets wrapped around him. She tried to get him to stand on his thinned legs, and Dr. Pi realized how much weight he'd lost since the last visit. Tank had difficulty standing, yet his tail wagged from side to side as he continued to look up at Dr. Pi. Constance picked him up again and placed him in her father's arms. Dr. Pi held him firmly and gently rubbed his bony head.

"You've got to drink and eat Tank," he said lovingly. "You're withering to nothing. We're going to get you better."

Tank continued to wag his tail and rested his head in the crook of Dr. Pi's arm, never taking his eye off his old friend.

"He really loves you," Constance said. "Bernardo says he's letting go. He says we should make him as comfortable as possible. Seems he's lost his will to live."

Bernardo, Constance's boyfriend, was working at the restaurant and would stop by later to meet Dr. Pi and have dinner with them.

"We need to get him to the hospital," Dr. Pi said. "I'll pay for it. He's dehydrated and needs attention. Come on, we have to get him there as soon as possible."

Constance agreed and put Tank's coat on to keep him warm and comfortable for the ten-block journey. Before long, Dr. Pi drove with Tank and Constance to the VERG animal hospital. He dropped them off out front, found a parking spot in front of an isolated warehouse two blocks away, and walked to the hospital quickly, battling a blustery, nasty wind that ripped through his leather jacket. Soon, he sat in the waiting room next to Constance, talking more encouragement to Tank, who cuddled on her lap almost motionless.

"We're gonna get you better, little guy," Dr. Pi urged. "Don't give up, Tank. You'll be a hundred percent soon. Trust me."

Constance remained quiet and gently rubbed his head and long ears. She kissed him often, and each time she raised her head back up, Dr. Pi noticed the tears that pooled in her beautiful hazel eyes.

The vet came to take Tank inside, but first she indicated that they had to pay at the front desk for the preliminary treatments and an overnight stay. Dr. Pi told the vet to take Tank in, and then walked to the desk. It would cost $1,837 just to secure a bed. The previous time Tank had been sick, Constance had paid over five thousand dollars to get him better, money she'd had to charge. Dr. Pi pulled out his phone and saw that it was 8:38 p.m.; he called Chase Bank, waited a few minutes to talk to a representative, told her about the large charge he was about to make, and then handed his credit card to the clerk.

He signed, took his receipt, rejoined Constance, and tried to reassure her. "They'll do everything they can, sweetie. We have to try."

"I know. But he's in bad shape."

The vet came back and informed them that Tank was resting comfortably for the time being. They'd run some tests to check his kidney values. They'd know by the following day how best to proceed.

"Call us late afternoon," the vet said. Constance and Dr. Pi agreed to and drove home, where they ate a simple supper when Bernardo arrived. The three chatted for over an hour. Dr. Pi found Bernardo a warm-hearted, wonderful young man, exactly as Constance had portrayed him. Most of their conversation focused on Tank's illness, but they also talked about Bernardo's relatives in Mexico and about soccer, his favorite sport. After Bernardo left, Constance and Dr. Pi retired to bed early.

Rather than calling the next day, they drove to the hospital before noon to see how things stood. The vet walked them upstairs to the sick ward for a visit with Tank. They found him sedated and cuddled under blankets in a small metal cage. He was hooked up to an IV, and by his head there was a small container of drinking water. Tank's eyes were half-closed, and his bony little body rose and fell slowly as he breathed. The barking, whining, and whimpering of the other sick dogs was constant and unsettling. It was easy to get agitated amidst that noise, stemming from the fear and pain of several sick animals. The vet said Tank had been given a sedative so he could rest.

Constance and Dr. Pi accompanied the vet to a consultation room on the ground floor, and it was there she told them of the seriousness of Tank's condition. They couldn't treat him until they could draw a blood sample to see how his kidneys were functioning. The problem was that they'd been unsuccessful in locating a vein because of how skinny and dehydrated he was. The only possibility left was an experimental and costly procedure, which could kill him — cutting into his aorta.

No sooner had those words come out of the vet's mouth than Dr. Pi was looking at Constance and shaking his head no. There was no way they'd agree to subject Tank to such pain; there was no guarantee it would work anyway. Both Constance and Dr. Pi agreed right then that the best and most humane thing to do was to put Tank to sleep. The vet agreed and explained the process and told them that Tank wouldn't suffer. The cost of the euthanasia and cremation would be included in the amount Dr. Pi had already paid. Constance agreed to return with Bernardo later that evening to be by Tank's side while he was put to sleep. Dr. Pi mulled over whether he should stay and see Tank one last time, though he was certain it would break his heart to see him again so weak and vulnerable.

Dr. Pi drove Constance back to her apartment. They ordered lunch and talked about Tank. Each reassured the other that the decision to let Tank go was the right one. Neither wanted him to suffer. Tank had lived a good life. They'd all loved him, and he had loved them back. What more could they ask?

As Dr. Pi was holding Constance's hand and reassuring her, his phone rang. At first, he couldn't fathom who it could be and thought about letting it go to voicemail. But then he recognized it was from the sheriff's office and picked up.

"Hi Dr. Pi," the familiar voice said. "This is Sheriff Wilks. Are you home in Pleasant Hills?"

"No Sheriff," Dr. Pi responded, looking up at Constance briefly. "I'm in Brooklyn visiting my daughter."

"Oh," Wilks said. "I have some sad news. There's been a shooting and a fire at the Brayden property this morning. Janet was shot dead. Ebenezer's at Bassett Hospital in critical condition. The shooter is still at large. The attack may be linked to your assault."

"Oh my God," Dr. Pi uttered, grasping the enormity of what he'd just heard. He looked at Constance, who was staring at him with worry. "That's just not possible. I left them both at Ebenezer's lake house yesterday afternoon. Does Phillip know?"

"Yes," Wilks said. "We called him. He's coming up later today. Would you stop in when you return home? We need to establish a timeline of the couple's whereabouts in the hours before the incident."

"I'm leaving now. Should be there in five hours."

"No need to rush back," Wilks replied. "Stop in tomorrow. Please be vigilant."

Dr. Pi hung up, looked at Constance with a pained expression, and told her a good friend had been shot to death.

"Oh my God, Dad, I'm so sorry," she uttered. "This happened in Cooperstown?" She was shocked that any violent crime could occur in such a beautiful town.

Dr. Pi nodded grimly. "I have to leave, sweetie." He gave her an intense, prolonged hug; she felt his body tremble. "I love you so much. Sorry about Tank. And that I can't stay to say goodbye."

"It's OK, Dad. Bernardo and I will be there with him. Tank knows how much you love him. Please drive safely."

"I will, sweetheart."

CHAPTER 43

By 6:30 p.m., Dr. Pi was road weary; though he'd only been driving two hours, he felt as if he'd been in that seat all day. With every passing mile, his head felt more like a wood block that was having nails driven into it by a broad-headed hammer. His back ached; his legs felt like heavy logs. But it was the mental strain that weighed on him the most. He agonized about Janet's death, couldn't accept he'd never hear her voice again, or feel her warmth. He tried listening to some classical music to relax, but gave up and shut off the radio in frustration.

Just as he turned onto Route 145 near the Catskills, his phone lit up and beeped. He pulled into a Valero gas station, parked, and saw Constance's text:

Tank is gone. Bernardo held him, and I rubbed his back. Hope he's in a better place.

Dr. Pi was overcome with emotion.

Glad you were both with him, sweetie, he texted back. *Really sad we couldn't do more. Made no sense to put him through more pain. He's no longer suffering. You gave him a good life. Love you.*

Please don't text and drive, Dad.

I never do. Parked at a gas station. Text you when I get home.

Dr. Pi shut off his phone, closed his eyes, thought about little Tank and the joy he'd brought him the previous autumn when they'd toured around in the Monte SS on beautiful sunny afternoons. He recalled walking him and how excited he got when Dr. Pi served him his dinner. Most of all, Dr. Pi remembered how Tank would come by his side when he was writing and whine gently when he needed to go outside. The good memories converged with images of Tank at his weakest point, huddled, listless, in that metal cage in the hospital. Dr. Pi also thought of his last moments with Janet and broke down to cry. Why hadn't he stayed with her and Ebenezer? Maybe she'd still be alive, he thought. For minutes, he felt as bitter and empty as he'd ever felt.

Dr. Pi dozed off, woke suddenly fifty minutes later, collected himself, and drove on in a zombie-like state. When he finally got home, he was emotionally depleted. He cut the engine, grabbed his phone, and texted Constance just one word: *Home.*

Thanks for coming down, Dad, was her instant response. *Love you.*

His big house was dark, had a haunting air about it, for when he'd be away for a while he never left any lights on. But since being assaulted at Council Rock Park, he'd been more mindful of possible intruders out to hurt him, and before entering the house he'd comb its perimeter looking for any sign of a break-in. He knew the home's vulnerable areas and purposely left things specifically arranged so at one glance he could tell if there'd been an intrusion. Mindful that no suspect had been apprehended in Janet's and Ebenezer's shootings, and fully aware that he and not Ebenezer may have been the intended target, Dr. Pi walked around the premises and inspected all of his markers before opening the front door. Everything looked undisturbed, especially the heavy slate rock he'd left at a specific angle atop the basement hatch doors. Initially, he'd placed it there to stop strong winds from blowing the doors open. Now it was part of his inexpensive security system. This was the surest way intruders could enter, if they were intent on doing so, since the hatch doors had no lock, and he'd never felt the need to install one, given the almost non-existent crime rate in Pleasant Hills.

In a short while, Dr. Pi was certain no one had been there, so in the darkness he found the second key on his keychain, unlocked the front door, entered, and then locked it behind him. He didn't perform any of his nightly rituals before bed. He was too depressed, too exhausted even to undress, or cry again. Before falling asleep, he kept thinking about how devastated Phillip would be. He said a prayer, and asked God to save Ebenezer's life, so that the lonely road ahead for Phillip would be more bearable. And then he forcefully buried his head in the pillow, yearning for the air to be snuffed out of him for good so that he could go to Maria, Miriam, Pablo, and Janet, once and for all, wherever they were in the vast, cosmic eternity beyond earth.

CHAPTER 44

When he awoke to his iPhone's alarm the next morning, Dr. Pi noticed there was a direct message from Katerina on his Instagram.

I see both packages arrive in Warsaw post office this morning. Soon I will have. Thank you! I work many hours at the restaurant these days. A very busy time for me. Work twelve to fifteen hours this break to pay for school. Little time for rest or relax. I let you know when I have. Sending my love. (Three red hearts, one smiley face, and a kissy face emoji).

A week earlier, this message would have left Dr. Pi feeling euphoric and propelled him to the stratosphere. Today, however, though he was happy to hear that Katerina's gifts had finally arrived, he felt somber and downcast, for he couldn't stop thinking of Janet.

Dr. Pi went downstairs, turned on his computer, and checked the USPS website. Both packages had indeed arrived and were in transit to Katerina's address. He was relieved because he thought for sure the first package had been lost.

Dr. Pi drank his coffee, shaved, dressed, and drove to Cooperstown. As soon as he reached Richfield Springs, he became aware of a strong police presence. There were troopers at various locations on Route 28, and the closer he got to Cooperstown the greater the number of law enforcement vehicles he saw. Once in town, the number grew even further. He stopped by Schneider's Bakery for some pastries to bring to Wilks, and the conversations he overheard were mostly about the shooting. Residents wondered whether it was a random act of violence, a burglary, a drug deal gone wrong, or something more sinister. The most common phrase Dr. Pi heard was "that just doesn't happen here." One could sense the fear that had suddenly gripped the community. Dr. Pi grabbed his pastries and cookies and walked out.

Wilks was grateful for the pastries. Dr. Pi detailed for him the last moments he'd spent with Janet and Ebenezer. He explained how he'd gone with her to return four of Ebenezer's paintings.

"She wanted to reconcile with Ebenezer, Sheriff," Dr. Pi said. "And to return his paintings. She brought him the purchase receipts and ownership documents proving they were rightfully his. These, she explained, she'd hidden and not disclosed during the divorce settlement. She wanted to make amends, do the right thing by Ebenezer. I thought it a noble gesture, so I went to offer support. Their reunion was wonderful. Peaceful, respectful, and harmonious. They both seemed happy when I left."

"That's good to hear," Wilks said. "I'm glad to know they reconciled, for Phillip's sake. May make this tragedy easier to bear knowing his parents had settled their differences and healed their wounds. That's, of course, if his father pulls through. Hope he makes it. He's under continuous police surveillance at Bassett."

Wilks paused, reflected, and briefly explained what was known and surmised about the shootings. Janet and Ebenezer had each been shot twice in the chest at point blank range with a .45 caliber handgun just outside the barn. Detectives believed the attacker had surprised them as they exited the barn. Janet was killed instantly; Ebenezer survived because the shots had missed his major organs. The attacker then torched the barn and took off. Ebenezer was bleeding profusely but somehow managed to call 911. All he said was, "Fire at the Brayden property. Casualties," before passing out. Fifteen minutes later, the EMT squad and fire trucks arrived, but by then the barn was completely engulfed. Ebenezer was given an immediate transfusion and rushed to Bassett. Janet was pronounced dead on the spot. One of the bullets had blown through her heart.

Dr. Pi listened in horror. He'd never felt such inner rage, and he vowed to get even, if the opportunity afforded itself.

He was startled out of his trance by Wilks's question: "Did Janet ever mention her involvement with Anthony in a forgery scheme to defraud art investors?"

"Yes," Dr. Pi responded. "She did. On the last night I spent with her she told me everything. She brought me to the barn's tack room where she created the forgeries, showed me the equipment she used, and explained how she did it. The room housed a valuable collection of abstract expressionist art — the subjects for her forgeries — acquired by Ebenezer's father, and which she also planned to return to Ebenezer. Said she regretted it *all*. Admitted it was a big mistake. She meant it."

"Oh," Wilks said. "I didn't know any of this." He wrote down these details in a small notepad on his desk and added a series of questions: *Did murder suspect come to destroy evidence in barn pertaining to forgeries? To steal valuable art? To kill Janet and Dr. Pi?* and added: *Suspect may possess a valuable collection of art.*

"Did she mention Anthony had been apprehended by police in Lower Manhattan selling a forged Picasso for fifty thousand to a Wall Street exec?"

"She said he'd been arrested. Never mentioned any particulars. She did tell me Anthony used his mob ties to sell the art."

Wilks scribbled down this last admission, queried in his notepad: *A mob hit? Mob involvement?* and then elaborated further to Dr. Pi:

"Caught selling fake art Janet made. He's confessed to peddling Janet's forgeries. Will likely get ten to twenty years solely for that crime. Maybe life if we can prove he was involved in Janet's murder. Or in destroying evidence. We're not sure if he's the one who ordered the hit, or if it was done independently by one of his henchmen. Now, if the mob is behind the shootings, trying to cover up their bigger forgery enterprise, things do get more complex. Nevertheless, Dr. Pi, regardless of who orchestrated the shootings, it's highly probable that, in addition to Janet, you were the other intended target. It just so happened Ebenezer was with Janet when the two were surprised. Our hunch is they expected you'd be with her."

"I see," Dr. Pi said. "Guess they'll be coming for me then."

"We think so."

Dr. Pi was now sure he'd been a target. He remembered there were two men in the old Ford truck that blocked the road, and one driver tailing him, on the night he'd been surprised when leaving Janet's house. Then there was the driver in the pick-up following him on Route 20 who'd been killed by the jack-knifed tractor trailer on Christmas Eve, just east of the Route 51 juncture. Since Anthony was in custody, he surmised that the third man, the one left, could perhaps be the one who'd assaulted him at Council Rock Park, the same one who'd maybe also shot Janet and Ebenezer. He told the sheriff his suspicions.

"Precisely, Dr. Pi," Wilks said. "That's our best guess too. Anthony's partners in crime are the Trotter brothers, Buddy and Benny. Buddy Trotter, whose identity we have finally verified through fingerprint records, was the driver killed in the tractor trailer accident. If you recall, a shotgun was found in his truck. He could have been looking to kill you that night. You got lucky."

"I did," Dr. Pi said.

"Buddy's got a record a mile long," Wilks continued. "Most recently served ten years of a fifteen-year sentence for armed robbery. The list is long; cocaine possession, aggravated assault."

"So his brother Benny killed Janet?" Dr. Pi asked, a heavy sadness weighing his query.

"That's what we think. Yes."

Dr. Pi agonized in realizing that had he killed Benny, Janet might still be alive.

"We'll get him," Wilks said confidently. "He'll do life, I can assure you. We have some good leads. We believe he's still in the area. It won't be long. From experience, I can say that criminals like Benny don't run off and hide. They return to finish jobs. That's why Ebenezer's under surveillance. But we want to ensure your safety, Dr. Pi. Chances are he'll be gunning for you."

"Let the fucker come. Soon as possible. I'm not hiding from anyone, Sheriff, or going under police protection, thank you."

"I understand, Dr. Pi. Not what I'm suggesting. Just wanted you aware. Vigilant."

"I appreciate the information, and I'll be careful."

"And I appreciate the details you've shared," Wilks said.

"Think they'll let me see Ebenezer?"

"He's still in a coma. But Phillip's there. I'm sure you'll want to see him."

"I do. Thank you, Sheriff."

CHAPTER 45

"If you don't have friends, you don't have anything in this life," Pablo used to say. His father's words echoed in Dr. Pi's mind as he drove slowly through the lovely Cooperstown streets towards Bassett Hospital. He wished to be there for Phillip in this trying time, for he well understood the unbearable pain of losing one's mother tragically and unexpectedly. The violent circumstances of Janet's death added another layer of horror that Dr. Pi could barely comprehend, but he would try to wrap his mind around this loss, for Phillip's sake. Light snow had begun to fall when Dr. Pi parked and then found his way to the ICU corridor. Police vehicles and foot officers were everywhere on the hospital grounds. Wilks had given him a special ID pass which Dr. Pi showed the desk attendant and then the detective who stood outside Ebenezer's room.

"Go right on in, Dr. Pi," the detective said, and he entered. Before uttering a word, Dr. Pi crossed to Phillip, who stood by the bed, and wrapped him in a tight embrace. When Dr. Pi pulled back and looked at his face, he saw a pale, disheveled young man in absolute crisis. The bright blue had faded from Phillip's eyes, and a thick stubble covered his cheeks and chin. Dr. Pi pulled him back in and cradled the back of his head with his hand.

"I'm truly sorry, Phillip. Your mom was a good, good woman who didn't deserve this."

"I know," Phillip said, as he held him tightly, and began to cry.

Veronica, who sat by Ebenezer's bed, came to console him. She was dry-eyed and dressed elegantly in a long brown knitted dress and a beige button-down cashmere sweater, and Dr. Pi noticed, with surprise, that her hair and make-up were perfect.

After Phillip calmed down, the three sat in silence. Next to them, Ebenezer lay hooked up to monitors and an IV drip. Dr. Pi put his arm around Phillip's shoulder.

"Any news on your father's recovery?" he finally asked. Phillip stared ahead and spoke softly.

"His vital signs have stabilized, and his organs are all functioning. Doctors can't say when he'll come out of the coma, but they think he will. He'd lost a lot of blood before they reached him."

"Sounds promising," Dr. Pi said and glanced at Ebenezer. A large breathing tube jutted from his mouth, just like the one the doctors had inserted in Miriam's mouth in her final hours.

"Still could be days," Phillip said. He glanced out the window at the heavily falling snow. Ten to twelve inches had been predicted for that evening, with strong winds and a severe windchill.

"Will you be staying at the farmhouse?" Dr. Pi inquired.

"We'd planned to," Veronica replied.

"Didn't anticipate these nasty conditions," Phillip said. "We can probably make it there, but getting out may be impossible tomorrow. Mom's service at Christ Church is at three. Might as well just stay at a hotel in town and not chance getting stranded."

"I have a friend who can plow you out in the morning," Dr. Pi offered.

"Thank you," Veronica said. "I'd much rather stay at the farmhouse tonight, Phillip. If it's possible."

"Me too," Phillip replied.

Dr. Pi stepped outside and called Randy, his next-door neighbor who plowed for him and other residents in the nearby counties. He explained the situation to Randy and offered him two hundred dollars if he could come this far out to do him this big favor. Randy said he'd do it at no extra cost, and Dr. Pi gave him the address.

"I have a customer in Richfield Springs and can swing by Cooperstown after that," Randy said. "I'll be there by nine. Storm should be gone by then."

"Perfect," Dr. Pi said. "And thanks. These are my good friends. I owe you."

"Nothing but a firm handshake," Randy replied.

Dr. Pi gave Phillip and Veronica the news, and they insisted that he stay with them and that they all go to Christ Church together. Within the hour, before the heaviest of the snow fell, they drove to the farmhouse. It seemed odd that not many days earlier they had celebrated Christmas in Janet's company. But here they were, keeping one another going, with Janet's funeral service set for the following afternoon. Sitting in the parlor after dinner, they were finally able to talk about their emotions, and each took turns speaking about Janet. Dr. Pi glanced at the empty wall spaces where the Cole and Church paintings had hung and fought hard to keep himself from bursting into tears.

Dr. Pi related what had happened when he'd accompanied Janet to Ebenezer's.

"Thank you for being her trusted friend, Dr. Pi," Phillip said with emotion. "She told me she cared for you, and she really seemed happy around you. It'd been a while since I'd seen Mom joke and laugh the way she did on Christmas Day, with you there."

"We did care for one another in the brief time we spent together. But on that last day I realized the depth of your parents' feelings for each other. Their bond was unmistakable. I felt happy for them. I just wish you'd been there to see it."

"And she brought the Cole and the Church to Father?"

"Yes. She said they were his. I helped her. They're at the lake house, along with a Picasso and a Warhol from the barn. Not all was lost in the fire."

"Thanks for telling me. And being there for Mom."

"She was there for me too. Shone a bright light on my life, if only briefly. I'll be forever grateful."

Phillip affectionately embraced Dr. Pi and then walked to the baby grand piano. He played distractedly at first, beginning with some of Chopin's saddest nocturnes. Then he transitioned to Rachmaninoff's more turbulent melodies, and Dr. Pi had the feeling that the young man's soul was purging itself of sorrow with each note. Phillip ended with Mozart, and the somber to liberating, hectic flourishes of the master's *Requiem*. He improvised, combined parts in unusual ways, made the piece his as he spanned through its richness creatively and expunged his deep pain in the way he knew best.

Dr. Pi closed his eyes and saw Maria playing her piano when she was twelve, heard Miriam's words of encouragement, and observed Pablo's warm, appreciative expression, loving the harmony of his once beautiful family with all his heart. Janet was also there in his mind, her spirit, now free, asking that he encourage her son to find strength and move forward. Dr. Pi was sure she was there with them. When he was done, Phillip said goodnight, and walked slowly up the staircase to bed. Veronica said goodnight and followed. Dr. Pi remained on the couch and again stared at the wall with the missing paintings; without the art, the wall looked like a face without eyes, without warmth or expression.

***

Like clockwork, Randy's pickup could be heard plowing the long driveway by nine the next morning. Dr. Pi had fallen asleep on the couch and the rasping plow woke him. He was thrilled to see his trusty friend's big blue GMC pushing the fresh white powder into tall mounds. He freshened up and went into the kitchen to make coffee and breakfast. A half hour later, Phillip and Veronica joined him for a meal of eggs, sausage links, and wheat toast.

The storm, now past, had left a foot of snow on the ground. The sky cleared slowly, and a brisk wind blew. It was a chilly twenty degrees. As the sun suddenly appeared and shone through the kitchen window, its warmth was welcoming. Dr. Pi gazed through the window and saw the charred remains of the big barn, near where Janet had been murdered. He took a long gulp of his hot coffee and let the liquid scorch his throat. A desire for vengeance possessed him, as it had when he'd sought Eddie; the anger was familiar. Though he'd experienced such emptiness before, it was the very first time he'd *truly* desired to kill anyone. He yearned to take the life of the coward who had ended Janet's.

**

The Cooperstown shootings had made the national news, and reporters from several major networks and cable outfits lined up outside Christ Church to report on Janet's service. The police presence alone was overwhelming. Townspeople were used to high security, especially late in summers when high profile baseball personalities filled the Otesaga Resort Hotel. But it was nothing like this law enforcement presence. Detectives, state troopers, and local police were stationed throughout town and on the church grounds, as parishioners and residents gathered to pay their respects. The church was packed to capacity, and some parishioners and residents lined its aisles and spilled outside its central doors, which, despite the cold temperature, were kept open until the service began. Dr. Pi was moved by the huge crowd offering support and recognized how important it was for Phillip to feel the community's love for his mother. Many residents knew and admired the Janet who'd worked in the library, and though most were well aware of the difficulties she'd faced in life (for gossip of her and Ebenezer's divorce abounded), they were there to honor her on this day and wish her wonderful son well.

Reverend Dorset started the service at 3 p.m. Janet's cremated remains were in a lovely red and white ceramic vase atop a table near the pulpit, surrounded by white daisies and chrysanthemums, red roses and carnations, and numerous condolence cards from local parishioners. The reverend spoke of Christ's enduring love and mercy, and he celebrated Janet's life as wife, mother, and painter. "Her talent," he said poignantly, "was a gift from the creator, one which she shared with the world, and through which many were brought joy and inspired into the heavenly realm."

A motive for the shooting had not been established, and few knew anything about the forgery scheme she'd orchestrated with Anthony. In the large audience, only Wilks and Dr. Pi were aware of this. Even Phillip knew nothing of it. As he listened, Dr. Pi understood the truth of Dorset's words, for Janet's art did inspire and elevate. He treasured the pieces he'd bought from her. If only she'd trusted her talent more, and not gotten involved with Anthony in forging art. Hers was a natural and unique talent. The real sadness lay in that she did not have enough time to make amends for her error and build a new artistic future and legacy for herself.

Dr. Pi battled with his conflicting feelings; he yearned for vengeance. His gut feeling was that Benny had done this, and he wanted Benny to suffer for his heinous crime. Though Dr. Pi understood all humans were flawed and deserving of forgiveness, he wouldn't grant Benny that hope. Being caught, brought to justice, and allowed to rot in a jail cell didn't seem adequate. He deserved to die, in unbearable pain, and soon, very soon. As Dr. Pi rifled through these unsettling thoughts, he dug his fingernails into his palm and stared straight ahead. He'd temporarily lost focus on the service proceedings and tuned out the Biblical passages that were being read, but he snapped back to the present upon hearing Phillip's loving voice from the pulpit celebrating his mother's virtues. With a heavy heart, Dr. Pi listened intently.

Phillip's voice trembled as he delivered his mother's sermon. He spoke candidly of how blessed he was to have received her love, and about how supportive she'd been as he pursued a music career, even when their family fell on hard times. He proudly announced that before her death she'd reconciled with his father, who now fought for his life at Bassett. "I love them both," he said poignantly, choking back tears. "They did their best, and always loved me." After a brief pause, he added: "And one another." He asked fellow parishioners to pray with him for his father's recovery.

After the service, Dr. Pi did not want to leave Phillip's side. He insisted that Phillip and Veronica join him for dinner at Alex's New World Bistro on Main Street. He had always loved their food and suspected that the restaurant's serene atmosphere was exactly what they all needed. The two agreed, and Dr. Pi asked Sheriff Wilks to join them. Afterwards, they had drinks at Sherman's Tavern, one of the town's oldest bars. As they were set to leave, both Phillip and Veronica excused themselves to use the restroom, and Dr. Pi was left alone with Wilks.

"I must head home tonight, Sheriff," Dr. Pi said. "I'm worried about leaving them alone. Can you have someone keep an eye on the farmhouse?"

"Of course," Wilks replied. "Been close by them since they arrived. You stayed with them last night?"

"I did."

"And a plow truck from Pleasant Hills, registered to a Mr. Rover, passed by early this morning, correct?"

"Yes, that's my friend, Randy."

"I figured. We have police cameras on the premises. Security ran the plates as soon as the truck was spotted. A state trooper is stationed less than a minute away. They're safe. Rest assured."

"Thanks, Sheriff," Dr. Pi said, relieved. "I appreciate knowing that."

"Just watch your back in your neck of the woods."

"I'll be ready if Benny shows," Dr. Pi said, and casually drank his beer.

Wilks sipped his beer. "Any trouble, I want you on that phone, understood? I'll call if I learn anything."

"Sure, Sheriff," Dr. Pi said. "I'll be fine."

Before leaving Phillip and Veronica, Dr. Pi promised to visit Ebenezer the following Wednesday evening. Hopefully, he'd see them there. By then, he hoped he'd be out of his coma.

Before leaving town, Dr. Pi got one more drink at The Black Sox Bar and Grill. He wanted to scope out the premises where Anthony used to work. He yearned for a surprise, any surprise. Janet was on his mind, and the beer's buzz made him feel invincible, belligerent — eager for a fight. But the bar was dead — just one old man in military fatigues drinking whiskey at the counter's far end, a lanky, reserved bartender, and himself. He ordered a beer and drank it slowly, stared at the counter, and glanced up occasionally at the bartender, whose face was glued to his phone. Dr. Pi's mind churned with angry thoughts. He knew Anthony had friends there and wondered whether the bartender knew him, Buddy, or Benny. If so, he wanted him to let Benny know he wasn't hiding, or afraid of anyone. He replayed Benny's assault at Council Rock Park in his mind and agonized about not having landed a crippling blow to Benny's head. Why hadn't he finished him?

He finished his beer, paid, and left. He walked around town to sober up before driving home. All of Cooperstown was blanketed in snow, and the sight of it, pristine and glimmering, raised his spirits. He headed towards Council Rock Park. He hoped Benny would show up to confront him, as he'd done once before. When he reached the park, there was too much snow on the stairs to descend to the famous arrow or sit on a bench and wait. He stood there for quite some time, glanced around, and stared at the lake waters in the distance. It was dark, but the perimeter lights revealed its outline, and he could hear the soft lapping of waves against the shore.

Suddenly Dr. Pi felt cold, so he walked briskly towards his car, observing parked police cars at each street corner he crossed. There'd be no battle tonight, he thought. An hour had passed, and his buzz was gone. Exhausted, he got in his car and drove home carefully. As he hooked left onto Route 20 at Richfield Springs, he saw four police vehicles with their red and blue flashing lights in the corner Sunoco, parked in front of the McDonald's. Sirens approached in the distance, and as he drove west on the two-lane highway, two state trooper cars passed him at high speed headed east. He found a classical station on the radio and focused on the dark road. This day had been long, depressing, and dreary; thinking of Phillip's loss was suffocating. He thought of Janet and the pleasant days they'd shared, but the shock of her death weighed on him. He knew this day would stay with him as long as he lived and became ever more aware of how little time anyone had on this earth to make a difference. He felt grateful that he'd meet a hundred new students in the coming week. It'd be another opportunity to impart knowledge and wisdom gained through harsh experience to young minds in need of guidance. He'd be ready Monday, he vowed optimistically. *This is what I live for*, he thought. *I'll be ready.*

CHAPTER 46

Pleasant Hills had gotten much more snow than Cooperstown, and the wind had created high drifts all around his house. Dr. Pi pulled into his driveway, listened to the engine's hum a few minutes, and then shut it off. He walked around the premises and performed his routine inspection. The back hatch doors were completely covered in snow, and there was no sign of a break-in anywhere, so he went inside and started his routine, charging his phone, preparing for bed, putting on his Netflix universe documentary, and finally trying to fall asleep. But a nervous agitation kept him awake.

He wondered what would've happened had he flown to Poland to meet Katerina and not gotten involved with Janet. Would she still be alive? It was, after all, his arrival in Janet's life that had aggravated Anthony, as Janet had mentioned, and led him to conspire with the brothers to scare Dr. Pi away. Suddenly, he felt enormous guilt and profound regret. He pulled the covers off, grabbed his phone, and combed through Instagram. He needed an escape from his crushing thoughts. He found it odd there was no message from Katerina acknowledging receipt of her gifts. He scrolled through her page and stared intently at her most sensuous photographs and videos. This action served as a calming, soothing narcotic. Right then, he understood why his students used their phones as self-medication for their anxieties and felt profound empathy for them. He vowed to be more tolerant of their needs from then on.

Scrolling through Instagram made him sleepy, less agitated. He put down his phone, shut off the bedroom lamp, and fell asleep by the glow of the TV screen while the show's narrator explained the magnificence of the sun's corona and how powerful solar flares could disrupt communication satellites and our technological world, should their intensity persist for a long enough period of time.

Dr. Pi dreamed of flying with Katerina from Moscow to Irkutsk. In the dream, they huddled together on a crowded airplane, surrounded by families and small children. Katerina inched closer to Dr. Pi and kissed him, telling him she'd try to be a good wife and make him happy in the coming years. As they chatted and snuggled, a stewardess approached, and when Dr. Pi looked up, it was Janet speaking in Russian to Katerina and asking what they wanted to drink. Dr. Pi's heart sank. He felt ashamed, guilty that he'd left Janet, declined her invitation to come for Christmas dinner, and chosen to fly to Poland instead. Suddenly he was in Katerina's apartment, and she had a big diamond engagement ring on her finger. He held her hands and told her he wanted to raise another family with her, in Irkutsk. She could return to America with him, get a student visa, and finish her degree, but the goal would be to return to her home city as soon as possible. When he spoke to her in the dream, it was already in fluent Russian. He kept telling her, in Russian, that he'd retire, live comfortably on an excellent pension and the proceeds from the sale of his house. Once they were living together in Irkutsk, he would write novels, while Katerina would become a professional pianist, play in Russian, European, and American orchestras, and travel the world sharing her musical gift. Their children would have all the freedom and support they would ever need to become successful artists, writers, or musicians, depending on their skills and interests.

Soon, he was no longer talking to Katerina, but to Constance, to Christopher, then to Dean O'Rourke, then to Bellows, telling them all, one at a time, that these were his plans, that as long as Katerina loved him and wanted him as badly as he wanted her, there should be no obstacle. *Why not?* he asked everyone in the dream, multiple times. *It can happen!*

Just then, his phone rang. It buzzed and vibrated. Sleepily, Dr. Pi picked up and mumbled, "Hello."

"We caught the bastard, Dr. Pi," Sheriff Wilks said.

"What?" Dr. Pi asked, as he severed himself from his dream.

"Caught him with a cheeseburger in his mouth," Wilks said excitedly. "Trying to recruit an accomplice at the McDonald's in Richfield Springs, about three hours ago. We just booked Benny. You there?"

Now wide awake, Dr. Pi replied, "That's great news Sheriff! So that's what the commotion was at the Sunoco."

"The .45 was in his van, along with some paintings taken, we assume, from Janet's barn before he torched it. The local man he tried to recruit heard his proposal, went to the men's room, and called police. So, you can rest easy."

"I will, Sheriff."

"Benny's missing a front tooth and a canine. Forensics will do a DNA analysis in the morning. Need you to stop in to file charges against him in your assault case."

"Wednesday night, okay?"

"Yes. See you then. He'll serve a very long sentence if I have anything to say about it. Good luck with school."

"Thanks, Sheriff," Dr. Pi said, ended the call, shut off the lamp, and wondered how he could return to his pleasant dream.

He tried but couldn't fall back asleep. Awake and wired at 2 a.m., he went downstairs and sat at the kitchen table to eat a bowl of cereal. It irked him that Benny had been apprehended in such an uneventful way — eating a cheeseburger at McDonald's, while his van was parked outside, with the murder weapon and other incriminating evidence just sitting there, waiting to be found by the police. It was not what he'd envisioned happening. Anti-climactic, for sure, but it seemed almost poetic, really, for such a scoundrel and lowlife.

Dr. Pi reflected on the missed opportunity to give Benny what he deserved. He finished his cereal, placed the bowl in the sink, and grabbed a big, bloody piece of raw red meat from the bottom of his refrigerator. Prime Angus steak. Next, he filled a plastic bottle with water at the sink. Finally, he walked into the dining room, pulled open a nearby door, turned on a light, and stepped down a rickety staircase into his basement with the meat and water. He snapped his right fingers three times — it was a custom, a powerful signal, always necessary for him to invoke the Trinity whenever possible. Immediately, he heard hectic movements from within a large metal cage that sat on the basement floor. He greeted his pals, a fierce, dynamic duo, ravenously hungry female rats, whom he'd named Sarah and Sabrina (after two of his closest childhood friends), trained to dine on raw flesh, and to be vicious on command (the finger snapping let them know that food would follow). They kept each other company and Dr. Pi safe in his comfy home. This was his security detail lately, if ever any visitor chose to enter uninvited. What Dr. Pi had learned in rat lab at college while studying psychology was very useful; in fact, every scrap of knowledge he'd ever learned had proven necessary for daily survival. A little Pavlovian conditioning had done the trick. Whenever Dr. Pi took a long trip, he'd leave the rats plenty of water to avoid dehydration, but no food; it was the food deprivation, and not knowing when they'd be fed next, that kept them ravenously hungry and vicious. Of course, he knew he couldn't deprive them too long or they'd attack one another.

Dr. Pi pulled open the cage's feeding tray and placed the hefty piece of meat on it. He pushed the tray in and watched happily as his dutiful friends devoured their meal. They bit either end with scissor-sharp teeth, tugging and gnawing at the bloody piece till just bone was left. Even then, they continued to chew and tug at it. In less than ten minutes, nothing remained. Dr. Pi filled their separate water containers. Contentedly, he watched Sarah and Sabrina suck their individual nipples, the way young toddlers do their milk bottles and pacifiers.

Dr. Pi rose and walked towards his old, asbestos-covered furnace, which was six feet away from the steps leading out of the basement to the outer hatch-doors. The furnace operated with the precision of an eighteenth-century German clock, its pressure gauge perfect at twenty pounds, and its hum pleasing in that chilly basement. He glanced at the floor and stared intensely at the peril which Benny had avoided. After Dr. Pi's assault at Council Rock Park, Randy had lent and helped him set up one of his prized possessions — a formidable and deadly bear trap whose teeth were like a shark's, and whose torque could crush through a human shin bone like it was a stick of butter.

How sad that Benny hadn't come to visit, Dr. Pi thought. This is where he should've wound up, trapped like Poe's Fortunato in the catacombs, an animal in unbearable pain, screaming, bleeding, and begging for his life, and waiting in darkness and utter terror for Dr. Pi to open the basement door, turn on the light, slowly descend the stairs, snap his fingers three times, and bring his hungry pals Sarah and Sabrina over to introduce themselves.

Benny being devoured alive while begging for mercy would've proven a proper punishment, a vengeance that Poe would have approved of and that would have spared New York taxpayers the expense of keeping him caged in perpetuity.

Dr. Pi went back upstairs and lay awake in bed till morning. At dawn, he loaded the rat cage in his Audi's trunk, drove ten miles out of town, found a huge, forested field, and released Sarah and Sabrina into the wild, snow-covered wilderness. He planned to dismantle and return Randy's bear trap later that afternoon.

CHAPTER 47

Standing in front of the classroom on Monday morning felt strange to Dr. Pi. It reminded him of how he felt years earlier on his first day back at teaching after his mother's funeral. So much had happened over the break that he wondered whether he'd ever again muster the optimism needed to inspire students. With Janet gone, his world felt strangely empty. He knew his job was to make students think, reflect, evaluate, and conclude intelligently — precisely what he needed to do with his own experiences. But where would *he* even begin to assess what he'd just lived through? He did his best that first morning, spending a little more time than usual listening to student introductions, then briefly outlining for them the semester's plan. Yet the energy wasn't there, and there was nothing he could do about it.

He thought about Janet continuously as he walked home to lunch. His emotions were conflicted; though he'd forgiven her for the falsehoods she'd told him, he had trouble understanding why she'd feed him such a litany of lies. It had all been so unnecessary. From the outset, he'd been frank with her, appreciative of her art, grateful to be in her presence. She had to have sensed his receptiveness. She didn't need to portray herself a victim at Ebenezer's expense to win his sympathy. He felt humiliated at how easily Janet had hoodwinked him, how systematically she'd smashed through his stalwart confidence that no one could fool him. He'd certainly been taken in by her lies and was appalled to recognize his weakness and the weight he'd given to her words. He'd sensed something didn't feel right, but Janet's physical charms and his pervasive melancholy had made him ignore his gut feelings.

His phone rang and seeing that it was Constance, he answered.

"Hi sweetie. How's everything?"

"Bernardo and I are doing great. Thanks, Dad. Was just thinking about you. Wondering how you are."

"Oh I'm fine, sweetheart," Dr. Pi said, almost choking on his words, for his soul was in agony and felt like a shattered vase. He recouped and continued: "Getting a new semester started. You know how much I love my students. Just finished classes."

"Well, I was just thinking how nice it'd be if we all visited Christopher and his family this spring. Spend a little time together. Play some music like we used to. I miss that."

"I do too, sweetheart," Dr. Pi said, his eyes tearing. "That's a fabulous idea. Let's make it happen and surprise him. I miss spending time with you two. Bernardo will love Vermont."

"Oh, and Pixie will too," Constance said, with a wink in her voice.

"Pixie?"

"Our new dog. A gift from Lena. She's a handicapped Chihuahua with one bad eye, but so loveable, Dad, and resilient — like all us females!"

Dr. Pi laughed and rejoiced for a moment, forgetting his troubles. "That is so true," he said, reflecting on how resourceful, and determined Constance was. "Well, that's wonderful news. Glad you've given Pixie a home. Give her a big hug for me. Can't wait to meet her. Can we Facetime tonight and plan our get-together? I just got home and am going to make lunch."

"Sure," Constance replied. "I know Christopher will be thrilled to see us. I'm excited, Dad."

"Me too. Love you sweetie. I'll call you later."

"OK. Love you too," Constance said and hung up.

***

On Wednesday afternoon, Dr. Pi drove to Cooperstown, saw Wilks, and learned that Benny had confessed. Anthony had indeed ordered the hit and barn burning; Janet and Dr. Pi had been the targets. In return for guilty pleas in the Council Rock Park assault on Dr. Pi, Janet's brutal murder, and the attempt on Ebenezer's life, Benny would receive a life sentence, with possible parole after serving thirty years; for ordering Janet's murder, the arson, orchestrating the forgery enterprise, and numerous other crimes, Anthony would get life without parole. Formal sentencing would take place in Manhattan in early April. An interesting fact gathered, which led to Benny's arrest at the McDonald's, was that he'd been trying to recruit someone to help him kill Dr. Pi in Pleasant Hills. Wilks grinned as he relayed this information.

"He was afraid of you — of kung fu professor. Figured an extra set of hands would do the trick."

"It wouldn't have helped him," Dr. Pi said confidently. "Wish he'd come. I know I'd feel better right now, though I'd be the one in the slammer."

"He'll get his," Wilks said reassuringly. "There are lots of rats in federal prison."

"I'm sure," Dr. Pi said. "But not like the ones I had ready for him."

***

An hour later, during visiting hours at Bassett, Dr. Pi sat with Phillip by Ebenezer's bed and talked about the crime and about Ebenezer's road to recovery. Veronica was not there, but Dr. Pi didn't ask why. Ebenezer looked physically wan and worn, and the nurses kept coming in with his medicine and to check his vitals. The good thing was that he was awake, and his mind was clear, even if his body would take weeks to be fully functional again. Phillip planned to stay with his father through his recovery. It was clear as the conversation ensued that Phillip now knew about his mother's clandestine affairs with Anthony. Ebenezer spoke forthrightly about Janet's mistake; however, he was not accusative but understanding and forgiving. Dr. Pi sympathized with Ebenezer's "survivor's guilt" because he'd felt it himself, first when Maria died, and later when he lost Miriam. None of it was Ebenezer's fault. Nevertheless, Dr. Pi didn't speak on this score; he just listened.

"Janet and I had just gone to the barn," he explained, "to dismantle the equipment, and protect the valuable art for transport to the lake house, when we heard a vehicle coming up the driveway. Janet recognized the burly man as one of Anthony's close friends. He pulled out a gun, instructed us to load the art into his van, which we did at gunpoint, and then he turned and shot us both. I fell forward in severe pain and became disoriented but heard our assailant rush past us. Minutes later, he rushed past me again, smelling of gasoline, jumped in his van, and disappeared down the driveway. I'd kept my head down and remained motionless. He'd apparently doused the barn floor in gasoline and set it ablaze. Before passing out, I managed to call 911. Can't remember anything else."

"Very glad you made it Ebenezer," Dr. Pi said. "Phillip has my number in case I can help either of you with anything."

"Thank you, Tobias. The sad part," Ebenezer continued, "is that the farmhouse may be taken from Phillip and auctioned off to pay back the art investors who Janet and Anthony swindled. Plan to talk to my lawyer to prevent that. Perhaps strike a deal with the court."

"All I want is Mom's art," Phillip said. "The pieces she created while inspired. Ones she made when we traveled the world together."

"They're beautiful," Dr. Pi interjected. "She showed me a few. Original."

"Yes," Phillip said. "That's when Mom was at her best. And how I'll remember her."

CHAPTER 48

His students called it *ghosting* when a person with whom you've had communications on social media suddenly disappears, stops engaging, or purposely ignores you. To Dr. Pi, it was a curious term, like much of the new language used to relate, explain, or understand interactions using modern technology — selfies, emojis, posting on your page, creating a profile, getting followers, or following influencers. It felt strange when Katerina went completely offline because she disappeared when Dr. Pi needed her the most. The winter days were draining, the memory of Janet's death was still fresh, and his own children were far away; their planned get together in Vermont was not until spring, and a lingering loneliness had set in.

The afternoons were short and dark, many overcast or permeated with constant cold and falling snow. He'd get home from classes, office hours, or meetings, take a brief nap, cook, watch some news, a hockey game perhaps when there was one, read a little, and before long it'd again be time for bed. Katerina had disappeared without letting him know whether she'd opened his gift boxes. In one of her last direct messages, she'd said she'd been working fifteen-hour days at the restaurant to save money for school and hadn't had the time for anything else.

Dr. Pi was a patient man. He understood Katerina's difficult situation, and working fifteen-hour days for anyone, anywhere, seemed excessive to him. So, he remained hopeful after a week, even after two, had passed that soon he'd hear from her. He was certain she'd love his gifts and that they'd bring her joy. But after a full month had passed and she hadn't answered any of his direct messages, a little gloom set in, and he began to wonder what had happened. Had the new man in her life found out about the packages and forbidden her to communicate with him? He couldn't be sure, but after a while this "ghosting" began to hurt. If she could no longer message him, why not just say so, and then vanish for good? He would understand. But no explanation was provided, no closure to what they'd shared, as in a physical relationship when someone tells you to your face, "It's over!" Such a declaration was preferable, even though it hurts deeply, to this "ghosting" stuff. Disappearing like this seemed outright cruel.

***

February came and went, and then a long March passed. These cold days with little sunshine, persistent snow squalls, and general natural bleakness wore on Dr. Pi's spirit. Sometimes at night before bed he played guitar to cheer up, but after a few songs he would lose his desire to sing. Meanwhile, he went in each day, taught writing and literature, and did his best to be inspired, to work on his new novel when he came home, but once his Russian muse had gone offline, it wasn't long before he stopped writing completely. Inspiration left him, and his turbulent emotions plunged him into depression. He also hadn't heard from Phillip in quite some time. At first, they'd talked twice a week, then once a week. Now, they hadn't spoken in three weeks. He was afraid to call or bother Phillip and figured that he needed time to heal emotionally and to reconnect with his father. Often, Dr. Pi thought of driving to Manhattan and inviting them to dinner but changed his mind.

A few Fridays, Dr. Pi met up with Curt Warrens for lunch at the Copper Kettle. Once, late in March, Dr. Bellows had joined them. Heather seated them in the coziest booth and brought their menus and drinks. Bellows knew the whole story and congratulated Dr. Pi on his heroic foiling of the Council Rock Park assault, while Curt shook his head in disbelief.

"Didn't know you were an action hero, Tobias," Curt said.

"I'm not. Just lucky the sucker didn't pull the trigger faster and blow my brains out."

"Wilks told me you wished you'd finished Benny off," Bellows said. "Don't let it haunt you. You did what you thought was right. No one can see the future."

"Janet would still be alive had I finished him," Dr. Pi insisted.

"Wasn't your fault," said Bellows. "He'll pay. Believe me, he'll pay. Not many places to hide inside the penitentiary."

Dr. Pi drank his beer and understood Bellows's implication. One way or the other, Benny would get his. Though he was happy to learn that Dr. Pi had pursued Janet, despite the strange events that had unfolded over break, Curt was curious about what had happened to Katerina.

"So did your Russian girl get your gift?" he asked.

"Gifts," Dr. Pi corrected him. "I sent two. The second for Russian Christmas."

"Two! Wow! Now that's making a statement. And?"

"They both got there," Dr. Pi said. "Finally."

"What did she think?" Curt asked.

"Don't know," Dr. Pi said. "She disappeared. Went totally offline. Don't know if she even opened them."

"She ghosted you? That's crazy."

"Strange, isn't it?" Dr. Pi asked. "Gone. Goodbye."

"You should've flown to Poland to see her," Curt said.

"Yes, I should've gone," Dr. Pi said, gulping down what remained of his beer. Tears pooled in his eyes, as he contemplated how going to Poland, rather than getting intimate with Janet, may have changed her fate.

When Heather arrived with their lunches, Dr. Pi ate his fish and chips in silence, which was unusual for him.

CHAPTER 49

"April is the cruelest month," the ironic opening of Eliot's *The Waste Land*, had stayed with Dr. Pi since he'd first read the complex poem as a college sophomore. They were strange words because he'd always equated the month with optimism and renewed hope. April ushered in spring, nature's rebirth, and the promise of coming summer. In April, one celebrated Christ's resurrection and marched onwards with a positive purpose. That had held true for him till this April, when disillusionment hit him like an iron pipe in the gut, as it once did to Eliot. Just as Eliot wondered how Western civilization would recover from the Great War's devastation, Dr. Pi pondered how to cope with Janet's death and the lingering gloom left in him. This April was "cruel," as he battled pervasive emptiness. Being alone made it worse.

After classes on Thursday, April 4, Dr. Pi drove with a heavy heart to lower Manhattan for the formal sentencing of Anthony and Benny. The day marked the fifty-first anniversary of Martin Luther King's murder, a preacher whose words he'd always revered, who'd voiced for a generation, with a martyr's resolve, Christ's teachings of love and forgiveness. Reflecting on King's optimism, despite the racial injustice prevalent in his time, gave Dr. Pi hope that the rage which had lately consumed him could perhaps be erased from his own soul permanently and replaced with God's goodness. He vowed not to allow his inner peace to be destroyed by the hatred he knew he'd feel the next day at 10 a.m. when he looked at Anthony and Benny.

Dr. Pi had respectfully declined Phillip's offer to stay at his Upper West Side apartment and instead had gotten a room at the Waldorf. At court on Friday, he'd sat by Phillip and Ebenezer and heard the judge announce the criminals' punishment. As expected, with no chance at parole, Anthony would die in prison; Benny, however, for cooperating with investigators, could be paroled after serving thirty years of his life sentence.

While the judge spoke, Dr. Pi found it difficult seeing these two disgusting derelicts, standing by their lawyers, dressed in orange jumpsuits, as if unfazed by what they'd done. Anthony was stone-faced, his black hair slicked back with a greasy gel, his beard now long, his heavy jaw jutting out arrogantly, and his eyes occasionally darting around the room, as if he were amused by the proceeding. Benny was a much bigger man, with broad shoulders, a military crew cut, and several gross tattoos around his thick neck — daggers, chains, guns, numbers, and dates — which blended into some mysterious meaning. His vulture's nose stood out because his mouth was small and his jawbone sunken.

Dr. Pi wanted to ask Anthony just one question: *If you cared so much for Janet, why have her killed?* Only someone motivated by jealous rage, Dr. Pi thought, could be so heinous. As he reflected on this, he pondered his own rage, which had consumed him since he'd learned of Janet's murder. He knew how hard it was to keep those angry impulses caged, especially now as he stared viciously at these beasts whom he wished to kill with his own hands.

After the sentencing, Dr. Pi invited Phillip and Ebenezer to lunch at the Waldorf restaurant and they accepted. The three men bonded over their shared grief. Dr. Pi inquired about Ebenezer's rehabilitation, and Ebenezer said he hoped to regain full use of his partially paralyzed left arm. Both men invited Dr. Pi to join them in Cooperstown mid-

June, when they planned to honor Janet's wishes and spread her ashes on Lake Otsego. Dr. Pi said he'd be honored. At one point, Phillip cursorily mentioned that he and Veronica had parted ways. Since he did not elaborate, Dr. Pi did not inquire further.

"What about the farmhouse?" Dr. Pi asked. "Will you keep it?"

"Sure as hell going to try," Ebenezer said, his blue eyes brightening. "That's Phillip's inheritance. It's a complicated mess right now."

"What's the problem?" Dr. Pi inquired.

"Several of the investors that Anthony and Janet swindled have sued Janet's estate. They want their money back, plain and simple. And I can't say I blame them."

"I see," Dr. Pi said. "How many lawsuits?"

"Too many," Phillip said sadly. "About twenty so far. Maybe more. Millions in total. And no one knows where the money from the fraudulent sales wound up. Detectives suspect it's in some offshore account, but it's hard to trace, and Anthony hasn't been cooperative. Probably never will be." Dejectedly, Phillip resumed picking at his food.

"Doesn't matter," Ebenezer said energetically. "They'll get every damn cent back. I promise you that. But that house will never go up for sale. Not if I can help it. My lawyer has arranged to auction off one of my Picassos at a private sale end of this month."

Dr. Pi wasn't aware Ebenezer owned two Picassos. He'd only seen one — the cave bull, which Janet had forged, the one he'd brought with the Warhol to Ebenezer's lake house.

"Dad, that's yours," Phillip interjected. This was the first time he'd heard of Ebenezer's plan. "The stolen money will turn up."

"It may," Ebenezer said. "But all that money won't cover damages. And that painting doesn't mean anything to me. The barn will be restored to its original splendor in Janet's honor. Insurance money from the fire will help us rebuild it. And the painting will fetch a good sum."

"It sure will," Dr. Pi said. "The Cave Bull one we brought you?"

"No. My other Picasso. From his Rose Period," Ebenezer answered. "Painted 'round 1905, and not well-known because it was in a private collection for a hundred years before I bought it. At a small, poorly attended, estate sale in Wisconsin, if you can believe that. Never thought I'd find a Picasso there."

"That's amazing," Dr. Pi interjected.

"Only one other bid. Not many there believed it real. But I knew it was."

"How?" Dr. Pi asked. "Janet said you're an expert."

"His scripted signature was authentic, underlined — though not all are — angled slightly upward, and each letter was spaced consistently and proportionally apart. The best part is what I paid." He smiled, paused, and added: "*Not much!* Let's just say I walked away whistling and smiling."

"Incredible," Dr. Pi said. "A rare piece?"

"One of the rarest. Well, you've seen it, haven't you? It's hanging in my small dining room at the lake house. She sat with us while we had our coffees that afternoon."

"Think I did," Dr. Pi said. "You mean the nude young woman, with a red rose in her long black hair, laying on a couch with an open book?" He thought of Katerina's Instagram post with her long red hair and grey-green eyes sitting in bed holding an open copy of *Yellow Bird*.

"Yes," Ebenezer said. "That's her. Has kept me company the last few years."

"Didn't look like a Picasso to me. Nothing like *Les Demoiselles d'Avignon*."

"Not at all," Ebenezer agreed. "Precisely why I was able to buy it. Few recognized it."

Dr. Pi was shocked that Ebenezer would have such a valuable painting — a museum piece — hanging in his dining room as if it were an inexpensive T.J. Maxx print, but he was highly impressed with Ebenezer's detailed knowledge. "What about the Church and the Cole?"

"I'll never sell those," Ebenezer said with a gleam in his eyes. "They're going right back up where Janet hung them. She had impeccable taste. An eye for elegance. They're the heart and soul of that farmhouse. I want everything maintained as she had it. Starting with that beautiful grand room."

"I couldn't agree with you more, Dad," Phillip said.

"Hope the auction goes well," Dr. Pi added, and proposed a toast to a successful sale.

"'A thing of beauty is a joy forever,'" Dr. Pi said, echoing Keats.

***

After lunch, Dr. Pi checked out of the Waldorf and drove to Brooklyn. He had dinner with Constance and Bernardo and met their new Chihuahua, Pixie. Though her right eye had been damaged by another dog at the pound, Pixie's spirit was strong, and her lively presence in Constance's apartment filled the void left after Tank's death.

***

Teaching this semester became a challenge for Dr. Pi because everything became a dull routine. After classes and meetings, he left campus quickly, didn't feel like talking to anyone or spending an extra second in his office. Once home, he napped longer than usual, often past dinnertime, which disrupted his regular sleep. Instead of cooking nutritious meals, most evenings he made sandwiches, went out for Chinese, ate pizza, or had a bowl of cereal. And while wide awake at three in the morning, he mulled over what he'd lived through, and agonized endlessly about costly decisions he'd made. Not killing Benny at Council Rock Park when he had the chance to was one. He knew the reason he'd not delivered the death blow to Benny's head had much to do with what he'd once done to Eddie and vowed never to do again. It was this haunting episode that held him back from killing Benny, though the consequences of his inaction had proven disastrous.

A deep depression gripped him with a boa's bite, and Dr. Pi gave in to its malaise. For days, he'd stopped checking his Instagram. Katerina had become a phantom. There were fleeting moments when he believed she'd reappear, when he'd nostalgically comb through his many saved photographs of her, and then listen to the Russian songs she'd sent him. But frustration would suddenly wipe away that tiny bit of optimism, and he'd put down his phone angrily, jump in bed, and bury his face in his pillow.

On the night of April 15, he watched the nightly news in horror and saw the great spire of Notre Dame Cathedral engulfed in flames. This iconic structure burned while the world watched, helpless and in dismay. So many art treasures could be lost, so much history destroyed. As he observed part of the roof collapse in real time, Dr. Pi felt sick. This April's cruelty was indeed one he'd never forget. He shut the television, grabbed his copy of *Bleak House*, and read for the rest of the evening. Dickens's stories, he knew, were sad, but in the midst of all the suffering, there was a glimmer of hope, some optimism, something redeeming about individuals, some bright light towards which to walk. That is why he loved Dickens — because he reassured one that human suffering was never in vain. Dickens's words filled one with hope. He closed the book at midnight and felt better. The added bonus was that his eyes and brain were tired from all the reading, so he slept soundly, and in the morning felt refreshed.

Later that day, Dr. Pi found a small ray of light to cheer him. He read what he could about the fire and learned that many of the cathedral's priceless works of art had been saved. But most importantly, Notre Dame's altar, its thirteenth-century stained-glass rose windows, and two pipe organs had survived. He also learned that over a billion dollars had already been pledged to rebuild the beloved cathedral. Its great towers would again stand for future generations to behold — a beacon of art's majesty, beauty, and enduring power.

That same evening, Dr. Pi walked into his office and glanced at Janet's paintings. He remembered the wonderful moments he'd spent in her arms, the peaceful Christmas they'd enjoyed with Veronica and Phillip, and realized that though they were gone, he must treasure those experiences. He decided to call Phillip on the following day. April was only half gone. Perhaps in the days left, a positive outlook was the ingredient needed to recast the great bard's words to "April is the most joyful month."

CHAPTER 50

"Dad's a miracle worker," Phillip said happily to Dr. Pi over the phone. They hadn't spoken since the sentencing. "Got the insurance company to pay for a complete barn restoration. They've been haggling with us for weeks. You believe that? Work will begin later this month."

"That's fabulous news. How'd he manage that?"

"His lawyer, Mr. Wolfsheim, is a hound. Manhattan royalty when it comes to attorneys. Third generation. His grandfather prosecuted gangsters, Dad says."

"Wow. Some lineage! A big shot!"

"Sure is. He's already gotten the go-ahead from police detectives and the fire marshal to remove the barn debris. Sadly, everything was lost, except for the paintings Benny stole, which were found in his van. But the investigations are over. A local contractor is clearing the site now. Dad's also hired a prominent architect to draw up plans from numerous old photographs. An identical structure will go up. And a memorial to Mom will be built where she died."

Phillip's excitement warmed Dr. Pi's heart. Hearing Phillip's optimism lifted his spirits. Finally! A glimpse of April joy.

"Just wonderful news," Dr. Pi reiterated.

"The best part is what it'll be used for," Phillip said.

"An art studio for local artists?"

"Better," Phillip said enthusiastically. "A music recording studio which I'll manage. Hideaway Hills at Cooperstown. Doing the paperwork right now. Already talked with Ivo."

"The famous Russian pianist?"

"Yes. He'll be the first musician to record there. Said he'd do everything he can to help promote our venture. Dad says I'm at the right age to become a businessman. He'll teach me some of the tricks of the trade. He's been very successful."

"He has. Great name. An excellent project. Janet would be proud of you. How's your Dad's rehab going?"

"Better than expected. More feeling has returned to his left arm."

"Fantastic," Dr. Pi said. "When's the private auction?"

"Are you buying?" Phillip asked humorously.

Dr. Pi laughed. "A Picasso? Me? That's for millionaires."

"Well, you're coming," Phillip said. "As our guest. I insist. Next Friday at Wolfsheim's Park Avenue residence, corner of Seventy-Fourth. Dad likes your company. Say you'll come."

Dr. Pi hesitated, quickly searched for a good excuse to not attend, but then reconsidered. He'd vowed to be there for Phillip.

"I'd be honored," he said. "I don't teach Fridays. And my grading's done till finals. What time?"

"One o'clock on the twenty-sixth," Phillip said. "I'll tell the doorman to put you on the guest list.

"Perfect. See you both there."

***

Phillip's news was elevating, and Dr. Pi's despair subsided. The idea of turning the barn into a recording studio was brilliant. It was such a peaceful, quiet, and romantic setting, and he imagined the many talented musicians and singers coming to this cozy, Cooperstown hideaway. Suddenly, Katerina's lovely face flashed in his mind, and he had the irresistible urge to message her, tell her about the studio, and invite her to come record there some day in the future. He'd promise to pay for everything — her flight, travel expenses, recording fees, and provide her with a comfortable place to stay. In his mind, it registered as the perfect plan. The only problem was that he'd sent various messages to her over the past three months, and not one had been answered. Though now gone and so far away, the thought of her still inspired him. Perhaps one day she'd return.

***

Dr. Pi had a dull weekend taking care of household chores, but on Monday he set off to teach with more enthusiasm than he'd had all semester. The thought of seeing Phillip and Ebenezer at week's end and sneaking another Brooklyn visit in to see Constance was a big motivator. He was also excited about teaching *The Great Gatsby* for the first time in years, a novel he'd had a strange relationship with. As a high school freshman, he'd hated it — was disappointed with the story's conclusion and wondered why Fitzgerald had brought Jay to such a tragic end. It was years before he reread the novel when it was assigned in an undergraduate course. By then, he'd forgotten many of its details, and the twenty-two-year-old Tobias had also had his first romantic relationship, which didn't end well. He'd suffered the pangs of lost love and understood Fitzgerald's vision better. The novel's ending still irritated him, but he appreciated Fitzgerald's artistry, his tightly woven sentences, vivid scenes, and perfectly wrought dialogue. These days, teaching *Gatsby* energized him, for he understood its greatness.

On this April morning, he explored with students why readers fall in love with Jay Gatsby — with his loving heart and ability to hold past joy in his mind. To end his lecture, Dr. Pi focused on a key exchange of dialogue:

"'You can't relive the past,' Nick tells Jay; to which Jay responds, 'Why of course you can.'"

Dr. Pi paused and let the clause hang in the room's silence. He smiled, then resumed animatedly:

"What marvelous confidence Jay has. So buoyant and uplifting!" He paused again, then summarized what he thought true: "Despite any coming darkness, harshness, pain, or failed opportunities in human life, one's memory of love — *lived* and *felt* — endures. Past joy lives in memory and has mysterious, magical power. The romantic vision *never dies!*"

When class concluded, Dr. Pi walked home in the bright sunshine. He felt happy, looked forward to having lunch and perhaps doing some writing that afternoon. Suddenly, he felt his phone buzz in his pocket. He stopped, pulled it out, and squinted at its screen. There was a direct message from Katerina on Instagram. He couldn't believe his eyes, and his elated heart leaped to the stratosphere. The emotions which coursed through his soul were the same ones Gatsby felt when casting his loving eyes upon Daisy after a long, five-year absence. He rushed home, sat at the kitchen table, and read her words:

Hi Tobias. I am OK. Thank you for concern and kind messages these many weeks. Sorry you worry so much. I think of you a lot these days. My phone was lost, and I just work long hours at restaurant. Then I found phone but forgot password for Instagram. I try many and none work so I give up. Been long time since I made account. I then used to life without social media and don't miss. I remember password one night and again was able to use account. Saw your many nice messages. I receive your gifts weeks ago. Beautiful gifts, the soaps, and headphones, which I love, and Polish money. I really appreciate. I smile a lot. And your cards and words which I read a hundred times. Thank you so much...

There was more, much more Katerina had written, so many emoji hearts, smiley and kissy faces, that Dr. Pi was overwhelmed with emotion. He felt relieved to know nothing bad had happened to her — for he'd worried a great deal. He was also happy she'd received his gifts and had liked them. But it was strange resuming his communication with her after the long absence. It didn't feel as it once had. She'd been gone three months, and, just as she'd gotten used to life off social media, he'd gotten used to life without her there daily. It was as if they'd been in a relationship and broken up, and though at first the separation had been difficult, especially since he was coping with Janet's death, he'd adjusted and stopped expecting her to be there.

Katerina posted a few Instagram pictures and explained for her followers what had happened and what she'd done in her absence. Like Dr. Pi, many had worried or expressed concern. In one photograph, she stood knee-deep in water on a Pacific Ocean beach, sunglasses in hand and wearing a baby-blue T-shirt with a big tiger's face imprint. She'd traveled to America for the first time and twice to Germany in those three months. Dr. Pi direct messaged her and asked about her trip to San Francisco, and she'd explained its purpose involved getting culinary training. For her restaurant to maintain its prestigious standing, it was essential to have its chefs gain valuable culinary experience abroad. The second photograph showed Katerina sporting the Bose headphones Dr. Pi had sent her. Her makeup and colorful outfit were perfect, and her expression beamed happiness; seeing that contentment warmed his heart. Katerina — his Russian muse — was back.

Throughout the week, Dr. Pi and Katerina shared brief messages. She asked about his writing and music and children; he asked about her chef's training, university classes, and yes, her lover.

Dr. Pi learned she'd left the university and taken a good position as a sous-chef at the restaurant. It was impossible to do both because of the job's demands, so she'd taken a leave of absence from her studies. After he'd asked early in the New Year, Katerina had mentioned to Dr. Pi that she had someone but had not elaborated. Now that she was back, he thought to ask about him again:

Is he still there? Is the relationship strong? And are you happy? I'm only asking because I want to know you're happy and loved.

Yes, he is still with me … He's a good man … he works every day as a driver, he does his best. He does everything in the house. I rarely clean the house — he does. Also, all the worries about the shopping, and cooking — he does the same. Since I cook a lot at work — I don't want to do it even at home ... He, doesn't regret, often gives flowers ... He is a multi-musician, he plays 5 instruments, sings, and composes music.

He sounds like a wonderful man Katerina, Dr. Pi wrote. *You're fortunate to have him to love you. Hold on to him. I wish you much happiness together.*

I'm happy you like him, Tobias.

I do, Dr. Pi wrote earnestly.

The time apart had changed Dr. Pi's amorous longings. His passion had transformed into friendship. He felt happy she had someone to look after and support her — someone who truly loved her! That's what mattered, ultimately — that she felt joyful, appreciated, and loved. In Katerina, he'd found a genuine friend. In Phillip, another. Suddenly, Dr. Pi felt rich, fortunate, and content, as Rochefoucauld's maxim rang true in his mind: *Rare as true love is, true friendship is rarer...*

CHAPTER 51

At Wolfsheim's spacious, elegant Park Avenue apartment, a small group of wealthy art collectors from various countries — Saudis, Indians, Germans, and Japanese, mostly — gathered to bid on the Picasso. They walked around with wine and champagne glasses in hand, picking on the caviar and fancy snacks provided, and talking about their art collections and latest purchases. In a secured part of the room, which was further back and away from the intense sunlight entering four large windows, sectioned off and guarded by two armed attendants, the Picasso took center stage. By it, on the broad table, and leaning on secure stands, Dr. Pi recognized the Warhol, the Rothko, and the Pollock Janet had shown him. The four paintings were front and center, but behind them on either side, and resting on two other tables, three in each, were six of Janet's original paintings. Dr. Pi knew these; he'd seen them at her farmhouse studio when he'd first come over to purchase her art. She never made a fuss over these, despite their obvious beauty and style. There was a colorful intensity in all her pieces, a delicacy of style, a consistency of technique. Three of them showed Lake Otsego in its natural splendor. The lake's vibrant, seasonal personality emerged, as did the rich history lived by natives and settlers on both its waters and shores. But Janet's eyes and masterful hands captured a more ethereal quality, an eternal tranquility and spiritual essence that made the lake sacred. The other three celebrated Cooperstown, on bright, sunny, weekend afternoons in summer, when visitors from around the world came to see its Baseball Hall of Fame and fell in love with its loveliness, its patrons, buildings, and charming streets. Janet captured the town's peaceful, busy ambiance, cozy niches, and the smiling, happy children wearing their favorite teams' uniforms and caps, and carrying souvenir bats and gloves.

Seeing Janet's paintings on display surprised Dr. Pi; he knew right away something special was in store. He'd arrived early, greeted Phillip and Ebenezer, and thanked them for inviting him. He was given a name tag but no bidding number. There were only thirteen bidders there, plus four other guests — Dr. Pi and three representatives from major NYC art museums: the Metropolitan, the Guggenheim, and the Whitney.

Dr. Pi took it all in, so excited to be there and to see Phillip and Ebenezer happy together after all they'd been through. He stood in front of the paintings with them, and Ebenezer informed him they were waiting for Wolfsheim; he'd conduct the auction, but apparently he was in an Uber still stuck downtown in traffic.

"I know all about that," Dr. Pi said. "Might take a while. The noon rush can be rough. Worse today than when I drove."

"A cab?" Ebenezer asked. Phillip smiled at his father's surprise.

"Yes," Dr. Pi replied. "My novel, *Yellow Bird*, tells all about it. I'll bring you a signed copy next time we meet."

"Ah," Ebenezer said and smiled. "You're a writer. Makes sense. I see why Janet liked you. And why Phillip talks highly of you. Painters, musicians, and writers find one another. The love of art is a glue which binds those with similar spirits."

"Couldn't have put it better," Dr. Pi said and smiled. "So, will you read it?"

"Why, of course I will," Ebenezer said. "Be glad to. I'll just pick one up on Amazon later."

"Please don't," Dr. Pi said. "I'd rather give you a gift copy. I love giving that book away."

"Glad to hear it. Generosity defines the soul," Ebenezer said. "In that case, I'll wait. There'll be some gifts handed out here today as well."

"Oh," Dr. Pi remarked. "Janet's paintings?" He pointed at them.

"Some," Phillip said. "You'll see. Mom was a lot like you. Liked giving away her work."

"She was very generous," Dr. Pi said. "Looking forward to seeing who will get those treasures."

Wolfsheim arrived finally and the auction was soon underway. Dr. Pi suspected that the delay had been purposely orchestrated to build anticipation and excitement in the room. Having the bidders spend a little time together, casually discussing their collections over caviar, whet their competitiveness. Wolfsheim stood on a small podium before the paintings, looked around the room with a highly dignified air, and waited for everyone to settle down. He was dressed in traditional Orthodox Jewish garb, an embroidered yarmulke atop a bed of fluffy, curly black hair, with long ringlets spiraling down the sides of his face, and his intense brown eyes peered into his audience. He had a handsome face, with high cheekbones, a strong chin, and thick mustache and beard. At forty, he was already one of the most prominent and successful of all Manhattan attorneys. He hadn't achieved such stature through generosity but rather through tact, intelligence, and savvy as a dealmaker. He wasn't thrilled with what Ebenezer had asked him to do on this afternoon, had tried to convince him not to give *anything* away — there was too much money to be made — but ultimately, he'd relented and set out to make his client happy. For Ebenezer, though money was important and needed, so was his desire to restore Janet's good name, reputation, and, perhaps, legacy in the art world. Wolfsheim knew his commission depended on his ability to raise the stakes and price of this "rare" Picasso. He'd do this, as in the numerous auctions he'd run previously, by making the bidders wait. The longer, the better. It was a proven, winning strategy.

Wolfsheim pounded the gavel heavily and only once. He was in command and certain that by afternoon's end there'd be a record price set, one which the famous auction houses would drool over.

"Esteemed collectors," Wolfsheim said, "I will begin this auction, held in loving memory and honor of artist Janet Brayden by my distinguished client, Mr. Ebenezer Hendricks Lancaster and his son Phillip, by asking representatives from the Metropolitan, Guggenheim, and Whitney museums to step forward."

Two women and a man walked to the podium. Wolfsheim stepped down, handed each of them two official documents, and then returned to his microphone.

"It is my sincere pleasure to announce that each of your museums will receive *two* gift paintings here on display — either a Warhol, Rothko, or Pollock — which I randomly selected for your museums, plus a painting by Janet Brayden, who, at this point in time, is a relative unknown in the art world. However, it is my belief that after this auction, her name will resound loudly and one day be as familiar as these others. Today, she will posthumously receive the recognition she rightfully deserves. In addition, your museums will receive an undisclosed donation from the newly formed Brayden Foundation to maintain and exhibit her art for years to come."

Each of the representatives thanked Wolfsheim, shook his hand, and then retreated to the back of the small gathered crowd. The bidders were getting anxious, seeing that six paintings had already been given away. Only the Picasso and three of Janet's paintings remained. Wolfsheim, sensing their desire to get in on the action, decided to auction off each of Janet's three paintings next. A great manipulator of language, Wolfsheim spoke with self-granted authority, for he was neither an art connoisseur, nor in any way able to predict the future relevance of art pieces.

"Dear collectors," he said warmly, paused briefly, and resumed with a dignified air. "Step forward and glance carefully at the three paintings on the right table beside me. In one hundred years, these unknown pieces, I believe, will be as famous as the Picasso you will soon bid on. Their artistry is unmistakable. Masterful! Just look closely at their elegant, rural scenes. Look at that peaceful, sacred lake. I've never seen one as lovely. Not even by the Dutch or Hudson River School masters. The rich, bright colors of these pieces will be beacons through time, a testament to a humble artist — Janet Brayden, whose reputation you will make today by purchasing them for your grand collections. I'll begin by asking for fifty thousand for the first. Do I hear someone offer fifty?"

"Fifty," said a Japanese investor, an elegantly dressed young woman with an accent.

"Fabulous," Wolfsheim cried. "Do I hear seventy-five?"

"Seventy-five," a Saudi man said.

The investors were hungry. The competition intense. In less than an hour, Janet's three pieces had fetched one and a half million dollars, not bad for the first public showcasing of a relative unknown's art. Dr. Pi was thrilled as the bids soared. He felt proud that Janet's legacy was secure, that her work would finally receive the attention it deserved. He was also aware that the pieces he'd bought from her months back had suddenly escalated in value. Of course, they would remain priceless to him, sources of inspiration on his office walls, for he had no intention of ever selling them.

In the end, the early-period Picasso garnered from a Bombay investor, Mr. Ganguli, a record one hundred and seventy-five million dollars — fifty mil for Uncle Sam, naturally, a cool twenty-five for Wolfsheim, thanks to his manipulative eloquence, and a solid one hundred million for Ebenezer. The Metropolitan, Guggenheim, and Whitney museums each received five million dollars with which to create a special wing named after Janet, displaying her art and preserving her legacy. Ten million were used to fund the Brayden Foundation in Cooperstown, most of which would support art, music, and writing programs at local high schools and scholarships at local colleges. Twenty-five million were used to settle all the pending lawsuits and any debt incurred by Janet to maintain her farmhouse. The remaining fifty million were put in a trust for Phillip, money which Ebenezer made readily available to him for his business ventures, travel, or whatever he wished. But what was most important to Ebenezer was making sure that what remained after taxes of the one and a half million dollars Janet's paintings had earned would be donated to Cooperstown village for the maintenance and preservation of Otsego Lake, which she had so cherished.

CHAPTER 52

On Friday, June 14, a beautiful and bright sunny day, Dr. Pi drove happily down Route 20 towards Cooperstown. He arrived at The Inn at Cooperstown, where he'd made a reservation, at 4 p.m., and after he'd settled in, he phoned Wilks. He invited Wilks and his wife to dinner at the Inn, and an hour later the three sat comfortably, perusing their menus. The couple ordered Angus steak specials and Dr. Pi his usual fare — fish and chips. While Dr. Pi drank his Ommegang beer, Wilks inquired about his teaching and writing.

"Just have one summer class, a little house-painting money. Back working on my second novel. Hadn't written for several months, but now I'm in the swing of things."

"Nice to hear," Wilks said. "Returning to some normalcy, after what you went through."

"Yes. Nothing compared to what Ebenezer and Phillip have suffered, but the past few months have been tough. Meeting them tomorrow, in fact. Haven't seen either for several weeks, but they've invited me fishing."

"Wonderful," Wilks said. "Glorious weather for it. The lake will be crowded. Tourists have been filing in all month."

"Phillip plans to spread Janet's ashes on the lake. Then, they've promised to show me the progress on the barn restoration."

"Wait till you see the farmhouse grounds and barn. Almost completely framed. Local Amish carpenters. Exceptional craftsmen. Ebenezer insisted on hiring community talent. He's always supported this town financially. A truly generous man."

"Sure is," Dr. Pi said, having witnessed Ebenezer's generosity first-hand at Wolfsheim's. "Can't wait to see it."

"Did you hear the best news of all?" Wilks asked, smiling, and glancing lovingly at his wife.

"What's that?" Dr. Pi inquired.

"The Black Sox Inn closed in late April. Ebenezer bought the building and has donated it to the Cooperstown Library to promote the arts in Janet's memory."

"That's fantastic," Dr. Pi said, and joy filled him.

"They plan to run a small coffee house on the ground floor," Mrs. Wilks said. "Exhibit works by local artists on the second and run an art school on the third. So many will benefit. All costs will be covered by the Brayden Foundation.

"Perhaps you'll teach a course in creative writing there, Dr. Pi, for us soon-to-be retired seniors. I've read *Yellow Bird*, along with several fellow nurses at Bassett. We've loved it, and someday hope to ask you questions about the story. Would you consider doing a reading at the library later this summer?"

"I'd love to, Mrs. Wilks."

"Fabulous," Mrs. Wilks replied. "And just so you know, from the day you paid for my husband's pastries at Schneider's, he's considered you a member of our community. Ever consider moving to Cooperstown when you retire?"

"Be honored to, Mrs. Wilks. It'd be a dream come true. Though retirement's not in the picture just yet."

Wilks raised his beer to toast Dr. Pi. "You're a member of our town, Tobias."

"I'm grateful. I've made many friends here."

At eight that evening, Dr. Pi said goodbye to his guests and read for a couple of hours in bed before falling asleep. He looked forward to spending the following afternoon with Ebenezer and Phillip.

***

On Saturday morning, Dr. Pi was up early. When he stepped onto the Inn's broad porch, he took in the splendor of his surroundings. It was sunny and mild out, and a light breeze felt good on his face. Though it was just past ten, tourists were out and about. Dr. Pi headed towards the Hall of Fame and soon found a perfect diversion, a huge book sale on the grounds of the public library. For over an hour, he became absorbed in perusing all kinds of books, until he finally found a literary treasure — a first edition copy of Wharton's novel *A Son at the Front*. He purchased it for fifteen dollars and kept looking around for other bargains, but he soon quit and meandered to Council Rock Park to read for an hour. He sat by an old willow next to the water and tried to immerse himself in Wharton's narrative, but soon became distracted. He stared at the calm lake and reflected on the day he'd left Janet and Ebenezer together. It had seemed to Dr. Pi that a harmonious future lay ahead for them and Phillip, yet that promise had been cruelly snatched away in a single act of violence. Dr. Pi lamented the chaotic randomness of lived experience and the absence of any real harmony, let alone security, in this life. It all seemed so unfair. Life itself was an infuriating shell game. Still, despite knowing this painful truth, what options remained? To give up entirely, to quit trying, was not worth considering. One could only battle on, searching and striving forward against all odds. Tennyson's words from "Ulysses" suddenly came into his mind, revived him — the heroic heart *must* maintain an unfaltering optimism. The only logical answer was *"To strive, to seek, to find, and not to yield."*

***

Dr. Pi greeted Ebenezer and Phillip punctually at one. The dock was crowded, and the lake was so busy with small sail and motorboats that it took almost an hour for them to find a quiet, cozy place to fish. Ebenezer maneuvered his mid-sized outboard expertly towards the lake's deepest part, where he knew most of the fish would be; he found a serene spot, a quarter mile from the eastern shore, and cut the engine. The sun shone intensely on the glassy water, and in the distance the low-lying hills surrounded and embraced the lake as a loving parent would a young child. It had been ages since Dr. Pi had gone fishing; an entire lifetime had passed since his uncle Cristóbal, Miriam's brother, had taken him to Yankee Lake in upstate New York one summer when he was seven. Ebenezer helped him set up his gear, and Dr. Pi lowered his line into the water. It took him a while to feel comfortable, to get the hang of operating his reel, but his mind and all his senses were awake to the beauty of the scene.

The three men shared casual conversation while they waited patiently for a bite. Ebenezer's physical therapy had been successful; he'd regained feeling and movement throughout his left arm. Phillip would resume working part-time for the philharmonic in September, until they could find a suitable replacement; he planned to start recording at Hideaway Hills before Christmas. Dr. Pi talked optimistically about teaching summer class and finishing his new novel, *My Russian Muse*.

For well over an hour, the three men spoke little and concentrated on catching fish. Finally, Phillip's voice pierced the stillness with a shrill boast — he'd hooked something, and it felt fairly big. He started reeling in his line carefully, then pulling more aggressively, until a flapping, squiggling yellow perch soared above the water. It was about a foot and a half long; Ebenezer eyeballed it as at least a two-pounder. The three men rejoiced briefly. Phillip waited for it to calm down, carefully unhooked it, and threw it back in the water. Not long after that, Ebenezer hauled in a three-pound whitefish, and after its wild struggle subsided, he stood up, held it up in admiration, and flung it back in the lake. He admonished and blessed it happily as he did this, telling the creature to "go make your second chance count."

By three-thirty, most of the other boaters and fishermen had headed back to shore, and Phillip told his dad he was ready to release Janet's ashes. Phillip brought out the vase holding Janet's ashes, said a prayer, and then emptied the contents into the water. There was no wind, so the ashes fell gently on the lake's surface, as if Janet's spirit wished to remain close to those she'd loved. Phillip stared at all the ashes as they dissolved and disappeared. Finally, he turned to Dr. Pi and spoke.

"Why do you think she gave up on her art, Dr. Pi?"

"Phillip," Ebenezer admonished. "That's unfair. She made a mistake, son. We all do. We're beyond that now. Let it go."

"I don't ask disrespectfully, Dad," Phillip said, his voice thinning, as if he were about to cry. "I just don't understand. She was a great painter, as good as anyone. I remember you telling her that often when I was a boy. How could she not know it?"

Dr. Pi bowed his head, thought hard, and finally answered him compassionately:

"All artists question their talent, Phillip. They doubt their abilities, and compare themselves to others, and sometimes convince themselves that they're not good enough — that their contribution isn't sufficient, or their own vision isn't unique. Dante, Mozart, Picasso — all of them lost their way once. Some recover and press on. Others, unfortunately, don't. It's like trying to maintain faith in a power greater than yourself — in a God, for example. Doubt will creep in, and reason will make us question our beliefs and our instincts. We'll lose our inner certitude. Making good choices is difficult for all of us, and especially for sensitive artists with high expectations. In the end, however, we're not the best judges of our own work. Our only job is to create. Keep at it, as best we can. Produce and believe that we have something worth sharing. Transmute the beauty we see into beautiful, timeless art that speaks to future generations. Janet did that. She produced a great deal. She did her best. Not many accomplish what she did."

"Wish I'd known what she was going through," Phillip said. "Been there to reassure her and help her financially. She never asked."

"Me too, son," Ebenezer concurred. "I have many regrets also."

"We do what we can for those we love," Dr. Pi said. "You both have done immense good in her name, established a great legacy in her honor. Because of you, her art *will* live, and her memory endure. *Be proud of that!*"

CHAPTER 53

Dr. Pi did not return to Cooperstown for months. He spent the long, quiet summer teaching, trying to write his novel, reading on the porch, and painting the house. On the last week of June, he, Constance, Bernardo, and Pixie drove to Vermont to see Christopher and his family. They celebrated Constance's birthday on the twenty-sixth, which, sadly, was the same day Pablo had died thirteen years earlier. Despite the turmoil he'd lived through over the past half year, and the lingering melancholy which still clung to him like moss on stone, Dr. Pi reveled in this joyous get-together with his children. He was determined to live in the moment and not allow this precious time to be marred by *any* sadness. For a week, they played music and sang, went boating on Lake Champlain, cruised through the beautiful, Vermont countryside in Christopher's classic '66 Land Rover, stopped for fish and chips and ice cream, and stayed up late to tell stories by a bonfire near the crick behind Christopher's house. Dr. Pi told his children everything he'd lived through in his relationship with Janet, including the attempt on his life and her murder. He even shared his romantic yearnings for Katerina. Constance rolled her eyes, and Dr. Pi laughed. When he mentioned he'd entertained the idea of marrying Katerina and moving to Irkutsk to raise a new family, both Constance and Christopher looked at one another in shock, but then smiled, and Christopher said, "It's okay, Dad. We'll come visit." Everyone laughed, and Constance chimed in to say, "You know you can't get rid of us." Dr. Pi's eyes suddenly teared up, and he pulled them into an embrace.

"Don't ever worry about me," he told them. "I'm just an old-world romantic like Gatsby. Gloomier than most, but happy. Sadness comes and goes, but I live aware of each blessing I've been gifted. And you two are my greatest inspiration."

After that memorable trip, Dr. Pi settled into his usual routines. Some weekends late in July, especially when loneliness crept in, he drove into New York City to visit Constance, and even took a few motorcycle driving lessons from Will on Long Island. Other times, he drove to Pennsylvania to play music with his graduate school roommate, Mathias. These excursions were preferable to singing late at night for the house spirits — a ritual which, at times, made him feel as though he'd lost his mind. Mathias was a gifted, inventive pianist with a Latin soul — a fellow Cuban who had a knack for livening up Dr. Pi's songs with crisp harmonies and a touch of Mambo flair. He welcomed Dr. Pi into his home as if he were a brother. When he arrived on Fridays, Dr. Pi would treat Mathias's family, his wife, Penelope, who cooked like Julia Child and decorated their house impeccably, and two children, Jasmine and Stella, to dinner at the Dimmick Inn in Milford. At seventeen, Jasmine was highly creative, a budding graphic artist with a love of animation and storytelling; Dr. Pi marveled at her lively imagination when she shared details of the story she was writing or showed him her visual creations. Ten-year-old Stella, with her natural warmth, instantly won Dr. Pi's heart, and he dubbed her Queen Stella. Their lively puppy, Luna, a Siberian husky, pounced in her cage and barked with wild energy each time she heard Dr. Pi's voice upon arrival; she'd not stop until he took her outside to do her business and play a game of fetch.

When Dr. Pi visited Mathias, old Dionysus bandmates, guitarist Fred and bassist Hutch, would often join them, and the four would jam for hours in the living room. Hutch would record some of their sessions and afterwards send Dr. Pi fifty-second clips, which he'd occasionally post on Instagram. These always drew plenty of enthusiastic comments, and it was good to know that people liked their music. Katerina had pointed to the fun melody in his latest post and wrote: *This is great! … Looks like a real pleasure!*

These sessions happened frequently in the late summer and early fall, and Dr. Pi appreciated the company. He and Phillip had begun to text less, and music was a welcome diversion from the haunting memories of Janet's death and all the other sadness he housed in his heart. His communications with Katerina had also dwindled to one or two messages every two weeks. And he'd completely lost touch with Ebenezer. Dr. Pi struggled to write during this time and sought inspiration wherever he could find it. Among his friends he felt imaginatively nourished. Playing their old songs and working on new ones reinvigorated him, like Katerina once had. Though he still longed for and wondered about her, she no longer was a pervasive presence in his life.

On his way to Milford, Dr. Pi would stop at Hancock for two McDonald's apple pies. This small ritual brought him comfort, as did driving south on the long, isolated but scenic Route 97, which snaked along the Delaware River on the New York side. This road imbued him with nostalgia for Wordsworth's poetry, for everywhere his eyes turned, nature's beauty beamed, and his heart swelled with joy — the changing colors of the sky, flourishing trees, and the call of birds awakened old memories with an irresistible charm.

While driving on one of these trips in late September, Dr. Pi unexpectedly received a long direct message on Instagram from Katerina. His phone buzzed, and he pulled over to read her happy words, punctuated throughout with abundant smiley face emojis and bright red hearts. Katerina explained that she'd be coming to New York for her birthday in December. She'd returned to school at Chopin University in August to finish her coursework (this fact alone brought Dr. Pi much joy) and had been told by one of her professors about a job opportunity to teach the following spring at Barnard College. She'd applied and been granted an audition for the visiting instructor's position in early December.

When I come, I wish to see you, Tobias. Is a dream come true! Can you believe it? Now I know more English. I hope is enough (five smiley face emojis). I plan to play Mozart Facile and other pieces. Of course, Chopin and Beethoven also. Maybe I get job, and with work Visa stay many months in America. You will show me New York? Drive me in taxi from airport? I want to visit your house in country. See the snow like in Irkutsk when I was child. Your photographs show lots of snow. Winter warms my heart (ten red heart emojis and five kissy face ones).

Dr. Pi closed his eyes, pictured Katerina in his arms, making love to her on a cold, wintry Pleasant Hills night. A year earlier these were the only thoughts that occupied his mind before he fell asleep, as he listened to the Russian rock songs she'd sent him. So much had happened since then to sober such sensuous longings. For one, he knew she had someone, yet he decided right then not to ask about him. She said she wished to see him, Tobias. She did not mention anyone else. It was best not to inquire. She wanted to be shown New York, to visit his house. She didn't say how long she'd be staying, but he wouldn't ask about that either. She could stay as long as she'd like, whether she got the job or not. He'd take care of her, pay her way as he'd once imagined. What he wanted was to feel her warmth and kiss her lips. Maybe this would happen. It took him a quarter hour of thought to compose a four-sentence response:

I'm here for you Katerina. We will do as you wish. Let me know when to pick you up. I'm thrilled to hear of your visit (a smiley face and three red heart emojis).

For the rest of that trip to Milford, Dr. Pi felt bewildered. His emotions were a jumbled mess. A year earlier he could see a clear future for himself and Katerina, but now he wondered whether there could be one. The experiences he'd had with Janet, he knew, had changed him. He'd gotten used to being alone again for long periods of time and wasn't sure if there was anything genuine that he could offer *anyone* long term. Still, the thought of holding Katerina in his arms and seeing her lovely smile made him happy.

When he arrived at Mathias's in the late afternoon on this Friday, Dr. Pi's emotions were still roiling. Yet he was hopeful and upbeat. He remembered how much he'd yearned a year earlier to see Katerina. Soon, he'd get his chance. After taking Luna out for a walk, Penelope made him a cappuccino, and he relaxed. While they all waited for Mathias to get home from work so they could head to dinner, Dr. Pi sat in the living room with Jasmine, and she told him about her developing story. Seeing her youthful enthusiasm inspired him. He asked her questions about her characters, Dream and Nightmare, and was genuinely curious to know more about them, for it seemed to Dr. Pi that they perfectly symbolized the two great sides of life. Where he stood at that precise moment was somewhere in between — though he wished to reach for Dream (to love Katerina), he felt that Nightmare (who'd taken Janet) wouldn't allow it, and would, once again, intervene to crush his hope.

***

After October break, Dr. Pi's weeks got busy. He visited Pennsylvania less often and struggled to keep up with schoolwork, grading, and departmental responsibilities. Work on his novel ceased, yet again. On October 15, he went to Ray's in Bouckville for barbecue ribs and beers to celebrate. A year earlier, *Yellow Bird* had been published with Joe's help. Remembering how thrilled he'd felt then, and his developing passion for Katerina, brought Dr. Pi hope that his new novel would get done and find its way into readers' hands. While he was on his second Blue Moon, Dr. Pi received a text from Phillip. It'd been quite a while since he'd last heard from him.

Hi Dr. Pi. I apologize for losing touch. Been very busy these past few months finishing work at the philharmonic and on the studio. We're throwing a party at the farmhouse on December 13. Would love for you to come. Celebrating the grand opening of Hideaway Hills. Ivo will be there. We start recording on the 16th. Stay with us. Ebenezer's been asking about you. We miss your company.

Of course, I'll come, Dr. Pi texted back quickly. *Thanks for inviting me. I may bring a friend.*

Whomever you like. Glad to hear it. Looking forward to your visit.

Hearing from Phillip had made his night. It dawned on him immediately how amazing it would be if Katerina could meet Ivo, a luminary in the classical music world. Perhaps play for him and display her prodigious talent. Though Dr. Pi didn't know her itinerary yet, he hoped this meeting would come to pass. Just as Joe had been there and helped him publish *Yellow Bird*, Dr. Pi wished to help Katerina forge the connection she needed to perhaps realize her dream. She had an immense musical gift. He remembered Phillip's stunned reaction the previous Christmas when he heard her original piano composition. The thought of bringing Katerina into contact with a world-renowned pianist produced an excitement in Dr. Pi which he hadn't felt in years. Such a meeting could be life changing. For days, Dr. Pi beamed with happiness in anticipation of what might happen with his help. He kept this event a secret, just in case it didn't come to pass, but in his communications with Katerina, he asked if she'd consider staying for Christmas. He promised he'd take care of her, show her every inch of New York, and go shopping on Fifth Avenue for whatever her heart desired. Many of the initial romantic feelings he'd had for her a year earlier returned, and every other night they flirted more intensely on Instagram Direct as the day of her visit drew near. Dr. Pi drove down to see Constance on Thanksgiving, and before heading upstate he cruised the city, looking around for places to take Katerina, and putting together a plan for her visit.

CHAPTER 54

What Dr. Pi loved most about Katerina was her honesty and forthrightness. He was an expert at analyzing writing, and not once in all his communications with her had he detected that she was lying, being underhanded, or hiding the truth. In one of her posts, for example, she'd expressed how overwhelmed she was with the growing number of followers she'd gained, for it seemed that most, in one way or another, wanted something from her. Dr. Pi had sympathized with her exasperation, and commented that he perfectly understood, knowing he'd never asked anything from her. She'd replied: *If I can tell you the truth, you are the only person, like an exception to the rule ... You never asked for anything, didn't try to limit my freedom, but you stayed close to me. You're a magical, wise man. You're the best (red heart emoji) and I'm happy you're with me!* He appreciated this admission and the respect she'd shown him. It didn't surprise him then when a week before her visit she told him she was engaged to be married in the New Year to her longtime boyfriend.

Dmitry shocked me, just two days ago. Wasn't expecting such proposal. Asked me to have his children, wants to care for me always. I'm sorry if this news is disappointing, Tobias. But is true. I accepted. He gave me beautiful ring and many red roses.

That's wonderful news, Katerina, Dr. Pi responded. *I'm happy. I remember you said he was a hard worker and took good care of you. I'm glad you accepted him. If he loves you and you love him, it is perfect. Great news.*

I feel sad because we made plans. He wants to come to New York with me. You don't need to show us the city.

I'll show you both the city, Dr. Pi insisted. *Doesn't matter. We will celebrate together. And if you two can stay a couple of weeks, I have a big surprise for you.*

Tell me, what? Please, she implored.

It's a secret. A special birthday gift. You'll both be my guests.

***

Katerina's Barnard interview was on Friday, December 6 at one in the afternoon. She and Dmitry had been granted a fifteen-day visa and would head back to Poland on the twentieth. Dr. Pi picked them up at Kennedy on the fifth at 6 p.m. and drove them to the Morningside Heights apartment that the college had reserved for her for the weekend.

From the outset, Dr. Pi liked Dmitry; he was courteous, kind, and appreciative. In his best English, he thanked Dr. Pi profusely for helping them and shook his hand many times. One could tell he was thrilled to be there. Dmitry was dressed elegantly in a black suit and long woolen coat. He wore his dirty blonde hair short and sported a mustache and full beard. He'd just turned thirty-two, a full eight years older than Katerina, had a solid, athletic build, and at six foot two looked imposing like a mixed martial arts fighter. His boyish smile made him appear much younger than the mature man he was. But it was the kind, loving way he treated Katerina that won him Dr. Pi's respect.

When Katerina emerged from the terminal door, Dr. Pi realized how truly beautiful she was; none of her photographs fairly captured the natural splendor before him. Her magnificent grey-green eyes were large and hypnotic, and her face glowed with a tranquil, pleasant expression that took his breath away. If he'd been smitten online while perusing her lovely pictures over the past two years, now he was even more amazed at her beauty. She looked taller than her five-foot-seven frame, for her slender legs, caressed by tight-fitting blue jeans, with polished, stylish, high black boots, carried her forth with a fashion model's grace and sensuousness. Her long red hair was gathered into a fashionable ponytail that fell softly on her lavender woolen coat. Dr. Pi was surprised when she dropped her travel bag upon seeing him, rushed towards him excitedly, and wrapped her slender hands around his neck, then planted a big, soft kiss on his lips. Dr. Pi squeezed Katerina tightly, held her several seconds, and breathed in her delicious fragrant perfume. Dmitry did not seem bothered by this intense, affectionate display on both their parts. He seemed a confident and happy man, and when the two separated, Dr. Pi saw a warm smile brighten Dmitry's face. Right then, he perceived his inner goodness, and knew Katerina had made a good choice; Dmitry loved her and would support her dreams. Dr. Pi yearned to show them both a great time, and to make this trip one they'd never forget.

Katerina's interview ran into the late afternoon, and afterwards they were free. She'd told him they'd made no other plans and left it up to him to show them the city he knew best. Dr. Pi had made weekend reservations for himself at the Waldorf and planned to show them as much of New York City as he could. Friday evening, he treated them to dinner at the Waldorf, and afterwards they took a carriage ride through Central Park. Katerina sat between them and pulled them each closer to keep warm. It was a magical ride and the lights from surrounding buildings and skyscrapers glowed like stars across the Milky Way. Early on Saturday, after breakfast uptown, Dr. Pi took them by taxi to Rockefeller Center, and then they spent a leisurely afternoon walking through Grand Central Station, the New York Public Library, and around Times Square. They also strolled in and out of the avenue stores and shopped on Fifth. Katerina bought an elegant red dress and Dmitry a pair of leather gloves at Saks. Later that evening, after dining on Broadway, with a phone call to Phillip, Dr. Pi secured VIP seats at Lincoln Center to hear a New York Philharmonic concert. Phillip was busy and couldn't meet Dr. Pi's Russian friends before or after the show but asked that he bring them to his Cooperstown get-together the following week, and Dr. Pi agreed to. On Sunday, after brunch, he got tickets to a Broadway show matinee, then they visited the Metropolitan Museum of Art before dining uptown near Columbia University. On Monday morning, Dr. Pi checked out of the Waldorf, picked up his friends uptown, grabbed some sandwiches at a nearby deli, and then headed upstate.

The three friends communicated fairly well in their conversations. Katerina's English had improved greatly since they'd begun their friendship over two years back. She was now more fluent, and Dr. Pi complimented both her progress and beautiful accent. Dmitry understood just about everything Dr. Pi said. Hand and facial gestures often helped clarify or emphasize points, and whenever things reached an impasse, Google Translate came to the rescue. It helped that all three had the desire to share their thoughts with one another; the technology proved to be a breath of fresh air — so useful in bringing those from faraway lands, backgrounds, and cultures together to celebrate the beauty of life.

When they arrived at Pleasant Hills, Dr. Pi immediately made his friends comfortable and showed them to his biggest guest room. He brought up their bags and got them settled, then took them out for dinner at the Copper Kettle. Dr. Pi, aware that Katerina's birthday on the eleventh was two days away, called in a cake order at Café CaNole in New Hartford. At the Kettle, since it was his birthday, he ordered a bottle of their best Riesling. At every opportunity, he introduced his Russian friends to the waiters and waitresses who knew him there, especially Heather, who always greeted him with a grand smile. Afterwards, they returned to his house and watched two of Dr. Pi's favorite Woody Allen films: *Midnight in Paris* and *Vicky Christina Barcelona*. The films had no Russian subtitles, but the humor came through regardless, and in many of the funniest scenes, the three friends would look at one another and smile — smiles of joy and mutual understanding. Dr. Pi was pleased that Katerina and Dmitry were having a good time. After saying goodnight to the two, Dr. Pi went to his bedroom. He texted his children goodnight as usual but was surprised to see a direct message from Katerina on his phone screen. Her words touched him:

This is a special December day, magical and wonderful, because this day was born such a good person like you! I wish you always to have cheerful mood, good health, strength to resist difficulties and patience, big success in all your dealings and great personal happiness! May your new year of life bring many wonderful things: your new novel I am sure will be finished, your musical creativity will grow, develop and have its listeners, and your work with students will be interesting and grateful! Thank you for the bright light you give me! I'm very happy to have you, and I really appreciate, and love you (red heart emoji).

Though Katerina wasn't in his arms, her warm words held him firmly, satisfied his deepest longings, and diminished the sadness in his heart.

On the following morning, Dr. Pi showed them the beautiful nearby towns and lakes — Skaneateles, Cazenovia, and Hamilton. He took them shopping later in the day at the New Hartford Mall and before heading home picked up Katerina's cake. They ate some Greek cuisine at Symeon's restaurant and then drove home. That night, they watched *Doctor Zhivago* with Russian subtitles. Neither of his guests had ever seen the film, and Dr. Pi could tell how moved they both were by the emotionally turbulent story. Katerina marveled at how much the wintry landscape resembled the one she'd experienced as a little girl in Irkutsk. She cuddled up to Dmitry as the story's tragedy unfolded and intensified. Katerina's eyes were beautiful and intense like Julie Christie's, and Dmitry seemed as warm-hearted as Yuri from the film. Looking at the two in that loving embrace, Dr. Pi prayed inwardly that happiness would be forever theirs, and that nothing in the years ahead would sever the profundity of the love he witnessed there.

The three friends celebrated Katerina's twenty-fifth birthday the next day with cake and wine. After she blew out the candles, Dr. Pi told her the big secret he held — his gift to her and Dmitry on their engagement: they'd be going to a big party that Friday, attended by the Russian pianist Ivo Pogotov. Katerina was immensely excited to meet Ivo, whose fame she was familiar with, for he'd graduated from the Moscow Conservatory and was a Russian legend. She thanked and hugged Dr. Pi intensely, and then danced wildly with her fiancé around the kitchen. It was a dream come true to meet the legendary pianist. Dmitry was familiar with all of Ivo's compositions and the honors he'd received. The three celebrated late into the night. Dr. Pi and Dmitry took turns playing songs on his custom Martin guitar, and Katerina made Constance's old piano come to life, despite how out of tune it was. Before retiring, Dr. Pi sang "Lady Stay," the original song that Katerina had inspired, with all the soulful energy he could muster.

***

The three spent the day Thursday relaxing and lounging by the fire, which raged in the grate. It snowed heavily and the roads were icy and dangerous. Katerina joyfully dragged Dmitry outside to prance in the snow and build a snowman. Dr. Pi, meanwhile, cooked them a delicious chicken dinner, and after showering and getting comfortable, they ate and listened to some Russian rock music; both Katerina and Dmitry found interesting selections. All three took turns sharing their favorite classical pieces and did their best to communicate the passion felt for the selections chosen. Randy arrived at six and could be heard plowing the driveway. Dr. Pi opened the side door and waved his gratitude. Randy cleared over a foot of snow in under fifteen minutes, careful not to destroy the funny snowman Katerina and Dmitry had built.

After lunch at Suzie's restaurant in Bouckville on Friday, they came back home and got dressed for the Cooperstown party. Katerina wore the beautiful red dress she'd bought on Fifth Avenue and Dmitry his elegant black suit, which gave him a dignified air. He looked like an orchestra conductor, a position he very well could fill, since he could play five instruments expertly. Years earlier, he had abandoned his dream of playing music because further schooling was too costly, jobs were scarce, and such a career seemed impractical. He'd begun driving an ambulance and not looked back. Nevertheless, music occupied his soul, and he supported Katerina's dreams of playing music professionally. In his opinion, Katerina was a prodigy. Dr. Pi could tell Dmitry was as excited as Katerina was about meeting Ivo.

Dr. Pi drove happily towards Cooperstown, and before long he entered the impressive gates of Janet's farmhouse — the newly named Hideaway Hills Recording Studio. The grounds looked magical, with Christmas decorations and colored lights everywhere. The barn had been impeccably restored, and a lovely memorial for Janet had been erected in front of it — a large granite easel, displaying a painting in progress, with her name carved beneath. Gas-fired sconces lit the sculpture with a warm light that reflected brightly in the surrounding snow.

Dr. Pi and his guests were greeted by Phillip and brought into the grand room to meet his other visitors, including Ivo. Ivo stood surveying the Church and Cole paintings with his wife Tanya when Katerina and Dmitry were introduced. They instantly began speaking in Russian as if they'd been long-lost friends, and this was promising. Dr. Pi understood the excitement his friends must have felt to find a fellow countryman and speak in their native tongue after days of struggling to speak English.

Dr. Pi walked into the kitchen and greeted Ebenezer, who poured him a glass of wine. He mused about how much had changed in a year. He remembered his intimate moments with Janet, the deep love she'd had for her King Phillip, and the joy she'd felt when she'd chosen to make amends with Ebenezer. As Ebenezer spoke on about the lake-house renovations and Phillip's new business, Dr. Pi's mind drifted, his eyes teared, and a heavy sadness crept in. Soon, he was far away, missing Maria, Miriam, and Pablo. A whole lifetime had passed, and, though so much happiness had been lived, experiences he genuinely cherished, there was a lingering loneliness which just couldn't be lifted permanently from his consciousness.

He felt his phone buzz and read Will's text message:

Hi Tobias. Join us for New Year's. Stay the weekend. Estella's birthday is on the 28th, and we're throwing her a huge party — Colombian style — lots of food, drink, and dancing. Come see the new kitchen I built for Adriana. Bring Constance and Bernardo. It'll be fun.

Dr. Pi smiled widely, happy to have received such a wonderful invitation. He typed his reply quickly: *Sounds great, Will. Count me in. I'll bring some wine and a cake for Estella. Look forward to seeing all of you soon. I'll tell Constance.* He put away his phone.

Suddenly, the opening notes of a Rachmaninoff piece floated freely in the grand room. Holding his wine glass with both hands up near his chest, as if embracing a sacred chalice full of Christ's blood, Dr. Pi walked in a dazed stupor towards the magical music. He entered the room and saw beautiful Katerina in her red dress playing on the grand piano. Phillip, Dmitry, and Ivo stood close by, mesmerized, it seemed, by her graceful performance. One by one, conversations stopped, and the room grew silent as the piece's emotion intensified, as all became hypnotized by the notes produced by Katerina's fingers. Dr. Pi smiled, knowing Ivo and Phillip were impressed. He felt deeply happy that his and Katerina's friendship had brought them here.

Dr. Pi closed his eyes, let the music elevate him, fill him with pure love. He felt the sadness, wrought from all the pain he'd ever felt, slowly lifting. Maria was there. Center stage with Katerina. The two were now one. He didn't need to prove it. He knew it! Maria lived in his mind.

Nourished his heart. Awakened his soul. She was omnipresent — like Jesus. She'd brought Katerina to Tobias. And magically, he'd brought Katerina here to her destiny.

As Katerina's fingers ceased playing, Dr. Pi opened his eyes. The small audience burst into wild applause. He placed his glass on the floor and clapped vigorously, looked towards Katerina happily as she stood and gently bowed. She turned and fixed her eyes on him. But it wasn't Katerina he saw. It was Maria. She smiled and softly waved.

THE END

ACKNOWLEDGEMENTS

I would like to thank my editor, Lee Parpart, for her brilliance and hard work. Lee, I appreciate your invaluable questions, commentary, and suggestions for improvement. Your expertise, attention to detail, and insights have helped me make this a story I'm proud of.

To my dear friend, Joseph Sciuto, for his loyal support. Joe, each time we talk, I'm reminded of what great professors helped shape our thinking and desire to write literature. We are fortunate to have learned from literary masters: Thomas Flanagan, Louis Simpson, Rose Zimbardo, and so many others. What bright minds! What incredible mentors!

To my colleague, Dr. Roxanna Pisiak, for editing an early draft. Thank you for giving the story a good haircut, and for listening for months to my endless rambling about the story's characters and themes. I'm grateful for our friendship.

To my dear children, Catherine and Andy, my very own Constance and Christopher, and to their loving mother, Christine, for years and years of love, inspiration, and support. In my heart, the three of you *are* my holy trinity.

To my brother Hutch and sister Elena, for buoying me through the hardships with your love. You two are the central, supporting pillars of my life's edifice.

To Alcides and Adriana Diaz, and their beautiful daughters, Camille and Isabelle. Your hospitality is boundless, and I am deeply grateful for your generosity and love. I edited much of this story in your Milford kitchen. Yours is truly my second home!

To Will Aguila, for introducing me to Natasha and suggesting Colombian food dishes. And to the Aguila family, Adriana, Nicole, Angelica, Marta, and Estella. Thank you for your generosity and support, and for hosting a memorable New Year's celebration — Tank's last. I'll never forget it. As Capra wrote, "No man is a failure who has friends."

To my colleague, Warren Costantine, for your friendship and support. Once you print a hard copy, I know I'm halfway there. I'm reassured, re-animated with the sense that "this is really happening" — that it won't be long till my story is offered to the world.

To Kristina Wolska, for your inspiration and love, for helping me with Russian names, and suggesting Katerina Kotova and Dmitry. Thank you for giving me permission to use your words and our communications in creating this fiction.

To Fred Falchook, for your friendship, and for making my songs come to life with your guitar, and to Randy Groves, for being there whenever I've needed a helping hand.

To the Cooperstown community. Your village and Otsego Lake are heaven on earth, a joy to visit — a true inspiration in all seasons.

Finally, a very special thank you to Meghan Behse, for believing in my work, to Toby Keymer, for proofreading the manuscript with such care, adding polish to the story and improving its rhythm and style, and to the rest of the wonderful staff at Iguana Books.

www.ingramcontent.com/pod-product-compliance
Lightning Source LLC
Chambersburg PA
CBHW031154050726
47495CB00019B/1735